PRAISE FOR *WHEN FRANNY STANDS UP*

"Smart and wickedly funny, *When Franny Stands Up* is a timely and timeless story that will whisk the reader away on a joy-roaring ride through mid-century Chicago."

—Wesley Chu, #1 *New York Times* bestselling author of the War Arts Saga

"A debut novel that's fresh and contemporary while feeling like an old favorite. An instant classic. Funny, unsentimental, brave, and silly without being unserious. What a book!"

—Cory Doctorow, author of *Walkaway* and *Radicalized*

"A showstopper of a novel, it is the story of a misunderstood comedian learning to embrace her identity in a world determined to hold her back. *When Franny Stands Up* is touching, funny, and smart as hell. You'll be standing up and cheering for Franny!"

—Ann Dávila Cardinal, author of *The Storyteller's Death*

"This novel is freaking magic in every way, and it pulls off just about every kind of magic trick you can imagine: it's all about the magic of stand-up and the magic of mid-twentieth-century Chicago and the magic of friendship and community and family. It's also about *magic* magic. I adore Franny and am so happy I got to follow her extraordinary adventures and misadventures, and I'm sure you will too."

—Juan Martinez, author of *Best Worst American: Stories*

"*When Franny Stands Up* is a riot of a book. Its characters burst with life and wit, even as they bristle against the hard edges of their world. Wielding humor and unabashed heart to steer us through a tale of what it means to find real family and what it means to heal, Robins navigates by every true comic's North Star: comedy comes from pain. She is a gifted storyteller."

—Rob Ziegler, author of *Seed*

"*When Franny Stands Up* is a goddamn delight, a can't-put-it-down page-turner about a girl who has the audacity to tell the truth about her own life at a time in our history when it wasn't acceptable or appropriate or even safe to do so. But she does it. Against all odds—class, race, faith, gender, and family— she gets on a microphone and stands the hell up. We should all be so brave."

—Megan Stielstra, author of *The Wrong Way to Save Your Life*

WHEN FRANNY STANDS UP

EDEN ROBINS

sourcebooks landmark

Published by Sourcebooks Landmark, an imprint of Sourcebooks
P.O. Box 4410, Naperville, Illinois 60567-4410
(630) 961-3900
sourcebooks.com

Library of Congress Cataloging-in-Publication Data

Names: Robins, Eden, author.
Title: When Franny stands up / Eden Robins.
Description: Naperville, Illinois : Sourcebooks Landmark, [2022]
Identifiers: LCCN 2022006659 (print) | LCCN 2022006660
(ebook) | (trade paperback) | (epub)
Subjects: LCSH: Women comedians--Fiction. | Jewish comedians--Fiction.
| Magic realism (Literature) | Chicago (Ill.)--History--20th century--
Fiction. | LCGFT: Jewish historical fiction. | Magic realist fiction.
Classification: LCC PS3618.O31765 W44 2022 (print) | LCC PS3618.
O31765 (ebook) | DDC 813/.6--dc23/eng/20220331
LC record available at https://lccn.loc.gov/2022006659
LC ebook record available at https://lccn.loc.gov/2022006660

Printed and bound in Canada.
MBP 10 9 8 7 6 5 4 3 2 1

For Dad, the thief of bad gags

CHAPTER ONE

Christmas Eve, 1944

IF A DOORMAN WOULDN'T OPEN THE DOOR, WAS HE STILL A doorman? It was like one of Papa's groaners: When is a door not a door? (When it's ajar.)

Franny Steinberg wouldn't have let herself into the glitzy Palmer House Hotel either. She looked shifty. Frizzy. Raccooned by mascara. She rubbed her eyes but just made it worse. Feet were numb from running in her awful, too-small boots. Bare, frozen wrists jutted from her ratty old peacoat. Stupid growth spurt couldn't have waited until after the war?

But Franny had vanquished bigger foes than a measly hotel doorman. She had big plans for this particular Christmas Eve, and she had already twisted the truth in many terrible ways to get here. Lied to her parents about spending all evening downtown with her best friend, Mary Kate Finnegan, and then lied to Mary Kate, saying she had to rush home early for—and Franny was not proud of this—a "Jewish thing."

"Aren't Jewish things at sunset?" Mary Kate had held her palm out like it was raining. "It's been dark for hours."

"Don't be rude," Mary Kate's handsome brother, Peter, had said. "Not everyone's religion makes sense."

Two lies didn't make you a liar, not if the cause was righteous enough. At least that's what Franny told herself, out of breath and at the mercy of the reluctant doorman.

And this cause was righteous. Tonight and tonight only, comedian Boopsie Baxter was in Chicago to perform at the Empire Room.

Franny had been following Boopsie's headlines for *months*— arrested on obscenity charges, arrested for doing comedy in a segregated nightclub, arrested for being obscene, handcuffed in her elegant floor-length mink or her spangled gown, smiling slyly, directly into the camera.

Franny wanted what Boopsie had. A grin in the face of danger. More devil-may-care, less knots-in-the-gut. A belief in winning, even when it looked a heck of a lot like losing. Franny *needed* to see Boopsie Baxter. Because Boopsie Baxter had a Showstopper. A legendary, famous, secret Showstopper that was too spectacular to talk about in the papers. And that Franny wasn't even completely sure she believed in.

Through the windows, twinkling lights and bows dangled from the ceiling, bored bellhops displayed themselves over countertops to the front desk girls. Wind and snow stung Franny's face, and her feet throbbed in her tight boots, thumping a staccato of *Showstopper*.

Franny just had to know if Showstoppers were real or phony, because if they were real, then magic was real. And if magic was real, she might just be able to bear this endless, dreary war. Dreariness was fine and dandy if it kept her brother, Leon, safe, but it didn't. Franny got all the safety, and he got bupkis.

The doorman relented. Franny ducked inside, melting gratefully into the entryway, wiggling her toes and trying not to think about sore thumbs. Everything in the Palmer House was gilded, marbled, bejeweled, or furred. The people were furred, anyway. Franny took the marble stairs two at a time, up to the landing, nearly skidding into a sculpture of Romeo and Juliet, forever batting eyelashes at each other. Poor suckers had no idea how their story would end. The stairs split at the landing, each side curving up to the bustling lobby bar.

Pillars, ceiling frescoes, Juliet balconies, sconces, chandeliers, gold, gold, gold. The ceiling had been painted with scenes from ancient Greece, when apparently girls got away with being naked all the time. You could barely see any of it through the fog of cigarette smoke.

Across the way, a towering Christmas tree covered in silver balls and white lights glinted hazily. The elevators to the hotel rooms were down there, and Franny squinted through the smoke, trying to glimpse a celebrity come to take in the famous Randolph Street nightlife on Christmas. It all felt very European. Not that Franny had ever been to Europe. And the way things were going over there right now? No, thank you. She had a bone to pick with that particular continent.

The lobby tinkled with champagne glasses and expensive jewelry. A tuxedoed waiter glided through the room with the hotel's famous brownie and ice cream, delivering it with a flourish to a woman draped, predictably, in furs. Franny must have stared for too long, because the woman glared back, silver spoon poised over its fudgy prey.

Franny's stomach rumbled. Mary Kate had promised her hot cocoa, and instead, Franny had run away and come here. Franny, who would have sold off the family silver for a teaspoon of sugar.

Mary Kate had linked arms with Franny as they looked at the Marshall Field's Christmas windows, rattling off all the desserts they could get Peter to buy for them. Some of which Franny had never even heard of. Pavlova? Like the guy who tricked his own dogs?

"You pick," Mary Kate said, patting her hand. "Your mother has such trouble finding sugar."

As if there weren't a sugar ration for *everyone*, or a war, as if money were plentiful and the neighborhood boys were playing baseball in Greenfield Park instead of shivering on a European battlefield.

Meanwhile, Peter had recently been honorably discharged from his post in Hawaii after losing his pinky finger in an air raid that turned out to be a false alarm. Somehow, he still received a Purple Heart. Which he took every opportunity to remind you of should you so much as *mention* the war. Or the word *purple*.

"Sure you don't wish Leon was here instead of me?" Franny said. Just saying her brother's name filled her mouth with bees. "I know you're sweet on him."

"Am not." Mary Kate squeezed her tight. "Don't worry, he'll be back. He could come back tomorrow."

Franny's grin had felt like a grimace. "He's probably back now, wondering what happened to *us*."

Laughter detonated behind Franny. This was no time to think about Leon. Not when a single flight of carpeted stairs led to the

Empire Room. Not when a single set of French doors separated her from Boopsie Baxter.

She took a deep breath and tugged open the door, releasing more laughter and smoke. A doorwoman half her height and twice her width blocked the entrance. She wore a black wool suit and Christmassy red tie, her hair slicked back like a mobster. She grinned crookedly.

"You got a reservation?" she said.

"Oh," Franny said, patting her coat pockets blankly. "I didn't know I needed one."

"We're full."

"I won't be a bother," Franny croaked. "I don't even need a seat. You'll forget I'm even here."

She looked Franny up and down. "How old are you, kid?"

"Eighteen," Franny lied.

The doorwoman sucked on her cigar and contemplated Franny's face. Finally, she stuck out a free hand. "Two bucks. And no crying to Mommy about the show. It's Christmas."

"I'm Jewish," Franny said.

"I wouldn't spread that around."

Franny dug into her purse—two dollars! If she gave the woman two dollars, she would barely have enough to take the train home. Definitely nothing left for a hot drink. Franny wiggled her frozen toes in her boots and handed over the money.

The doorwoman pointed Franny to a tiny round table in the back corner of the room, up a small set of stairs and at the farthest point from the stage. "You'll have to share the table with the cocktail waitresses on break."

"I'm good at sharing," Franny said.

"I'll bet," the doorwoman said with a low, manly chuckle that tickled Franny somewhere in her lower gut region. She didn't understand the joke, but since she seemed to be the butt of it, she wasn't about to ask.

Women in red lipstick chatted animatedly over starched white tablecloths. Franny squeezed past, apologizing constantly, jostling candles and forcing the women to protect their jewel-colored drinks from sloshing. Heavy velvet draped the stage, and two massive blooming chandeliers flickered from the ceiling. It was cozier than the lobby but just as glittery. Face hot, Franny finally reached her humble, wobbly table.

Her fingers and toes began to thaw, and the quiet murmur of feminine voices, the rustle of satin, and the clink of rings against martini glasses felt oddly...relaxing. In fact, Franny noticed her shoulders weren't hunched up by her ears, her jaw wasn't clenched. *If this is how Boopsie's Showstopper feels*, she thought drowsily, *I could definitely get used to it.*

Franny reluctantly removed her ratty coat—the dress underneath was only barely less ratty—and touched the magazine article tucked in her pocket for luck. Boopsie Baxter had been interviewed in *Ladies' Variety*, a salacious rag out of Miami that Franny had gone through a lot of trouble to get her hands on. The most information about Showstoppers that Franny had ever found was in this interview, now tucked in her coat pocket as a kind of talisman:

Boopsie: Showstoppers are real as your magazine. But they don't work on men, so men don't believe in them. They call them hallucinations if they call them anything at all. If you ask me, that's for the best.

LV: But what is a Showstopper, really?

Boopsie: If you come to one of our shows, and you laugh? You'll feel something that only we can give. Comedian Ida Horne makes her room feel love at first sight, NYC's Lucy Goosey has her room flipping tables and screaming battle cries like Joan of Arc...

LV: So the Showstopper is unique to each comedian.

Boopsie: Exactly right.

LV: But where did Showstoppers come from? Why us, why now?

Boopsie: Let me put it this way. A man pinches your rear and you really want to let him have it, but you pretend to be flattered. Been there, honey?

LV: I'm sure our readers can relate.

Boopsie: You swallow those feelings, and they sink down deep, stick to your ribs. They shake you up like a beer bottle, and that pressure can suffocate you. Comedians are like bottle openers. We relieve the pressure by making you laugh. Pressure can be painful, but it also has power. And potential. The world doesn't want us girls to have either.

The evening had begun with a set by the Palmer House jazz band, broadcast for the hotel's Christmas radio show. The comedy that followed would not be broadcast. Only those ladies lucky enough to see it in person would know it even happened.

The all-girl band packed up their instruments, chatting animatedly with the stage crew as they tested the spotlight. If it hadn't been for the war and its insatiable appetite for men—including artists and comedians—would Franny be watching male musicians right now? A man comedian? Impossible to imagine. Emily Post complained in her etiquette book that wartime comedy marked the death of good old-fashioned femininity: *Alas, American morals are fraying at the seams even as our boys are fighting—and dying—to preserve them.* Franny read the whole book, hoping for some mention of Showstoppers, but Emily Post either didn't believe in them or didn't consider them worth mentioning.

A cocktail waitress swooped over to Franny in a stylish but surprisingly skimpy getup and set a glass mug with a lemon wheel floating in it on the table.

"But I didn't order anything." Franny politely tried and failed not to stare at the waitress's jiggly décolletage.

"On the house," the waitress said in a shockingly high-pitched voice. "Courtesy of Diane at the door."

Diane's suit bunched up around her ears as she relit her cigar.

Franny turned back to her drink. "What is it?"

"Hot toddy," said the cocktail waitress, holding out her palm.

"I thought you said—"

"Tip?"

"Right." Franny dug into her purse and pulled out a nickel. "Thanks."

"Boopsie's on next," the cocktail waitress squeaked. "I never miss her for anything."

"Sorry if I took your seat," Franny said.

"I prefer to watch her in private anyway," the waitress said, jiggling away before Franny had a chance to ask what she meant.

A red-haired beauty, probably the singer from the house band, grabbed the microphone. "Ladies. Without further ado, it is my pleasure to introduce the girl who started it all, the comedian who needs no introduction," she said. The audience clapped harder. Some cheered and whistled. Franny could barely breathe.

"Please welcome to her Empire Room debut—"

Franny couldn't believe she had pulled it off. She was really about to see, with her own two eyes—

"Boopsie Baxter!"

Chairs scraped the floor, and dozens of elegant ladies hopped to their feet to cheer. Franny stood and cheered too, even though her voice sounded funny in her ears. She froze midclap as Boopsie shimmied onstage. Her red sequined dress hugged her every curve, winking like fish scales, black hair laid close to her scalp, shiny and finger waved. Her neck was drenched in diamonds. She embraced the singer who introduced her—Franny was surprised at how small Boopsie was—then waved demurely at the audience. She was more captivating than even her newspaper photos. She probably smelled terrific. Franny had never had the chance to clap for a Negro woman before and did so with vigor.

"All right, all right," Boopsie said in a smoky voice that sounded many years older than she looked. "We're all thrilled about the birth of Jesus, now sit your asses down."

The crowd tittered and sat. Franny felt prissier than Mary Kate, blushing in the dark at the word *ass.*

"Siddown," hissed a voice right below Franny. It was Diane from the door, looking up at her. Franny was the only one still standing. She plopped into her chair. "And drink up, it'll get cold."

Franny took a sip of her drink and coughed. "This has alcohol in it!" she said.

Diane laughed. "No kidding. Merry Christmas, kid."

Two extremely handsome men in tuxedos wheeled out a glossy baby grand while Boopsie ogled them. "That's right, fellas," she said in that husky voice. "One of these days, if you're lucky, these fingers will practice on you." She settled in at the piano. "Let's warm up with a little holiday music, get those juices flowing." The audience clapped their approval.

Franny attempted a second sip. The drink was warming and lemony and vaguely spiced, and now that she was expecting alcohol, it wasn't too bad.

Boopsie tinkled a few notes on the piano and started to sing.

When you see a pretty fella
With a certain kind of asset
And you wanna get a hold-a
The eggs in his basket
Just remember this one trick

The best way to get his stick
Smash your boobies
Smash 'em together
Squeeze those titties
In any weather!

Franny laughed and blushed at the same time. She took a big gulp of her drink for courage. It warmed her fast, spreading low into her belly. So low, in fact, that if she were being honest, it wasn't really her belly at all.

Boopsie tinkered on the piano, smiling that sly smile. "Thanks so much for coming out on Christmas Eve. Christmas is a special time, a very special time. When else can a respectable woman sneak a strange man into her house, accept gifts, and wiggle around on his lap, asking for more? Oh yes, Santa, I've been a very bad girl. That, my friends, is the real Christmas magic."

The room exploded in an atom bomb of laughter. Imagine Mary Kate listening to this! Franny pictured Mary Kate shaken to her core, her sweet, heart-shaped face frozen in an expression of horror. Franny laughed until her ears ached. What was there to worry about again? Life was grand. And hilarious. She relaxed into the laugh, felt it bubbling up from deep inside her.

And then her giggle became a moan. A *loud* one. The kind of noise Franny would never *consider* making. She slapped a hand over her mouth, but the moan continued behind her hand. She grabbed her mug for another gulp, but it was empty. Was this what being drunk felt like? She could see why winos existed, if so.

A warmth filled her entire...*lower region*...but mostly a certain spot between her legs that pulsated like a tiny heart. The physical sensation was irresistibly exciting, and Franny desperately wanted to give in to it. But what if people noticed? What if she ruined everyone's nice, relaxing evening by yowling like a tomcat? She forced herself to sit painfully still and keep the feeling inside until it passed. But on and on Boopsie went, her words barely comprehensible over the sound of Franny's own heartbeat. Franny's breath came ragged, and suddenly she was yelping like the Finnegans' Yorkshire Terrier, Noodles, and then an explosion rippled upward from her nether regions through her chest and arms and head and down to her tingling toes, and Franny melted into her chair. She had never felt so good. Which felt bad. She wanted to leave. Her limbs were empty fire hoses, and she could barely stand. What had she done?

Immediately after the heat evaporated, it started to build again.

"Oh no," Franny said, in a voice that didn't sound like her own. What was this place? They had slipped her a Mickey Finn Special, that was for sure. Franny forced herself to stand and ignored the heat building up again. She stumbled, knocking the chair over on her way to leave.

"What did you put in my drink?" she said to Diane, whose cheeks were rosy and eyes unfocused. "Let me out."

"Slow down, sweetheart," Diane said. "Remember our deal. I let you in, you be cool."

"Cool? I'm sweating through my dress. And I am not your sweetheart."

Diane looked her up and down, and Franny crossed her arms over her chest to hide…what?

"I don't believe it. A Showstopper virgin," Diane said, grinning. "And *Boopsie Baxter* popped your cherry. If that ain't the limit. Hey, Dolly"—she nudged the cocktail waitress—"get a load of this."

But Franny would *not* be gotten a load of. She pushed past Diane and tugged open the French doors, squinting in the dim lights of the lobby. She oozed down the marble stairs, dashed through the gilded doors so that the doorman had to jump out of her way, until finally she was standing in the middle of Monroe Street in the blistering cold night, letting the snow cool her cheeks, and sucking in the fresh air until it burned her lungs.

Franny shrugged her coat on and refused to cry. Whatever happened in the Empire Room was *not* magic. Magic was supposed to transport you out of yourself, not sink you deeper into it. Magic was supposed to give you courage, not something else to worry about.

From now on, no more Boopsie Baxter, no more Empire Room, forget all about Showstoppers. But how could Franny forget *that*? She would make herself forget. Boopsie who?

Mama and Papa would never have to know. Leon would never have to know. It would be so secret that Franny would keep it a secret from herself. What secret?

Franny hustled down State Street to Adams, keeping her coat open as punishment, which was awfully Catholic of her, something Mary Kate would do. But Mary Kate would never allow herself to be…consumed by whatever had consumed Franny. Boy, whatever it was, it sure felt great. Franny wished she had stayed at the Empire

Room long enough to ask Diane—what was Boopsie's Showstopper, exactly? Would it have killed her to ask? *Stop thinking about it. Forget it, remember?*

Franny hopped up the slick steps to the L platform at Adams and Wabash and gave all her remaining pocket change to some scrawny urchin who couldn't believe his luck.

What happened happened; forget about it, Papa would say. *The future doesn't care about the past and neither should you.*

Franny most definitely did *not* want to think about Papa right now.

❦

The downstairs lights were still on at Steinbergs' boxy brick four-square home at 504 North Euclid Avenue. That meant Mama and Papa had waited for her. Franny tried not to look guilty. She would just say she had gone to a dance at the Servicemen's Center with Mary Kate and lost track of time. Not a punishable offense, surely, since Peter had been there to chaperone?

She took a deep breath and opened the door. There, in the entry-way, stood Mama and Papa...and Mary Kate and Peter. Her throat clenched tight. Caught in the crosshairs of a lie she hadn't even told yet. Why couldn't she catch a break? They looked grim; Mary Kate and Peter still wore their coats. Franny was in so much trouble.

"I can explain," Franny began. But they barely noticed her. They were all huddled around a small yellow square of paper. A Western Union telegram. The house was a scratchy sweater they were all wearing. Papa's pipe dangled, unpacked, from his fingertips. Franny's heart stopped dead in her chest.

"Leon," she croaked.

Leon's entire division—the 106th—had been dumped some-where in Belgium, swapping in for some bored soldiers who had, Leon promised, seen absolutely no action. And true to his word, his last letter was all about the excitement of winning two cigarettes in a chess game against people who called themselves *Smitty* and *Buster*.

Papa looked at Franny as though he had never seen her before in his whole life. Mama reached for her, pulled her close. "He's miss-ing," Mama said. "He's been missing for three days."

Franny wanted it to be two hours ago, before she lied and ran away, when Peter suggested they go to the Servicemen's Center dance.

"My buddies will be there, on Christmas furlough," Peter had said. "Who knows the next time I'll get to see them? You don't get a Purple Heart for turning your back on your brothers."

"Yeah, you get it for blowing off your own finger lighting a road flare," Mary Kate had said, rolling her eyes. "On a sunny beach in Hawaii."

"What did I say about disrespecting—"

"*Meanwhile*," Mary Kate continued, "Leon is risking real limbs in Belgium, right now." She slapped a hand over her mouth and looked sidelong at Franny, who felt herself go a little weak in the knees.

"Now you've done it." Peter had grabbed Franny around the shoulders, and she had been grateful the stinging wind covered her flushed cheeks. "Leon's just fine, Franny," he said, holding her tight. "He's stationed in the absolute dullest part of Europe right now. Snooze fest. I promise." He had smiled his brightest, most trustwor-thy smile.

Snooze fest. He *promised.* Stupid, handsome, not-missing Peter who enlisted his way into a tropical vacation because his father played golf with rich people.

"But Leon was playing chess." Franny's voice wobbled. "He was supposed to be bored."

"Nu, Ruth, you want to lie to the girl, that's your business, but I won't." Papa crumpled the telegram, squeezing it tight in his big fist like he could make it a diamond. "He's dead. They lost the body. That's what this means."

Franny had never heard Papa talk this way. Papa, always quick with a joke, no matter what.

"That's not true," Peter said hoarsely.

Papa turned to Peter with a fierce look. "This from the war hero who got a Purple Heart in schtupping Polynesian girls."

"Isaac," Mama said. "Please."

Tears dribbled down Mary Kate's cheeks, and Peter's jaw muscles worked, but he held his tongue. All Franny could think was that if she hadn't lied, if she had just stayed with Mary Kate and Peter and never set eyes on Boopsie Baxter, somehow this telegram would not have arrived, and Leon would be fine. Winning cigarettes off Smitty and bored out of his skull in Nowheresville, Belgium.

She had only wanted to relieve a little pressure, have a little laugh. Take her mind off the nightmares and the dread, the constant hum of worry about Leon. Just one night off. Just for a moment. But this was what happened when Franny took her mind off things. She lost them.

CHAPTER TWO

June 1951, Seven years later

THE FINNEGANS' HOUSE SPRAWLED ACROSS TWO CITY LOTS, kitty-corner from the Steinbergs' modest brick foursquare. The house had cost Mr. Finnegan almost ten thousand dollars to build—and that was during the Depression, don't forget. Mr. Finnegan's memories were the clearest when they were about how much he had paid for something. The lawn was smooth and lush as carpet, uninterrupted by trees, and they still hired a person to do their land-scaping, which was just so unfair. The Steinberg lawn was cramped with white oaks, as was the vacant lot next door, and who had to rake those giant leaves? *And* mow the lawn? Franny.

"Don't fidget, dear," Mrs. Finnegan said. And then, to the tailor, Mr. Epstein, "I told you, she's at least a size larger on the bottom half." She whispered *bottom half* as though it were a curse word. Franny's face prickled. That familiar pain gripped her insides, gur-gling demonically and earning a glare from Mrs. Finnegan.

"Honestly, Franny," she said. "You can't possibly be hungry *again.*"

It was hot for early June, a stuffy, sticky August-y heat. Even with all of Mary Kate's bedroom windows open, Franny's girdle pricked her flesh, sweat trickling maddeningly down her ribs. It was hard to breathe in the thing on a good day, and this was not a good day. She looked like a gelatinous undersea creature in the bridesmaid dress. Its ruffled shoulders and seafoam-green chiffon made Mary Kate's other bridesmaid, Agnes, look dewy and diaphanous and positively goddess-like but turned Franny's olive skin moldy.

"We take in the bodice, fit the shoulders like so, no problem," Mr. Epstein said around a mouth of straight pins.

"Mama says I'm full of hot air," Franny said. "Poke me with one of those pins and I'll pop like a balloon. Problem solved." Mr. Epstein chuckled politely. Mrs. Finnegan grimaced.

"Honestly, Franny, this is no time for jokes."

"Does she have it on upside down?" Agnes cracked.

"Nothing we can do about it now," Mrs. Finnegan said. "If there's any…anything you can do about the hips…" She threw up her hands and stalked away. "Twenty minutes, girls, then we absolutely must leave if we want to have high tea."

Franny suddenly wanted nothing more than to stand on that chair forever. A day with Mrs. Finnegan, on top of everything else, was not her idea of fun. "Are you sure you have all the measurements you need, Mr. Epstein?" Franny asked. "Did I mention the shoulders feel a little loose?"

Mr. Epstein helped her off the chair. "Don't worry, shayna maydel, I make sure you look good for the wedding."

"I don't want to rush things," Franny said. "These days it's all hurry hurry, rush rush rush. Whatever happened to taking our time?"

Mary Kate smiled sweetly. "Franny's not used to being forced to do what she doesn't want to do."

Franny's guts punched her from the inside, and she willed herself not to show it. Mary Kate was just nervous about her wedding. That was probably her idea of a compliment. But she didn't know the half of it; she didn't know a *tenth* of it.

The truth was, Mary Kate had abandoned her right when Franny needed her most, so how could she know anything?

The two of them hadn't spent more than an hour in the same room since high school, but really, they had drifted apart even before then, when the war ended. Had Mary Kate even wanted Franny to be a bridesmaid, or had Mrs. Finnegan made her do it? Franny said yes because saying no would have required an explanation. Keeping the peace was easier. Of course, it also meant there was no way to avoid crossing paths with Peter.

Nat King Cole crooned from the record player as Franny shimmied out of the dress behind Mary Kate's Japanese room divider. Franny was always a little surprised that Mr. Finnegan allowed jazz music in his household. He had spearheaded the campaign to keep the handsome Negro doctor—Dr. Avery—and his family from moving into the neighborhood, still a sore point between him and Papa a year later. Mr. Finnegan had tried to wheedle Papa into signing a petition to "keep coloreds out of the neighborhood," to which Papa replied, with mock concern, "Why, what color are they?" The Finnegans now shared a property line with Dr. Avery, and Mr. Finnegan was always picking fights with him about the lawn.

"Come here. Hurry, before Mommy gets back," Mary Kate whispered.

"Wait," Franny said, "I'm getting dressed." She grabbed Mary Kate's Mary Kate–sized kimono, which barely covered the important parts. She cinched her arms across her chest to make up the difference.

Mary Kate looked like a tidy garden flower in her bright-blue dress with trim yellow belt and full skirt. The cap sleeves accented her narrow shoulders, and the blue of the dress was reflected in her bright eyes. Franny's belly did an unexpected little leap of nervousness when Mary Kate slipped an arm around her waist. Her glossy curls smelled of rose water. How had so much happened since Mary Kate left for Saint Mary's? Since before then, really? Awkward silences had filled up the space between them like balloons. Franny missed her friend but had no idea how to get her back.

And was she really old enough to be married? Franny could not believe the wedding was this weekend. Though how could she forget; Mr. Finnegan took every opportunity to remind anyone who would listen how much he'd had to pay to allow the Steinbergs into the restricted Rose Valley Country Club. (Twenty dollars per Steinberg, on the condition they didn't go off wandering.)

"I have a surprise," Mary Kate said, huddling in close. "Franny's right—high tea at the Drake is for little girls."

Franny frowned. "When did I say that?" It was true, she didn't want to go to high tea, but only because she didn't really want to *do* anything. *Doing* meant time was passing, which meant eventually she would have to go home, where what awaited was far worse than dainty sandwiches.

"I can read between the lines," Mary Kate said. She held up a hand before Franny could protest. "If this is one of my last days to do what I want, I'm not spending it with Mommy glaring at me every time I put a sugar cube in my tea." Mary Kate's chin jutted out, daring them to object.

"Naughty, naughty MK," Agnes said. Her slanting green eyes were set wide in a porcelain face where not a single pore was visible, and her black hair was flawless, even after putting on and taking off the bridesmaid dress a thousand times. She and Mary Kate had been roommates for all four years at Saint Mary's College. Their matching, delicate gold cross necklaces dangled in unison as they huddled. It was hard not to feel replaced by a newer, souped-up model.

"But you love high tea," Franny said, suddenly committed to the idea. "All the little pink sandwiches?"

"I used to love high tea," Mary Kate said, rolling her eyes. "But I overheard Peter talking about the party they're throwing for Walter. If he gets to do *that*, I want something fun too."

Peter. The name sounded like an air raid siren and brought on the same sick feeling. But this weekend, Franny had two options: suck it up or choke. She couldn't be undone by the sound of his name. At some point, she would be in the same room with him, possibly even making *conversation*. Just the idea made it difficult to breathe. Franny plastered on what she hoped was a grin. "Why, what's he doing?" she asked in a weird voice.

Agnes smirked. "If you don't know what men do at bachelor parties, there's no point in telling you." She grabbed Mary Kate's hand. "We'll do something even juicier, really make him jealous."

"Oh, we can't tell Walter," Mary Kate said. "We can't tell anyone. I just want to have a little fun, that's all. Who knows the next time I'll be able to?"

"Don't be so dramatic, MK," Agnes said. "You're getting married, not dying."

The record ended, and Mary Kate flipped it solemnly. "There's a comedian in town tonight at a nightclub called the Blue Moon, and I want to go." She reached into the pocket of her skirt, pulled out a folded newspaper page. "A colored gal called Boopsie Baxter."

Franny nearly died, right then and there. They were going to have to call Mama and Papa, tell them their twenty-three-year-old daughter had a coronary *and* a stroke *and* spontaneous cancer. Of all the newspaper clippings for Mary Kate to magic out of her skirt. Of all the days for her to bring this up. Franny seriously considered hiding behind Mary Kate's folding screen until the weekend was over, but Agnes was speechless, and someone had to say *some*thing.

"Why would Boopsie Baxter be in Chicago?" Franny said.

"What are you, an expert or something?" Agnes asked.

"Agnes has a car," Mary Kate said.

Franny's heart skipped more beats than seemed advisable. "Me? Expert? No way."

After that Christmas Eve, after high school, Franny was desperate to forget that night. But she had no idea what to do to fill the space. At a particularly low point, Mama convinced her to volunteer for the Red Cross Gray Ladies. She managed to dabble in blood and chunks for a few weeks but didn't have Mama's zeal for it. Too many grabby hands, too many sick people needing to hear they would be okay. Who was Franny to decide that for them? When the factories shut down after the war, Franny was kind of at a loss for what to do with herself. Papa didn't push it; he made a good, steady living as a plumber, so she didn't try too hard to find work. Mama seemed content to wait for the right nice Jewish boy to appear. Franny thought about college, but the lack of enthusiasm had been deafening, so she thought better of it. How had she spent all those days? How was it possible for years to slip by like a Cadillac on ice, but a single night could change everything?

Not that Franny wanted to think about nights that changed everything.

"According to this," Mary Kate said, unfolding the article, "Boopsie Baxter opened a club in Miami after the war, but she got her start at the Blue Moon, so she's coming back to do a show."

"Papa's a comedy connoisseur," Franny blurted, even though no one asked. She had never said the word *connoisseur* out loud, and by the glance Agnes shared with Mary Kate, deduced that she had pronounced it wrong. "*Texaco Star Theater, The Colgate Comedy Hour*, basically all he does when he's not working is laugh at the television set." He'd been trying to get her to appreciate his taste in comedy, but Franny didn't quite get the appeal.

"That's pathetic," Agnes said. "Male comedians aren't even funny."

"I don't know," Franny said. "I've enjoyed your jokes today."

Had that just come out of her mouth?

"Excuse me?" Agnes said.

"Showstoppers were invented at the Blue Moon, and I want to

see—" Mary Kate avoided their eyes, "I want to see Boopsie Baxter's Showstopper. Tonight." Her arms were folded, her little chin lifted. Even after all these years, Franny recognized Mary Kate's stubborn face, knew she wouldn't be budged.

"Showstopper?" Franny said hoarsely. "What's that?"

Agnes and Mary Kate looked at each other and burst out laughing. "Do you live under a rock?" Agnes said. "It's not 1945 anymore."

"You've heard of Boopsie Baxter"—Mary Kate frowned—"but not Showstoppers?"

Franny had a real talent for unforced errors. She tried to carve an Agnes-quality scoff into her face. "No, I have," Franny said. "It just sounds like a lot of hocus-pocus to me."

She couldn't go. She just couldn't feel...*it* again.

Mary Kate glared, but she wasn't very good at it. "That's not true," she said. "It *can't* be. Because Boopsie Baxter's is...that it makes you feel..." Her face got redder and redder and redder.

"Geez, MK, spit it out before your head explodes," Agnes said.

Mayday, mayday, don't say it, Mary Kate. Franny pulled out all the stops. "The Blue Moon's not just a nightclub. It's an *integrated* nightclub. You really want to do that to your daddy, the day before your wedding?"

"Gosh, Franny, are you twenty-three or sixty-three?" Agnes said. "Roger's not going to find out. Unless *you* tell him."

Mary Kate's shoulders slumped. "No, she's right. Daddy would have a coronary. Peter would be furious with me. He says being funny is a man's job."

"Peter would say that," Franny muttered. Mary Kate looked at her oddly, like she couldn't decide if her feelings should be hurt.

"Well, I'm not afraid," Agnes said. "You only have two days of freedom left, and I'm not going to let you squander them."

"That's not true," Mary Kate said. "Do you think that's true?"

"Just follow my lead," Agnes said.

"Do you think that's true, Franny?" Mary Kate said.

Franny glanced at her watch, which frankly was too dainty to read the time. There *was* another option, a way she could escape Boopsie's Showstopper. But it could not have been less enticing. Avoiding it, in fact, was the reason she was still here.

"I should...go home," she said miserably.

"Oh, Franny, are you sure?" Mary Kate said, reaching for Franny's hands. "No. Come with us. And I'll go to the party with you when we get back."

"I thought you would do anything to miss that party," Agnes said. "That's what you said."

"Don't you think you could use a laugh?" Mary Kate said. "Especially today?"

Yes, Franny could definitely use a laugh. What she didn't need was to feel *that* again. In front of Mary Kate and Agnes? How could they be so calm about it? *If you don't go, you'll lose Mary Kate for good*, a little voice said. Was there a way to see Boopsie and not feel her Showstopper? Franny sighed.

"I just can't."

Agnes slinked an arm around Mary Kate's shoulder and looked right at Franny. "Come on, MK. I'll take care of you, don't worry."

"Who's worrying?" Mrs. Finnegan burst into the room in a

flowered day dress with gloves up to the elbows and a hat with an ostrich plume that matched her shoes. She spun in a circle.

"Oh, Mommy, you look gorgeous," Mary Kate said.

"Franny, you're not even dressed yet," Mrs. Finnegan said.

"Franny was just leaving," Agnes said.

"Leaving? *I'm* paying for high tea, you know," Mrs. Finnegan said. Franny opened her mouth to say something she'd regret, but then Agnes moaned bovinely. She doubled over, stumbling toward the bed, dragging Mary Kate with her.

"Agnes!" Mary Kate said. "Are you all right?"

"Bad," Agnes said in a voice like a consumptive actress, "oysters."

"Oysters," Mrs. Finnegan said. "When did she have oysters?"

"Should we call a doctor?" Mary Kate said. "What should we do?" She looked wide-eyed at Franny, who tried to give her a meaningful eyebrow raise. It was like they had never tried to do anything sneaky in their whole lives.

"I think she just needs some rest," Franny said. "And probably no finger sandwiches. Or *tea*." Mary Kate mouthed an *oh*, which Mrs. Finnegan somehow did not see.

"Well," Mrs. Finnegan. "The three of us can still go!"

"Franny has to go home—it's Le—it's the anniversary," Mary Kate said, looking at Franny pityingly, which made Franny feel positively ill. "And...don't you think I should stay behind with Agnes? Make sure she's all right?"

"Do you think so?" Mrs. Finnegan said, her face falling behind the frozen smile. "I was so looking forward to our tea." She clapped her gloved hands together and spoke brightly. "Well, we'll do it another time! When you're a married woman. I'll just, oh, I'll go over the seating arrangements one more time, just to be safe." She removed her gloves slowly, and Franny felt sorry for her.

"Need," Agnes wheezed. "Water."

⤷◈⤶

Franny turned the doorknob to 504 slowly so Mama wouldn't hear it click.

"Where have you been?" Mama called from the kitchen.

"How did you hear that? You should have been a spy," Franny said. "Or a hunting dog." The house was even stuffier than the Finnegans', which meant Mama had the oven on. Franny's polyester dress, a goldenrod number from two seasons ago, felt like a shroud in this heat, like it had gotten tighter just in the walk across the street. The shoulder pads stuck like bandages.

"What a daughter I have, calling her mother a dog," Mama said, wiping her hands on her apron. "Where have you been?"

"I told you, I was at—"

"We're out of sugar."

"Oh, Mama, no," Franny said. "Please, no cake today."

"I won't let you rain on my fourth of July," Mama said.

"That's not the saying."

"Stop being a nudnik," Mama said.

"I'm not hungry."

Mama's eyebrows shot up into the stratosphere. "Not hungry for cake?"

Franny wiped flour from Mama's cheek. "If I eat one more of your cakes, I'll never fit into that bridesmaid dress."

"Don't be talking that shiksa nonsense," Mama said. "A husband wants a girl with a little something extra." She shook her hips to illustrate her point.

"Who's talking about husbands?"

"Your biology clock," Mama said solemnly, handing her a quarter. "Sugar. Two pounds."

As soon as the war ended, Mama had gleefully burned the rest of their ration stamps in a bonfire in the vacant lot adjacent to 504. There was still a burn mark on the ground that the landscape man, with his horse-drawn grass trimmer, grumbled about. He was trimming the grass there now. The sun flashed off his gold tooth and caught Mama's eye.

"Cut that dead tree down," Mama called, waving her hand at the giant dying elm in the lot. "One strong wind and our whole house is kaput." The landscape man grunted and turned his horse in the opposite direction.

"He doesn't listen," Mama said, shutting the door. "No one listens to me."

Franny sighed, pocketed the quarter. It was easier than fighting.

"And bring your brother. He needs the fresh air."

Franny's arms pricked up in goose bumps despite the heat. Her breath wouldn't go in, or was it supposed to go out? "Mama," she said in her most coaxing voice.

"Don't *Mama* me. It's his anniversary. Can't he at least pretend to be free?"

❧

Franny paused at the door of O'Hara's Grocery and looked Leon in the eyes. He glared back with a face just like hers. It looked better on him, even with the stubble and the dark circles under his eyes. His breath was already coming quick, and Franny forced herself to look reassuring.

"I don't want a cake," he said.

"Tell Mama that."

"You tell her."

"Leon," Franny said. "You're the only man alive who's afraid of pound cake."

Somehow, she had coaxed him out of his pajamas, but his curly hair was a wild mop, his handsome face dark with stubble. Sparse black curls of chest hair poked out of his collar. Franny looked away. On the seventh of June, 1945, he had rung the doorbell of 504, a skeleton in uniform. Franny had squeezed him gently, afraid he might snap. Or disappear again. He had stood there like a dead tree, and then he didn't say a word for three weeks. Even after he found his voice, he never spoke about what happened to him. But she was so relieved to have him back, it hardly mattered. She could almost forgive herself for that Christmas Eve. Almost.

"Okay, Leon," Franny said in her calm voice, looking him in the eyes. "First, I'm going to say hello to Mr. O'Hara, then he is going to say hello back. I will ask him for two pounds of sugar."

Leon nodded silently, his forehead slick with sweat.

"He's going to fill the bag, I'm going to pay, and then we'll walk right back out the door. Easy street." Franny smiled, and Leon tried to reciprocate. She pushed the door open and instantly knew they were doomed.

At least ten neighborhood women chatted in line, and the tiny store felt claustrophobic even to Franny. Leon squeezed her hand tight and wouldn't let go. Her older brother, clutching her hand like a child.

"Leon!" Mr. O'Hara cried. "We were just talking about you, weren't we? Your mother told me about your last episode, I'm so sorry to hear it." The women in line turned to look sympathetically or quizzically at Leon. "But you look hale and hearty today, doesn't he, Mrs. O'Hara?"

Mrs. O'Hara peeked around the aisle from where she was stocking cans of corn. "Leon!" she cried, wiping her hands on her apron and waddling toward them.

"Say something," Franny muttered. "Anything."

"I—" Leon rasped. Sweat had sprouted through his stubble, beading on his upper lip.

Everyone was staring. Mrs. O'Hara squeezed through the line of women with an *excuse me, dear*. She opened her plump arms wide, just steps away from embracing Leon, and there was nothing Franny could do to stop it. If she threw herself in the line of fire and took the hug for Leon, everyone would laugh, and Mrs. O'Hara would say, *Well, it's good to see you too, dear*, and then go to hug Leon anyway. And shouldn't Leon embrace a friend without falling to pieces? Her heart ached for him, but at the same time…did *Franny* fall apart just because bad things had happened to her?

Mrs. O'Hara dove into Leon's chest, and predictable as a book report, he started to hyperventilate. His face got slick and pale; and Franny regretted not jumping in, not speaking up. He slipped out of Mrs. O'Hara's grip and landed on all fours on the linoleum, whimpering. Mr. O'Hara came around the counter, all the women in line chirped around them. And now Franny had to step in anyway.

"Give him room," she said, holding her hands out. "Mrs. O'Hara, a wet cloth, please." She had her back to Leon. Her jaw ached from clenching it. She couldn't watch him do this again. He wouldn't talk about the war in private, but he would fall to pieces about it in public?

"Does he need a doctor?" Mr. O'Hara asked.

The doctor who could cure Leon did not yet exist. Franny gathered her courage and handed Mr. O'Hara the quarter. "We just need two pounds of sugar," she said. "Please."

He looked at her, shocked, possibly a little coldly, but he took the quarter. Mrs. O'Hara returned, sat Leon back against the wall. "There you go, lad, a nice cool cloth on you." She reached for him tentatively, like he might bite. Clearly, she had experienced Leon before.

"It's okay," Franny said. "If he's hyperventilating, he can't scream." It was meant to be a joke, but Mrs. O'Hara wasn't laughing.

"Don't talk about your poor brother that way."

Damn Mama and her cakes. She never had to watch Leon break down in public when someone shook his hand, or brushed his sleeve in passing, or dared to look in his general direction. Franny thanked Mr. O'Hara for the sugar, hugged the bag like a football she'd like to hurl across town. She thought about telling Leon the story of Mrs. Finnegan and the hideous dress, but he didn't look like he was in a laughing mood. Laughing moods weren't really in his repertoire anymore.

Leon managed to slow his breathing to a reasonable cadence. "Okay, I'm ready," he said.

"Sure," Franny said. "You look ready."

He smiled weakly but wouldn't let her pull him up from the floor. He struggled slowly to his feet. So slowly.

"Keep the cloth," Mrs. O'Hara called.

They left without saying goodbye but didn't shut the door fast enough to avoid hearing, "War's been over six years. What's wrong with the lad?"

"If Mrs. O'Hara had just stacked her cans like she was supposed to," Leon said, "everything would have been fine. Who does she think she is?" They turned the corner onto Euclid Avenue, and he chucked the rag into the street.

"She was just happy to see you," Franny said.

Leon stopped on the sidewalk in front of 504, where Mama could easily see them through the windows. "You think I'm doing this for attention? You think I want to be this way?"

"Can we please go inside?"

"Okay then, Dr. Freud, why would I want to be this way?"

"I didn't *say* that." A vivid memory from Franny's twenty-first birthday popped, without an invitation, without an RSVP, into her head. She pushed it back down, down deep into the dark sea of her mind. Couldn't Leon do that? Was it so hard to push away the bad and focus on the good? You couldn't just let yourself explode because of some crummy memories. It wasn't fair.

Franny spun around and clomped up the porch, but Leon lunged for her elbow, making her fumble the sugar, nearly spilling it all over the stoop.

"Leon! You want Mama to make us go back for *more* sugar?" Franny shoved the bag at him, and a spray of sugar crystals sprinkled on his stubble. She knew better than to engage Leon when he was in a mood. But when was he not in a mood? Didn't her moods count?

"Why not?" Leon said, his voice raising dangerously.

"Spare me," Franny said.

"If they would stop shoving their fat Irish faces where they don't belong," Leon said, "I'd go back for a thousand pounds of sugar."

"Oh, a *thousand* pounds?" Franny said. "Sure thing, Daddy Warbucks. You got a wad of bills in your pajamas or what?"

"I'm wearing," Leon said, "real pants."

They stared each other down. Leon, red-faced and sweating. He reserved all his anger and stubbornness for her, it seemed. He would stand out here all night if she didn't look away. Franny sighed. "Let's not fight, okay? Not where Mama can see."

"Mary Kate would never treat her brother like this."

Franny froze. She had offered an olive branch, and he pierced her in the heart with it. Not that he knew—

Before she could stop it, the memory of her twenty-first birthday popped up again, like a buoy on the sea, and she didn't shove it down fast enough—the backs of her thighs rubbing the upholstery of the Cadillac sedan, Peter's breath on her neck—no. She couldn't say it, she wouldn't *think* it. Certainly not on the porch in June with sweat dripping down her girdle. *Definitely* not when she would have to see Peter Finnegan in the flesh this weekend and somehow keep herself stitched together. Franny's gut was full of secrets, about to burst. She had to stay tidy, had to keep it all tucked in.

"Mary Kate is nice to everyone, even you," Franny said. "Mary Kate is sweet on the rats who eat their garbage."

"Not funny, Franny," Leon said.

"Say," Franny said, "do you think Rose Valley Country Club is restricted for rats or just Jews? Maybe there's still time for Mr. Epstein to hem some tiny tuxedos."

Leon's mouth twitched, and Franny took it as a victory. "Anyway, they'd look better than me in that dress," she said.

Mama flung the door open, and Leon just about jumped out of his skin. "What took you kids so long? Peter Finnegan is here, and Papa's not back with decorations yet." She took the sugar from Franny and padded inside. Franny froze in the doorway.

"Why is Peter here?" Franny said so she wouldn't vomit. Her guts were twisted into sailor knots—tighter and tighter the more she pulled on them.

"It's a party," Mama said drily, her arm sweeping to show the lack of decorations and general dishevelment. "Nu, can't you tell? Go entertain Peter while I make the cake."

"Why can't Leon entertain Peter?" Franny muttered, but Mama had already disappeared into the kitchen, and Leon was giving a decent impersonation of a deflated balloon. Then, without a word, he hopped up the stairs two at a time before closing the door to his bedroom. Franny wiped sweat from her forehead, wishing she believed in a god who would take care of situations like this with a lightning bolt or a plague of boils or something.

"I, for one, can't *wait* for the cake, Mrs. Steinberg. And Franny, look at you! More beautiful every day," Peter said, patting the sofa. "Tell me everything. Anyone special in your life?"

He sat back, ankle crossed over knee, strawberry-blond hair neatly combed, his handsome freckled face spread in a wide, friendly grin. She searched it for recognition. For a hint of the secret they shared. Nothing. Just everyone's favorite Peter, who volunteered his time at the Boys Clubs of America and told the neighborhood kids he lost his finger in a shark attack.

"I—can't stay," she rasped, her voice belonging to someone else. Someone in an iron lung, perhaps. She couldn't move, her feet were rooted to the spot, her insides snarled. "Mary Kate is expecting me. Wedding stuff."

"Oh, come on," Peter said. "Mary Kate gets the whole weekend; she can spare you for a couple hours. I came all the way from the city just to see you."

He was still patting the sofa, as if he could force her to sit by hypnotizing her rear end. "The city isn't even that far," Franny muttered.

"Sit on the sofa before he pats a hole in it," Mama called from the kitchen, making Peter blush. "Papa will be home soon, god willing with some balloons, and we're going to light candles and sing the 'Jolly Good Fellow'…"

"Sorry, Mama," Franny said, backing away. "She—Mary Kate needs me."

"And your family is what," Mama said, "chopped liver?"

How could she stay? How could she go? Franny's feet just wouldn't choose a direction.

"It's okay, Mrs. Steinberg," Peter said. "You know how girls are. They love you until the next big thing comes along."

If Franny stayed in this house with Peter Finnegan for one more minute, everything inside her would come rushing out, and that would be that. The end of everything. Worse than Leon's episodes. Worse than those first three months of 1945 when they thought he was dead. Worse than Fat Man *and* Little Boy.

Worse, much worse, than Boopsie Baxter's Showstopper. Franny spun on the heel of her Mary Janes and left.

"Was it something I said?" Peter laughed.

◦~❧~◦

As humiliating as it was to cross the street again, to pad up to Mary Kate's darkened bedroom where the girls were whispering, the shame of defeat was a relief by comparison. Franny slowly unclenched everything. Nearly kissed Agnes for her put-upon sigh.

"Oh good," Agnes said, the roll of her eyes almost audible. "She's back."

"Franny!" Mary Kate whispered. "The plan will work so much better with three." She thrust a sloshing bucket into Franny's arms. "It's Agnes's vomit! Oh, but don't worry, it's water. The oysters are just dollops of cold cream."

"You two are really bad at this," Franny said.

"You weren't here to help!" Mary Kate pouted. "I'm not as clever as you."

"Who needs to be clever? Just dump it in the sewer and make a big show of pretending it smells bad," Agnes said. "And then bring my car around the back alley. But don't let anyone see you."

"Can't I do that without the bucket?" Franny said.

"I told you she'd be useless," Agnes said. "I'll do it."

"No, I'll do it," Franny said. She balanced the bucket on one hip. "Give me the car key."

"Promise you won't wreck it," Agnes said. "It's brand-new."

"Isn't that what Jesus is for?"

"What's that supposed to mean?"

"Well, what's the point of believing in a ghost that doesn't protect your stuff?"

"Our Lord and Savior Jesus Christ is *not* a *ghost*."

"Girls!" Mary Kate said. "We have to hurry. Agnes and I will shimmy down the drainpipe when we hear the engine, just like high school."

"You sneaked out in high school?" Franny asked. "And didn't invite me?"

Agnes snorted.

"Well," Mary Kate said, "I'm inviting you now, anyway."

CHAPTER THREE

FRANNY RUBBED HER HANDS ON THE STEERING WHEEL OF Agnes's Pontiac. Mary Kate was afraid to drive in the city, and Agnes didn't know her way around, so Franny convinced them she drove all the time. In truth, Papa had a '48 Cadillac sedan, but she was only allowed to drive it from the garage to the street, and only because it was her chore to wash the car. That was a chore she enjoyed, wearing coveralls and a kerchief, spraying the water everywhere, buffing the car shiny as a mirror, seeing Papa's delight at a job well done.

"Don't drive too fast," Mary Kate said, leaning over the back seat.

Agnes rolled her eyes. "You're a drag, Mary Kate," she said. "Drive too fast, Franny."

A home run cracked in Franny's chest. As soon as Franny had gotten behind the wheel, Agnes had switched allegiances. Franny glanced back at Mary Kate's pouty face before guiltily shifting into higher gear. Agnes stuck her feet out the passenger window and wiggled them. "I love the feeling of wind in my toes," she said, leaning back, hair tickling Franny's forearm. Poor Mary

Kate hugged herself, hot wind whipping her curls around. Franny almost slowed down but then remembered Peter and pressed on the gas to outrun him.

"Come on, Franny, let loose," Agnes said. "You know you want to." She howled like a wolf into the wind.

Franny laughed nervously.

"That didn't sound like a howl to me," Agnes said.

"Oh," Franny said, "I never howl and drive."

Agnes laughed. "Mary Kate didn't tell me you were funny," she said.

Franny shrugged. "I'm no Boopsie Baxter."

"But it's not an opinion. Empirically, you're funny."

These Saint Mary's girls said things like *empirically* in casual conversation. Franny's humor slipped away like Mary Kate's tiny kimono, and she focused on the road.

"Hey, Agnes, you heard of…Fingers Marcone?" Mary Kate said dramatically.

"I can't hear you," Agnes said. She winked at Franny.

"Fingers Marcone!" Mary Kate hollered.

"Is that one of your little-girl tea sandwiches?"

Mary Kate snorted from the back seat. "I guess you don't have newspapers in Indy." Blotchy redness crept up Agnes's neck, and Franny was a little disappointed to see she was human.

"He owns the Blue Moon," Franny said.

"He's the *gangster* who owns the Blue Moon," Mary Kate said. "Comedians have been shot there. Just because someone doesn't like their joke."

That was mostly before the war, when it was men onstage and in the audience, but Franny didn't correct her. She had never been to the Blue Moon, but she knew its reputation.

Agnes made a gun out of finger and thumb and pointed it at Franny. "Bang," she said.

Franny swerved the steering wheel, pretending she was hit. Mary Kate yelped and grabbed the front seat. "Franny, be careful!" she said. Agnes and Franny shared a grin like an ice cream sundae.

Now that she was driving, hot wind in her face, putting miles between herself and…everything else, Franny let herself get a little excited.

"Forget about Fingers," she said. "Lottie Marcone's the one who's really in charge. She was the first person who put girls onstage during the war. No Lottie, no Showstoppers. Plus," and here, Franny paused for dramatic effect. "Rumor has it? One of her rich lovers proposed marriage by giving her a Bengal tiger."

"That plus a diamond and you're in business," Agnes said. Franny growled, and Agnes elbowed her chummily.

"Don't be absurd," Mary Kate said. "How do you know so much about the Blue Moon all of a sudden? You don't believe in that stuff, remember?"

"I don't live under a rock, Mary Kate," Franny said. Agnes laughed.

"Oh yeah? Since when?" Mary Kate asked.

"I didn't memorize my diary," Franny said, glad that Mary Kate couldn't see her flushed face. "But I did have a life while you were in college."

"Franny Steinberg," Agnes said, "you are full of surprises."

Mary Kate rolled her eyes and flopped back in her seat. She muttered something into the wind.

"Say again?" Franny asked.

"Is Leon coming to my wedding?" Mary Kate shouted then blushed. "He didn't RSVP. I wouldn't care, *obviously*, but there's a part for him at the reception and for you—"

"Of course he is," Franny said. Agnes smirked in her periphery, which emboldened Franny. "Why would he get out of it if the rest of us have to go?"

Mary Kate's face crumpled, and Franny instantly regretted her words.

Agnes roared, slapping the dashboard with her palm. "I told you," she said. "Empirical!"

❦

Franny parked on the curb in front of the Blue Moon, as though she had been there a million times. The name of the club—Blue Moon Cocktail Lounge—was lit up in blue neon cursive and surrounded by flashing light bulbs above the door, as though it were Chez Paree instead of a tiny storefront club run by the Outfit. The neighborhood was all right in the daytime, but Franny had heard stories of mobster guys shooting people at night for looking at them funny, just innocent bystanders. Would the car be safe all alone here? It seemed so helpless, sitting on the curb with no one to take care of it. Franny hesitated, unwilling to let go of the door handle.

Agnes was already skipping up to the door, and Mary Kate hung back, as though torn between Franny and Agnes. Franny hugged

Mary Kate's arm, realized it was the first time they had been alone together in years. They used to talk for hours when they were girls. About what?

"Can you believe you'll be a married woman this weekend?" Franny asked. What a dumb question.

Mary Kate nodded absently, the lights of the marquee flashing on her blue dress. "Do you think it's a good idea?"

Franny was not even remotely prepared for this kind of conversation. "Cold feet are totally normal. Doesn't mean anything."

Mary Kate looked like she might reveal something frightening. But then she slapped Franny's arm and grinned. "Don't be silly," she said, "Every girl dreams about the kind of wedding I'm about to have."

"Oh, definitely," Franny said. "I dream about it every night."

Mary Kate rolled her eyes. They stared at the door to the Blue Moon, each waiting for the other to do something first. "I meant," Mary Kate said, "if this is a good idea. Boopsie Baxter."

That was not what Mary Kate meant. "I know," Franny said.

Nothing had been right in Franny's life after she walked into the Empire Room that Christmas Eve. She couldn't prove it was because of Boopsie Baxter, but she also couldn't prove it wasn't. And yet, now that she was standing right outside the door to the Blue Moon, she couldn't bear the idea of *not* going inside.

Agnes poked her head out the door. "You girls coming or what?"

Mary Kate took a deep breath and nodded to Franny, and they burst through the door into a cloud of smoke and jazz. The bouncer, a squat woman in denim and flannel who reminded Franny queasily of Diane from the Empire Room, took their money, patted them down with her ham hands, and then jerked her head toward the bar.

"After a petting session," Franny said once the bouncer was out of earshot, "I usually get offered a cigarette." Mary Kate blushed to her ears, but Agnes laughed and wrapped a slender arm around Franny's waist. Franny sucked in her stomach.

Just inside the door, the bar stretched dimly along the left side, eventually curving out of sight. It was crowded with girls laughing and shouting drink orders. Franny had never seen such a variety of girls together in one room—from stuffy-looking matrons to girls Franny's age, Negro girls, white girls, petticoats and pencil skirts and even pants, everyone gazing at themselves in the mirrored wall behind the bar, patting their hair, waving cigarettes dangerously close to each other's ears. The bartender, a petite blond girl in rolled-up shirtsleeves and a red bow tie, nodded at each order solemnly, shaking a cocktail mixer in one hand and pouring a champagne bottle with the other. Franny was an explorer in a girly jungle, peering through misty cigarette smoke, a garden of floral perfumes tingling her nose. Crinoline and satin rustled like the pages of Franny's ancient copy of *Robinson Crusoe*. Her shoulders relaxed. She hadn't even realized they'd been tense.

Past the bar, the long, narrow club opened slightly. Blue velvet booths lined both walls with round tables in the middle, huddled together and pressed right up against the stage. Two U-shaped booths sat side by side in the middle of the club, facing away from the stage and toward the door. Who would want to face away from the stage?

Franny was certainly not going to ask the girl sitting in that

booth. She looked like she didn't answer questions, only asked them.
No, she didn't ask, she *demanded*. The club was standing-room only,
but the girl took up the whole booth. Her arms stretched across the
back, one holding an old-fashioned ebony cigarette holder. Straight
bangs cut across her forehead, black hair curled slightly against her
neck. She wore a black dress with a high neck that exposed bare,
white shoulders, a diamond necklace glittering at her throat. She
had the carriage and clothes of a much older woman, but she was, at
most, a few years older than Franny.

It was Lottie Marcone; it had to be. Franny shivered in the hot,
stuffy room.

Lottie watched everyone and no one, bringing the cigarette
holder to her lips and blowing out a delicate trail of smoke. A martini
with three olives sat untouched in front of her. For a split second, she
seemed to notice Franny staring, but then her eyes slid past as though
Franny were nothing more interesting than one of the odd landscape
scenes painted on the wooden walls.

Franny was pulled away by Agnes. "Mary Kate got us a table,"
she said.

The nightclub was packed, but sure enough, Mary Kate was patting the seat in a cozy booth tucked up against the wall. Franny went
to slide in next to her, but Agnes shook her head.

"I'm sitting by Franny," she said. "You don't mind, do you,
MK?" She pulled Franny, laughing, into the booth with her, while
Mary Kate sat alone across from them.

"This place is unbelievable," Agnes said, lighting a cigarette.
"Negroes over here, suburban hausfraus over there, a group of *bull*

dykes, for Chrissake." Franny's gut flip-flopped at that frightening word—why should it scare her so much? It was just a word—while Mary Kate gasped at the name-in-vain-taking. "Then there's *that*—" Agnes pointed at the woman in the U-shaped booth and leaned in, narrowing her eyes. "Franny, is she...in the Mob?"

"That's Lottie Marcone," Franny said.

The three of them stared for as long as they dared. Mary Kate smoothed her hair and sat up straighter.

"Can you imagine," Mary Kate said, "being here that first time? Thinking you were just going to get a laugh, and getting—Boopsie Baxter's Showstopper?"

Imagine that! Franny forced a laugh that sounded a bit too much like a scream. "Boy, you sure are obsessed with that Showstopper."

"Am not," Mary Kate said. She fiddled with her manicure. "Just curious, is all. Is that a crime?"

"Not yet," Franny said.

"Personally, I'm glad *my* first time was with a man," Agnes said.

Mary Kate's red face warmed them from across the table. Franny tamped down a rogue bubble of a bad memory. Not here. Not now. Not ever.

"And here I thought you girls went to a Catholic school," Franny said.

"Exactly." Agnes tapped her cigarette in the ashtray. "So which is it, Franny?" she said. "Are Showstoppers real or not?"

The all-girl band finished their set to a smattering of applause, and Franny clapped too loudly, giving Agnes a phony apologetic look. The club felt so safe, so homey. Would these suburban housewives *really* come out here if Boopsie's Showstopper were as embarrassing as Franny remembered? But then again—the other women at the Empire Room hadn't looked terrified and embarrassed. Just Franny.

The all-girl band began packing up their instruments, and a tall girl in a colorful gingham dress hopped up to the microphone, swinging her ponytail out of the way.

Mary Kate frowned and leaned in. "Who's this?" she whispered. "Where's Boopsie?" Agnes shushed her.

"Good evening, ladies and degenerates," she said in a low, soothing voice. The room released an anticipatory chuckle. All except for Lottie Marcone, who continued to face the door, unsmiling, her body so still, she might have been a Marshall Field's mannequin.

"My name is Andy Grand Canyon, and I'll be your mistress of ceremonies for the evening," the girl onstage said. "Girls, we have got the lineup of a lifetime. Forget calisthenics, forget diet pills, the laughing you'll do today will melt the pounds off your waistline, guaranteed."

The audience whooped and clapped, and Andy Grand Canyon set up a portable record player on a stool, laying the needle on a record. A guttural chanting started, followed by a rhythmic wailing and an insistent drumbeat. Her face turned solemn, stony even. The strange rhythms of the chants washed over Franny. Then, suddenly, the comedian's mouth twisted into a bright, mischievous grin.

"Hollywood is just terrible," Andy Grand Canyon said. Even in the packed room, it seemed Andy directed her warm gaze at Franny alone. She felt like the center of the universe. "I'm serious. Because of Hollywood Westerns, you think all Indians live in tepees, but some of us live in hogans. Those are kind of like your 'cold-water flats.'" Andy flipped the microphone cord over her feet as she paced the stage. Franny was mesmerized. "You think we all hunt buffalo, but some of us grow squash. Me? Eat a buffalo? I'd be out of my gourd." A few light chuckles from the audience. "Worst of all, ladies, you think we say things like *how. Papoose. Smoke 'em peace pipe.* But we're just like you. We have high school dances, Fords, Grandma's Sunday dinner. We like to go to nightclubs and laugh just like you. And when a man likes us, he scoots across the bench seat of his Ford, puts his hand on our neck, and says, 'C'mon, baby, smoke 'em peace pipe for me.'"

The joke was blue, but Franny's laugh was faster than her embarrassment. It exploded out of her like fireworks. And in that moment, the booths and Lottie Marcone and Andy Grand Canyon faded from view. Now she was Cinderella, from the movie, two cartoon bluebirds in kerchiefs perched on her knees while she sat propped up in bed. The prince's castle taunted her from the open window, and her nightdress was a frumpy hand-me-down, but Cinderella didn't bother with all that. She took a deep breath, overcome by the need to express herself through song.

Franny realized she couldn't carry a tune to save her life…and then the scene popped like a balloon. Across the table, Mary Kate muttered tunelessly to herself, running an imaginary brush through her hair. Agnes poked Franny's chin with her finger, trying to get her to perch on it. Girls at other tables were dancing or admiring themselves, and across the club, one woman had stretched out precariously on the table and was starting to loudly warble "A Dream Is a Wish Your Heart Makes."

Andy Grand Canyon tried to make herself heard over the sing-ing. "And speaking of *jobs*…Uncle Sam promised me the Windy City was full of 'em. So what do I do? I take a Greyhound bus all the way to Chicago, just to find out our dear uncle loves to blow smoke even more than Hollywood Indians."

No one laughed. Franny wanted to be polite but didn't quite get it. And the singing droned on and on. Andy stopped pacing, openly glaring at the back of Lottie Marcone's head, but Lottie didn't seem to notice. She took a dainty sip of her martini, her posture straight as an arrow, not even the hint of a smirk on her face. She could have balanced a book on her head, like Franny had had to do in etiquette class. All the other girls could do it easy, but the book always slid off Franny's head and crashed to the floor.

Andy slapped the microphone. The squealing feedback finally stopped the woman from singing and snapped Mary Kate and Agnes out of it. Mary Kate clutched her ears and winced. Andy Grand Canyon grinned. "Don't forget who has the microphone, girls," she said.

"I was Cinderella," Mary Kate whispered. "From the movie! Birds and mice and deer were choosing my clothes for me. I'm not making it up, I swear." Mary Kate looked from Franny to Agnes, who was nodding dreamily.

"My fairy godmother just transformed me for the ball," Agnes said, "And the prince fanned me with a palm leaf and fed me grapes."

"When does that happen in the movie?" Mary Kate said.

"It wasn't a movie," Agnes said. "It was real."

"No, it was a Showstopper," Mary Kate said. "Wasn't it, Franny?"

Lottie was looking directly at them. She held a finger to her lips, and a chill jangled Franny from head to toe.

Then, right in front of the stage, a chair clattered to the floor. The girl who had been sitting on it fell backward with a plop, looking stunned. She scrambled up, looked wildly around the club, and then ran past the stage and out the side door.

"Happens every show," Andy Grand Canyon said. "Some girls just can't handle their Showstoppers."

Agnes gripped Franny's hand. "It *was* a Showstopper," she whispered. "I want my princey back."

This Andy Grand Canyon had a Showstopper Franny could handle. More than handle—she could enjoy it. Who didn't want to be Cinderella? The second half of the movie, anyway—not the scrubbing and insults.

"Before I introduce our next comedian," Andy Grand Canyon said, "I do want to note one teeny-tiny change in the program— unfortunately, Boopsie Baxter has come down with a rotten case of laryngitis, so she will not be entertaining you this evening. I know, I know, settle down," she said, over the groans and complaints. "But she promised me she'll be drinking nothing but hot toddies all day. She has decided to perform here at the Blue Moon on Saturday night, and you all get free admission." The crowd clapped and cheered. Franny, louder than any of them. No Boopsie? She could not believe her luck.

"But," Mary Kate said, "Saturday's too late. I'll already be married." Her blue eyes glistened, and she blinked rapidly to keep the tears in.

Sheltered, innocent Mary Kate, who had probably only let her husband-to-be kiss her on the cheek, wanted to feel Boopsie Baxter's

Showstopper—and Franny, who had lived through it, would give anything to forget it ever happened. Poor Mary Kate. She looked positively heartbroken.

"FDR won a war from a wheelchair, but Boopsie Baxter can't be funny with a throat tickle?"

Mary Kate was staring at Franny. Agnes was staring at Franny. The entire audience had turned to look at her. Franny had said this out loud, and she had said it *loudly*. She sank down in the booth and tried to disappear.

Two seconds of silence passed, five seconds, but then all at once, the whole audience—plus Agnes and Mary Kate—laughed. Some howled, some cackled, some chuckled, some even clapped. It felt…well, it felt *great*. Franny poked her head up from under the table.

"Do you all hear something? Something high-pitched and irritating?" Andy Grand Canyon said, cupping a hand to her ear. "Sounds like a mosquito about to get squashed."

Suddenly, Lottie Marcone was standing at their table, cigarette trailing smoke. Petite and glamorous and terrifying.

"Girls," she said in a smooth-as-silk voice. "There is no talking during the show, no exceptions. This will be your only warning."

Franny mimed locking her lips and throwing away the key. Lottie lingered for a moment then turned away.

"It's okay," Mary Kate whispered. "We tried, that's what matters." She discreetly wiped her eye but left a telltale smear of mascara and grinned hugely like Mrs. Finnegan. It was too much.

"Saturday is too late," Franny said. "She can't come back."

Lottie stopped and turned slowly. "You had better be dying."

"Saturday is," Mary Kate said, blushing for no reason Franny could discern, "it's my wedding day."

Lottie laughed. "Then you're the first girl in history to choose your husband over Boopsie Baxter."

The audience laughed, and Mary Kate blushed, looking at her fingernails.

Franny clenched her fists under the table. It wasn't fair. They came all the way out here just for a snooty Mob girl to make Mary Kate feel stupid? "Everyone came here for Boopsie Baxter. I think," Franny said, getting warmed up. "I think this is a scam."

Now that Franny had gotten indignant, she couldn't stop running her mouth. Even Agnes looked scared. Andy Grand Canyon was about to slap the microphone again, but Lottie held up a hand. Her mouth curled into a smile.

"That's quite an accusation. Barb, show this nice girl—Franny, was it?—out of my club. We only allow amateurs during Amateur Hour." Lottie smirked at the weak smattering of applause. But up close, her jaw pulsed, and her eyes flashed dangerously. Franny had done more than annoy her—she had hit a nerve. This was bad. This was the sort of thing that got a girl's fingers chopped off.

"No men allowed," Barb yelled at the door, thankfully drawing Lottie's attention away from Franny. Two pairs of feet scuffled, and Barb grunted, struggling to restrain a man who was trying to get in. Satin crinkled anxiously, and girls murmured, worrying it was their husband at the door, catching them in flagrante. Men did not show up unannounced at nightclubs. That was the whole point.

"Oh no," Mary Kate breathed. "It's Peter."

Peter's worried face popped up over Barb's head, searching in the darkness for Mary Kate and finally locking eyes with her. "Mary Kate Finnegan, you come out here right now," he said.

Lottie blew out cigarette smoke. "Well," she said, tapping her ash directly on their table. "Enjoy married life."

"That's her brother," Agnes said.

Lottie raised her eyebrows. "Two for the price of one," she said. "Lucky duck."

Mary Kate scooted miserably out of the booth, looked expectantly at Agnes and Franny.

Agnes shrugged. "He's not my brother."

"Sorry, Charlie," Lottie said. "Time for all three of you to skedaddle." She lifted her foot to the booth, revealing a tiny, stylish holster and pearl-handled derringer wrapped around her shapely ankle. Her mouth curled into a grin. "And don't come back. Ever." Franny and Agnes slunk out of the booth, and the room erupted into applause.

Papa's Cadillac sat on the curb, Leon slumped in the passenger seat. Papa had let *Peter* drive the Cadillac? It was so unfair. She tapped at the window to get Leon's attention, but he pretended he hadn't heard. He couldn't still be sore about the sugar argument, could he? He had shaved, looked calm, had pressed his pants. It wasn't fair that he'd save the worst of himself for Franny.

"I'll drive back with Agnes," Franny said. "She doesn't know her way around the city."

"Get in the car, Franny," Leon said through the closed window.

She slid into the back seat with Mary Kate, face hot with humiliation. "Least you could do is let me drive," Franny muttered. Leon turned to look at her. His eyes were red rimmed. Her voice caught in her throat.

Peter sank into the driver's seat and shifted into gear almost before he had the door shut.

"I'm sorry, Peter," Mary Kate said meekly.

Peter sighed. "I'm just glad I found you." He patted Mary Kate's knee, and she burst into tears. Franny looked at her, stunned.

"I was so scared," Mary Kate said.

"What?" Franny said, but the word stuck in her throat, came out as a cough. Mary Kate avoided her eyes.

"I know, sweetheart," Peter said. "It's not *your* fault." He handed her a handkerchief, and she dabbed at her tears.

Franny looked from Mary Kate to the back of Peter's head, to Leon's profile. Pain shimmied through her guts, and she was worried she might not make it home in time to deal with its consequences.

"How did you find us? Are you a KGB mole or something?" Franny said, clutching her belly. She had just heard this term on Papa's TV, couldn't help thinking of a whiskered snout in a teeny ushanka hat, hunched over a reel-to-reel in its underground burrow.

"That's serious business," Peter said. "And it's not ladylike to joke."

Leon said nothing. How could Leon say nothing?

Mary Kate snuffled into the hanky and stared out the window the whole ride.

"A spy *would* say that," Franny muttered.

❧

Papa was blasting *Texaco Star Theater* from the TV room—the breakfast nook, it used to be, before TV. Mama would not allow the television to become the centerpiece of the house, like it was at the Finnegans', but that meant the table was now stuffed into the small kitchen and everyone had to listen to Papa laugh at the television during breakfast. Balloons littered the floor, still trying to make the party happen.

Milton Berle emerged to cheers and squeals. "I'm a June bride, aren't I cute?" he said. "You're just jealous."

"How'd they get a wedding dress to fit him?" Papa cackled to no one. "Look at that!"

Slapstick and men in women's clothing and stale Borscht Belt patter—TV paled in comparison to what Franny had just witnessed.

"Ruth, is that you?" Papa's chair squeaked as he leaned forward to turn down the volume dial and wait for the answer.

"Just me," Franny called. "And Leon." Papa *hmph*ed, sat back in his chair. "Your mother has been kvetching with the Gray Ladies at the hospital for over two hours. Couldn't you kids eat the damn cake? I'm starving!" He turned up the volume again.

"I'll cook something, Papa," Franny said. Leon followed her silently into the kitchen, like a ghost, the shadow of a ghost. A ghost's ghost.

Franny sniffed an onion dramatically. "*Phew*," she said. "This is a strong one."

"What has gotten into you?" Leon asked in a low voice. A voice he did not possess before the war.

"What?" she said. "Smell it yourself. It's a real tearjerker." She turned around and held the onion under his nose, which he slapped out of her hand. It landed hard on the linoleum and rolled under the counter. "No onions," she said, saluting. "Roger that, Private."

He grabbed her saluting wrist, hard. "You're hurting me," she said. "Let go!"

"Kids?" Papa called over the TV. "No monkey business."

"Mary Kate is about to be a married woman," Leon said. "She had no business at a nightclub. An Outfit night club, Franny, what were you thinking?"

"She wanted to go," Franny muttered.

"Mary Kate will do whatever her friends say," Leon said. "She doesn't have her own opinions, you know that."

"It was her idea."

"That's not what Peter told me," Leon said. "And that's not all Peter told me." He let go of her wrist, and Franny rubbed it, picking up the onion as carefully as a family heirloom.

Leon looked over at the breakfast nook and then back to Franny. "He told me about your twenty-first birthday."

Franny's mind floated up and out of her body until it hit the ceiling, and then she was watching herself standing on the linoleum tile with her ugly, frizzy hair in her sweaty old dress. Stupid onion in her hand. Then her mind slammed back down into her body, hard, colliding with the memory of Peter pressing on her with all his weight, fumbling with the petticoat of her brand-new dress that Mama had bought for the occasion, fumbling with his belt. And then everything that came after.

◦~੭੭

"Why would you do that?" Leon was whispering, but his voice pummeled her ears. "He had to push you away? Like a—like one of *those* girls?" The memory kept coming, in full Technicolor, playing in front of her eyes like a movie that would never end.

"Franny, say something," Leon said. "You can't just ignore me." His face was blotchy, fists clenched and vibrating. What was he going to do?

Franny swallowed the memory, wrapped an old rusty anchor around it, shoved it in a pirate chest, tied the rope of her guts around it, watched it sink. "Think fast," she said, bobbling the onion and tossing it at Leon. It bounced off his chest and rolled to the floor again. "You'll never make the big leagues with those reflexes."

Leon punched the countertop and winced, clutching his fist.

"When's dinner going—oh," Papa said. "Strong onion?" He had his ratty cardigan on that Mama hated, his ratty house shoes that she kept trying to throw away. Papa had an entire wardrobe of new sweaters and house shoes that he never wore, his grease-rubbed work clothes squeezed into a corner in the back.

Leon straightened himself up. "Your daughter," he said, "went to a nightclub today."

War or no war, Franny was going to let him have it. He could sob on the linoleum of O'Hara's Grocery, and she would take that secret to her grave, but he just couldn't stand the idea of her laughing in public?

"You're kidding," Papa said, gripping Franny's shoulder somberly. "In the afternoon?" He winked.

Franny's anger evaporated in an instant. "Well," she said, "early evening, really."

"You're missing the point here, Pop."

Papa peered at them over his glasses. "This is really your mother's department. She'll be home soon." He patted Franny's cheek and nodded as though to reassure them of this inevitability then shuffled back to his seat in front of the TV, turning up the volume.

"Why are you always trying to get me in trouble?" Franny tested her voice to make sure the right words would come out. "You used to be nice to me."

"And you used to be nice," Leon said. He left Franny stranded in the kitchen, clutching the onion like a life raft.

❧

"A bissel too much salt in here, Franny." Mama coughed, taking a sip of water.

"I think it's delicious," Papa said, dabbing his forehead. "I'll never turn down a stew, even on the hottest day of the year."

"Did you use all the brisket?" Mama said. "I was hoping to make a roast. Did you save enough for a roast?"

"Maybe a bit too heavy for a summer meal," Papa said, "but a good hearty supper for a man who's worked all day, isn't that right, Leon?"

Leon hadn't touched his stew, and it was forming a beefy skin on top.

"Speaking of working all day," Papa said, "Leon tells me Franny went to a nightclub. In the afternoon! Why do they call them nightclubs, then, I wonder."

"What?" Mama said, dabbing her lips and turning to Franny. "When? After the cake?"

"Just forget it," Franny said.

"Why didn't you bring the cake with you?"

"This is what we're talking about?" Leon asked, standing up and tossing his napkin into the beef stew. "Everything's a comedy routine in this family. Do you know what happens at these nightclubs?"

"Don't speak to your mother that way, Leonard," Papa said. "We're not children. We remember vaudeville, don't we, Ruth? You want to see how the other half lives, wow. Take a peek backstage at a vaudeville theater."

"You were backstage at a vaudeville theater?" Franny asked. She knew this story backward and forward, but Papa wouldn't tell it unless someone expressed interest. He was shy that way.

"Well, let me just have my after-dinner mints," Papa said, dropping Alka-Seltzer into his water, "and I'll tell you. I was a lousy student, kids. Not because I was a putz. No! I was scared to go to school. The rotten neighborhood kids chased me and said I smelled like cabbage and drank Christian blood, and they'd make themselves so mad that they'd punch my lights out. Four or five of them at a time! And my papa—a rebbe's son!—selling pickles door-to-door. I couldn't tell him. Mama? Forget about it. I had to figure it out by myself."

Papa took a sip of his bubbling water, and Franny sat perfectly silent. Even Leon stood still, haunting the table. In all the times they'd heard this story, or any story, Papa had never mentioned anything about his childhood.

"I always had a stomachache, and sometimes Mama let me stay home. But when she made me go to school, I'd walk halfway there and then duck in the back door of the Grand Theatre at, ah, Grand and Chrystie. I can still see it. I can still smell it, not so good. Uncle Eli had a regular act there. He was a star in the Yiddish theater. I'll tell you, my stomach stopped hurting the moment I walked into that theater. The dancing girls would cuddle me, and boy, those comedians sure could drink. One time, Benny Birnbaum, he was three sheets to the wind, and as he went onstage, he grabbed me by the wrist and dragged me on with him! He could barely get the words out, but by this point, I knew the routines cold, so I told his jokes for him, and he was my straight man. The audience laughed so hard, it was intoxicating! I remember thinking I'd be the youngest vaudevillian to ever hit the Yiddish stage. But my papa caught wind of what Eli was up to, and he tanned my hide something fierce. I never got to go to the theater with him again." Papa sighed, finished his Alka-Seltzer. "I told myself when I was old enough, I was going to run away and join the theater. I was going to be famous just like Uncle Eli. There's nothing in the world like being onstage, making people laugh. It's a lot like fixing a clogged drain, if you can believe that. Maybe not quite as funny. Anyway, we moved to Chicago, and, well, things were different after that."

Papa always stopped the story here. Franny hoped for more this time, but Papa smiled at them in his satisfied way, and she knew he was done. Could she ask him about his childhood? Could she ask him about *things were different after that*? How was this story different from the other stories? So much of the family had been wiped out in the pogroms in that era, Franny didn't even know their names or relations. Sisters, grandparents, cousins? Kiev, Odessa, Vilna? She should ask. She would ask him.

"May I be excused?" Leon said, breaking the spell.

"Nu, you're a grown man," Mama said. "Excuse yourself if you like." She gathered up all the plates, clattering them loudly, and retired to the kitchen.

After Leon and Mama left, Papa put a hand on Franny's hand. His hands always looked dirty, from the grease and grime of people's plumbing, but it was just the ghost of the dirt. For all his falling-apart house shoes, he was actually quite tidy. "I remember when you were five and Lenny was nine," he said. "You had found your way into Mama's vanity and smeared her brand-new cherry-red lipstick all over your face. Too much, that lipstick cost. But you didn't mean anything by it. You just wanted to be pretty like Mama. We all need color in our lives, even little nudniks. But that tube of lipstick was supposed to last Mama through the Depression. You may not have been old enough to know that, but Lenny was.

"He found you in our bedroom with red smeared across your face, the tiniest nub of lipstick left in the tube, and in his little nine-year-old head, he thought you were in a lot of trouble. He took you into the bathroom, washed the lipstick off your face, and then painted his own lips with it. Then he marched downstairs and set the tube on the kitchen table. He looked at your mama and me and said, 'I'm sorry I used up your lipstick, Mama. I take full responsibility for my actions.' Like a little grown-up! What a mensch. Of course, we could see that you still had some pink on your little punim, so we knew exactly what had happened. But it was important to take a little boy seriously, and he had done a very good job protecting you, which he should! Your mama told him to stand next to her, which he did. She ruffled his hair and said, 'You are a brave boy to tell the truth. Now give your mama a kiss.' He grinned and smeared that lipstick all over her face."

Lipstick Leon would definitely have defended her today. "That doesn't sound like Leon," Franny said.

Papa nodded, patted her hand. "Lenny loves us," he said. "The anger will pass. Eventually, it will pass."

Franny didn't know about all that, but Papa looked convinced, so she nodded. Mama had stopped clattering to listen, and now she started filling the kitchen sink. Papa stood. "Do me a favor, though," he said. "Stay away from Fingers Marcone. Okay?"

"Don't worry, Papa," Franny said. "I got kicked out anyway."

A bowl crashed in the kitchen. "This goyische wasteland! Nu, now I should worry about the Mob too?"

CHAPTER FOUR

BELOW MARY KATE'S WINDOW, MR. FINNEGAN WAS MUTTER-ing to himself. He had hiked up his tuxedo pants and crouched on his property line, the bald spot on the back of his freckled head glistening with sweat, measuring the height of Dr. Avery's grass with a wooden ruler. Dr. Avery was nowhere to be seen, and Franny couldn't for the life of her see the difference in length between the Averys' lawn and the Finnegans'.

"If they can't take care of their property," Mr. Finnegan said to no one and everyone, "then they shouldn't be allowed to own property."

Franny had never once introduced herself to the Averys; it had somehow seemed like betraying the Finnegans. But also, what would she even say? They seemed like they preferred to keep to themselves anyway.

"What are you staring at?" Mary Kate asked through the mirror. "Do you think my hair looks too big?" She had just removed it from Coke can curlers and brushed it away from her face like Elizabeth Taylor, and it *was* a little strange to see Mary Kate without the cork-screw rag curls framing her cheeks.

"There are *so* many eligible men at the wedding," Mary Kate said. "From good families too. Rodney was captain of the crew team at Notre Dame, and he's tall, you'll like that. Agnes is a little sweet on him, but really, they would be a horrid match. Then Daniel, he's an Adler from Indianapolis, not terribly tall but broad shoulders, you know, which can give the illusion of height. Oh, but his father's family is German, never mind." She bit her lip and barreled onward before Franny could respond, listing out each bachelor and his attributes, leaving out, of course, that every single one of them would be Catholic. You never knew how the Finnegans' pursuit of Franny's eventual Catholicism would pop up in conversation. *Franny, you should come to Mass. Franny, it's so hot out, don't you want to sprinkle some holy water on your face? Franny, I bet five minutes in confession would ease your conscience.*

"I heard that," Agnes said, materializing in the doorway with Mrs. Finnegan and a platter of sweet rolls delivered from Strickland's. "You better not have your eye on Rodney," she said to Franny. Whatever tenuous rapport they had created had disappeared— *poof*—after the Blue Moon episode, when Agnes had been forced to drive through an unfamiliar city all alone. She had gotten horribly, humiliatingly lost, somehow ending up on Lake Shore Drive, all the way downtown.

Agnes squinted as though she was used to looking down imperiously at other girls, but Franny had an inch or two on her, so she had to squint up.

"Too tall," Franny said. "I'm into the little ones." Agnes laughed before she could stop herself.

"You sure are a weird duck," she said.

Mrs. Finnegan placed the platter of sweet rolls on Mary Kate's vanity, and Mary Kate wrinkled her nose.

"You didn't catch Agnes's tummy ache, did you dear?" Mrs. Finnegan asked, clamping a hand on Mary Kate's forehead to test her temperature. Agnes stifled a snort.

"Mommy," Mary Kate said. "Oysters aren't contagious."

"She hasn't eaten more than carrots in two days," Agnes said. "Won't be able to squeeze into that dress if she does."

"I won't eat a bite until the car comes to take us to Union Station," Mary Kate said.

"That makes one of us," Franny said, grabbing a sticky-sweet roll, ignoring Mrs. Finnegan's glare.

Mary Kate brushed her hair serenely, just like Cinderella. Any trace of cold feet had disappeared, and Franny found herself wondering if she had imagined it. Mary Kate looked calm and composed, a wife-to-be who wished to be nothing else. Franny couldn't remember the last time she had felt calm and composed. She took a big, sticky bite of sweet roll, straining to chew with her mouth closed.

Franny had met Walter only once. Mary Kate had brought him home for Easter, and they'd rung the Steinbergs' doorbell in the middle of the Passover seder, to which Papa had cried out, "Elijah, you don't need to ring the doorbell!" They made space at the table, but Walter had stammered an excuse about some fictional obligation, and the two of them rushed back out barely after they had said hello.

"That's the Irish goodbye for you," Papa had said.

The lawn situation had gotten heated. Or rather, Dr. Avery was now striding across his lawn, and Mr. Finnegan was shouting and shaking the ruler at him. Dr. Avery held his hand out for the ruler then snapped it in half and tossed it into Mr. Finnegan's manicured bushes. The way Mr. Finnegan grabbed his heart, you would think he had just been shot through it.

Mrs. Finnegan peered out the window and gasped. "Pardon me, girls, I have to save your father from himself," she said. "Who knows what kind of firearm that Negro has."

"Mr. Finnegan is the one with the shotgun," Franny said.

Mrs. Finnegan looked hurt. "That's for protection."

"I think I've figured it out," Agnes said, shutting the door behind Mrs. Finnegan and hopping up on the bed. "After you cut the cake, I'll pretend to pass out from the heat, and you two volunteer to take me home." She grinned back and forth from Franny to Mary Kate.

"I think *I've* figured it out," Franny muttered around her sweet roll. "You're cuckoo."

Agnes rolled her eyes. "Get with the program," she said. "Boopsie Baxter? Tonight?"

Franny laughed, but Agnes did not. "You think Mary Kate can run away from her own wedding? She can barely stand up straight in that corset."

"Can we forget about that night already?" Mary Kate said, powdering her face.

"I don't want to forget," Agnes said. "I want to go back."

"It's my wedding day, and I *don't*," Mary Kate said. "No one is to mention it. Ever. Didn't happen."

Franny had never heard Mary Kate use that tone of voice.

"You didn't even get in trouble," Agnes said. "Franny did. Why are you being such a pill?"

How did Agnes know what had happened to Franny? Franny polished off her sweet roll and licked syrup from her fingers slowly, delaying the inevitable second sweet roll.

"I'm a woman now. I'm done with childish things," Mary Kate said.

"You sound like Peter," Agnes asked.

"And what's wrong with that?" Mary Kate caught Franny's eye in the mirror and quickly looked away. Had Peter lied to her too? He wouldn't. Would he?

"Someone say my name?" A light rap on the door. "Am I allowed to see my little sis before her wedding, or is that bad luck?"

Franny's whole body tensed up. Everything was clammy. Her stomach started to do that knotted-up thing. She grabbed another sweet roll.

Mary Kate stood, fast. "Peter!" she squealed. She threw open the door and dissolved in the arms of her brother. "Don't mess up my hair," she murmured into his chest.

"Hi, girls," he said.

Franny nodded noncommittally, swallowed a piece of sweet roll. "Peter." She took another bite.

"Watch out," he said, pointing, "you won't fit into your dress if you eat too many of those."

Franny flushed. Where was her sharp tongue when she needed it? It filled her mouth like a chicken liver. Fat and dumb and dead.

"She already doesn't," Mary Kate said.

Death by a thousand tiny cuts. Who was this strange girl—pardon—woman?

Peter separated himself from Mary Kate and held her by the shoulders. "I'm about to pick up Elizabeth at the train station, and she doesn't know a soul at this wedding other than me. Do you girls think you can keep her company?"

"Who's Elizabeth?" Franny said around the crumbs of her roll.

"My fiancée," he said.

Franny barked a laugh, and crumbs went flying all over Mary Kate's flowered coverlet. She wiped them off and swallowed what felt like a saw blade. Everyone was staring at her. "Lucky girl," she muttered.

"Of course we will," Mary Kate said. "She's family."

"That's my girl," Peter said. He shut the door behind him.

Agnes sighed. "If only we went to college in Chicago," she said. "Maybe *I* could have been Elizabeth."

Franny almost, but not quite, lost her appetite.

"Ew," Mary Kate said. "That's my brother we're talking about."

⁓⊚⁓

Franny was wiggling into the seafoam dress when Elizabeth arrived, and Mary Kate ran to hug her as though they had been best friends forever. Mary Kate led her over to the room divider, hand chummily wrapped around Elizabeth's waist, and Franny tried not to stare enviously at the opening in Mary Kate's kimono. All her parts were the right size and in the right spot.

"Elizabeth, this is my oldest friend, Franny Steinberg."

Elizabeth had a sweet little face, a tidy figure, not so dissimilar to Mary Kate, but there was something sort of vacant about her expression. "She doesn't look that old." Elizabeth frowned.

Franny laughed, but Elizabeth did not. "She means we've been friends for a long time," Franny said. "We're the same age."

"I'm six months younger," Mary Kate said.

"Steinberg," Elizabeth said. "That's an interesting name."

"Feel free to drop your things in the corner over there," Mary Kate said, steering her around. "Peter can bring them to the hotel for you."

"This is my dress for the wedding," Elizabeth said, patting her garment bag. "Peter already brought my things to his apartment."

Mary Kate blinked. "His apartment?"

"Yes, he has an apartment on, oh, what did he call it, Halsted Street?"

"I know where Peter's apartment is," Mary Kate said.

"Oh okay, well, that's where my things are, then." Elizabeth smiled. "Do you think I could get changed when Miss Steinberg is finished? Gosh, what is that *name*?"

"Dutch," Franny said. "Used to be *van Steinberg*."

Agnes snorted.

⌘

Crossing the threshold into Saint Giles before the wedding, Franny had feigned solemnity. "So they let us into the church," she said, "will they let us out?"

"Don't be ridiculous," Leon said. "They're Catholics, not Cossacks."

"That's exactly what they want you to think!" Papa said, loudly enough to incur a jab from Mama's elbow.

They all got to sit together in the pews, while Franny had to stand the whole time, next to dewy, gorgeous Agnes and looking even more wretched by comparison, feet aching in her seafoam-green heels. Every time she happened to look over at the pews, Mrs. Finnegan mimed holding the bouquet over her hips. *You've got those peasant, childbearing hips, my dear. Nothing to be ashamed of.* Jesus eyeballed everyone from his perch. Trickles of sweat dripped down Franny's girdle. Somehow Mary Kate wasn't sweaty at all in her sweetheart neckline, lace collar-and-sleeve wedding dress modeled after Liz Taylor's dress in *Father of the Bride*, the massive skirt of which Walter had stepped on at least twice.

After only two hours of standing and kneeling and Latin mutterings, Mary Kate became Mrs. Walter Roberts.

But once it was over, two hours didn't seem like *enough* time. Only two hours and a person could suddenly have a different name and a new family? Beforehand, the wedding felt like the culmination of something, but now that it was over, Franny realized it was supposed to be a beginning. Of what? Did Mary Kate know? Was she happy about it? Franny clapped along with everyone when the bride and groom burst out of the church doors, she tossed uncooked rice on them, and when Mary Kate caught her eye, she smiled as big as she possibly could.

⚬─◈─⚬

No alarm bells had gone off when the Jews entered the Rose Valley Country Club, so even Mr. Finnegan started to relax. Franny picked a champagne flute off the tray of a passing waiter and took a fizzy sip. There was a slight breeze wafting through the tent the Finnegans had set up behind the clubhouse because, as Mrs. Finnegan said tightly, "The clubhouse *only* seats two hundred."

"Look at that car!" Papa said, as a 1939 Studebaker Champion in mint condition pulled through the gates, Mr. Finnegan's pride and joy. "I would give my firstborn for a chance behind the wheel just once. Don't tell Leon."

"I won't tell," Franny said, "on the condition you let me drive it."

He patted her cheek. "You look like a beautiful plant," he said.

"Thanks, Papa."

"Isaac!" called Mr. Finnegan in his booming voice. He threaded his way through the crowd to pump Papa's hand. "I want you to meet one of my top salesmen at Abbott, very ambitious fellow, very eloquent, this is Joe Wachowski."

"How do you do?" Papa said.

Mr. Finnegan smiled like he had just told a joke neither of them got. "Well," he said, "I'm sure you have a lot to talk about. And if anyone gives you any trouble for being here, any trouble at all, you call me over straightaway, and I'll take care of it. Lord knows it cost me a pretty penny." He gave them a meaningful look, dabbed his endless forehead with a pocket square, and disappeared back into the crowd.

Papa and Mr. Wachowski looked at each other. "Bist a yid, then, is it?" Papa said.

Mr. Wachowski smirked. "Where do you hide *your* secret Jew gold?"

"I'll never tell," Papa said.

A waiter thrust a platter of shrimp canapés between them, and Papa took two.

"Papa!" Franny said.

"What?" Papa said around a mouthful of canapé. "I want to make sure Roger gets his money's worth."

"Shrimp *is* the most delicious trayf." Mr. Wachowski pointed a shrimp at her like a yad. "So it is written."

"I bet this entire goyische wedding is trayf," Papa said.

"You can relax," Mr. Wachowski said. "I know Roger, and he—"

"They told our ancestors to relax too," Papa said, squinting at his second canapé. "And look what happened to them."

Mr. Wachowski laughed, clapped Papa on the back. "We'll get along just fine," he said.

Leon, like Peter, had worn his army dress uniform to the wedding, a shocking development, and not just because it was made of heavy, navy blue wool. Franny tried to push away the image of skeletal Leon at the doorstep of 504, that same uniform hanging off him, jangling with battle ribbons. How she could count his ribs through the thick wool as she hugged him and cried.

Franny thought he had burned the uniform in the vacant lot like Mama's ration stamps or at least hid it at the bottom of a box full of mothballs in the basement. Despite being surrounded by a swarm of pretty girls, he looked so utterly miserable that Franny almost felt sorry for him. His face was sallow and sweaty, and Franny knew, he was doing his best not to fall to pieces, for Mary Kate's sake. Agnes hung on his arm, along with two other Saint Mary's girls, three of Franny's high school classmates, and at least two of Mary Kate's spinster aunts.

He caught Franny's eye and gave her a pleading look she

pretended not to see. But he broke free of his admirers and made his way over anyway. Agnes glared daggers from across the room, and Franny gave her a friendly wave.

Franny grabbed another champagne flute and drank it fast.

"Slow down," Leon said. "Ain't much'll make you sicker than champagne on an empty stomach."

She grabbed a shrimp canapé from a passing waiter, and Leon raised his eyebrows.

"Papa's doing it too," she said. "Why don't you go nag him?"

"Did I say anything?"

On the other side of the tent, Peter wore an identical uniform, his hat in the crook of his elbow. He chatted heatedly with Mr. Finnegan, pointing at the band as they set up their instruments.

"I didn't have a choice. If I wore a suit, everyone would ask about the uniform," Leon said, answering her unasked question. "Especially because Peter's wearing his. But now everyone is thanking me. I can't stand it."

"Yeah, love and admiration sure are exhausting," she said. Then she really looked at him. His hair was neat and slicked back, but his olive skin looked gray, his eyelids drooped. "Leon, you look horrible."

"Thanks a lot," he snapped. Then he grabbed her shoulder to steady himself. The touch of his hand surprised her.

"I'll get you a chair," she said. "And a wet washcloth." But he wouldn't let go of her shoulder.

"I didn't want to make a scene," he said. "Peter gave me something to help."

"Like a pep talk?" Franny said, absently searching for an available chair.

Leon stared blearily at the wedding guests. "Barbiturates," he said. "Just to calm me down."

"You mean *pills?*"

"Remember…when you wanted to play ball with those older boys and they wouldn't let you, even though you were pretty good for a girl? But you kept going back, day after day, and eventually they gave in." He shook his head. "Peter and I used to watch from the bushes, ready to pounce if they ever tried anything."

"At least lean on me. Have some water," Franny said, holding a glass in front of his face that he wouldn't take. Her jaw hurt from clenching it.

He looked at her, eyes bloodshot. "Why did you do it, Franny?"

"Franny, Leon, *there* you are." Mrs. Finnegan materialized out of the satin and crinoline crowd. She fanned her face. "Is it hot in here? I've been searching all over for you." She grabbed their hands, led them along like farm animals.

"Isn't this just a lovely, perfect wedding?" Mrs. Finnegan huffed in her cropped ivory jacket and matching pencil skirt, elbowing their way through the crowd like a football player. "Just perfect. Almost three hundred people showed up. Isn't that incredible? Have you ever heard of a more perfect wedding?" She adjusted her beret as they hustled past giant tureens filled with sprays of ferns wilting in the heat. She pushed past gauze that hung from somewhere, and Franny stubbed her toe on a chair and nearly toppled over onto one of the dining tables, but still Mrs. Finnegan tugged at her arm.

Finally, they emerged on the dance floor, installed that morning, currently occupied by the five-piece band.

"So who was more expensive," Franny asked, feeling a bit tipsy now that she was moving. "The Jews or the band?"

"Franny!" Mrs. Finnegan said. "Don't be rude."

"You're here!" Mary Kate floated over, cake-like. She leaned in toward Leon, and he managed a kiss on the cheek, which made Mary Kate blush.

"You look nice," he said.

"Oh, Leon," she said, patting his cheek. "If I weren't a married woman."

Was this Mrs. Walter Roberts or Mary Kate? "Shouldn't you be hiding somewhere?" Franny asked. "Until they announce you?"

"Daddy is so old-fashioned," Mary Kate said. "He *insisted* on doing the father-daughter dance before I can dance with my husband—my husband, can you believe it? Anyway, stay here. Don't either of you move—you're up third."

"Up?" Franny asked, but Mary Kate had already flitted away, and Leon had gone full statue.

"Ladies and gentlemen," the singer of the band said, leaning into the microphone. "Please gather around for the father-daughter dance!"

Franny tried to wedge her body between Leon and the crowd that pressed against them. She searched his face for the pinched expression that led to screaming or hyperventilating, but he had no expression at all. He stumbled along, glassy-eyed, bouncing off shoulders and stepping on toes, not registering any of it.

So her two choices were either screaming Leon or lobotomy

Leon? Franny felt a surge of pure, cold anger at Peter and his drugs, which was a welcome change.

The band struck up "Clair de Lune," and Mr. Finnegan led Mary Kate onto the dance floor, clutching her hand so hard that she scowled and told him to readjust. As they settled into their Frankenstein sway, Mr. Finnegan looked mortified and grief-stricken and sweaty. Franny almost felt sorry for him. Mercifully, it was a short dance, and then Mr. Finnegan dissolved into the crowd, while Walter appeared to much careful applause around martini glasses.

"And now, for their first dance as man and wife, Mr. and Mrs. Walter Roberts!"

"You ready?" said a voice in Franny's ear. Her body froze before her ears recognized the whisper. Her own voice disappeared.

Peter sidled up next to her, shook Leon's hand. "How you feeling, buddy?" He winked hatefully then leaned into Franny. His cologne, that piney scent, wrung the air out of her like a sponge. She tried not to inhale; it was all wrong. "Mary Kate's always been sweet on Leon. I think that's why she insisted on this." He shook his head. "But it's her day, and if she wants to dance with her childhood crush, well, we'll make the best of it, won't we?"

Franny just stared up at him, guts roiling, lungs burning, hating every angle of his body, hating that he could stand so close, so casually next to her, that not a single person in this room could know how badly she wanted to scream. He didn't deserve the uniform he wore. Or the Purple Heart. Or Leon.

"I picked the song," he said. "I know it's one of your favorites."

"I don't know what you're talking about," Franny managed to mutter.

Peter looked genuinely surprised. "Mary Kate didn't tell you about the brother-sister dance?"

Is Leon coming to my wedding? Franny remembered the conversation on the way to the Blue Moon. Had she said something about a dance? No, Franny would have remembered. Because she would have pretended to be sick and stayed home. She would have actually been sick. She was sick now. Where was the bathroom again?

And what about Leon? He could barely stand, much less dance.

"And now, ladies and gentlemen, the bride would like to share a dance with her brother and her childhood friends." Walter turned red to his ears but stepped off to the side with Mr. Finnegan, as Mary Kate, too eagerly, tugged Leon onto the dance floor. Leon was not a dancer on the best of days; right now, he looked as green as a seasick sailor, but he held on to Mary Kate like an anchor and let her lead.

The band struck up Billie Holiday's "You Can't Lose a Broken Heart," and Peter held out a hand to Franny. Her heart pounded then gave up and turned to stone. Her legs tensed, her hands iced over. Sweat popped up everywhere. Her skin itched in a numb sort of way. Everyone was watching. Had an hour passed? A day? She watched herself slide her hand onto his; the touch of his skin hurt. She swallowed every instinct that told her to run and followed him onto the dance floor. He snaked an arm around her waist and began to sway. They turned too fast, and her head started to ache. Peter gripped her back tightly, pressed himself to her. She could feel his hot breath on her ear. The room began to sway and sparkle.

"I can't breathe," Franny said.

"Is the dress too tight?" Peter said, concern on his face.

"You're hurting my hand."

"I'm just dancing with you, Franny." He chuckled. "This is how dancing works."

Franny nodded because she couldn't speak. She tried to remember how to foxtrot, ended up slamming her heel on Peter's toe. He yanked her arm, and the momentum sent them tottering across the dance floor.

"What's gotten into you?" Peter looked around. "Everyone is staring."

"I'm sorry," Franny whispered, even though she wasn't sorry. Why did she say it? Her tears were lava hot on her eyeballs. She stopped swaying; her feet grew roots. Peter pressed a hand into her back, but who could dance with a tree? "I can't," she whispered.

Peter laughed uncomfortably. Leon squinted, dimly aware of where or who he was, meanwhile Mary Kate rested her head contentedly on his chest and noticed nothing.

"I need to sit down," Franny said.

"The song's almost over," Peter said.

"Franny, don't embarrass me." It was Leon now, suddenly aware of the world around him, leaning in, *scolding* her. Had Franny ever once scolded him for his episodes?

Franny's hand shot out before she could stop herself. She shoved Leon in the shoulder, which made him lose his footing, and Mary Kate stumbled into him. He stepped on the hem of her dress with a tremendous ripping sound, and everyone gasped.

"My dress," Mary Kate said, looking down. It had ripped at

the waist, so the outer layers of satin drooped and revealed the inner petticoats. Leon reached over to try to fix it, but his fingers dipped clumsily inside the petticoats, which brought Walter out of the wings.

"I've had about enough of this," he whispered to Leon.

"Don't talk to him like that," Franny said.

"Franny," said Leon and Peter simultaneously.

"Stop saying my name!"

The band stopped playing midnote, and time stopped too. Franny felt like the atom bomb about to explode and annihilate everyone. It was building inside her, the explosion; she wasn't big enough to contain it anymore. Everyone was staring and hating her, and somehow Franny always knew she had this inside her, this ugly, bloated, unnameable thing that would wreak destruction and turn everyone against her—friends, parents, neighbors, wedding orchestras—it was so exhausting, keeping that ugly thing locked away. But now, it was coming out. It was going to blow her whole life to smithereens, and there wasn't a damn thing she could do to stop it. Like hot vomit when she had the flu. She couldn't bear to stand there in that stupid dress and watch the world explode.

"I'm sorry," she said to Mary Kate.

She pushed through Peter and Leon, through Mama and Papa, through the three hundred perfect guests, whose martinis splashed on her seafoam-green dress. She kicked off her heels and ran barefoot across the tent, through the golf course, and out of the gate, the tears that she should be crying stopped up in her throat like a wine cork.

She couldn't go back to the wedding. She couldn't go home. She couldn't stay here, panting like a miserable mutt in the middle of a busy street. Franny wished she didn't have a body at all. She wouldn't be doubled over right now, like a sawed-in-half magician's assistant. She wouldn't have to take her body anywhere. She could just disappear, evaporate like a mermaid into seafoam. She was the right color and everything. This made her laugh, the ridiculous dress and the fact that everyone just *had* to comment on how it didn't fit. And laughing made her see how ridiculous she looked—standing alone, barefoot in the middle of busy Thatcher Avenue, cackling at nothing. The knot in her belly eased just slightly, which gave Franny an idea.

If anything in this world could make Franny forget who she was and what she had done, it was Boopsie Baxter's Showstopper.

Franny hurried along the grassy side of the road, tucking up the dress so she could run faster. She had to catch the streetcar before anyone had a notion to follow. She got to the stop just as the streetcar pulled up and could not believe her luck. Ignoring the raking eyes of the young men on board, she sat and tried to catch her breath, fanning herself with that silly little matching hand purse. She had just enough money to get to the Blue Moon, at which point she could either buy a martini or a return trip to Oak Park. As the country club grounds disappeared from view, Franny thought the martini might be the better choice.

But then, how was she even going to get through the door? Lottie Marcone had told her never to come back. The wicked little derringer winked in Franny's memory. Was she really prepared to bet her life?

The young man next to Franny put a hand on her knee and waggled his eyebrows.

"How much?" he asked.

She was just about to tell him where he could shove it, when she realized—she knew this guy. They had been high school classmates, and he didn't recognize her from Adam.

Franny laughed. The solution was obvious—Lottie would never recognize her in this dress, with her hair like this, the rouge and lipstick. And with the size of the crowd coming to see Boopsie, Franny would probably be able to slip in without her even noticing in the first place.

She lifted the man's hand from her knee, dropped it like an egg in his lap. He called her a couple of foul names and scooted away.

This body, she thought, *is nothing but trouble*.

CHAPTER FIVE

A GIRL IN WRINKLED NYLONS GRIPPED THE MICROPHONE and warbled dirty parody lyrics to a record of "Oh My Darling, Clementine." The record was louder than her voice, so mercifully, her jokes about the miner schtupping his sister were drowned out—unfortunately, not entirely.

Franny stood in the doorway to the Blue Moon and thought maybe she had made some mistake. Barb the bouncer was napping with her head pressed to the door frame, cap as a pillow, a lit cigarette sticking to her bottom lip as she snored lightly. All the lights were on, and without the mysterious cover of darkness and smoke, exciting perfumes and the chatter of women, the club felt too real. Embarrassingly so. Like catching Eleanor Roosevelt on the toilet.

The club was nearly empty, except for the girl onstage, two skinny girls smoking at a side booth to the right, and Lottie Marcone, slumped over a highball glass at a barstool. She looked up when Franny entered, and Franny froze with a dumb smile on her face, but as she had anticipated, Lottie didn't recognize her, just picked up her highball and clinked the ice cubes, which brought out the bartender from around the hidden corner, wiping her hands on a dirty towel.

The record ended, and the thin girl finished her song on a sour high note then paused as if waiting for applause. When none came, Franny clapped enthusiastically, but the girl scowled at her, heaved the record player off the stool, and stalked offstage.

Lottie wore white pedal pushers and a green plaid blouse tied at the midriff, and Franny didn't see an ankle derringer, so that was a good sign. When she applauded, Lottie turned to glare at her. "What are you anyway, a princess?"

It was one thing to face Lottie Marcone in the dark, in a crowd, and a whole other thing to pretend she was just a regular person.

"Somewhere between princess and frog, really," Franny said.

Lottie lifted her highball for a sip but then slammed it back down. "You're that smart-ass I tossed out on Thursday," she said. "This day just keeps getting better and better." She tilted her head back and downed the drink. Barb the bouncer chuckled, adjusted her posture, and somehow never lost the cigarette.

Franny took courage from the fact she had neither been thrown out or shot and heaved herself onto a barstool.

"I could be wrong," Lottie said into her empty glass. "But it appears you're even closer to me than you were before."

"And here I thought barstools were for sitting," Franny said. After everything that had happened, here she was, sassing Lottie Marcone to her face. *Again.* What was it about this place that loosened her tongue, but when it really mattered, when she really had something important to say, her voice took a permanent vacation?

Franny became very interested in pretending to read the bar menu, felt Lottie's eyes boring into her.

"That is a ghastly dress," Lottie said.

"I was going for *aquatic enema bag*," Franny said, not looking up. "How'd I do?"

Lottie laughed. "You won't make it on the cover of *Vogue*," she said. "I'll say that much."

"You'll see. Next season this look will be all the rage. Girls everywhere clamoring for a dumpy, Jewish tuchus."

This seemed to really tickle Lottie, and she let out a girlish, tinkling laugh that lit up her whole face. The laugh burrowed inside Franny like a tapeworm. It terrified her to realize she would starve herself to feed it.

The occasional rumor about Lottie Marcone popped up in the papers—the tiger engagement, nonsensical comments about preferring girls over boys (who didn't?), an unwanted come-on from one of Fingers's men that ended in bloodshed from Lottie's pocket nail file—and seeing Lottie face-to-face should have exposed them as absurd fables. But somehow, these rumors now seemed exceedingly possible.

There was something about Lottie that was both real and unreal. You would think all her mystery would evaporate with the harsh lighting, but Franny just wanted to look closer. Glossy black hair pulled back in a ponytail that curled slightly at the ends, narrow honey-colored eyes, lips in a mean smile, making an arrow of her Roman nose. She was pretty, sure, but it was more than that. It was the reason Franny humped up on the stool instead of running away again. That *something* made her chest warm—she wanted to be near it, she wanted some of it for herself.

Franny felt...great? Was that a feeling a person could have?

"Get this Jewish princess a glass of bubbly, Enid," Lottie said, relighting her cigarette. "My treat. What's your story, pretty enema bag?"

The blond bartender slid a flute of champagne across the bar. Franny took a big gulp, blushed, and struggled with the knotting of her tongue. She would not clam up, not now. "I couldn't hack it as a bridesmaid," she said. "Cold feet."

"The *bridesmaid* ran away," Lottie said. "That's a new one." She leaned back, regarded Franny with a smirk.

"Hello? Which one of us is next?" one of the girls in the booth called. Franny had forgotten all about them.

Lottie ignored them, held out her free hand to Franny. "Lottie Marcone," she said. "I run the place. What was your name again?" she asked. "Steingold? Goldstein?" She said it in a mocking Yiddish accent.

"Franny Steinberg."

Lottie snorted. "That will not do," she said.

"Sorry to disappoint."

"Too Jewish. Too..." She made a face. "You need something lighter, more fun. Jews aren't any fun. What about...Peggy?"

"What about her?" Franny said.

"Yeah, Peggy. Peggy... We'll think about a last name. Something quick, one syllable. Easy to remember."

"Blake," Barb said.

Lottie Marcone took a drag of her cigarette and nodded. "You're a pro, Barb. That's perfect. Peggy Blake. Okay, Peggy Blake, you're next."

"I'm lost," Franny said. "Who are we talking about?"

Lottie shoved her shoulder. "You. This is Amateur Hour. You're the next amateur. Tell us all about being a runaway bridesmaid. Make me laugh again. I could use a laugh today, I'll tell you what."

Franny was not finding any of this even remotely funny. "I'm here to see Boopsie Baxter," she said. "Ideally from the audience."

Lottie's smile faded. "Gosh, and for a second there, I had forgotten how we met," she said. "Too bad I left my piece at home. I bet that would convince you."

"I dunno, Lottie, looks like you got a piece right there next to you," Barb said.

Franny could still feel Peter's handprint on her sweaty back. And there it was, the twinge of an oncoming bellyache. What was she even doing here? Franny didn't tell jokes; she was the butt of them.

Lottie grabbed Franny's forearm before she could slide off the stool. "Make me laugh and you can stay."

"And if I can't?"

Lottie ashed her cigarette into Franny's champagne. "Let's not be morbid, sweetheart. Maybe they'll have you at the Velvet Swing."

"*Have you* is right, a little 'spicy entertainment.'" Barb puffed out a guffaw. "Damn, dropped my cig."

Papa loved to point out Fingers Marcone stories when they popped up in the *Tribune*. *Fingers Macaroni strikes again!* he always said.

Getting a little handsy, *isn't he?* Franny would say. It was fun because it was like a movie, a drama unfolding in an imaginary life, far, far away.

But now Franny sat knee to knee with the real gangster's real wife, whose closet seemed like it might contain even *more* skeletons than her husband's, with Franny one wrong decision away from becoming a headline herself. And yet. The door to the Blue Moon was more than just a door. It was a portal: Here or there; uncertain future or painful past. Possible finger loss or definite bellyache.

Franny had ten fingers and hardly used them all on a regular basis anyway.

She smoothed her gauzy dress, patted her flyaway hair, and took the longest walk of her life, to the stage of the Blue Moon.

"How come she gets to go?" a girl whined as she passed their booth. "We was here first."

A microphone was set up on the small, low stage, in front of the house band's snare drum, with very little room in between for standing. There was, Franny noticed, a naked Greekish statue of a woman glaring from over her right shoulder. They were *all* glaring at her: the three girls, Lottie with her burning cigarette—even Barb had cocked an eye open to watch, and the bartender had stopped wiping glasses. Franny's legs started to shake. What words did she know? Her brain was full of thoughts, none of them useful. Time sped up and stopped. She forgot how to breathe. How did sentences work again? Somehow she was even watching herself, sweaty, mouth breathing. Just perfect, she thought. Two Frannys, neither of them capable of speech.

"Say *something*," one girl whined.

"Hello, ladies and germs," Franny tried. She had heard Milton Berle start that way on *Texaco Star Theater*, but the girls in the audience groaned. Lottie clinked the ice in her empty glass. The clinking echoed in Franny's head like chattering teeth, like dice rolling out the odds of her getting out of here alive.

The microphone was so far away it was practically on another planet, and yet her heart pounded so loud she was sure everyone could hear.

"What's, uh," Franny said, "a man that crawls in the morning, walks at noon, and has a cane at midnight? Wait." She shook her head. "Let me try that again—what's something—"

"That's a riddle," a girl shouted. "Who is this joker, Lottie?"

"*Not* joker, more like," said another.

Lottie slid off the stool like a dancer and started a slow, determined walk to the stage.

"Wait, no," Franny said. "I got one."

The girls started to boo. Someone threw an ice cube at Franny, missed, and it cracked against the wall behind her.

Lottie was maybe five steps away from the stage, and she did not look like a person who would be sympathetic to stage fright. She had told Franny to make her laugh, and Franny had failed, and...well, just because a person didn't have a derringer didn't mean she wasn't dangerous. Franny was being stalked like prey by a tiny woman in a ponytail. Anything could be a weapon in the right hands. Even jokes.

Franny yanked the microphone up to her lips so fast, it banged against her front teeth. The feedback reverberated through the bar. Lottie stopped, hands on hips. All eyes were on Franny.

"Anyone hear about Fingers Marcone's collection?" Franny said, her voice like a trumpet blasting Lottie Marcone into oblivion. "He has so many fingers, he doesn't even use his own hands to touch a girl. Best part is no one can accuse him of adultery. They dust his girlfriends' tits for prints and all that comes up is dead men."

Not a sound. Not a snicker. The girls had matching jaw drops. Even Barb's mouth dangled. Franny had Lottie's attention now, her face frozen in naked shock.

Franny's whole body vibrated. She was challah right before it rises. She was a scream stuck in her own throat. She was that dead elm in the vacant lot, about to crush a house.

She lowered her voice to a near whisper, felt bodies lean in. "But he's put all that finger business behind him. He's a new man, and he's got a new plan," she said brightly. "Now he wants us to call him *Peckers* Marcone."

The girls gasped and then erupted in laughter. Barb coughed around her cigarette in an honest-to-goodness chuckle. The laughter felt real as breath, and Franny realized she hadn't been breathing. Her body sucked air in, cool and refreshing, like taking your girdle off.

The laughter ebbed, and the knots in her gut started to tighten, the too-small bodice squeezed her like a juicer, and Franny just had to make them laugh again; the sooner, the better.

Lottie leapt to the stage like some kind of jungle animal. But Franny wasn't ready to let the microphone go. She pulled the stand backward with her, forgetting the bass drum, which boomed as her heel struck it. She stumbled and tumbled to the floor, knocking over a cymbal with a screamy crash. The microphone howled with feed-back, and Lottie yanked Franny up by the neck of her ugly dress, the whites of her eyes glowing.

"Are you trying to get us all killed?" She pointed to the back of the bar. "He was just here. Right before you walked in. Jesus Christing Christ, girlie, you got some nerve."

"And how," said a girl from the audience.

"Get off my stage," Lottie said.

"Wait, give me a chance," Franny said. The old fear was return-ing, the old tightness. "Please."

"I oughta toss you out on your fat behind. Your—what was it—tuchus?"

She pronounced it *tuck-ass*, but Franny didn't think it wise to tell her so.

"Never should have let you up here. I'm a pushover for a girl who can make me laugh, isn't that right, Barb?" Lottie tightened her grip on the neck of Franny's dress. "Get out of my club. And do me a favor, make it forever this time."

"Oh, put those claws away, Lottie, honey, you're scaring the poor thing." Boopsie Baxter herself burst through the door of the club, a kerchief over her hair, her impossibly long legs clad in short denim beneath a neatly tucked white blouse. "Hiya, Barb," she said, sweep-ing past with a garment bag over her shoulder that revealed a glimpse of red satin. Her other hand dangled cherry-red heels.

"Boopsie Baxter?" Franny asked hoarsely.

"It's just comedy, Lottie," Boopsie said, draping her clothes over the back of the U-shaped booth. "It's supposed to be funny."

"Tell that to Ed," Lottie said, dropping Franny with a *thump*. Franny exhaled for the first time in about an hour.

"Oh no, what has your dear hubby done now? Don't tell me the fuzz finally nabbed him," Boopsie said.

"I wish," Lottie said, hopping offstage and giving Boopsie a kiss on the cheek. "Forget it, doesn't matter."

Now that there was an intermission in the threat of physical violence, Franny wondered if she might manage to squeeze in one more joke. She rolled around onstage, trying to stand without splitting the dress.

"This is too hard to watch." Boopsie walked up to the stage. "Need a hand?"

Franny touched the real hand of the real Boopsie Baxter. It was cool and dry. She struggled to her feet with an undainty grunt and then hopped off the stage, trying to parlay the help into a clumsy handshake. "Uh, Miss Baxter. I'm Franny Steinberg."

Boopsie smiled politely and retrieved her hand, wiping it discreetly on her shorts. "I got pulled over *again*," she said to Lottie. "As soon as I cross Roosevelt, like clockwork. They're waiting for me, the bastards. I know they are. You'd think the cops would be bored of this game by now, but no, they just squint at my license and lick their lips at me until I fork over some cash. I hate this city."

"Join the club," Lottie said.

Boopsie narrowed her eyes. "Oh yeah? And what club is that, Lottie? The married-to-the-Mob club?"

Lottie waved her hand dismissively and sat in the booth. "No real-world talk," she said. "I'm not in the mood."

Right about now, Mary Kate and Walter would be cutting their five-tier bone-white wedding cake while everyone clapped. So much clapping at weddings, Franny always left with her hands throbbing. Weddings were supposed to be an expression of love, but maybe they were just a performance of it. Or maybe no one wanted to clap, but no one wanted to be the only one *not* clapping.

In any case, Franny didn't have to think about any of that, because she was here, at the Blue Moon, having a casual, breezy conversation with Boopsie Baxter. She leaned against the booth and tried to look breezy.

Boopsie looked from Lottie to Franny and back again, a smile curling her wine-red mouth. The smile alone was enough to make Franny blush. "So, anyone worth a damn at Amateur Hour?" Boopsie asked.

"What do I know?" Lottie said. "I just run the place."

Anticipating a glowing review, Franny had already put on a bashful smile and modest shrug. All dressed up for the wrong party. Boopsie laughed.

"Don't pay any attention to her, kid," she said. "Lottie thinks she's a tough cookie, but you just have to dip her in the right milk."

This embarrassed Franny even more, though she couldn't quite explain why. She fidgeted with her dress, wishing she had something, *any*thing else to wear right now.

"You gonna introduce us to Boopsie or what?" the Clementine girl said.

"Or what," Lottie said. "Amateur Hour is over. You want to stay, you gotta pay."

The girls packed up their things, grumbling. "You're a washed-up cunt," one of them called to Lottie as they left. "Everyone knows it."

Franny had heard enough curse words not to be a total Mary Kate, had even used some words herself, but had never heard *that* one out loud.

They pointed at Franny as they left. "Mazel tov," one said. "You got some balls."

"Oh, these old things?" Franny said, cupping empty air like a baseball. The girl looked at her, puzzled. Franny imaginary pitched the imaginary ball, which didn't help.

Boopsie eased herself into the U-shaped booth and sighed, laying her head against the back. "You're lucky I'm a nice person, Lottie," she said. "Coming up here is not worth it anymore. You know, in Miami, no one gives me trouble? I can run my own club and people treat me like a damn human being."

"They don't treat you like a human being, Boo. They treat you like a celebrity, and only when it suits them." Lottie shrugged casually. "Ed can talk to the cops for you, you know. Fix that whole problem right up. You should come back, work for me again. Remember how much fun we had?"

"Thanks, but no thanks."

"You'll be back," Lottie said, sliding into the booth. Boopsie just rolled her eyes.

Franny hovered awkwardly in their orbit, hoping to become a planet or at least a moon. "Do you really think I'm funny?" she asked.

"Did I say that?" Lottie said.

"No, I mean," Franny said. What did she mean? "You said I made you laugh." Lottie glared, and Franny lost all ability to speak.

"Oh, let the girl stay," Boopsie said. "She's making me nervous, clomping around like that. Anyway, she looks like she could use a good time."

"Lucky you, the lady of the house wants you to stay," Lottie said then patted the seat next to her. "Enid, whiskey sour for the new comedian. Extra cherries."

New. Comedian. Was this real life?

"Hope she knows Fingers ain't the only Marcone with wandering hands," Boopsie said.

Lottie laughed, and once again, Franny was the butt of some joke she didn't understand.

"Actually, I should go," Franny said. Instead, she plopped down on the seat next to Lottie, who sat so close, Franny could smell her vanilla perfume.

Boopsie snatched Lottie's cigarette case and tapped a cigarette on the table before putting it to her lips. The bartender, Enid, brought Boopsie a light and a martini with five olives.

"Thank you, sweetheart," Boopsie said around her cigarette. "You're a doll." Enid blushed.

Franny just couldn't stop grinning.

"Take a picture, it lasts longer," Boopsie said.

"Gosh, your voice sounds great," Franny said. "I had the flu once and lost my voice after? And it took a month before I could speak again."

"And I want to hear the story of your life because?" Boopsie said.

"*Because*," Lottie said, "you had to cancel your show on Thursday. For laryngitis."

"Did I now?" Boopsie said. She regarded Lottie with narrowed eyes. "And here I thought it was because some hack comedian guy stole my jokes and performed them on *The Ed Sullivan Show*, so I had to fly out to New York with my lawyer at the last minute and fork over a whole lot of my own cash to do it too, just to be told that said comedian and his *Chicago Mob* lawyer had never even *heard* of a gal called Boopsie Baxter. And how did this fella get my jokes, I wonder?"

Stolen jokes? Ed Sullivan? *New York City?* This was way juicier than laryngitis. Franny tried to remember every tiny detail to tell Mary Kate…once Mary Kate got over the whole wedding thing and was speaking to her again.

"Ed's a real ass," Lottie said, "but he does not sell jokes."

Boopsie *hmph*ed. "Ed would sell his own mother for a nickel. All I know is, every time I come back to Chicago, things get worse for me. And look at you. Chartering buses to fill seats with suburban housewives? Giving away free drinks? It's embarrassing, Lottie. How many new comedians have you found through Amateur Hour? And I mean real comedians."

"We got Gal Gardenia," Lottie said. "She already has a Showstopper—less than two weeks onstage and she's already got a Showstopper."

"Is that the one who makes you feel like you're waiting for the bus?" Boopsie said.

"She makes you feel like you showed up just in time to *catch* the bus." Lottie ashed her cigarette so hard, it bent in the middle. "It's a fine Showstopper," she said. "Not everyone can be Boopsie Baxter."

"Lottie, the comedy we love is dying. There's no way around it,"

Boopsie said. "And if you can't let it go, you're going to starve. We had a good run, you and me, but it's over."

Dying? Over? Franny just got to the party in her terrible dress; it couldn't be over already. She looked from Boopsie to Lottie, but they weren't looking at each other.

"It is not dying," Lottie said.

"If you can't get on television, it is. For girls, especially Negro girls, it is," Boopsie said, blowing out a delicate curl of smoke. "How many girls you fit into this club? Sixty, seventy? *Millions* of people watch Ed Sullivan every time his ugly mug is on TV. You're way out of your league."

"It can't last. Men just aren't funny," Lottie said. She looked miserable. "What do they have to be funny about? They own everything, they run everything, someone else feeds them, dresses them, massages their filthy feet. Comedy comes from pain, and what pain does a man have?"

What did pain have to do with being funny? Laughing made pain go away. Pain was dancing with Peter, pain was Leon panting on the floor of O'Hara's. Franny had left all that behind to come *here*.

"*White* man," Boopsie corrected. "A Negro man has it plenty hard."

"They're still not funny," Lottie said.

Boopsie gave her a look but said nothing.

"Valentine's Day, 1942," Lottie said. "Do you remember, Boo? You're up there doing your thing, and suddenly all these girls in their coveralls and kerchiefs are moaning, eyes rolling back in their heads."

"Don't you try to woo me with nostalgia, you harpy," Boopsie said, but her face softened into a smile.

Franny remembered spending too much money on those old

magazines, scouring them for one measly drop of information about Showstoppers, and here she was now, bathing in a waterfall of it. She sternly resolved to keep her mouth shut. She would be barely there, a dust bunny under the bed, an eyelash on a cheek.

"I thought for sure I was bombing. But after the show, dozens of girls gushing at me, calling it the best night of their lives." Boopsie chuckled. "I mean, I knew I was good, but this was a whole new level."

"The cops beat our doors down. I forked over more cash than we made, just to keep you out of jail," Lottie said. "That was a good night. Things haven't been the same since you left, Boo."

"Face it, hon. War's over, and you're the only one who misses it." Boopsie touched Lottie's hand, but Lottie pulled away.

"I saw you on Christmas Eve. 1944?" Franny blurted out. "At the Empire Room?"

So much for being a dust bunny.

The two of them blinked at her like they had forgotten she existed.

"One of the first high-class hotels that ever let me onstage," Boopsie said. She cocked her head at Franny. "You must have been knee high to a grasshopper. They let you in?"

"Your Showstopper was." Franny stopped. "You made me feel…" She wanted them to finish her sentence for her, but Boopsie and Lottie stared expectantly until Franny looked away.

"Hold on," Lottie said. "Did Boopsie—" Lottie and Boopsie and Barb and even silent blond Enid burst out laughing. Lottie took big gulps of air to compose herself, meanwhile Franny's face was hotter than Hades in August.

"Did Boopsie—give you your first orgasm?"

First? Was she supposed to have had more than one?

But just knowing the feeling had a name was a strange relief. After years of trying hide from it, naming it meant it could be knowable. "Yes?"

"Oh, honey," Lottie said, and then her hand was resting on Franny's gauzy thigh, higher up than one might expect. "No wonder you're so obsessed. You can give them to yourself, you know."

"You can also get 'em from a man," Boopsie said.

Lottie rolled her eyes. "That's the story anyway."

"Ignore her," Boopsie said. "Everyone has to have a first time. You could do worse, if I do say so myself."

"Best I ever had," Lottie said into her drink.

"Ain't a thing wrong with you, girlie," Boopsie said. "Except someone *really* should have explained all this to you before now." They both laughed at her again, but Franny was sick of being embarrassed.

"When will I know what my Showstopper is?" Franny said. It was a simple question, or so she thought. Lottie didn't answer; her strange honey-colored eyes just glared a hole in Franny's skull.

She poked Franny hard in the spot just below her ribs, right where the knots always were. "What's bottled up in here?" she demanded.

Lottie couldn't know. How could she possibly know about it? Franny laughed, but only so she wouldn't be tempted to cry.

"You think you're the only one with secrets?" Lottie said. "Welcome to womanhood, darling. You want to be special, like Boopsie Baxter, you let the world laugh at your secrets. And I don't mean the time you broke your mama's china platter. I'm talking the ugliest, nastiest ones. If you can do that—the Showstopper's not far behind."

Franny's belly curdled around the spot where Lottie had poked her. It had to be the whiskey.

"The comedians who can't dig deep," Lottie said, "they don't have much to offer in the Showstopper department. You may taste phantom chocolate or feel like you have a smart new hairstyle. Big deal."

Boopsie lifted her empty martini glass to Enid. "You forgot one," she said. "Feeling like you've arrived just in time to catch the bus."

"I thought I just had to make people laugh," Franny muttered.

Boopsie pointed her cigarette at Franny. "You can't escape yourself when you're up there, if that's what you're hoping. You don't want to put in the work, you should walk out that door right now because you're just wasting everyone's time." She turned away, like that was how normal people ended conversations.

"Thanks for letting me waste your time," Franny said.

"Let's not make it a habit."

Lottie was watching them with an amused smile, and Enid plopped down a martini for Lottie and a whiskey sour for Franny. It was a golden thing with three skewered pink cherries across the top like a bridge. Franny felt small enough to drown in it.

"Okay, listen up, kiddo, because I'm only saying this once." Boopsie closed her eyes and sighed hard. "My mama did her best to protect me from the world, because she knew that it chews up poor little Negro girls. Instead, she made me hate myself. And when bad things happened to me, I just hated myself more, because I thought I wasn't strong enough to stop them. You follow?"

Franny was afraid to nod.

Boopsie leaned back in the booth. "Valentine's Day 1942 started with a telegram—Mama was dead. I was devastated, obviously. But at the same time, a fog lifted. I could laugh. I tried a joke about her, and I told a joke about myself. And then—what do you know—the world's first Showstopper." Boopsie smacked the table, and Franny jumped. "Do you know how embarrassed I was that first time? I did *not* sign up to watch a bunch of girls get their rocks off. Do you know how long it took me to understand what a gift it is to be able to turn pain into magic? Some people spend years on a couch to figure out what I was just handed out of the clear blue sky."

Franny nodded, not understanding at all this time but knowing she should pretend.

"Meanwhile, I start getting calls from New York, Los Angeles, London," Lottie said. "I could practically hear the dollar bills crackling over the long-distance line. Suddenly everyone wanted to be at the Blue Moon. The war was dragging on, devouring male entertainers like hors d'oeuvres. Ed was slugging it out on an Italian battlefield. I was the queen of this dank little castle. God, it was exhilarating."

"I can't keep flying out here every time you need to make rent," Boopsie said softly.

Lottie looked at her watch for a long moment. "Doors open soon. Better get dressed."

"You know what would solve your money problems?" Boopsie said, arching her eyebrows. "Let men in."

"Don't start with me again," Lottie said. "Showstoppers don't even work on them."

"Exactly," Boopsie said. "They won't know what they're missing."

"And who says I have money problems?"

"Lottie—"

"A toast," Lottie said. "To a packed house tonight. No one can do what I do, certainly no bottle-blond floozy named Varla."

"Who's Varla?" Franny said.

"To Varla." Boopsie smirked, lifting her glass.

"Long may she reign!"

"Off with her head!"

They laughed and clinked glasses with Franny.

⁓⧸⁓

By the time Boopsie took the stage, the Blue Moon was packed, and Franny was squeezed into a tiny booth in the back between two middle-aged Negro women and a plump white girl who wouldn't stop yammering. Franny's body buzzed from all the whiskey sours, and she was ready to handle the Showstopper, even if she still couldn't call it by its given name. She tried hard to let go, just like Lottie and Boopsie had told her. "Just breathe through it," Boopsie had said. "Pretend you're in a Cadillac that someone else is driving." Franny squinched her eyes shut and huffed through her mouth. Was she doing it right? She kept opening her eyes to see what everyone else was doing. But the sound of women moaning all around her was embarrassing. Was that what she sounded like? Her muscles would tense up, and her brain would start running a million miles a minute and then she had to start all over again. Was it even going to happen this time? What was she doing wrong?

"Girls, you know what is absolutely absurd about modern life?" Boopsie paused for a sip of water, looking thoughtful. "Toilets. Think about it! A gleaming white pedestal to rest our dainty behinds on, pipes hidden in the walls to whisk our unmentionables away, but when you get right down to it, we're still just shitting in a hole."

Franny didn't even hear the rest of the joke. The shock of glamorous Boopsie talking about toilets obliterated her thoughts, and a laugh bleated out of her like a shofar.

And, finally, a trail of heat ignited like gunpowder from her thighs all the way up her chest, down to her fingers and toes, and exploded, releasing her to gulp down the diluted dregs of her whiskey sour. All this letting go was exhausting. Lottie, meanwhile, sat totally silent, draped like a silk sheet over the blue booth, the only sign a slight parting of her lips at the moment of release. She opened her eyes and smirked to see Franny watching. Franny looked away but not quickly enough to avoid blushing.

She felt tongue-bloated and buzzy, and she didn't want the night to ever end. She didn't want to think about home or how in the world she was going to get there. But too soon, the show was over, and girls filtered out the door to return home, preparing lies about PTA meetings and bridge clubs and whatever else bored their husbands out of asking questions.

Franny lingered at the door, stifling a yawn, reluctant to leave. She was an unpacked suitcase with everything tossed haphazardly back inside. Walking out that door felt utterly impossible.

Only Lottie and Barb and Enid remained, stacking glasses and wiping off the bar. Lottie had offered the service of her chauffeur to get Franny home at this late hour, but Franny hung around, waiting to be asked to return for the next Amateur Hour. Lottie was counting the till and didn't seem in any hurry to talk to her.

"A tip from me to you," Boopsie Baxter said, slinging her garment bag over her shoulder. "She's allergic to desperation." Franny opened her mouth, but Boopsie held up a hand. "Hey Lottie, I'll drive the girl home."

"No, you won't," Lottie said. "I already offered her a ride."

Boopsie winked at Franny. "Now look busy."

Franny thanked her silently and looked around for something to do. She opened her change purse, counted imaginary change, and then like magic, Lottie appeared next to her. "That's Carl outside. Nice meeting you, Peggy Blake." She shook Franny's hand.

"So Amateur Hour, tomorrow?" Franny asked. "I'll have better jokes, scout's honor."

"Look, you gave it a shot onstage, you got to see Boopsie—not a bad night for a good girl like you. You don't want the trouble of being a comedian, believe me. I'm doing you a favor." Lottie pushed her gently out the door. "Find yourself a nice boy, get married or something. And don't show your face here again."

Franny melted into a puddle of whiskey and disappointment. The flashing lights of the Blue Moon Cocktail Lounge marquee flashed once, twice, then shut off for the night.

CHAPTER SIX

SUNLIGHT STREAMED THROUGH THE WINDOW, AND Franny flung the blankets over her head and played possum. She was a stranger in her own bed, an impostor in polka dot pajamas. She was a whole new person who looked exactly the same.

Mama burst into the room, and Franny only just managed to pretend she was still sleeping. Mama paused next to the bed. Had she bought it? Finally, she set something down on the bedside table and tiptoed out, closing the door softly behind her. Franny peeked out of the blankets to see a cup of chicken soup accompanied by a pickle spear, which was what Mama gave to Papa after a particularly lively Passover seder, when he had indulged in the requisite four cups of wine, plus a few extra nips *for Elijah, who couldn't be with us.* How had Mama known? Guilt pierced Franny's belly, along with all that whiskey.

She reached for the pickle spear, and the saucer clinked. Mama threw open the door.

"Oh good!" she said. "You're awake."

Franny yelped and nearly dropped the pickle. Her head pounded. "Mama!" she croaked.

"Where did you go last night?" Mama asked. "No pickles until I have answers."

Franny's mind went blank and throbby. "You can't hold my pickle hostage," she said, clutching it to her chest.

Mama unfortunately took this as an invitation and sat on the bed with the sigh of a desert wanderer. Franny steeled herself for an Olympic guilt trip. "Mary Kate and Walter left for Hawaii this morning." Mama shook her head. "Poor girl."

"Yes, however will she survive a tropical vacation," Franny said.

"After Leon destroyed her dress and you ran away," she said, as though Franny hadn't even spoken, "she stood alone in the middle of the dance floor—alone! A new bride at her wedding! And then"—Mama paused for effect—"she burst into tears and ran off into the night."

"I'm so sorry." Franny covered her face.

"To me, you're sorry? After you left, Mrs. Finnegan poked her with a safety pin, trying to save that dress—and last I saw, she was sprawled out on the grass outside the tent—"

"Okay, enough, Mama, I get it." Ruining weddings then running away to nightclubs? Who was this person? Last night, which had felt so utterly life-changing, seemed silly and embarrassing in the daylight. She would have to come clean. When Mama decided to dig for gold, she'd hit a gold vein eventually.

But this time, Mama hugged Franny close and stroked her hair, rocking her like a baby. "Oh, ketzeleh, when my best girlfriend got married, I thought about running away too," she said. "I thought it would never happen for me, can you believe it? And this in Lawndale, full of nice Jewish boys!"

Maybe if Franny stayed very, very quiet, Mama wouldn't notice that she had completely misunderstood Franny's reaction.

"Nu, your father wanted to move to this goyische wasteland with its Catholics, and I told him! I told him our daughter would feel like an ugly duckling when really she is the swan, but when there are no other swans, how will she ever learn? Well." Mama held Franny out by her shoulders. "I'm going to find you a swan, and that's that."

"You won't even let us get a dog."

"The Bermans' boy is home from Harvard Medical School for the summer, volunteering for the Red Cross," Mama said. "Very handsome. Michael."

"You're buying a swan from a medical student?"

"Don't be a nudnik. Mrs. Berman said he's not interested in the B'nai B'rith Girls she's tried to set him up with."

"Oh," Franny said, "you're talking about a *date*."

"I'm talking about a *future*," Mama said. "None of this silly Peter Finnegan nonsense."

"Who said anything about him?" Franny pushed away that sneaky memory, down deep in the deep, dark sea. "Why would this handsome Michael Berman be interested in me and not the BBGs?"

"Because you're a swan, pupik. And swans marry other swans." Mama patted her cheek. "Now go fish your brother out of the basement. He's being impossible."

⌘

Papa looked up from behind his newspaper. "Is this my daughter or an impostor?"

"Definitely an impostor," Franny said. "I climbed through the window and sucked up your daughter's soul."

"Ah, so you're a dybbuk," Papa said. "A dybbuk *would* make a shiksa cry at her own wedding, stay out all night, then come to breakfast smelling like old whiskey."

"Papa," Franny said, flushing.

"You're a grown woman, dybbuk Franny. Let your husband discipline you."

"Isaac," Mama said.

"What?" Papa said. "We have two grown children—one sneaks out of weddings, the other hides in the basement. Franny, get your brother out of the basement."

"What's he doing down there?" Franny asked. The basement was cold and dark, without electricity, and full of spiders. It was where they threw all the stuff they didn't use anymore but didn't want to throw away.

"You think I didn't ask?" Papa said. "When was the last time Lenny answered a question?"

Franny remembered his slurred speech at the wedding, his drooping face. She didn't want to see him, not even in the dark. But if she stayed up here, she'd face the grilling of a lifetime. Two guilt trips? No thank you. She'd try her luck with Leon. Franny grabbed a mug of coffee and turned the knob of the basement door.

"Coffee on an empty stomach is a recipe for indigestion," Papa said.

"You do it all the time."

"And"—Papa raised a finger—"I always regret it."

A whiff of stale, spidery air brought back more memories Franny wasn't interested in. She took the first step on the rickety wooden stair and then the next, and suddenly she was five years old again, and Leon's friends had convinced her to play hide-and-seek in the basement. They were all hiding, and she had to find them. Franny was not a particular fan of the dark at the age of five, but her love for Leon overrode everything, and all she could think about was how proud he would be when she found him first, before any of the other boys.

Franny had moved cobwebby furniture, opened powdery old boxes, dug through corners where not even a nine-year-old boy should be able to hide, and the more she looked, the more scared she got, convinced the evil basement had eaten Leon and his friends, and it was going to eat her too unless she could find Leon and bring him back. She didn't know how long she was down there searching and crying, but suddenly footsteps had tumbled down the stairs, and Leon scooped Franny up in his arms. "I didn't know, I swear. I swear I never would have told you to play hide-and-seek in the basement."

Franny had clung to him as he carried her back up the stairs, where the four nine-year-old boys, fully grown men to Franny's eyes, looked sheepishly at the floor.

"No one treats my sister like that," Leon had said.

"Aw, come on," Hank had said. "I play jokes on my kid sister all the time."

"Yeah, she doesn't belong in the club anyway," another boy had said—one who moved away two years later; Franny forgot his name.

"Is that how you all feel?" Leon had asked.

The boys nodded. Leon gripped Franny by the shoulders as she sniffled and looked at the floor. She knew this moment had to come. She was a little kid, after all, and a girl. She didn't belong in the club.

"Franny," Leon said.

"Yeah," Franny said, looking at his sneakers, grimy and formerly blue.

"Looks like it's just the two of us in the club now."

Now, Franny called Leon's name, half expecting to dig through boxes again.

"Over here," he said.

He was sitting cross-legged on the cold concrete floor in the darkest, spideriest side of the basement, but his hair was combed smooth, and he wore summer slacks and a polo shirt. He was surrounded by old toys. Franny's dolly in her starched pinafore, a pile of alphabet blocks, a windup tin soldier, Lincoln Logs. He was stacking the alphabet blocks, one on top of the other, hunched over his work like an architect. It scared her more than the spiders, seeing him on the floor like this.

"You used to love these," he said. "Do you remember? I would make a pyramid of them, and you'd stomp over on your chubby legs and knock them all down. You thought it was hilarious, every single time."

"I remember," Franny said. She didn't. "Should I knock them over, for old times' sake?"

He paused his block stacking to look at her. In the dark, his face had hollows where eyes should be. "I'm just trying to remember what it felt like," he said.

The basement was a place for old things to get chewed up or

disintegrate into dust. It was a place for memories to fade and be forgotten. Leon was always trying to stir up Franny's dust but wouldn't let anyone touch his.

"How's about you do your remembering upstairs? Where we can both suffer Mama's guilt trips?" Franny said. She touched Leon's shoulder, and he jerked out of reach.

"I took those pills for Mary Kate," he said. "I couldn't live with myself if I had—" He slammed an alphabet block on top of the tower, and the whole thing toppled.

"Leon, hey, it's okay—"

"If I had done something like what you did."

Franny's chest tightened. Her heart beat like a trapped bird. "That's not fair."

"To whom? You have to face your mistakes, Franny. You can't keep running away."

"I guess I should just follow your example, huh?"

"What's that supposed to mean?"

Leon's voice was rising like a fever. Soon, someone would open the door and holler down the stairs. It would turn into a fight. Dinnerware might even be thrown.

I don't mean the time you broke your mama's china platter. Secrets wrapped Franny's tongue like spiderwebs, too sticky to speak out loud. She stomped up the stairs.

"Is he coming?" Papa asked.

Mama pressed the phone to her ear and beckoned Franny over. "Yes, I'm sure she'd love to attend the symphony with you, *Michael*," she said meaningfully, but Franny brushed past her and climbed the stairs to her bedroom two at a time. She fished out an old padlocked diary from high school and crumpled up the first two entries from March 1944 without even reading them—that was before Leon enlisted, before Peter, before barbiturates and alphabet block stacking and runaway bridesmaids. She would storm into the Blue Moon, and she wouldn't leave until Lottie let her up onstage again. *How's that for running away, Leon?* Franny stuffed the book in a handbag with her change purse. She was out the door as Mama laughed into the phone.

"What a coincidence! Franny adores the early Baroque masters," she said.

CHAPTER SEVEN

Surely, the Blue Moon couldn't be closed? That was *not* an option. Franny shoved the door with her shoulder, but it didn't budge. The door was locked; how much evidence did Franny need? She threw herself against it again, just in case, and the comedian Andy Grand Canyon opened the door at the same time. Franny stumbled into her, nearly knocking them both over.

Franny was nothing if not great at first impressions.

Andy Grand Canyon's hair was tied back, a flowered scarf covering it, a pair of sunglasses on top of her head. Her mouth puckered like a lemon in her square face.

"Looking for honey?" she said. "Buzz off."

The lights were on inside, relieving the Blue Moon of its mystery. Franny scanned discreetly for Lottie but didn't see her. A pair of cowboy boots stuck straight out from a booth to the right of the stage, the booth where the Amateur Hour girls had been sitting yesterday. Facing Franny sat a girl with stylishly short curly hair. She looked vaguely familiar, in a Jewish sort of way.

Franny tried to unknot her tongue. "You're—" Franny said, "You made me feel like Cinderella." The friendly little birds, the glittering castle just out of reach...

"Ooh, which scene?" Andy clapped her hands. "Wait, you aren't one of those girls who sing at the top of their lungs, are you? I *hate* that." She pulled back to look at Franny. "What was your favorite punch line?"

"I—"

"Never mind, whichever one you pick, I'll wonder why you didn't like the others." Andy tugged on Franny's arm and dragged her inside. "Is a movie without songs too much to ask for?"

Was she supposed to answer? Franny shrugged and hoped it was the right response.

"I miss the days when *Sunset Boulevard* was the most popular movie. Much quieter. Hey Helen, you got a pen? Kid here wants my autograph."

"I'm sorry," Franny said. "I'm actually looking for Lottie Marcone?"

Whoever was attached to the cowboy boots snickered. An arm thrust upward from the booth, waggling a pen. "Hey, now, that chicken scratch will be worth something one day. Andy Grand Canyon is gonna be a star, isn't that right?"

Andy crossed her arms over her chest and squinted at Franny. "Does it look like Lottie Marcone's here? Do I look like a secretary to you?"

Franny looked over at the Jewish girl, hoping she might intervene, but the girl just smiled pleasantly, as though she were watching a movie and not a real argument.

"Anyway, we were just leaving." Andy Grand Canyon spun around and returned to the booth, nudging the cowboy boots.

"Two seconds ago, you would have signed my bare ass," Franny said, regretting it instantly. Just who controlled this mouth?

But the cowboy boots swung to the floor, and the top half of the girl exploded in laughter—swingy, stringy hair and a flannel blouse with the sleeves rolled up. She had a skinny chest and a ratty face Franny didn't care for. "I like this one. Hair of the dog?"

Andy groaned.

"Pardon?" Franny never said things like *pardon*, and the primness of it made the rat-faced girl smirk, revealing too many teeth, or maybe the right number of teeth but all jumbled together wrong. She quickly closed her lips and popped to her feet.

"It's a drink, genius. To help you get over a hangover? Boy, you are green," she said. She shook Franny's hand vigorously. "Helen Angel."

"She's no angel," said the other two in unison.

"These girls," Helen said. "Like putty in my hands." She led Franny to the booth but didn't offer her a seat. The Jewish girl still smiled pleasantly, and Andy slumped across from her, arms crossed. Also in the booth: a beach ball, a stack of towels, a straw picnic basket. "Gal, Andy, this is, I can only assume, another of Lottie's new girls. Uh, what was your name?"

"Fr—"

"Uh-uhh!" Helen wiggled a finger in front of her face, a worm Franny was supposed to get hooked on. "Stage name, no real names here. Verboten."

"Peggy Blake?" Franny said. The new name felt screwy, weirdly dishonest. Like getting a new haircut and then meeting someone on vacation who'd never seen her regular hair.

"Yeah." Helen *hur-hur*red, smacking her too hard on the back. "You look like a Blake."

"You said—" Was she *trying* to make Franny feel stupid? "It's a stage name," she muttered.

"No shit." There was a hole in the shoulder seam of Helen's blouse, and up close, her stringy hair had an unpleasant tang. "Anyone else? Drink? My treat."

"You're not hungover," Andy said.

"I will be if I stop drinking." She skipped over to the bar and started clinking through bottles.

"We all have stage names, Peggy." The Jewish girl spoke, finally. "Lottie's old-fashioned that way. I'm Gal, short for Galit, which is actually my real name, so that's not a great example now that I think about it." She thrust out a soft, manicured hand, and Franny realized this was one of the BBG girls Mama had mentioned. Franny shook her hand. What was she doing here? She wore an expensive-looking emerald pencil dress with matching bolero—Franny had seen this same dress in the window display of Marshall Field's.

Had she tried to woo the famous Michael Berman? She could have him, as far as Franny was concerned.

Helen dropped a bottle of whiskey and four shot glasses on the table and then made as if to sit in Andy's lap, but Andy grimaced and scooched over.

"Andy chose *Grand Canyon* for herself, can you believe it?" Helen said. "All the names in the world and she picks *Andy Big Hoo-Hah*."

"It was either that or *Organ Rock*." Andy shrugged. "Which felt like false advertising."

Franny laughed and hoped it sounded like she understood what was going on.

"Helen Angel is also a nom de plume, in case you're wondering."

"Well, la-di-da," Andy said. "What do you call a French cracker?"

"Oh, I know this," Gal said, squinting at the ceiling. "Biscuit, right? But they pronounce it funny."

"I'll show you something French," Helen said, waggling her tongue between two fingers in a gesture that made no sense. V for… victory? Very…French?

"Repugnant." Andy sniffed.

"Oh, lighten up.."

"Girls, don't fight," Gal said. "Please?"

"We're not fighting," Helen said solemnly. She filled her shot glass and downed it in a single gulp. "So what's your set, new girl?"

Franny felt interesting as furniture, lurking next to the booth. Was this a test of some kind? And if so, what kind?

"My set?"

"Your act, your tight five. Your jokes?" Helen said. "Ya missing your ventriloquist, dummy?"

The alarm bells rang so loud in Franny's head, she could hardly think. What was she doing here if she didn't know a simple word like *set*? "Oh, my *set*," she said. "Well, it's mostly, uh—"

"She doesn't have a set," Helen said to Andy.

"No set whatsoever," Andy said, suddenly interested. "She is thoroughly set-less."

They peered up at her curiously. "But you've been onstage here," Gal said. "Otherwise Lottie wouldn't have told you to come back."

It was…half true anyway, the first part. She plopped down in the booth next to Gal. "Last night was my first time," Franny said. "Onstage, I mean."

"Wait, I do know you," Andy said. "You interrupted my set the other day. Boy, you got a lot of nerve coming back here."

"So she's *not* a fan after all," Helen said, *tsk*ing. "You should be more discerning with your John Hand Cock."

"You can kick rocks with your hand cocks," Andy said. "And take 'Peggy' with you, while you're at it."

"I think it's pronounced Hancock?" Gal said. No one responded. "Without the *d*?"

"Oh, you know I think you're the tops, sugarplum," Helen said, tugging Andy close. Franny was surprised to see Andy rest her head on Helen's shoulder. Helen looked surprised too. She held perfectly still, like a butterfly had alighted on her.

Classic Franny, offending someone before they ever met. Only way to win these girls over would be to impress them. Time-honored recipe for making friends.

"Boopsie Baxter said I was funny," she said.

Andy rolled her eyes. "She'd laugh at paint if that made it dry faster."

And just like that, Franny's one trump card turned out to be the wrong suit.

"Last night," Gal said, squinting at the ceiling. "Hold the phone, that was you? *Peckers Marcone* was you?" She grabbed Helen's arm. Helen tried to shake her off and only succeeded at shaking off Andy's resting head. "Helen, she was the one I was telling you about— Margot heard about her from Betty, who heard from Myrna at the Oneg after Havdalah services last night? Remember?"

"The Heeb grapevine strikes again," Helen said.

"That took nerve," Gal said. "I could never be that brave, not in a million years."

"It just came out," Franny said. She arranged her face to look modest, but inside she was doing flip-flops. Brave? Franny?

"Jokes don't 'just come out,'" Andy said. "They take work. And practice. No one just waltzes up there and kills."

"I didn't *kill*," Franny said, the word feeling phony in her mouth. "It's just, I get nervous… I either freeze or blurt out something crazy."

"Cheers to that." Helen lifted another whiskey and downed it with a grimace.

"All I know is that Myrna said the girls can't stop talking about it," Gal said. "So I say you must have real talent."

BBG or no, this Gal gal was all right.

"Okay," Andy said, clapping. "Well, it's been a treat, but the three of us have got a date with Foster Beach. And then a *professional* comedy show to do. That we've worked for."

"Why, Andy," Helen said. "Don't tell me you're…jealous."

Andy barked a laugh. "Of an amateur? Give me a break."

Helen shrugged. "New girl's got the gift. First time up, and Lottie's already got her coming here to learn the ropes. Remind me, how many Amateur Hours did you do before she summoned you after hours?" She tugged gently on Andy's silky ponytail, but Andy hopped out of the booth, grabbing the beach ball.

Franny's guts flipped, a marquee spelled out *LIAR!* on her forehead. "That's not *exactly* what happened—"

"What BBG chapter are you?" Gal said, worrying on a swizzle stick. "City or suburbs? I don't recognize you, but then, I haven't been to a meeting in at least a month. What with being here every evening. Have I missed anything good?"

Franny didn't want to offend, but she wouldn't touch the B'nai B'rith Girls with a ten-foot pole. "I'm not really—"

"So!" Helen slammed her palms on the table and grinned at Franny. "Where were we? Oh yes, you need a set."

"I hate to keep you from the beach," Franny said. "Don't worry about me. I'll just, ah, I'll wing it. Did she...did Lottie say what time she'd be here?"

"Wing it? Oh no, Lottie will not tolerate winging. Unless you're me, right, girls?" Helen flapped her arms; another joke Franny didn't get. "But here's three hardened comedians sitting right in front of you, ready and willing to help. Darn it if it ain't your lucky day."

Andy had hopped up onstage and was bouncing the beach ball loudly off the back wall, narrowly missing the drum set Franny had knocked over the night before. "Helen Angel," she said, "you *promised*."

"I also promised Lottie I'd watch the joint till she got here," Helen said. "The beach will be there when we're done."

"Lottie asked you to watch the place?" Gal asked.

"Hardly," Andy said. The bass drum boomed rhythmically in time with the beach ball, fraying Franny's nerves. "Helen's got it in her melon that if she never leaves the Blue Moon, eventually Lottie will just give it to her."

"I don't want no handout," Helen said. "I'm buying it off Ed fair and square."

"Need money to buy things," Andy said, kicking the ball hard. "Getting onstage occasionally might help."

Helen blushed blotchily from the neck up. She slid out of the booth, and the two of them argued in hushed voices.

Things had sure taken a turn and fast. "Is this my fault?" Franny whispered. "For not having a set?"

"No, they're always going on like this," Gal said, rolling her eyes. "Helen loves Andy, and Andy loves the attention. Other than that, arguing is the only thing they have in common."

"Wait." Franny frowned. "*Loves*, as in—"

The beach ball kicking had mercifully stopped. Onstage, Helen played with Andy's hair. They were standing awfully close to each other.

"Take a picture, it'll last longer," Andy called.

Either Franny really had a staring problem, or all these comedians used the same quips. Franny turned away and sank low in her seat. What she really should consider doing was the *opposite* of whatever felt natural.

"This is going to be so much fun," Gal said, resting her head on her fists. She had an honest-to-goodness diamond bracelet circling her wrist. "And a BBG too. You have to tell me everything I missed. Do you know Sarah Beckmann?"

"Gosh, there are so many Sarahs, I—"

"I suppose I could spare a few bits of wisdom," Andy said, sliding haughtily into the booth, "since you're so green. But you could have at least asked politely."

"That is awfully nice of you, but—"

"And since you ruined our beach plans," Andy said.

"You're pretty lucky," Helen said in a boozy stage whisper. "Andy Grand Canyon is the next Boopsie Baxter. No. *Better*. I'll make sure of that."

Andy smacked her playfully. What just happened? First, they were at each other's throats, and now they were united against Franny?

"Look, I just came here to talk to Lottie, so—"

"Peckers Marcone was a pretty good joke," Gal said. "You girls have to admit it. That just popped in your head?"

Franny sighed. "Sure, I got a million of them," she said. "And no control over when they come out."

"Stage fright." Gal nodded. "Happens to the best of us."

"I wouldn't say I'm afraid, exactly..." Franny started, hoping to be interrupted, but instead, she just trailed off in silence. First time she could have actually squeezed in a full sentence, and this was the one she picked.

"You got something to write on?" Helen said finally. She dug an arm into Franny's purse without asking and pulled out her diary. Franny tried to stop her but got a sloppy grin in return. "Price of admission," Helen said. She pawed it open, drawing a wobbly circle in the middle of a blank page.

"You don't do it right," Andy said, yanking the diary away. Franny flinched but didn't protest.

Andy pointed at the circle. "This is a joke tree. First, we start with a topic. Name anything. Childhood. Sex. Marriage. Religion. School. Scrotums. Puppies. Stop me any time."

"How do I know what to choose?" Franny said. What was a *scrotums*?

Andy yawned. "Just choose something. Anything. Doesn't matter. I feel like Rip Van Winkle over here."

"Childhood," Franny said.

Andy scribbled *childhood* in the circle. "Now tell me some stories about your childhood. Anything that comes to mind."

"*My* childhood?" Franny asked. "No, that's not—my childhood was boring. How about something like…how little girls think kissing a frog will turn it into a prince."

"That *happened* to you?" Gal said.

"That's not funny," Helen said.

"Is too," Franny said, face hot as a stove top. "With the right words, it is."

"Now, Peggy," Andy said in a big-sisterly voice that made Franny want to slither under the table. "Anyone can write a cliché. You, or me—well, not me—"

"Or a male comedian on television." Gal nodded.

"What's wrong with that?" Franny asked, thinking of Papa guffawing in the breakfast nook.

Gal gaped. "Only basically everything," she said.

"Television stole from radio, which stole from vaudeville," Andy said. "The only thing new about any of it is that you can watch it in your house shoes."

"You're not a three-piece suit filled with punch lines and pratfalls," Helen said. "You're you. Tall, twenty-five, frizzy Hebrew hair, big ass—"

"That's not very nice," Gal said.

"Do I look twenty-*five*?" Franny asked.

"The point is," Andy said, removing the sunglasses from her head and folding them neatly on the table, "everywhere you go, you bring *you* with you, so you might as well figure out how to work with it. Can't leave yourself behind when you go up onstage."

Franny remembered Lottie's fingernail skewering her breastbone, Boopsie telling her she was wasting everyone's time. What was so great about being yourself when there were so many other things to pretend to be?

"Are you sure?" Franny asked. "Have you tried?"

Andy sighed. "I can't work with this."

Helen leaned across the table, her little ratty lip curled. "You want a Showstopper, don't ya?"

And there you had it—the sixty-four-thousand-dollar question. The idea frankly made her a little queasy. "Yes," Franny blurted. "No. I don't know."

"You need *authority* to conjure a Showstopper." Helen slammed her fist on the table and made everyone jump, including the shot glasses.

"Careful!" Gal said, wiping whiskey off her wrist. "This is a new dress."

"If you can't command a room," Helen said, "you can't conjure a Showstopper. And if that's the case, you might as well walk out that door right now."

Everyone looked at the door, some (Andy) more hopefully than others.

"Ever wonder why Boopsie Baxter doesn't hand out orgasms on the street?" Helen asked. "Plenty of willing ears out there, plenty of girls who need to feel good."

Franny really hoped the question was rhetorical.

"You think Boopsie has any authority on the street? Any of us? We could scream at the top of our lungs, and no one would hear us. Or at home? You know any comedian conjuring a Showstopper in her house? Not a chance, sister. Out in the world, we're nothing. A pair of legs, a pair of tits, an empty head," Helen said. "But here? In the Blue Moon—if you got the microphone, you got power. And the one with power conjures a Showstopper. Hell, you don't even need a microphone. Watch."

Helen jabbed a skinny arm across the table and grabbed Franny by the collar. Her stringy hair hung like yarn, and her nose was shiny, but there was something about her that Franny didn't mind being close to. "Tell me a story from your childhood," Helen murmured. "Now."

Franny choked, tried to free her neck, but Helen gripped it tighter. "I can't breathe," she croaked.

"Aw, let her go, Hels," Andy said.

"Life's ticking away," Helen said. "Better make with a story before you kick the bucket."

This wasn't really happening. Was this really happening? "My—" Franny wheezed, racking her brain. She blurted the first thing that came to mind. "Uncle Hymie told me if I didn't eat my string beans, I'd turn out pigeon-breasted."

Helen grinned and released her. Franny rubbed her neck and coughed into a napkin.

"Growing up is a bitch," Helen said. "Luckily I had an Uncle *Hymen* to show me the ropes. He says, if I didn't eat my string beans, he says, I'll end up pigeon-breasted. Well, I shoulda listened." Helen paused. "'Cuz I'm pigeon-breasted all right. All I got now is one giant tit." Helen mimed squeezing one breast in the middle of her chest.

A laugh burst out of her like a shot, and suddenly Franny wasn't Franny anymore. She was a pigeon. What was Franny, the pigeon, doing at a nightclub? She had better flap her wings and fly away, pronto. Find a tree or a nice garbage can. She just had to hop up on this table here and take a good long leap, flap them wings, and go.

Helen snatched Franny by the collar, yanked downward, and Franny smashed her funny bone on the table.

She yelped, rubbed her elbow, which was no longer a wing.

"And *that* is authority," Helen said, arms wide, shit-eating grin spread across her face. "That has got to be some sort of record—new joke to Showstopper at the speed of sound."

"And what was the point of that?" Andy said.

"That's your Showstopper?" Franny asked, still rubbing her elbow.

"Try not to laugh," Gal said. "You can't feel the Showstopper if you don't laugh."

"I see right through you, sweet tits," Helen said, beady eyes skewering Franny, triggering a full-body shiver. "You got some juicy pain in there, and it's gonna pop no matter what. All I'm saying is, you can man up and let it pop onstage, conjure yourself a Showstopper, or you can let it pop out there"—Helen jerked her thumb doorward—"and get carted off to the loony bin."

Franny nodded politely, but that's where Helen was wrong. Franny knew *exactly* how to keep that fragile balloon intact. She was something of an expert at it.

"Take Andy here," Helen said. "If she's not the center of attention, she might as well not exist. Wants to be a starlet, but Hollywood would toss her in the back of a tepee, and that's that."

"Watch it, Hels," Andy said.

Helen did not watch it. "Her folks are Navajo; Daddy lost his life to Jerry in the war. Uncle Sam barely said thank you, and then he got real nervous, like he always does about Indians. The *rez* was looking a bit *red*. And anyway, it had a little too much oil under it."

"Tell your own sob story, huh?" Andy said.

"So he forked over bus money to get 'em to move to the city. Promised jobs and utopia but was dreaming about annihilation, same old story. Andy left Arizona and ended up in this lousy joint. And now she goes up on this stage and gets to be a star. And when she feels like a star, she can make *you* feel like a star. Cinderella. Gloria Swanson. Liz Taylor."

Andy glared daggers at Helen. "And Helen," she said, "wishes she was a man."

"Shut up, Andy."

"Her daddy hoed corn when he wasn't whacking her with his belt. But Mama was even worse—she made Helen wear *dresses*," Andy said, face in a mockery of horror. "She escaped in Daddy's overalls, two dollars and a loaf of bread wrapped up in her Sunday pinafore. Day one in Chicago, she got on the Marcones' bad side, and Lottie gave her a choice: stand-up or cement shoes."

Helen flicked away a fake tear. "Nicest thing anyone's ever done for me," she said.

"Helen's best trick is saying what she means but *pretending* it's a joke," Andy said. "Second best is her Showstopper. Makes you feel like you can fly. Not that she's allowed up anymore. Not after last time." Andy crossed her eyes and mimed guzzling a bottle.

"What is this, Nuremberg?" Helen slumped in her seat.

"They just kept laughing...and flying...and falling." Andy shuddered. "We tried to pull you offstage, but you wouldn't stop. It was horrible, Hels. You were so drunk, you thought you were killing. And you were."

"Exaggerate much?" Helen muttered. "No one died."

"Girls broke bones because of Helen," Gal said. "Lottie had to call an ambulance. It was like the Saint Valentine's Day Massacre."

"Whose side are you on, huh?" Helen said.

"Your elbow gave me a black eye." Gal touched her cheek like she could still feel it.

Helen grimaced. "It was an accident."

Gal lowered her voice. "She doesn't remember a thing. And she's not allowed back up unless she stops drinking."

"I can hear you," Helen said.

"Anyway, she's pretty much immune to other girls' Showstoppers. So don't expect much encouragement," Andy said.

"Sue me for having a refined sense of humor."

"Immune to a Showstopper?" Franny asked, thinking about Boopsie. "Is that something you can learn?"

But Helen regarded Gal through her eye slits. "And then there's our Gal."

Gal shrugged. "Some of us don't have dirty secrets," she said good-naturedly. Helen snorted; Andy rolled her eyes.

"Oh!" Franny pointed at Gal. "You're the one who makes the audience feel like the bus showed up at the right time."

"You know about Gal's Showstopper?" Andy said. "Who was talking about Gal?"

"I'm sure they were just talking about how boring my Showstopper is. Right, Peggy?" She sounded oddly enthusiastic about this possibility, but still. Franny didn't want to hurt her feelings.

"Not exactly. Sort of? Actually, I can't remember."

Gal smiled. "It's okay! Comedy's just a lark for me. I'm happy to be the stepsister to Andy's Cinderella."

Andy and Helen burst out laughing. "Say it often enough, maybe you'll believe it," Helen said.

Gal shrugged, twisted her diamond bracelet. "It's a good way to pass the time. I'm just not ready to marry a doctor and sit around a mansion all day painting my nails. I'm not ready to be that...bored."

Franny remembered Michael Berman and the Baroque masters.

"There must be something to this comedy thing," Franny said, "if a Jew would rather be funny than rich." She grinned, but the three of them just stared. Good old Franny! Always running her mouth at the exact wrong time.

But then they burst out laughing. Andy's shoulders shook. Helen smacked the table, jostling the whiskey in her shot glass. "She got you good, Gal Gardenia!"

Gal giggled and elbowed Franny chummily. "Now you're cookin'. What else you got bubbling on that stove?"

It felt good. Really good. Franny took a deep breath and nodded. She was going to do this. She was going to write some jokes about herself. Right now. Any moment now.

They waited for Franny to say something. Franny waited for Franny to say something. She fidgeted in her seat, her childhood slipping around like a fish she didn't really want to catch. "I guess comedy is more scientific than I was expecting," she said instead.

"Exactly," Andy said. "Isn't comedy scientific? One injection and you're cured of ever being attractive to the opposite sex."

Everyone laughed, except for Helen. And then there were the friendly little cartoon birds at the foot of Franny's bed, just where she left them. She reached out to let one perch on her finger.

"Do you think," Gal said, holding her arms out, "this dress is made of real diamonds?"

The scene popped, and Franny was back in the booth. Back in her own body. Still jokeless. Andy sat back, grinning. "What was that about the speed of sound? Chew on that, Helen."

"Chew on my rear end," Helen said.

If they would just start arguing again, maybe resume kicking the ol' beach ball…

"Girls, this isn't about you, it's about Peggy," Gal said, patting her hand. "You can do it. We've taught you everything we know."

Good evening, ladies and germs. Take my wife, please. Boy, are my arms tired. Panic filled Franny's mind with the world's worst punch lines. It was pointless. Jokes either appeared or they didn't. She couldn't dig for them. Who knew what she'd find down there?

"Will you write my jokes?" she blurted out. They gawped relentlessly, like goldfish. "Just this once? I swear after Amateur Hour, I'll go home and write a whole book of them."

Andy shook her head. "That's called stealing jokes, Peggy Blake. We don't do that."

"I don't want to steal anyone's jokes," Franny said quickly, "I just mean—"

"Doesn't matter what you *mean*," Andy said, suddenly serious as a heart attack. "It's what you *do*."

"I'll do it," Helen said, snatching the notebook. Andy gawped at her. "I wish someone had helped me when I started out."

"Lottie will be furious," Andy grumbled.

"Not if you don't tell her," Helen said.

"I'm not a snitch," Andy said. "But she'll figure it out."

"Oh, lighten up, girls," Gal said. "Lottie's not that smart."

Franny could have just about kissed her for saying that. Andy looked stunned.

Helen laughed. "Did she just say what I think she said?"

"Will you two stop fighting," Gal said, "if I buy lunch?"

❧

Several hours later, paper wrappers lay crumpled on the table, remnants of Francheezies and Dagwood Burgers from the Peter Pan Snack Shop across the street, along with several empty soda bottles with straw snorkels and another half-empty whiskey bottle. Back at 504, Mama was probably starting to think about supper and wondering where Franny had got to. When would she start to worry? Franny's belly twanged, not just because of the hamburger. She should leave now. She should have left hours ago.

Franny was not going to leave any time soon.

Gal nodded at her diary with approval. "It's rough, but not bad for your first day on the job."

"Not bad? Not bad?" Helen said. "Boopsie Baxter herself couldn't have had a better first set."

"Let's not get carried away," Andy said. "Now get up there and show us what you got."

Franny coughed up soda fizz. "Up?"

"We're an hour from Amateur Hour. Grab the mic and take this set for a test drive," Andy said. Gal handed her the diary.

"Why don't I do it at Amateur Hour?" Franny said. "Isn't that what amateurs do?" She looked around for sympathy, but even Gal shook her head.

"Even an amateur comedian needs to practice," Gal said.

"For *Amateur Hour*?" Franny asked.

"Come on," Helen said. "If this sourpuss can do it fresh off the bus, so can you." She lunged at Andy, arms wide, smacking her lips, and Andy pushed her away.

"You sure know how to woo a girl," Andy said.

Helen's mouth curled in a grin, and she looked like she was about to say something terrifying, so Franny hopped out of the booth and began her death march to the stage. Helen followed and adjusted the microphone for Franny so she didn't have to hunch over.

"Thanks," Franny said.

Helen clapped a hand on her shoulder. "A bit of advice from me to you," she said. "Toughen up. If the room thinks they can laugh *at* you, they'll never stop."

Franny nodded, but her hands shook so hard that Gal's loopy writing was barely readable. The papers crackled in the microphone. "What if I screw it up?" she said.

"There's a trapdoor right under your feet," Andy called from the booth. "We feed you to the crocodiles."

"And the ghosts of gangsters in the old rum-running tunnels," Helen said. "They love fresh blood."

"Would it help if we booed?" Gal asked earnestly. Helen giggled, and even Andy chuckled a little. Franny managed an embarrassed laugh, and then she was arriving, breathlessly, at the corner of Oak Park Avenue just as the bus pulled up. She felt pleasantly satisfied, as though there really were meaning and order to the world, if only one took the trouble to notice it.

And now, miraculously, she felt ever so slightly more confident. Had Gal done that on purpose? "Wow," Franny said. "That is an extremely specific emotion."

Gal shrugged. "Can't nobody do what I do. Why would they bother?"

"Bet she conjures a Showstopper on the first go," Helen said.

"Even faster than Gal. Of course, Gal's Showstopper bores everyone to tears—"

"I resemble that remark," Gal said.

Franny tried not to pant like a creeper into the microphone. "Let's not get ahead of ourselves," she said. She was already sweaty. Why was she so sweaty?

"Anyway," Andy said, "it's not quantity, it's quality."

"Now, now, don't be jealous," Helen said.

"Of Street Corner Jane here? Hardly."

Gal smoothed her expensive dress. "I went up every day for two weeks, Andy. I worked hard for my Showstopper."

"I thought this was just a lark," Andy said. "A way to pass the time?"

Gal pursed her lips but then turned to Franny with a big smile. "You'll do great," she said.

Franny held her diary right up to her face. "Childhood isn't all it's cracked up to be," she read.

"Anyway, *Helen*, you can't conjure a Showstopper with someone else's jokes," Andy whispered, loud enough for Franny to hear.

"Speak up," Helen called. "And don't *read*. Try to do it from memory."

"They're Peggy's stories," Gal said. "We just wrote the words."

"Doesn't matter," Andy said.

"This is literally the first time I have looked at this paper," Franny said. "I can barely read your handwriting." Why were they talking about her like she wasn't there?

"Yes!" Helen said. "Like that. That sounded natural."

"I was just…talking."

"Exactly," Gal said. "Tell the jokes like they just occurred to you. Like you're suddenly dying to tell a bunch of strangers about your menstrual history."

Franny scanned the page and then reluctantly lowered the diary. She could do this. She *would* do this. "Childhood isn't all it's cracked up to be. Eleven years old, I wake up in bed—blood *everywhere*. 'I'm dying!' I call out. 'Help!' I cry. Mama tells me I've been visited by the Curse. The *Curse?*" Franny saucered her eyes wide. "Whatever happened to the tooth fairy?"

She had talked too fast and still ran out of breath at the end. They weren't going to laugh.

But they *did*. Politely, and okay, it sounded a little forced, but the laughs sent a shiver through her whole body. Franny had never felt exactly right—always a little too this, a little not-enough that. She hadn't even known *exactly right* was a feeling a person could have. But the drips of laughter felt like Moses's manna, and Franny considered that she (almost, maybe, possibly) was meant to wander in this particular desert.

CHAPTER EIGHT

LOTTIE BREEZED INTO THE BLUE MOON IN RED PLAID TROU-sers and a black short-sleeved blouse, waist cinched with a wide leather belt. Her heels clapped the linoleum, stuttered to a stop, then regained composure and walked slowly through the club. By the time Franny could see her full silhouette in the sweaty stage lights, Lottie was leaning casually against her U-shaped booth, lighting a cigarette, cool as can be. Franny finished her set with the closer Helen had written: "Got a stomachache? Thank Peggy Blake!" to a smattering of applause and Helen's spitty attempt at a wolf whistle.

"Not bad," Andy said, "but don't mumble. Really bite off each word. You won't get a laugh on jokes they can't hear."

"Lottie," Helen said, pulling wet fingers from her mouth. She hopped out of the booth, grabbing food wrappers and empty bottles, suddenly nervous as a baby giraffe at Lincoln Park Zoo. "Everything's running smoothly," she said, hiding the bottles. She cleared her throat. "I've been working on new material too."

Lottie's fingers drummed the blue velvet booth, and she nudged the beach ball away with her toe with a smirk.

"From one dipsomaniac's girl to another, Andy," she said. "You'll never make it to the beach."

Andy flushed like a novice chameleon. "I'm nobody's girl."

"Keep telling yourself that, sweetheart."

Lottie joined Franny onstage, and Franny lost the ability to breathe.

"You're here," Lottie said.

"So far," Franny croaked. She was going to get kicked out, for the third time, right when things were starting to get good.

"It's easier to get rid of bedbugs," Lottie said. She thumbed away a dribble of sweat from Franny's upper lip, which somehow felt more violent than Helen grabbing her collar.

Franny saw Andy straining to listen. Her heart pounded. "Please, give me a shot. Just one more time."

"How in the world did you convince Andy Grand Canyon to give you comedy tips? She's not a fan of sharing, especially the stage." Lottie cocked her head. "And somehow Helen's not falling-down drunk. Yet. What are you, a miracle worker?"

"I have a set," Franny said. "For Amateur Hour."

Lottie raised her delicate eyebrows. "A whole set? Well, now," she said. "How could I say no to that?" She patted Franny's cheek and left her off-balance. Then Lottie walked behind the bar and, casual as anything, lowered herself into the floor and disappeared. Was she... some kind of magician? What had just happened?

"Did she say anything about me going up?" Helen asked. "I really do have new material."

"I swear, if you told her we wrote your set——" Andy said.

Helen shushed her. "She's still here, dummy. Jesus, work on your stage whisper."

"She," Franny said, lowering herself off the stage, "she apologized for being late."

"She *apologized*?" Andy said.

Franny shrugged, avoided Andy's glare. "You asked me what she said."

"This is like a real-life *Pygmalion*," Gal said dreamily. She turned to Helen. "I just love Leslie Howard, don't you? What an absolute dream—"

"Please," Helen said, miming indigestion. "Not while I'm drinking."

"Good news, everyone," Lottie said, popping up behind the bar with a shit-eating grin. "The book clubs are coming."

"Oh, Lottie," Gal said. "Not for her first Amateur Hour?"

"They're not *that* bad," Andy said. "I like the book clubs."

"Kiss-up," Helen muttered.

Franny leaned against the table, trying to look like she knew what was going on. She was always lagging, would never catch up. Her good feelings evaporated, and, ah, there it was—that familiar sense of having too many arms, all of them wrong.

"If you can make the book club ladies laugh, Miss Peggy Blake, you can do anything," Lottie said, sliding onto a barstool and reaching over for a vodka bottle. "You *can* make them laugh, can't you? You don't know the meaning of the word *no*."

"Sure thing." Franny tried out a breezy laugh, but it was just a lot of hot air. "As long as they're not reading books."

"They're phony social clubs," Andy said. "Housewives who got a taste of freedom during the war and couldn't let it go. They started the clubs as a ruse for leaving the kids behind and doing things their husbands wouldn't approve of."

"Like stand-up," Gal said.

"Used to be all the clubs would fight over them. Now there aren't many left—nightclubs *or* book clubs," Andy said. "If they do come here, it's only after a long, hard day of shopping. They want an easy laugh. Who doesn't want to forget snot-nosed kids and needy husbands? Every girl wants to be a star, so I do okay." She looked at Helen for validation, but Helen was squinting hard at Lottie.

"I feel sorry for them," Gal said. "They've forgotten what it's like to have fun, and who can blame them?"

"When I run this place, no more old-fashioned book clubs," Helen said.

Lottie barked a laugh. "You're too wet to run a bath."

"I got lots of good ideas, Lottie," Helen said. She toppled her empty glass and watched it roll around in a circle. "You'll see."

"You say *husband* like it's a dirty word," Franny said.

Andy looked at her hard. "You might consider doing the same," she said. Helen rested a hand on Andy's knee, and only Franny saw that she didn't move away.

It occurred to Franny that maybe Gal and the BBGs had turned down Michael Berman and not the other way around.

Franny helped Gal set up the small round tables at the front of the stage. "Don't be nervous," Gal said, wrapping an arm around her shoulders chummily. "Last new girl we had? She was this pale, mousy little thing but had a doozy of a Showstopper—might've even given Boopsie a run for her money. Laugh at her jokes and suddenly you're being pawed by the world's greatest lover—Casanova himself! And he knew exactly what to do, if you know what I mean. Wowza! What a feeling. But her first time going up for the book clubs, *phew*." Gal shook her head. "Had a nervous breakdown right there on that stage, got fitted for a straitjacket, and was carted off to the loony bin. Never told a joke again."

Franny blinked. "Is that supposed to make me feel *better*?"

Gal grinned. "Oh, you'll be fine. Just, whatever you do, don't let them heckle you." She started wiping down the tables and draping them with white tablecloths.

"How do I keep them from heckling me?" Franny asked. But her question was drowned out by the flinging open of the door, which released a wave of lively giggles. Was it time already? Franny glanced at her watch. Now that strangers were here, strangers with shopping bags who expected to laugh, Franny felt a yearning for Michael Berman. He didn't expect to laugh. Boys didn't even like funny girls.

The crinoline horde burst through the door, and Barb tried her best to order them around, but eventually she gave up and tossed tickets at them, worth one free drink each. Girls chatted animatedly in clusters of four and five, flocking to the bar and elbowing each other to squeeze in their order first. Helen rushed back to their booth before someone took it.

"Did I just hear someone order a Mai Tai?" Franny asked.

"They milk Lottie dry for those free drinks," Helen said over the din. "She loses money with the book clubs, every time. When I'm in charge—"

"Lottie's showing off. She's threatened by us—always trying to get me to bomb. But what housewife doesn't dream of being Cinderella?" Andy grinned. "I'll never bomb, Lottie, never!" Her taunt was swallowed in the noise.

Franny bit her cuticles, an old habit from childhood that she thought she had outgrown. Back then, she'd chewed her thumbs to bloody nubs when she was nervous, or excited, or bored. Or breathing.

Andy swatted her hand away. "If you're hungry," she said, "go get a Francheezie."

"Yeah," Helen said. "Ed Marcone may need those fingers someday."

"Then he knows where he can stick them," Franny said.

Andy raised her eyebrows. "Look who's funny all of a sudden." She smiled, and warmth spread through Franny's chest.

"What if I forget all my jokes?" Franny said.

"We told you," Andy said, miming the motion of a trapdoor and a snapping crocodile.

Franny flipped through the diary pages so she wouldn't succumb to the siren song of her bloody cuticles. But her mind just slipped across the surface of the words, not absorbing anything.

"You're going to do great," Helen said.

Franny scratched her knee, which did not itch. "Gal said not to let them heckle me."

"We'll be right here in this booth, cheering you on," Gal said.

"But—"

"Don't think about it too hard," Andy said, "At least you're not that broad with the Clementine act."

"In a cavern, in a canyon, excavating for a mine, poked a miner in the 'giner of his sister Clementine," Helen twanged. Franny laughed, and Helen snatched her collar again so she wouldn't fly away.

"Enough with the choking," Franny said. "It wasn't *that* funny."

Andy laughed. "Our little bird has flown the nest," she said. "We've created a critic."

❦

"And now, ladies and degenerates, a brand-spanking-new *virgin* comedian—it's time to have your way with her—Miss Peggy Blake!"

Andy clapped into the microphone to encourage the crowd—no, the *room*, that's what the girls called it—to do the same. Andy had warmed them up, they'd laughed and twirled in their Cinderella dresses, two or three had belted out songs from the movie, much to Andy's annoyance—"I'm the one with the microphone here, girls."

There was a smattering of applause, but mostly the audience had their heads bent together in groups of fours and fives. Lottie had made them wait, had made Franny wait to go up until the bitter end, and now everyone was several Mai Tais in and couldn't care less about Amateur Hour. As Franny approached the stage, the chatter crescendoed. Some had taken articles of clothing out of shopping bags and held them up, asking each other for opinions and praise. Several huddled near the bathroom door, chatting.

"We want Andy," one of them slurred into her sticky Mai Tai glass. "I need my Prince Charming!" shouted another.

Franny stood up straight, holding the microphone close to her mouth, projecting to the back of the room just like the girls had coached her. "Childhood isn't all it's cracked up to be. Eleven years old, I wake up in bed—blood *everywhere*. 'I'm dying!' I call out. 'Help!' Mama tells me I've been visited by the Curse." Franny revved up for the punch line. "The Curse, she says. Whatever happened to the tooth fairy?" She paused for the laugh. No laugh came.

Paper rustled. Someone knocked at the bathroom door and whined about having had too many piña coladas. Someone else was complaining loudly about her husband two-timing her with their lady mailman. "It's mail*man*," she whined. "That's the whole point!"

The whole time, Lottie sat perfectly erect in her U-shaped booth. Franny could almost feel that smug smile emanating from the back of her sleek head. She made no move to stop the chatter. Helen kept frowning over at her, and even Andy looked surprised. Only Franny knew better. This was the point of summoning the book clubs, after all. Not to throw hecklers out but to throw Franny out.

Not this time, sister. Franny planted her feet on the stage and decided it was time to kill.

"So, uh," Franny said, "It ain't easy being born right before the Depression—"

"What year?" a voice shot out from the dark.

Franny froze instantly. Did dealing with hecklers mean she *should* respond or she *shouldn't*?

The whole room shut up for a moment, staring up at Franny

to see what she would do next, exactly at the moment when Franny wished they would keep talking. Franny forgot her punchline. She forgot what joke she was telling. She scanned the diary page in her mind, couldn't remember a single word written on it. Her armpits tingled, every nerve in her body exploding in panic.

"Nine months after your husband fucked my mother."

Oh no. Not again. Franny had cursed into a microphone in front of a room of strangers. A collective gasp sucked all the air out of the room until it was positively Martian. The silence lasted a thousand years.

And then a wave of laughter crashed over Franny and swept her away. Over and over, it crashed, but oddly enough, with each wave, Franny felt a little more solid. Here was the microphone; here were her fingers gripping the stand. Here were her feet sticking to the stage, and here was a breath. Glorious breath! Like life's girdle freeing her ribs. She let the wave of laughter tug at her as it ebbed, and just as the last foamy giggles sucked back to sea, Franny leaned into the microphone.

"Hey," she said, "man's gotta eat." The wave crashed again. Out of the corner of her eye, Franny saw Helen pounding the table with her fist, Gal covering her mouth. She had made Helen laugh! Only Andy sat in disappointed silence, arms folded.

Her lines came back to her one after another, and now she had the room's attention. They were on her side, and they seemed to find her genuinely funny, but the thrill of delivering her own punch line, of getting pummeled by waves, never returned. Then suddenly it was all over, and Andy was tugging her offstage to raucous applause.

"You did great," Gal whispered across the table. "A hundred times better times better than I did my first time."

Helen nodded slowly. "You did good. Real good."

"How do you feel?" Gal asked.

"You're grinning like a baboon," Helen said.

"Man's gotta eat," Gal said, shaking her head. "Inspired. I knew you could write your own stuff."

"Are you kidding?" Franny said. "If it weren't for your jokes, I would have been toast. Next time, though. If there is a next time."

"Why wouldn't there be a next time?" Andy asked, eyes narrowed. "You made them laugh. Lowest common denominator laughs, but laughs."

Lottie materialized at the booth and gestured to Franny with a twitch of her head. Gal elbowed her mercilessly, eyebrows waggling. Franny stood and tried to smile, but her guts were heaving. Lottie probably, definitely hated it. Franny had insulted the audience, and Lottie knew the rest of the jokes weren't hers. And yet, Franny was determined not to be thrown out. She would fight, she would beg, she would do whatever it took. They weaved between the housewives, who had gone back to ignoring Franny. Lottie slapped the bar, and Enid tossed up two martinis. Lottie clinked her glass against Franny's and took a sip.

"Come back tomorrow," she said. "I've got some notes." And then, just as swiftly, she turned away. Like peekaboo with a baby; if Lottie wasn't looking, Franny didn't exist.

Franny tried to think of something to say, something that might prove her continued existence, but instead, she grinned like a clown, floating all the way up to the sky, higher than the Wrigley Building, higher than humidity in August.

❧

The front door to 504 squeaked no matter how carefully you opened it. Franny paused, and when no voices emerged from the darkness, she floated up the stairs, two at a time.

Leon switched on a flashlight from the top of the stairs, and Franny yelped, heart pounding.

"Leon?" she whispered, shading her eyes.

"Who was driving that car?"

"Why are you awake?"

"I'll ask the questions," Leon said, waving the flashlight nauseatingly. "Mama's been worried sick. No one knew where you were or when you'd be back, and I agreed to call the police if you weren't home by midnight."

The dash clock in Lottie's chauffeured car had said eleven-thirty. Franny should have been worried, but even this couldn't puncture her spirits. "Looks like I foiled your plan, Truant Officer Steinberg."

He didn't say anything. His eyes were glazed over, and when Franny looked closely, his head was swaying slightly on his neck.

"Are you okay?" she asked.

"I said I'll ask the questions," he said.

"Well, if it isn't Sam Spade, Private Detective. 'You're a good man, sister,'" she quoted. Leon cracked just the tiniest smile. "Come on, Leon, let's go to sleep, huh? I don't want to wake Mama and Papa." She leaned in close and gently slid the flashlight from his grip, turning it off, but not before she caught a sour, boozy whiff on his breath. "Whoa," she said, waving her hand in front of her face. "Did I miss the party?"

He popped up from the step. "You win," he said. "But next time I'm not covering for you." He disappeared into his bedroom and shut the door.

Franny sank onto the top step and weighed her head in her hands. The warmth Leon left on the step was the only evidence that he was still her flesh-and-blood brother.

Franny was restless, couldn't possibly go to sleep, so she flipped through her diary, whispering the lines to herself. The laughter had felt like a force of nature, one that she, Franny Steinberg, had caused. No less real than a blast of wind—invisible but also physical. But it was more than that—the laughter was a cartoon anvil lifted off her chest. An iron girdle she hadn't noticed until now. And now, the pressure was unbearable, squeezing the air out of her lungs, the blood out of her heart.

She shouldn't risk going back to the Blue Moon, though. Not tomorrow, maybe not ever. Not with Leon so suspicious, threatening to call the police. Not with Mama so worried. Franny's heart felt sick.

She would, though, obviously. She would risk it again and again.

Families are so strange, Franny thought. *As in, live together long enough and you become strangers.*

She pulled the pen out of her handbag and turned to a fresh page of the diary. She could do this. She promised.

Franny drew a big, shaky circle. She would have a set written before she even got tired. If she could pull a joke out of thin air that made the book clubs laugh, she could write her own set.

Franny wrote *family* in the middle of the circle and drew a line spoking out of the side then tried to think of a story to use. Such as that time Leon jumped out from behind the bushes at Greenfield Park like a charging rhino and socked the boy who wouldn't let her join their baseball team. "My kid sister is a great pitcher," he'd hollered as the kid clutched his bloody nose. "You just try to hit her curveball."

Franny scratched the words out. That story was off-limits. She poised her pencil. Oh, how about the time Leon tried to teach ol' two-left-feet Mary Kate to jitterbug so she could go to her first Gym Jam at school, but she clomped on his foot so many times, three of his toenails turned black and blue, and no one knew until they all fell off a few days later because he never stopped smiling?

Franny's eyes filled up, and her nose tickled threateningly. She closed the diary. Not Leon. There were plenty of other stories to use. Tomorrow, maybe. Once she had a little sleep. She was just worn out, that's all. Franny filled the bathroom sink and dunked her face in ice-cold water so her eyes wouldn't look puffy in the morning.

CHAPTER NINE

MICHAEL BERMAN HAD A BIG BROWN MOLE IN THE MIDDLE of his cheek but behaved like someone who didn't. Franny didn't realize how intently she had been staring at it until he got up to use the restroom and she couldn't recall what the rest of his face looked like. He had sawed through half his steak—charred and brown all the way through, the way Papa liked his (according to Mama, he once ordered steak tartare well-done)—while Franny had already finished hers, plus the baked potato and dinner rolls, folded and refolded her napkin on the lap of her new pink dress that supposedly put some color in her cheeks. He hadn't stopped talking long enough to eat and looked at her empty plate with some trepidation.

"I like a girl with an appetite," he said, but he didn't mean it.

Michael Berman played doubles tennis and had, while at Yale, placed third in the state. Not as impressive as first, but Connecticut was a small state packed with men in tennis shorts, so it wasn't nothing. At Harvard, he was studying to be a heart surgeon, which was the future of medicine. This future meant artificial hearts, pig hearts, open hearts diced and filleted on a table with a man's ribs cracked wide open. The heart was a machine, nothing more romantic than that. It was a clock, a bomb; all it did was keep the time, none of this nonsense about feelings—those lived in the brain—so the heart could be fixed with a steady hand and the right tools. Michael was going to save lives, but he couldn't take all the credit, as he would be standing on the shoulders of giants.

That was a Sir Isaac Newton quote, by the way, whom he assumed Franny had only heard of because an apple fell on his head.

Speaking of giants, why didn't anyone yet realize how *completely* Hemingway had revolutionized twentieth-century American literature, and did Franny know he was born in Oak Park?

Now that Franny was trying to write her own jokes, what if these embarrassing situations could be something to dissect, like Michael Berman's hearts? Mole marks the spot... Apple doesn't fall far from the tree? *First dates are terrible...*

"Got a pen?" Franny asked. Michael gave her an odd look and kept talking.

It wasn't fair to hate him. Neither of them wanted to be there, but at least Michael ("Mike, if you don't mind. May I call you *Frances*? It's much more elegant, don't you think?") was working doggedly to have a good time. Franny didn't even want to *want* to have a good time. She couldn't stop checking her unreadably dainty wristwatch, hoping this whole thing would wrap up in time for her to make the tail end of Amateur Hour. If she got up for five shows in a row, Lottie had promised to buy her the famous flaming crab at the Pump Room. Tonight would be her fifth.

Lottie had hitched her wagon to Franny so fast, it felt more ominous than flattering. And Andy, whom Franny had thought was warming up to her, had gotten considerably less friendly when Lottie took her off the lineup of next Saturday's show and replaced her with Peggy Blake.

"I'm sure my fans won't mind," Andy had said, "once they feel *your* Showstopper… What was it again? Sitting in a room where nothing happens? How avant-garde."

Saturday's show would be a real show, not an Amateur Hour. The end-of-the-month show. Franny didn't have a whiff of a Showstopper, and boy, had Lottie been sniffing for it. And other than blurting out a punchline to that heckler, she hadn't told a single one of her own jokes, which Lottie didn't know. Yet.

"They're not ready," Franny had said at Amateur Hour two days ago. Andy had sunk into the booth, looking like she had completely given up on Franny. Gal had fidgeted with anything within reach. Helen had been out, supposedly sick. "The bourbonic plague," Andy had called it, cracking a swizzle stick into her ice.

"Practice makes perfect," Gal said, ripping a cocktail napkin to shreds. Again.

"What if we tell Lottie?" Andy said. "We can massage the story so she won't be mad. This isn't about me, Gal, don't give me that look. It's about all of us. Even you, Peggy. If Lottie finds out on her own…" Andy threw down the swizzle stick. "Why'd she take me off the lineup, anyway? I always close the end-of-the-month show."

"I've written a few jokes," Franny said. "But they're rotten apples compared to what you wrote for me. If I go up there and do my own set now, she'll figure it all out for sure." It wasn't a complete lie.

Franny's diary was filled with stories and half-baked punch lines, it was just that she had crossed them all out and then crumpled up the pages and thrown them in the trash bin. It was just that every time she tried to write, she ended up blubbery as Moby Dick. The only joke she'd managed to squeeze out was when Mama taught her about the birds and the bees with mayonnaise (*Here's the egg, here's the, ah, oil, that's the man, and when you mix them, nu, it's mayonnaise!*), but that reminded her of Peter, which was not going to happen. Her memory was full of land mines; her heart was one of Michael Berman's ticking time bombs. Franny had to tread carefully. Didn't they understand that?

"Can I see?" Gal said, reaching for Franny's handbag. "Maybe we can help."

Franny yanked the bag out of her hands so fiercely, she bent Gal's pinky fingernail and made her yelp. Franny apologized, of course, but Gal fell into a funk anyway.

Even worse, when Andy thought Franny wasn't listening, she pulled Lottie aside. "She's not ready," Andy said. "She still freezes at the mic; she doesn't have a Showstopper. You really think she can hack it for a Saturday crowd? She'll bring the whole show down."

"Jealousy isn't a good look on you," Lottie said.

"What if there's TV producers in town? You think they'd come here to see a rotten show? She's only been doing this for a few weeks. I've been—"

"You've been? You've been writing terrible jokes is what. I don't know what's gotten into you," Lottie snapped. "'How about *thanks* for *giving* us syphilis'?"

"Smallpox," Andy muttered.

"What kind of a joke is that? You want them to laugh or feel guilty?"

Andy's face fell, and Franny felt positively ill. She hadn't shared this new material, but if a joke was funny and personal and punched up instead of down, as Andy sometimes said, what did it matter what it was about? Franny wished she could pipe up in Andy's defense, but that would require admitting she was eavesdropping.

Andy toed a patch of old gum. "And here I thought the point was to dig deep. Which Peggy is *not* doing, by the way."

"Eyes on your own paper. And dig shallower next time," Lottie said. "Then we can talk about lineups."

Franny pretended to look for something in her purse as Andy buzzed past, wiping her eyes. She should say something. But what? Andy didn't believe in her, didn't trust her, and didn't think she belonged onstage in the first place. Franny felt protective of, sorry for, and angry at Andy all at the same time. What a mess.

Helen Angel's Showstopper materialized after fifteen shows, but she herself admitted that she had been holding it back, deliberately, out of fear. Fear of what? Helen didn't fear anything.

Case in point, Helen had finally showed up again at Amateur Hour just yesterday, hair chopped clean off, all of it—presumably with a push mower or else with the aid of Picasso the barber. But it looked good on her, and she knew it. Or maybe she knew it, and *that's* why it looked good. She'd worn a sport coat and smelled like cologne and pomade and ordered drinks for everyone, paying with a wad of cash instead of putting it on a tab, all the while admiring her silhouette in the dirty mirror behind the bar. For herself, she'd ordered a soda water, loudly, so Lottie could hear.

Wasn't the whole idea that the Showstopper released something ugly that had been bottled up inside? What if Franny released the wrong thing? God, what if she released the *right* thing? What if Andy was right and Lottie was wrong, and Franny stood onstage next Saturday and sweated through her girdle in silence, breathing lewdly into the microphone?

◦◦◦

Franny looked at her watch again. Either Michael Berman had escaped out the window of the men's bathroom, or he was doing things in there she didn't want to think about. She just had to get to the Blue Moon in time. She mouthed her set to herself at the table, gesturing under the table.

Michael sat down and pushed away his half-eaten steak, and Franny clamped her mouth shut. "Couldn't eat another bite," he said. He tapped out a cigarette and offered one to Franny.

"No thanks," she said.

"Suit yourself," he said, lighting up. "What do you say we catch *Bedtime for Bonzo* tonight? I've heard it's a real gas."

"The monkey movie?"

"Actually," Michael said, blowing out smoke, "chimpanzees are apes, like humans. Monkeys are a totally different species of primate."

"What happened to the early Baroque masters?" she said.

"Oh, that," he said. "I tell that to all the mothers."

"Maybe you should take my mother on a date," Franny said.

"Fine, if you want Bach, we can go listen to Bach."

"I don't want to listen to Bach," Franny said. "I just don't appreciate being tricked."

"You make it really hard to have a good time," Michael said. "You know that?"

"I don't know," Franny said. "You seem to find yourself pretty interesting."

"Excuse me for trying to have a nice conversation with a wet mop. I took you out as a favor, you know."

"I see your mole got all the personality," Franny said. "The rest of you could use some work."

He threw his napkin dramatically onto his half-eaten steak. "I liked you better when you were stuffing your face, and that's not saying very much."

Franny eyeballed her clean plate like it, and not Franny's unladylike appetite, was responsible for its own emptiness. The white tablecloth was dribbled with dots of mushroom sauce from when she'd missed her mouth. A grease spot marked the straining bodice of her new pink dress. She'd dabbed at it with water and made it worse. Well, what was she supposed to do, order food and stare at it?

Michael sighed. "I'll drive you home if that's what you want."

"No thanks," Franny said. "I have other plans."

❧

Helen cheered when Franny opened the door to the Blue Moon, and it felt pretty damn good, even if Gal just smiled politely and Andy stood by the bar, stewing in her own sour puss.

"Just under the wire," Helen said, straightening her tie. "You girls have to call me *Hal* from now on."

"That was your wager?" Franny cried. Her absence was worthy of discussion, of being the subject of a bet! Franny bounced into the booth. "What about money? We could have made out like bandits."

"First of all, this is my bet, and I set the terms," Helen said. "Secondly, horses don't get a cut at the racetrack, so why should I give you anything?"

"Who you calling a horse, tough guy?"

Helen grinned. She liked that kind of talk. Maybe *Hal* was a better fit after all. Franny warmed up to the idea.

Andy tapped on the table with red fingernails. She wore a pair of high-waisted trousers and a white blouse, and her long hair was tucked up in victory rolls.

"You don't have to doll yourself up just to impress me," Hal said.

"If I wanted to impress you, you'd know it, *Hal*," Andy said.

"Like music to my ears."

"You're in my seat," Andy said to Franny.

"Why don't you sit on my lap?" Hal said.

"Do I get a present?"

"Have you been a good girl?"

"Cool it, you two," Franny said. "Or my steak's coming up the way it went down."

"Steak!" Hal said. "I hope you put out."

Franny pretended to lose her lunch, and Hal laughed.

The crowd for Amateur Hour was just Lottie and Enid and any rats and cockroaches who could sneak a good seat. Lottie couldn't afford to truck the book clubs in again, and who wanted to pay for their own Mai Tais? Not one of them had returned. Lottie's anxiety could be measured in martini olives, which were currently plentiful. She said nothing, but her mood dripped everywhere like melted wax.

Since the crowd was so sparse, Franny shared a nice experiment that might make everyone happy—what if she just *tweaked* the jokes in her set? That would show the girls she meant well, without exposing herself too much.

"Don't touch those jokes," Lottie called. "Not until after Saturday."

"Gee, I'd love to hear Peggy's new material," Andy said. "Wouldn't you, girls?"

"Yeah, what's the harm?" Gal said.

"She wants my job so bad—what does Helen Angel say?" Lottie asked to much groaning.

"Hal," said Hal.

Lottie poked Hal's soda water and smirked. "Lake Michigan don't dry up in a day, sister."

"Hal agrees with me," Andy said.

"Out with it, then," Lottie said. Instead of answering, Hal peered curiously at Lottie, like she was looking for something hidden or like she had just found it and was trying to decide what it was worth.

"Last I checked, you need to get onstage to get a cut of the door," Lottie said, rubbing imaginary money between finger and thumb, or maybe a tiny violin. "And you need money to buy this place."

"Maybe I have a secret job you don't know about," Hal said.

Lottie snorted. "Good luck finding a job in that getup," she said, but Hal just smiled sweetly, which irritated Lottie more. "Has it occurred to any of you that sometimes, god forbid, weather permitting, I know what I'm doing?"

Franny squinted into the darkness, trying to figure out what to do next.

"Stick to the script," Lottie said, pointing at her.

Franny telegraphed *see, I tried!* in fluent shoulder shrug.

"Childhood isn't all it's cracked up to be. Eleven years old, I wake up in bed—blood *everywhere*. 'I'm dying!' I call out. 'Help!'"

"You sound like you're sick to death of your own jokes," Lottie interrupted. "Comedy's not about jumping ship for every shiny new thing that crosses your path."

Hal stood and cupped her hands around her mouth. "Are we talking about Peggy's comedy or your love life?"

The girls laughed, and that's when they noticed a single audience member who sat in a shadowed booth all the way in the back. No one had seen her come in, but her hyena laugh was unmissable.

She climbed up on the booth then took a precarious step onto the wobbly table. Hal sprang into action and grabbed the woman's arm just before the whole thing toppled. She wrapped an arm around the woman's waist and lowered her back into the booth, talking to her in a low voice. Franny strained to hear what she was saying.

"Goddammit, Barb," Hal said. "Why didn't you say something? I woulda kept my big mouth shut."

"Oopsie daisy," Lottie said, eyes widening in mock concern. "Poor Hal can't control her Showstopper, even when she's sober."

"That's not true," Andy said. "If she had known, she would have prepared for it. Like we talked about, right, Hal?"

"Lottie doesn't care," Hal said.

"Lottie cares," Lottie said, "about the Blue Moon."

Franny watched Hal slink back into the booth, feeling a strange little flutter in her belly. What was it? Envy at how easily Hal conjured her Showstopper? Must have been envy.

Lottie had been watching her this whole time, a little curl at the corner of her lips. Franny blushed because, boy, were the stage lights hot. "Barb, let's close up for the night," Lottie said. "I'd hate for someone to get hurt. Again."

"Should I finish?" Franny asked.

"What do you say, *Hal*?" Lottie laughed. "Should one of us help her finish?" Franny didn't understand the question, but it made her feel squirmy. "That's part of the job too, you know. Can't be hung up on just one of your girls. Gotta love them all equally."

Bedtime for Bonzo was sounding pretty good right about now, even with Michael Berman's inevitable arm slung over her shoulder, fingers creeping down her chest. Franny's belly curdled.

Hal didn't answer, just chugged her soda water and glared at the empty glass like she might find the future in it.

❦

Franny helped Gal unplug the microphone and turn off the stage lights. Gal wore a black satin cocktail dress that Mary Kate would have died for. She removed her pristine white gloves to wrap up the microphone cords without smudging them. Franny tried not to look at Gal's one ripped pinky nail. "I thought I might try to convince Andy and Helen—Hal—to go dancing at the Aragon," Gal said. "Want to come with?"

Franny felt a pang of jealousy. "I wish," she said. "If I get home too late, my family thinks I've joined a Catholic circus harem. Or worse."

Gal paused in wrapping up the cords and sighed. "My mother used to check my neck for hickeys any time I came home past ten," she said. "You haven't told your family."

"About hickeys?"

Gal opened her eyes wide. "About this! Stand-up, the Blue Moon, Lottie Marcone, all of it."

"Are you nuts? My mother thinks I'm on a date with a Harvard medical student right now."

"Michael Berman?" Gal said, grinning. "Did he remember to tell you Hemingway is the most underappreciated of all twentieth-century masters?"

"It's possible," Franny said. "I couldn't stop staring at his mole."

"The mole got all the personality," Gal said. Then her face got serious. "If you can go out with him again, do it."

Franny laughed.

"I'm serious." Gal touched Franny's arm. "You don't want your family finding out about all this. Believe me. I can barely afford my hotel room. The whole building shakes when the L passes, my bed frame squeaks, and the only roommate I have is the occasional roach."

"You don't—live at home?" Franny took in her stylish clothes, her perfectly set hair.

"It's tempting," Gal said. "You think *I'm pretty good at this*. You think *maybe they'll be proud of me*. Don't do it, Peggy. They think stand-up is worse than being knocked up. Go out with the Michael Bermans, pretend they're funnier and smarter and more interesting than you, and don't ever let anyone figure out where you go after the date ends. Even if it means everyone thinks you're easy. In fact, that's the ideal situation. He'll never correct the rumor, and it's better than the alternative. You can still live this life, as long as you also live a lie." She stared at nothing, cords dangling from her wrists. "You won't tell the other girls, will you? You'll keep this between us?"

❦

Franny kicked pebbles onto Lawrence Avenue, hoping if she waited around long enough, Lottie would ask Carl to give her a ride home. If she took the bus, she would get home so late, Leon might actually call the police. If Gal's family gave her the heave-ho, would Franny's family do the same? Gal must have been exaggerating. It couldn't be that bad.

"Waiting for your prince to whisk you away?" Lottie asked, locking up the Blue Moon behind her. "What was his name again—Bore-man?"

If Franny went home now, Mama would be expecting a full report of the date. She would be expected to go on another one. If not with Michael Bore—Berman—then with someone else. Franny could either lie to her family or lie to herself. What a choice. On the other hand, Gal didn't have to lie to anyone anymore. Sure, there was no one to lie to, but still.

"Or is your prince named…Helen, excuse me, Hal?" Lottie stood so close, Franny could see the pulse in her neck.

Lottie slid into the back seat of her car, leaving Franny on the curb. Alone. In Uptown. At night. Without Carl driving her, it could take an hour to get home.

Franny realized she didn't want to go home at all, no matter what the consequences. But where else was there to go?

Lottie poked her head out the window. "Are you coming or not?"

❧

The Palmer House concierge called Lottie *Mrs. Marcone* and gave her a suite overlooking the lake. It seemed impossible that the Empire Room would be in this hotel, just sitting there at the far end of the lobby, the same Empire Room where Franny had seen Boopsie Baxter and everything had changed. Franny imagined that if she walked into the Empire Room right now, she would see her younger self, grimacing at the taste of the hot toddy, ragged peacoat tossed over the back of her chair, oblivious to everything that was about to happen. She hated that girl. She also desperately wanted to be that girl again, frozen in time. Instead, she followed Lottie obediently into the elevator.

Lottie watched Franny as the elevator *ding*ed at each floor, a look on her face that Franny couldn't quite place, but it made her heart and belly flop around like slimy pink puppies. She pushed Franny gently out of the elevator, forcing her to walk backward, then Lottie leaned across her to unlock the door before closing it gently behind them.

Lottie's eyes raked every part of Franny's body, slowly, like she was thinking about buying it or devouring it. Michael Berman had looked at her that way when she opened the door to 504, but it had made her want to slam the door in his face, and now she felt— something else. Lottie stood so close, Franny could smell her musky vanilla perfume. In heels, Lottie was nearly as tall as Franny was in her ballet flats. She pressed a cool hand to Franny's hot bare arm, traced her finger down it, leaving a trail of goose bumps.

"You're tickling me," Franny said to break the silence. She felt warm in some places.

"That's the idea," Lottie said. "If you're willing."

Lottie held her by her hips (*those peasant, childbearing hips*— Franny banished Mrs. Finnegan from her mind) and pressed her soft lips to Franny's. A zing zipped up Franny's middle. The tip of Lottie's tongue darted between Franny's lips, and Franny's darted out to meet it. She couldn't breathe. She started to panic then realized she wasn't actually scared. Who needed to breathe when you had fishy gills, when you were a plant that only needed the sun?

She touched Lottie's face, which was soft, Lottie's hair, which parted between her fingers. Lottie's hand slid lower, cupping Franny's bottom, and Franny thought of Hal's arm around the audience member's waist, and suddenly her own hands were peeling back Lottie's emerald dress, revealing a brassiere (black!) with no girdle and her garter and stockings, and then Lottie pulled away, gently unzipping Franny's new pink dress with the grease stain that Mama had bought for her date with Michael Berman.

"Wait," Franny panted, but in one smooth motion her old girdle was revealed, her panties and lack of garter, and next to Lottie, she looked like someone's grandmother, someone's naked grandmother being undressed by a notorious mobster's *wife* in a lakefront suite at the Palmer House Hilton with the curtains wide open. This was the most naked Franny had been in front of anyone; Peter had kept her dress on. As soon as Franny thought of Peter, her body was crushed under that hated anvil.

"Don't think about him," Lottie murmured into her neck. "Whoever he is, he's dead to you."

"How—"

"Life is terrible, nothing to be done about it. But we're alive." She paused her caresses, cool fingers hovering over Franny's back. She waited to see what Franny would do next, and Franny felt like the ticking clock that could stop or start the march of time. Lottie, the heart surgeon; Franny, the half-eaten steak.

She pulled Lottie close and tossed them both playfully onto the bed.

"I thought so." Lottie smirked, unhooking Franny's girdle and relieving her of it. She traced her fingers down the indentations the girdle left on Franny's ribs. "All this pain, and for what?"

"What girl doesn't want to look like a dowdy grandmother with her clothes off?"

"You're not onstage." Lottie put a finger on Franny's lips. "Show's over." Franny, not even thinking, wrapped her mouth around the finger. Lottie raised her eyebrows. "Look who decided to join the party." With her free hand, she traced Franny's belly, around the curve of her hip, across her thigh, and then, lightly at first, began to trace a circle in a spot just between Franny's legs, and the zing of recognition almost made Franny leap right off the bed.

"Boopsie's Showstopper," she gasped.

"No shoptalk either," Lottie said, pressing harder, faster...then stopped entirely. "Tell me your name."

Without Lottie's touch, the world zoomed back into harsh focus. Franny's mind zoomed back into her doughy body. "My name?"

"Say it," Lottie said.

Franny immediately started to feel weird again, lying naked on a bed, being touched by a girl. "Actually, you know, I should probably—"

The electric warmth returned. "Say it. Say the name I gave you."

Franny's mind went blank. She had no mind at all. "P-peggy?"

"Your full name."

"Peggy Blake?" Franny squeaked. "I'm Peggy Blake."

Hotter and hotter, the spot burned and throbbed; it spread outward and upward and downward until there was only the feeling and no Franny at all.

"Who are you?" Lottie licked her lips, pressed her body to Franny's. "Who are you?"

Franny wanted to shout, *I don't know anymore,* but her body vibrated, tensed, clanked like a radiator on the first day of winter. Franny couldn't take it anymore and tried to tell Lottie to stop, but she didn't really mean it, and she couldn't get the words out anyway, and then—the release, the grand finale, the Showstopper.

⌒⌢⌒

The sun smeared up oily behind the lake. Franny's whole body ached. She hadn't slept, hadn't moved, had barely shut her eyes. She wasn't the sort of girl who did this sort of thing. *What sort of thing, Franny?* Oh, just some probably deviant, definitely illegal hanky-panky with another girl in the bed of a fancy hotel. She might throw up. Was she going to throw up? Franny rubbed her face with her hands. She had to get out of here. Was the L train running yet? Was that a slow clanking off in the distance?

Franny scooched her legs closer to the bed, but then there was an arm around her middle with a cigarette at the end of it.

"Good morning, sweet thing," Lottie murmured. "Sleep well?"

Franny froze. "Yes, thank you," she said. "Like a brock. Like a raby... It was a very adequate slumber." She shot up off the bed and searched, head down, for all the strewn pieces of her clothes. Lottie propped herself up on one arm, watched her with those narrow honey eyes.

"I'm ordering scrambled eggs. You want some?" she asked, pulling the phone off the bedside table. "Pancakes? Coffee? Anything. My dime." The pinkish morning light made Lottie's skin glow—*all* of it, and boy, there sure was a *lot* of skin glowing at the moment. Franny looked away. Last night was in the past, and it would stay there.

"Oh, thank you, I couldn't eat a bite," she said, clutching the girdle over her growling stomach. "But thank you."

"You said that already."

"I meant it."

"Well, fine then, you're welcome."

"Thank you."

They stared at each other, Franny pasting girdles and stockings over her private areas and Lottie stretched out on top of the comforter like some bohemian artist's model. Franny cleared her throat to speak.

"This can stay between us," Lottie said. "I can keep a secret, if that's what you're worried about."

Franny hadn't even thought to be worried about *that*. But now that it was out there, she didn't find the reassurance particularly reassuring. "Thanks," she said.

"Stop thanking me already," Lottie said. "Can we be a couple of girls, having a good time? Just for a second?"

Franny felt queasy with all her clothes off. Would Lottie be tender or prickly? Sweet or sour? If she could just put some clothes on, this would be a lot easier. She sank onto the bed and tried to pretend she was just hanging out with Mary Kate, with clothes on. Just a regular couple of girls who hadn't done anything weird.

"Okay," she said. "What are you, uh, going to do today?"

Lottie groaned. "Just forget it. This was a dumb idea," she said, picking up the snakeskin of her nylons from the floor. "Let's chalk it up to too many martinis and move on."

Lottie's vertebrae poked out as she hunched over her nylons. How could she loom so large when she was so small? Her vulnerability made Franny afraid, suddenly. "What am I going to tell my parents?" she said.

"We are *definitely* not there yet."

Franny blushed. The very idea.

"I mean…about where I was all night."

"Tell them you fell asleep in the park, necking with Michael Boreman."

Franny laughed, but Lottie didn't. Was she serious? "Mama would faint," Franny said. "Papa would faint. Everyone would be unconscious."

"They'll be so worried about the necking, they won't wonder about whether the story makes any sense," Lottie said. "You got a family that loves you. They want to believe you. And even better— they want to forgive you. Necking, they can forgive. The truth, not so much."

Franny thought of Gal again, wondered if Lottie had had this exact conversation before.

"You don't know my brother," she said. "Even when I don't do anything, he's angry."

Lottie slipped into her dress then presented her back for Franny to zip. She hoped Lottie couldn't feel her hands tremble.

"Where was he captured?" Lottie said.

"Battle of the Bulge," Franny said, startled. "How did you guess?"

"What happened?"

Franny thought about getting into it. Lottie was better than nobody. She shook her head. "He doesn't talk about it."

"You've asked, though," Lottie said. Franny didn't answer, and Lottie raised her eyebrows. "You have asked him about it, haven't you?"

Enough was enough. "I really have to go," Franny said, humping into her girdle as fast as her skin would allow, followed by the dress and nylons. She made a vaudevillian production of looking for her shoes. The quicker she was dressed, the quicker she could forget she had ever been undressed.

"One day, I came home from school," Lottie said, "all the furniture—gone. My parents, brothers, and sisters—*poof*, disappeared. Closets empty, pantry bare. They didn't tell me where they were going. And I never saw them again."

Franny paused, one shoe on, one hand jazzing. "That's terrible. How old were you?" she said. "What did you do?"

Lottie smirked, tapped cigarette ash into the ashtray. "Oh, I'm fine, just peachy—look how great I turned out."

She leaned across the bed and clamped Franny's arm.

"You're not the first girl I've kicked out of the Blue Moon. And you're definitely not the first girl who tried to muscle her way back in. But when I saw you up on that stage—I thought about clocking you, I really did. I even thought about summoning Ed—"

A lump the size of Lottie's diamond ring lodged in Franny's throat.

"But you surprised me. Talent *and* nerve is a rare mix, and a set like that your first time up—" Lottie whistled low, "I'm not blowing smoke up your ass."

"That's good. I spend enough time in the bathroom as it is," Franny said. Boy, Lottie really had a grip on her arm.

"Franny," Lottie said. "I need you to be serious right now." The sound of her real name raised embarrassing goose bumps on Franny's arms. Lottie pulled Franny down so they were both sitting on the bed. "Your head is a mess. Who are you? What do you want? You can't answer, can you? But I can."

"I know who—"

"I know you're scared of me. I get it. But now that you've seen what a sweetheart I am, you don't have to be afraid," Lottie said. "You can let 'er rip. Let that Showstopper sing."

Was this some sort of pop quiz? Had Franny passed? Did she want to?

"I thought you said no shoptalk," Franny said finally. "I thought we were having fun."

"It's all shoptalk, baby," Lottie said, releasing Franny's arm to light another cigarette. "Even when it's not."

⁓☙⁓

A squad car sat outside of 504, along with the nondescript Pontiac of the neighborhood's undercover police officer, whom everyone called Undercover Rod. The whole neighborhood recognized the car, undermining the whole undercover thing. Franny cursed herself for staying out all night. Somehow, she had walked out of the Palmer House more confused than when she had walked in, and that was saying something. Of course, her family would worry. Of course, they would call the police. In fact, Leon had basically promised to do it. Franny hardly recognized herself. She was an egg with scrambled insides and the shell intact. Franny wished she could go back in time and do the whole night over again. *A movie about a chimpanzee? Why, that sounds like a hoot, Michael Berman.*

Inside, Mama and Papa clutched each other's hands on the sofa while a uniformed policeman stood by, scribbling on a notepad. Undercover Rod had pulled over a kitchen chair and talked softly to them.

They looked up as she walked in. "Franny, you're back," Mama said. She swept Franny up in her arms, and Franny knew it would all come out; she was a flooded dam about to burst.

"Mama, I'm sorry—"

"Is Leon with you?" Mama asked.

"Does it look like Leon's with her?" Papa said, out of breath. His face glistened with sweat as he sat back on the sofa, propped by pillows. Alka-Seltzer fizzed in a glass of water on the coffee table. Mama had the telltale Steinberg dark smudges under her eyes, as though she hadn't slept at all.

The flood receded, replaced by a slurry of relief and shame. Had they not even noticed she was out all night?

"No one has seen him since you left with Michael Berman," Mama said.

Suddenly, Franny was standing in the entryway again on Christmas Eve, eyeballing a telegram with icy wrists. She shivered. It almost seemed like every time she went to a nightclub, Leon ended up missing.

Papa's Alka-Seltzer looked awfully enticing right now. Franny had never mentioned her stomachaches, but now didn't seem like the best time to start.

"He usually has to be dragged out of the house," Papa said. "How were we supposed to know he wouldn't come home?"

"We looked everywhere," Mama interrupted. "Finally, we called the police. Nu, your papa and I haven't slept a wink."

"If it's all right with everyone," Undercover Rod said, "I'll do the detective work. Where did you just come from, Frances?"

Franny lowered herself into the armchair, hands folded in her lap, trying to think of a good answer. The moment of truth had come. Maybe, just maybe, she could lie to her parents, but she was *not* prepared to lie to the police too. What if everyone packed up and left her in a bare house just like Lottie? What if they stayed and she had to find a hotel with a dirty mattress and cockroaches for roommates, trains clanging by at all hours of the night?

"I woke up early and went for a walk?" she said, not intending it to sound like a question.

"A walk?" Mama said. "Where?"

"Just around."

Undercover Rod looked at the policeman, who scribbled something in his notepad.

"What are you writing?" Mama asked.

"Have you spoken to Finnegans yet?" Papa said, gesturing to the door. "My family has been nothing but nice to the Averys."

"The Averys?" Franny said. "I thought we were talking about Leon."

"According to the Averys," Rod said, flipping the pages of the policeman's notepad, "you've never introduced yourselves."

"Can someone please explain to me what's going on?" Franny asked.

"Someone is threatening Dr. Avery over the telephone," Mama said. "Threatening bombs! In this nice goyische neighborhood."

"Anyone with a copy of the Yellow Pages can make a phony phone call," Rod said, patting Mama's shoulder.

Two years ago, the Steinbergs had been at a cousin's house for

Thanksgiving when someone threw a firebomb in the Averys' yard, right before they were supposed to move in.

"But it happened to them before," Franny said. "Couldn't it happen again?"

"You know how many of these calls we get per week?" Rod said. "Don't worry, Frances. It's summer break, probably just some kids blowing off steam."

This sat a bit funny with Franny, but she supposed Undercover Rod would know best.

"I didn't even sign the petition," Papa said. "Jews have suffered too much to have anything against coloreds."

"Mr. Steinberg, this isn't an interrogation. No one's accusing anyone of anything," Undercover Rod sighed, rubbing the bridge of his nose. "May I continue?"

Papa mimed locking his mouth and tossing away the key.

Rod turned to Franny. "So," he said. "No one heard you come home last night—"

"I didn't say that," Mama said.

"—but you got up early and went for…a walk?"

The seconds ticked by, and Franny was stuck. She had to say something. "Michael and I were necking in the park," she blurted, "and then we fell asleep. It was innocent, I swear. He was a perfect gentleman, but we knew everyone would think the worst. I walked home from the park so no one would recognize his car. Please don't tell anyone. I'm so embarrassed. I've never done anything like this before."

Franny's face heated up like Vesuvius and gave her away. They were going call her bluff, it was so obvious, she was caught red-faced. But Undercover Rod coughed, and Papa joined in throaty harmony.

"It's okay for a boy to stay out all night, but if anyone found out…" Mama said, eyes closed to savor the horror. "Officer, can't we keep this story to ourselves?"

Lottie was right. And even worse, Franny was relieved.

"Let this be a lesson, young lady," Rod said. "Your reputation is your most precious possession."

A loud knock at the door made Franny jump, and Mama shot up. Another police officer had Leon draped over his shoulder, dirt smudging his face, leaves in his hair, barely conscious.

The officer deposited him on the armchair across from the sofa. "The colored family said they heard a loud noise in the alley behind their house last night. They took the garbage out just now, found this one hiding in the trash bin. Dispatch didn't believe the story, sounded like a lot of hysterics, but I was in the area," the officer shrugged. "Said I'd check it out, get them to stop calling. But son of a gun, there he was."

Undercover Rod squatted in front of Leon, who stank to high heaven of garbage and whiskey, even from where Franny sat. Rod looked like he was trying very hard not to laugh. "Leon, can you tell me why you were hiding in the Averys' garbage bin?"

Leon didn't respond.

"It's not illegal," Rod said. "If it was, we'd have to arrest all the bums in town." The other officers chuckled, but Rod gave them a look.

"Now, I do have to ask you," Rod said. "Did you make threatening phone calls to the Averys' house?"

"That's enough," Papa said. "My Leon would never—"

"You don't have to answer him," Mama said.

Undercover Rod held up a hand. "Leon, we know you. You're a good boy. Just answer the question."

Leon squinted at him. "I didn't make any calls. I was looking for Franny," he said.

All eyes back on Franny. "Me?" she squeaked. "I was on a date."

Leon shot her a look that left her blistered. He could always sniff out the truth, except, of course, when she was telling it.

"Leon has combat fatigue," Franny blurted, hating herself for it. "He gets scared in public, and if no one was there to calm him..." With no one to stop him from panicking, Leon probably hid in the safest place he could think of: the garbage.

Leon's jaw worked overtime. "You don't know a thing about me. You don't know what I'm capable of."

"I'm trying to help you," Franny said.

"Help yourself," Leon said. "And see how you like it."

"Well, whatever you were looking for," Rod said, "look for it in your own trash next time, okay?"

Leon glared at Rod, squatting and smiling at his feet, and then pushed him. Rod fell backward. Mama gasped. Time stuttered to a stop.

Finally, Rod stood, brushed off his pants. "You boys think you're the only ones who ever saw action, but you never learned respect," he said. "I could arrest you for this, you know."

He pulled Leon from the chair as Mama cried out. "Don't worry, Mrs. Steinberg, Leon and I just need to have a little chat outside, that's all."

Franny had never been angry at Leon before—sad about him, sure. Scared for him, absolutely. But now. She wanted to scream like an air raid siren, launch a fist in his direction. She had never felt so alone, and that was saying something.

Papa trailed after Undercover Rod, gesturing unconvincingly with his Alka-Seltzer.

Mama leaned in close, coffee breath basting Franny's ear. "You don't think Michael told his mother?"

"A time like this, you're thinking about Michael Berman?"

"To think," Mama said, "a doctor! From Harvard, no less. Such a weight lifted off my shoulders!"

"Mama," Franny said. "Can it wait?"

"Oh, I know, I know," Mama said. "But what a beautiful bride you'll be!"

⁓◉⁓

Franny sifted the flour while waiting for the yeast and sugar to proof. She oiled one bowl and mixed the eggs, water, and oil in another. Franny hated making challah for Shabbos dinner—why spend so much time on a lousy loaf of bread?—but challah had a recipe, with all the steps laid out in the right order. All you had to do was follow that recipe, and you would get something wonderful and delicious and perfect that wouldn't go wrong or send anyone to jail or make anyone angry.

She had made enough dough for two challahs—the extra one was for the Averys. Even though Leon might be the kind of person who hid in other people's garbage, the Steinbergs were not the threatening-phone-call sort. Undercover Rod knew that, but did the Averys? Did they know the bored kids were just letting off steam?

The Steinbergs were the sort who made incredibly time-consuming bread for their neighbors, no matter what color skin they had. In fact, the Steinbergs didn't see skin color, only neighbors. She might even say that; that was pretty good.

Help yourself, see how you like it. The words were a rabid dog she couldn't shake off her leg. They were making her rabid too. She was seething and foaming, ready to bite.

Franny punched the dough until her arms burned, and then she punched some more, but it was just bread, and she couldn't hurt it. She peeled the dough off her fingers, smoothed it into the oiled bowl, and shoved it in the warm oven to rise.

She drummed her fingers on the stove top, leaving sticky clues for anyone to find. All this time, she was too scared to write a single measly joke about Leon, but it would just serve him right. He didn't want to be helped? Fine. Lottie didn't think she knew anything about him? Or *herself*? Fat chance. She was a comedian who made people laugh. And if her best jokes happened to be about Leon, then so be it.

Franny needed a pencil. Where were the pencils? She threw open drawers and left floury fingerprints everywhere. It was barreling toward her, the joke, and she had to be ready. Next to the phone, of course! A pencil. Next to the stove—an old recipe card for chocolate soufflé that Mama had never made and now never would. Franny grabbed it and hovered over the kitchen table. He was such a spoiled little boy. Sitting in the basement playing with blocks. Wasn't war supposed to make you a man?

They say war makes you a man, but my brother went to war and came back a boy.

Franny's heart *boing*ed against her ribs, as though Leon would materialize out of the wallpaper and catch her in the act, like she could conjure him with jokes. Franny pushed the recipe card away, tapping her pencil on the tabletop, watching the card like the joke might defy her and write itself.

Maybe it wasn't Leon's feelings she was worried about. Maybe she was worried about ripping the stitches she had worked so hard to sew. Worried what might still be festering underneath.

Franny stretched across the table and scribbled a sentence without looking. The world refused to fall apart.

Maybe terrible stories could be funny if you looked at them right. As arguments to be won instead of memories to avoid. Like Boopsie and her mother, turning her pain into magic.

Franny yanked Leon out of her head, splayed the memories out on the table like a carp. Poked it, sniffed it, felt its slimy heft. It was just a fish, for crying out loud, not the end times.

Franny wrestled her fish, the guts and scales and the entrails. The sugar, the barbiturates, the Averys' garbage. The jokes came faster than she could scribble, and some were even funny. She sweated like a marathoner next to the low heat of the oven. *Give me your worst*, she thought. *I'll wrestle all the fish in the sea.*

Something felt weird about her face—she was smiling. She had written a set, a tight five, an act. The hard part was over. She had won.

And then, suddenly, obviously: Peter. *That* was what happened when you dug too deep. You hit Peter. You unleashed a geyser and drowned. She shoved the memory down. It bobbed up again. Franny flailed, gasping for breath. Her vision sparkled. She pressed her thumb to the pencil and snapped it.

"Leave me alone," she whispered. It did not.

If Leon was a carp, what was Peter? He slipped out of reach. Animal, vegetable, mineral? Monster?

What if Peter had blown off his willie in the war instead of his pinky? Would he have accepted a Purple Heart? A Purple Head?

Franny watched her hand scribble down words. The hand erased and re-scribbled these words she had never let herself think, much less speak. The hated memory that had only ever appeared to her as a movie might—set on film, unchangeable—became dough she could shape as she pleased.

Franny laid her chewed-up pencil down and backed away from the recipe card, now a skunk with its tail in the air, threatening malodorous vengeance. But who was the skunk—the words or Franny? It was a standoff with no good outcome.

She had written a joke about Peter.

When the dough had finally risen twice, Franny braided the two challahs, brushed them with egg yolk, plumped them once more, and then baked them until they looked like buffed wood, soft on the inside like a feather bed.

Follow the recipe and you get bread; you get a set you can't possibly perform in public.

But if she did perform it? What was the worst that could happen?

Franny laid the Averys' challah on a plate and covered it with a clean towel. It couldn't be so different, talking to a Negro family. She had talked plenty to Boopsie Baxter, after all.

Hello, Dr. Avery, my, what a lovely home you have. I'm your neighbor, Franny Steinberg, and I'm so sorry for the trouble my brother caused you. I hope you know he would never make those phone calls. The Steinbergs don't see skin color, you could be purple for all we care! Why, yes, I did come up with that on my own. I'd love to come inside and join you for some lemonade!

All it took was Leon getting in trouble for a whole new Franny to emerge—one who took charge and Made Things Happen. She put on a fresh day dress, smoothed her hair, and walked across the street, repeating the script to herself and trying hard not to feel like she was being watched from every window on the street. Next door, Mr. Finnegan had come outside and was standing on his porch pretending to assess the height of his bushes.

Each step Franny took felt like walking through wet cement. Was the Averys' house receding? It never seemed to get any closer. Franny's hands sweated around the plate.

A shadow passed behind a curtain before Franny had even breached the sidewalk, and she froze, a dumb grin on her face. Had the Averys' doorknob turned? Maybe she should wait for them to invite her in. The door didn't open. Franny smeared sweat from her eyes. What if they thought she was planning to take up residence in their trash, that this was the sort of thing the Steinbergs did? Franny was too far away and too close at the same time. Another curtain rustled. The house pulsed like a living thing.

Franny forgot everything she had practiced. She was trapped, halfway across the street. Everyone in the neighborhood was whispering. Curtains rustled all up and down North Euclid Avenue. Phantom doors squeaked. Whispers disapproved. Mr. Finnegan was no longer even *pretending* to examine his foliage.

Franny stood at the wrong end of a telescope, a hundred thousand miles from the Averys' doorstep. She tripped on the curb, and the challah slid across the plate in slow motion, flipped over, and landed upside down on the Averys' neatly manicured lawn. She stared at it. Mr. Finnegan stared at it. The whole neighborhood stared.

If she picked it up, the Averys would think she served grass-stained challah to her neighbors. If she left it there—they'd think she dumped garbage on their lawn! She was a bread-hurling nuisance, and they were probably calling the police right now. She and Leon would both be in jail. A family of criminal trespassers! Franny picked up the challah, but it fell apart, leaving crumbs all over the nice green lawn. Could you vacuum a lawn? The neighbors shook their heads in unison. Franny's whole body was somehow simultaneously frozen and on fire. She smooshed the broken, green-smeared challah pieces on the plate and ran home, slamming the door to 504 behind her.

CHAPTER TEN

LOTTIE PACED BACK AND FORTH IN FRONT OF THE STAGE, sucking hard on her cigarette and picking tobacco bits off her tongue. Sweat trickled down Franny's temples under the hot lights.

"Again," Lottie said. "From the top."

"Can't we break for lunch?" Hal said. "I'm hungry enough to chew Andy's arm off." She pulled Andy's wrist to her mouth, and Andy pretended to be aghast.

"Eat your own arm."

"Too gamey," Hal said. She kissed the arm before letting go. "Lottie, I'm starving. Peggy's starving. We're all starving."

"I'm okay," Franny said as her stomach betrayed her with unholy grumblings.

"Something is off," Lottie said. She rubbed the air like fabric between a finger and thumb. "Show's tomorrow. It should be here by now."

"Our lunch?" Hal said. "I agree."

"It'll be here; why wouldn't it be here?" Andy said. Even her words were sweaty. "She's just hungry, like Hal said."

"You conjured your first Showstopper on two hours of sleep, Andy Grand Canyon," Lottie said. "And you"—she pointed at Gal— "you barely had your set memorized. And Helen—"

"Hal. I wasn't even wearing clothes," Hal said, leaning back, hands behind her shorn head. "That was a wild night."

"You weren't wearing clothes?" Franny said into the microphone. "Like onstage?"

"The point is," Lottie said, "where is her Showstopper?"

Silence. Except, that is, for the telegraph of Lottie's fingernails, tapping out doom. Franny had hidden the recipe card and her diary underneath her mattress, then worried that the jokes would infect her dreams, and jumped out of bed in the middle of the night to bury it in the back of her closet, at the bottom of a hatbox filled with hats she hadn't worn since high school. *This* set was good—she had it memorized, and it was written by experts. Who was she? Someone who couldn't even deliver a loaf of bread to a doorstep without incident.

Plus, anyway, she and Lottie hadn't spoken, not really, since that night at the Palmer House. Lottie wouldn't understand why she suddenly had a whole new, raw set. She'd have questions, Franny wouldn't have answers; what a mess. If only Andy could hold it together, they could make it through the big Saturday show, and then she could try out new jokes. It would be that easy. But Andy flickered like a guilty lighthouse, sitting in the dark.

"I think maybe I felt something last time," Andy said. "I'm sure of it. I felt a tingle."

"What kind of tingle?" Gal asked. "Like when you rub your feet on a carpet and touch a doorknob?"

"Didn't anyone else feel it?" Andy asked. "The tingle?"

"No one felt any fucking tingles," Lottie said. "Peggy, again. From the top."

Every word felt like a confession. Every confession came out as a joke. Franny had arrived early at the Blue Moon, thanks to the intense scrutiny Leon was currently under at home. Mama and Papa monitored his every flinch, and no one had a spare eyeball for Franny. And so, even considering the Michael Berman situation, she was able to slip out with a vague *be back later!*

Lottie had been sitting at her barstool when Franny arrived, drinking hot tea, of all things. She'd dunked the tea bag in the hot water and asked Enid for a slice of lemon. She had not yet put her makeup on and looked unfinished in a way that embarrassed Franny. She had been crying. She looked puffy. Franny had grimaced and tried to tiptoe back out the door before Lottie saw her.

"Gal tells me you're still seeing that Boreman kid."

"I see him at the grocery store sometimes"—Franny had shrugged—"but he never sees me."

Lottie had slammed her fist on the bar. "You know your problem? You shoot your wad before you ever reach the microphone."

"For someone who doesn't want to be feared, you sure do a lot of shouting." Whoops, that wasn't going to help.

Lottie swiveled around. Her malice was too fetching. "I've seen that dress already," she said. There was a cut on her lip. The derringer winked at her ankle. "I certainly hope you brought something else."

Franny rushed out and bought the first thing that fit—white

pants that clutched her hips like sausage casings and a red checkered blouse—spending her lunch and dinner money in the process.

❧

"Stop fidgeting with that blouse," Lottie said. "Is this your first time wearing a shirt or what?"

"I think Peggy should try some *new* jokes," Andy said. "Didn't she say something about having new material?"

Hal coughed. "Actually, I think she's doing great with this set. Why fix what ain't broken?"

Franny crumpled inside. Just a spider under the hot lights, minding her own business on the wrong side of a shoe. It wasn't that she wanted to tell her own jokes. That was the *last* thing she wanted. But the second-to-last thing she wanted was for these girls to give up on her. She'd had enough of that elsewhere, thanks.

Her stomach commenced its familiar clench. Hal wouldn't even look at her.

"Either my ears need cleaning or your clock does." Andy brandished a hopeless little fist.

Hal shrugged, unimpressed.

"Andy, you've been squirrelly all day," Lottie said. "You got something to say, say it already."

Franny panicked. Andy didn't need any encouragement to relieve herself of the burden of Franny's fakery. Sure, Franny hadn't *forced* anyone to write her jokes, but they wouldn't have done it if she hadn't begged. She had to save Andy from herself. She had to save herself

from feeling like a slice of moldy bread. She would save all of them...
with a joke.

"Hey, get a load of this!" Franny held up two fingers in a V shape
and darted her tongue between them. *V for Victory, we'll lick 'em good.*
Something like that, right? Something to make everyone laugh.

It did not make everyone laugh.

Mouths gawped like hooked fishes.

"What the hell?" Andy said.

"It's official. I'm rearranging deck chairs on the *Titanic,*" Lottie
said. She stalked over to the bar and slid onto her stool. "Enid.
Martini. A whole bucket of martinis. If the ship's going down, I
might as well start swimming."

Lottie gave full attention to her martini, turning her back on the
club, her face reflected in the mirrors behind the bar. The wicked
face had gone soft and sad. The reflection of a woman lost, more
frightening than her anger and the derringer combined. And somehow it was all Franny's fault. She fidgeted with her blouse. She would
have bought a thousand new ill-fitting outfits on credit to make that
face go away.

Eventually, she would have to get off the stage. Eventually, she
would have to marry Michael Berman or a facsimile of him. Franny
clutched the microphone like it was a lifeboat.

"You know, I'm not that hungry after all," she said in a tiny,
squashed voice. "From the top? One more time?"

A five-o'clock shadow in shirtsleeves stumbled through the door
to the club. Barb jumped to her feet with surprising agility for someone who had so recently been snoring.

"Evenin', buddy boy," the man slurred, patting Barb on the head, "who's a fella gotta drink to get a blow around here?"

"Sorry," Barb said. "We're closed."

"Bullpucky you're closed." He peered over her shoulder. "There's a girl right there at the bar."

"I know," Barb said. "It ain't closed for *her*." She nudged him with her folded arms until he stumbled backward out the door, swearing under his breath.

"Maybe he'll think I'm funny," Franny said. She had muttered it to herself, but the microphone was still on, and Lottie whipped around to face her, all softness gone.

"No men," Lottie said. "Not now, not ever."

"I was kidding."

"And once again, Peggy, no one's laughing."

Tears stung. She would not let them see her cry. She would *not*.

"Hey, girls, why the long faces?" Hal smoothed her hair back and hopped onstage, blocking Franny and gesturing for the mic. When Franny didn't hand it over, she finally turned around. She mouthed, *Let me help*. Franny pretended not to see.

"I think we could all could use a pick-me-up," Hal said. "Because Hal Angel…makes time fly." She grinned. Franny did not grin back. "What do you think, Peggy? It's my new catchphrase."

"It's a free country." Franny dropped the mic, and Hal fumbled it.

"Get off my stage, *Hal*," Lottie said.

"I haven't had a drop in a week," Hal said. "That was the original deal."

"The deal was, there was no deal."

"If there's trouble, I can stop a joke on a dime." Hal snapped her fingers. "I've been practicing on Andy."

Andy smirked. "That she has."

"Ew." Gal wrinkled her nose.

"And I bought pillows, lots of them, so if any girls"—Hal flapped her arms—"no one gets hurt. Lottie, I've got it all worked out. I can do this."

"No one gets hurt, what a gal," Lottie said. She stood in front of the stage, cocked her head. "Or actually, what *are* you, Hal?"

Every inch of Hal flinched.

"Because if you're a man, well." Lottie grimaced. "No men. No exceptions."

Lottie had a real talent for making people miserable. Maybe even better than her husband, and he removed actual body parts. Hal hurt Franny's feelings, but she didn't deserve this.

"I'd take a drunk vagrant over Ed 'Fingers' Marcone any day," Franny said.

Lottie turned on Franny. "Who said anything about Ed?"

"I'm just saying, if we're letting men in, let's be choosy."

"I'm not," Hal said, "a drunk."

How did she always manage to upset everyone? Maybe that was her Showstopper, ol' Foot-in-Mouth Peggy Blake. "I *meant* the guy at the door," Franny said. "The bullpucky guy?"

"Everybody knows how to run this joint except me, is that it? The one who has actually kept us alive?" Lottie downed her martini, motioned for a refill. "The indignities I suffer, daily, just to keep this place running. The Blue Moon wouldn't exist without me. *You* wouldn't exist." She pointed at Franny, who had always been worried about this, yes, this exact thing, the not existing, not really, not without outside help.

"The Blue Moon is your home; this is your family. Outside those doors, nobody cares what any of us think or say or feel, or haven't you noticed? Helen Angel, get off my goddamn stage." Lottie yanked the mic stand offstage, and the microphone screamed. She tottered backward, clutching the stand to her heart. "Fine, take a lunch break. Bring your boyfriends into the club. Be your own boyfriends! Get knocked up and scrub kitchen floors on your hands and knees until the day you die. You girls always march so gleefully to your own prisons. I don't get it, never will."

No quips filled the silence. Lottie closed her eyes and pressed the mic to her forehead, like those once-a-year ashes on Catholics that Franny always thought were dirt.

"Lottie," Gal said, "No one's saying—"

"Just go," Lottie said.

"Last one to Peter Pan's is a rotten egg," Andy said. She and Gal raced out the door. Hal glanced back at Franny and then followed.

If Franny got offstage now, would she ever get back on? She'd spent all her money on these stupid clothes she'd never wear again, and the thought of watching Helen—Hal—down two Francheezies while not being able to order one of her own was excruciating.

The thought of waiting alone at the Blue Moon while Lottie chewed on her anguish was even worse.

"Well, look who's the rotten egg," Lottie said.

⁓◦⁓

Franny squeezed into a red vinyl booth next to Gal, and as the wait-ress frowned at Hal's hair and sport coat, Andy quickly ordered for all of them.

"Let's see, one Dagwood burger—"

"What the hell are you supposed to be?" the waitress said.

Hal picked at her frayed cuffs.

"Whatever happened to *soup or salad*?" Andy asked.

"Andy," Hal muttered, "don't worry about it."

"Okay, wiseass." The waitress smirked. "What are you supposed to be, soup or salad?"

Andy examined the menu, making deciding noises in her throat. Then she examined Hal. "What if I want both?"

Hal beamed like a neon sign.

"So that'll be one Dagwood burger with soup *and* salad," Andy said, "four Francheezies, four french fries, a chocolate milkshake, and three Cokes. You got all that?"

"Yeah, I got it," the waitress said.

"Make that three Francheezies," Franny said.

"Your stomach's louder than a squealing pig," Hal said, pulling a flask out of her coat pocket. "Don't tell me you're on a diet."

"Four Francheezies and that's final," Andy said, shooing the waitress.

"I'm not hungry," Franny said.

"I don't blame you," Andy said. "But you gotta keep your strength up. Don't let Lottie get to you. She's not worth it." She patted Franny's cheek, and Franny tried to smile.

"That's not whiskey I spy, is it, Helen?" Andy said.

"Hal. You lost the bet, remember?"

"Well, is it?" Andy asked. "Whiskey?"

Hal unscrewed the flask and turned it upside down. Nothing came out. "Sue me for pretending. Beats the alternative."

Quick as a blink, Andy kissed Hal on the cheek. Hal blotched from the neck up.

"Don't worry, we'll cover you," Gal whispered to Franny.

There were the waterworks again—was she really crying over a hot dog? "I'll pay you back," Franny said.

"Our treat," Gal said. "Anyway, once you conjure that Showstopper, you'll be rolling in dough."

"Stop, you'll make me lose my appetite for real," Franny said.

Andy leaned across the table. "Forget about everything that just happened. New plan."

"Can't I eat first?" Franny asked. "I can't take another monologue on an empty stomach."

The waitress deposited their Cokes but hesitated with Hal's milkshake, clinging to the silver tumbler like she was deciding whether Hal deserved it.

"Oh, for Chrissake," Andy said, snatching it from her.

Hal dunked a straw in her milkshake and shrugged. "I just think," she said, "that Peggy should do the set we wrote."

"I keep hearing you say that, but I don't believe my ears."

"Me either," Franny said.

"It's nothing personal, Peg, I just—can't lose the Blue Moon."

"None of us want to lose the Blue Moon," Andy said.

"It's different for you," Hal said. "I lose this place, I got nothing."

"Peggy is basically stealing our jokes," Andy said. "Suddenly you're okay with that?"

Franny gaped. "I'm not stealing jokes! You said you'd help me!"

"Well, you did say," Gal said, "you did say—that you would write your own set."

"I'm going to," Franny said. She couldn't handle Gal's puppy dog eyes. "Look, I already did. I wrote a set, okay? But I can't do it."

Gal squealed and clapped. "I knew it! I told you she wouldn't break a promise."

"What do you mean you can't do it?" Andy said.

"She's scared," Hal said.

"Of what? She's been onstage a million times already."

"Our Peggy is a housewife in comic's clothing. She wants everything to look shiny and clean so no one will see what a mess she is inside."

Franny had never wanted to punch anyone in their rat face as much as she wanted to punch Hal. What right did she have to be right?

"No offense, Peggy, but it's too late," Hal said. "If we're still open for business next week, you can be a mess onstage then."

"Don't listen to Hal," Andy said. "We're not going to let you dangle up there, but jeez, Peggy, you see the pickle you've put us in?"

"No, Hal's right. Lottie's got me headlining. On a Saturday," Franny said. "What's worse, a great set and no Showstopper, or a rotten set and no Showstopper?" Why couldn't Andy understand this? How many different ways did she have to explain it? "Lottie's been so nice to me."

"Lottie is a lot of things," Andy said. "But *nice* is not one of them."

"She can be real nice when she wants to be," Hal said. "Flaming crab, nights in her Palmer House suite—"

"Hal." Andy grimaced. "Put a sock in it."

"What?" Hal said, gesturing at Franny. "She can't be that green. Everything is shoptalk with Lottie, even when it isn't."

A zing of shame. Hadn't Lottie said the same to her, almost verbatim? Franny became absorbed in the tabletop's boomerang design. There was a faded spot in the middle; why? From the ketchup hopper? The boomerangs overlapped like a magician's linking rings. She thought maybe she might slide down the vinyl booth, under the table, crawl to the door, and run away to Cabo.

"Nobody's judging you," Gal said. "One time is a mistake, not a lifestyle."

Hal downed the rest of her shake, wiped her mouth with the back of her hand. "Might be a lifestyle for Peggy," she said, waggling her hand in front of Franny's face. "'Who would want to get fingered by Fingers,' remember?"

"Suck eggs, Hal," Andy said.

"With pleasure."

"How often do you get to try flaming crab guilt-free?" Gal said. "That's about as trayf as it gets."

Franny groaned and pressed her hands to her face to hide the heat. "Not you too?" she said. Unbelievable. What an absolute rube.

Gal elbowed Franny, but Franny didn't feel much like laughing. Though, to be honest, it was a teensy relief to know just how meaningless that night at the Palmer House was. Franny tried to feel relieved.

Hal rolled up the sleeves of her sport coat to dive into her

Francheezie. "So Peggy will do our set Saturday and try out her new material next week," she said. "We're all agreed."

Andy poked Hal in the shoulder. "You can't chicken out now," she hissed. "This is not what we agreed on."

They all agreed on something? Without Franny?

"What do you mean, *agreed on*?" Franny asked.

"I've got it!" Gal said. "Maybe you tell *one* of your own jokes? Squeeze it in, and if it bombs, you have the rest to fall back on," Gal said, palms open like she had just brokered world peace. "We'll build a new set joke by joke. Isn't that a nice compromise?"

"Peggy just needs to relax. Boopsie told me she can't conjure her Showstopper at all if she's too nervous," Andy said.

"Here we go again," Hal said, "all hail the protégé of Boopsie Baxter."

"She says you have to *know* you'll knock their socks off. All you have to do is strap a rocket to your ass, and suddenly you're an astronaut. You understand?"

"Not even a little bit," Franny said.

"What do you say, Andy?" Gal said. "One joke?"

Franny looked from one girl to the other as they negotiated over her like she wasn't even there. All she could think about was that grass-stained challah. That was Franny in a nutshell—painfully constructed and utterly inedible. Who knew what horrors a Showstopper would reveal about her? *Not* conjuring a Showstopper was the best thing Franny had going right now.

Andy narrowed her brown eyes and pursed her lips like that first time they met, when Franny banged down the door of the Blue Moon. "Well, I suppose one joke is better than—"

"Peggy, Ed's coming to the show tomorrow," Hal blurted. "To see *you*."

Franny snorted, waiting for Hal's ratty lip to curl in a smile. No smile. No gotcha.

"A billion sentences in the English language," Andy groaned, "and you had to pick that one."

"She needs to know," Hal said.

Franny looked from Andy to Hal to Gal, total strangers in the bodies of her supposed friends. "It's true?"

"We weren't going to break it to you like this," Gal said, reaching for Franny's hand. Franny pulled away. "You don't need that kind of pressure."

"You girls don't know the half of it," Hal said. "Ed's coming to get his cut for the month and sticking around for the show. If Peggy can't knock the socks off everyone in the club, including his"—Hal's voice caught on the hook of her throat—"he's shutting us down and giving the Blue Moon to Varla."

Now everyone was staring at the table.

"He wouldn't," Gal said finally.

"Kill me now." Andy snatched the flask and pretended to chug until Hal wrestled it away.

Franny laughed. "Ed? Fingers Marcone? Quit fooling. Lottie didn't bet the Blue Moon on *me*." She waited for the girls to crack, but their faces stayed intact. Franny put her head between her hands and tried to squeeze it like an orange. She thought of Lottie, makeup-less and crying into a cup of tea, her relentless coaching. Even the night at the Palmer House. Franny was just some kind of Eliza Doolittle Hail Mary. If only it didn't make so much sense.

"The show must go on, right?" Andy faked a brilliant smile. "It only takes one laugh to conjure a Showstopper, so one real joke will have to do. Tell us some of your setups. We'll make it shine, don't worry."

"What does it matter?" Franny said. "Ed can't feel Showstoppers anyway. Who cares if I tell my joke, if I tell your jokes? I'm not in a joking mood."

"There's your problem," Andy said. "No such thing as a joking mood. Forget about Ed—this is about you. You're using jokes as a shield instead of a weapon."

"Am not."

"Then tell a joke about Leon," Gal said gently.

Judas. Benedict Arnold. It was a small Jewish world; of course, Gal would know about Leon.

"Who's Leon?" Andy smirked. "Your boyfriend?"

"I know you've written one. There's not a comic in the world who hasn't mined her family for gold." Gal laid a manicured hand on Franny's. Her diamond bracelet winked expensively. "What's the worst that could happen?"

Oh, you know. Chaos. Destruction. An atom bomb shot into space that explodes the whole dang universe.

"Leon's not funny," Franny said, shaking her hand off. "And he's off-limits." The jokes about Leon had scared her all right. They were too honest, funny because they were so painful to tell. But that wasn't even the scariest part, which was that Franny couldn't bring herself to throw any of them away, or even hide them. She had pulled her diary out of the closet at the last minute. The jokes were right there, in her handbag, if anyone thought to look.

A thought popped up like one of Mr. Finnegan's gopher nemeses—the joke she'd written about Peter. The Purple Head. The joke was ipecac, threatening the Francheezie she had just swallowed.

"What was that?" Andy said, pointing. "Just now, what were you thinking?"

"Nothing."

"Let's play poker sometime," Andy said. "I saw you think of something funny, and you're afraid to laugh at it."

"You guys are mind readers now?" Franny said. "I wasn't thinking about anything."

"Peggy." Gal leaned her head against Franny's shoulder and batted her eyelashes up at her. "No way out but through."

"What's that supposed to mean?"

"It means," Hal said, "just tell us the damn joke."

⟡

Lottie reeked of gin and olive brine. She pulled Franny aside and stroked her arm, her cheek, tried to pull her in for a kiss.

"Where are you, little Showstopper?" Lottie said, knocking on Franny's head before she could pull away. "I know you're in there."

"You smell like a wino."

"Better that than a corpse. And I forgive you, Peggy Blake." Lottie had refreshed her makeup, her posture straight and face composed.

"You'll be a star, just like Booksie Bapster. But you have to want it. I can't help you if you don't want it."

Lottie was so scared of losing the Blue Moon, she had to hide behind martinis and phoniness, and Franny wasn't even convinced she was drunk. In an instant, everything had just rotted like an old apple with Franny at the core.

She did not want to tell this joke about Peter. *You have to add a tag*, Andy said. *That's the punch line after the punch line.* Franny was the one who came up with the tag, and they had all nodded thoughtfully, with a slight tang of jealousy, which was the comic's version of laughing. It was her joke through and through, but she didn't want it. She didn't want to go onstage and joke about that memory. Or any memory. Franny was done with memories. Was that so much to ask?

She did not want to prepare for tomorrow, or see Ed, or conjure a Showstopper, or not conjure a Showstopper. But she was on a conveyor belt, a bomb pieced together by line workers, and there was no getting off now. She was built to explode, there was no way around it.

So she said: "I want it."

"You're a good girl, Peggy," Lottie said. "I'm never wrong about my girls."

Franny thought of the Palmer House suite, with its ghosts of Lottie and Gal, Lottie and Andy, Lottie and Hal, Lottie and the poor girl in the straitjacket who couldn't handle the book clubs.

༒

The Friday show should have been named the Terrible Foreshadowing

Show. The Show Where Everyone Ends Up Disappointed. Or, most accurately, The Friday Show Before the Saturday Show Where Franny Steinberg Would Be Responsible for Shutting Down the Blue Moon Forever and Maybe Also Losing Her Fingers.

Instead, it was advertised, recklessly, as a Showstopper debut. Some of the book club girls had returned on their own dime, tantalized by the idea of bragging that they had "seen Peggy Blake when." They drank free seltzer water and squeezed tiny limes into them, slipping flasks out of their purses when no one was looking. Gal had invited a group of BBG girls and bit her freshly manicured nails, waiting to see if they would actually show. Franny hoped they wouldn't. What if they told their mothers? Did Gal have space in her shabby hotel room for a human roommate?

Gal warmed up the crowd with her routine about dating.

"Dating is awful, isn't it?" she said. "We girls wear lipstick and set our hair, bat our eyelashes, eat melba toast, and squeeze into girdles. We pretend we're not funny so he can believe he is. A man can eat like a horse and dress like a bum. And—this is a true story—I once went out with a man who couldn't stop talking about his mother. A great cook. Sweet as pie. He says, 'I want a girl just like Mama.' Well, that was the last straw. I says to him, 'You schtup your own mother?'"

The room tittered, a few gasped. Gal's sweet face spread into a smile. She leaned into the mic. "Does that mean your daddy's available?"

The laugh exploded, and even Franny couldn't stop herself from laughing. Gal knew how to milk her Showstopper for all it was worth. Her punch lines were funny, the tags she hung on them even funnier, and the accumulation of small satisfactions—bus after bus after bus reaching the corner at just the right time—made Franny feel like she was perpetually in the right place at just the right time. Even Andy looked relaxed, but Hal sipped on her soda sullenly. If she could just find a way to enjoy herself, she could probably soak up Showstoppers better. But Franny knew better than to mention that. Anyway, she couldn't think about Hal right now. She had to focus. Gal was trying to help boost Franny's confidence with her Showstopper; that was just the kind of friend she was.

"And now, a very special treat," Gal said, and Franny's heart started pounding, even through the haze of her Showstopper-assisted confidence. "For the first time on the Friday stage, please welcome the very funny Peggy Blake!"

The crowd applauded politely, and Franny hopped onstage fast so they couldn't stop before she got her first line out—keep the energy up, ride that happy Showstopper wave as long as she could. She shook Gal's hand and pulled the microphone close. Under the lights, her body felt surreal, and it would be so easy to slip away and watch herself go through the motions, to wait on the sidelines until the body finished talking. Not this time, she thought. *I need to be here in case I have to run away and never return.*

"Childhood isn't all it's cracked up to be," she said, "but it's a cakewalk compared to womanhood." A smattering of applause. Franny screwed up her courage as Gal's Showstopper faded. No way out but through.

Her mouth dried up. *Say the words, Franny.*

"My twenty-first birthday, a family friend decided to make a woman out of me," she said. "He had his finger blown off in the war—and by the end of the night, I wished he had lost…a different appendage. Sadly, they don't call him *Peter* for nothing." Shocked, chirpy laughter, a few gasps like smoke. Sparks flew, looking for something to ignite. Was the Blue Moon on fire? Franny's guts started to churn. But it wasn't a stomachache; it churned and bubbled like primordial ooze, like a fish deciding to try out a pair of legs. Her insides sputtered and spun and created fire. The fire climbed out of the swamp.

"Forget the Purple Heart," Franny said. "An injury like that, we should award a Purple Head. To us girls."

They laughed! Not a lot, but definitely a solid chuckle-plus. The comedians laughed too, even Hal. It looked genuine, but she probably just did it to make Franny feel better.

But Franny didn't have time to doubt herself because the fire inside her spun brighter, bigger. She was a human X-ray, her insides illuminated for everyone to see. And then, just as she thought maybe she might actually, physically burn up from heat and radiation, the fire burst out of her mouth and was extinguished.

The room was dark, darker than it had been before, lit by measly stage lights and carved wood chandeliers.

Something heavy had been burned away. A tumor cauterized. Franny gripped the microphone, fearful in that hazy moment that she might float away without it.

Had it been her imagination?

Had it been her Showstopper?

Whatever her Showstopper was, it kept everyone sitting politely in their seats. No singing, no arm flapping, no one running away screaming. All this teeth-gnashing about her Showstopper, and she had nothing to worry about. But Franny couldn't help feeling a *little* disappointed—it was quite a lot of hoo-ha for not much payoff.

She kept going with the set the girls wrote for her and noted that she never felt the fire again. Curse Andy for being right.

"Got a stomachache, don't blame Peggy Blake!" She waved to the room and hopped offstage to mildly enthusiastic applause. Franny slid into the booth next to Andy and exhaled for the first time since June.

"I'm telling you, if you've got more jokes like that," Andy whispered, "then you really have been holding out on us."

This was the nicest thing Andy had ever said to her. Franny cleared her throat. The moment of truth. "Was my Showstopper as boring as Gal's?" She rolled her eyes in mock worry.

"Listen, Peggy, you didn't—there wasn't—" She shook her head. "You didn't conjure a Showstopper."

Impossible. The light? The fire? Everything? Franny's face must have looked dreadful, because Andy actually hugged her.

"I'm sorry I was so hard on you. Don't worry. We're in this together. We have until tomorrow night to figure it out."

"Oh, definitely." Franny tried to sound chipper.

Andy looked around the bar. "You see where Hal went?" she asked. "She laughed so hard at your Purple Head joke, snorting and everything. Wish she were here to tell you herself; must be in the bathroom or something."

Gal finished her interlude and introduced Andy to uproarious applause. Andy scanned the bar again then nudged Franny out of the way and ran up to the stage with a huge grin and a wave to the room.

As soon as Andy went up, Hal bounced into the booth and smiled sweetly at Franny, cradling her head in her hands.

Something felt off.

"Where were you?" Franny whispered. "What's the matter?"

"Matter?" Hal said. "No matter, mad hatter!" She giggled (giggled!), and Franny frowned.

"Did you feel…anything?" Franny asked. Hal didn't like to be reminded of her insensitivity to Showstoppers, but Franny needed a second opinion. "Maybe a little tingle?"

Hal stroked Franny's cheek. "You're pretty," she said.

And there it was, the only answer Franny needed. Hal was drunk. Franny's failure had driven her to start drinking again. Boy, she really had blown it.

The truth hit Franny like a Sherman tank.

In order to let herself bare her dirtiest, nastiest secret, Franny had to convince herself she could conjure a Showstopper. The spinning, the fire, the euphoria—it was all in her head. None of it was real. She trusted Andy, the other girls; she had believed she could be a real comic. In return, she'd lost her most precious possession: her own secrets.

Now Franny really felt sick.

Tears blurred her vision, and she wiped them away roughly, but they would not stop. She cried quietly at first, but this was not a dainty weeping. Her shoulders started to shake, and her breath came in gasps and gulps. She got up from the table and stumbled toward the door. She couldn't stay, not for one more second.

Lottie appeared, blocking her path to the outside and fresh air, swaying slightly. "My office."

"Sorry, Lottie," Franny said. "I'm not cut out for this. I'll show myself out."

But Lottie squeezed her arm hard, pinching the delicate skin underneath and pulled her behind the bar, lifting a trapdoor to reveal a ladder leading into darkness.

"Ladies first," Lottie said. She peered closely at Franny. "Are you crying? Jesus. I'm the one who should be crying."

Franny climbed reluctantly down, her feet clanging on each rung of the ladder, her sniffles echoing in the darkness. Down below, it was pitch-black and impenetrable. She blinked as though she could clear the darkness from her vision. Lottie struck a match and lit several candles to reveal the outline of two armchairs and a low table with a telephone on it.

"Pretty big for a dungeon," Franny said.

"They're old rum-running tunnels. Now they're my office," Lottie said. She sat in one of the armchairs and motioned for Franny to do the same. "It's my private spot," Lottie said. "I come here to disappear when things get extra rotten." She leaned forward, eyeballs glowing eerily in the candlelight. "You sure screwed me over good."

"The girls said—if I just added a new joke—" No, she couldn't throw them under the bus for trying to help her. "It was my idea."

"You've been stealing jokes," Lottie said. "Right under my goddamned nose. You made me think you were a real comedian, and I fell for it, hook, line, and sinker. Congratulations, you got me. You fooled Lottie Marcone."

Franny's mouth stopped working. "I didn't. I would never," she said finally. "I just—I asked the girls for a little help. Just until I got comfortable onstage. I—I should have written my own set, sure, but I didn't *steal*. Ask them, ask any of them."

"I didn't have to," Lottie said. "They came to me."

Andy.

Lottie lit two cigarettes in a candle's flame, offered one to Franny, like they do in Westerns right before the outlaw gets hanged. Franny took it and sucked so hard, she started coughing. Lottie gazed at the candle, which gave Franny a moment to compose herself.

"The Blue Moon is in trouble," Lottie said. "Money trouble. Ed wants to flush it all down the toilet and turn it into an underground casino run by his new girlie, Varla. She's got less business sense than a cockroach, and he knows that. But Ed thinks it's my fault this joint is losing money. He doesn't understand stand-up, never appreciated what I built. But he was okay when it made him rich."

So it was really true. Franny shivered. "If it weren't for those lousy male TV comedians..." Franny stopped. This was not the time to remind Lottie of how mad she was about Boopsie's stolen jokes.

"It's not just the male comedians," Lottie said. "It's the obscenity laws, paying off the cops. It's the suburbs, the happy homemakers, the dullness that comes from having all the comforts you ever wanted. We used to have regulars, if you can believe that." She snorted. "Now they're up to their tits in kids and Jell-O molds."

"What if we—"

"Please. Let me finish," Lottie said. "So, next thing I know, I'm begging Ed for more time. I'm on my hands and knees on the sticky bar floor. He's telling me Boopsie Baxter was lightning in a bottle, and I'm saying I made her happen and can do it again." She grabbed Franny's hands in a death grip, and Franny's cigarette was trapped, burning down her fingers like a fuse.

"Not five minutes later," Lottie said, "you show up in your bridesmaid dress, cracking jokes about enema bags, and stupid me, I think it's some kind of sign. You've been handed down to me like manna from heaven to save the Blue Moon. I don't believe in signs. But you just kept coming back. So I started to believe." Lottie ground out her cigarette. "You probably stole that enema joke too."

"Actually—"

"Save your breath to blow on your coffee," Lottie said.

It wasn't fair. And worse, it wasn't true. Franny wrenched her hands free. "It's not like I planned any of this."

"Vesuvius didn't plan to erupt, but tell that to Pompeii."

"What about that night in the hotel, did you plan that?"

Lottie took her sweet time tamping out her cigarette. She shrugged. "I felt sorry for you. So timid for such a big girl."

It stung worse than a slap.

"Feel sorry for yourself next time," Franny said. She whipped around and clomped up the ladder, expecting Lottie to chase her, to protest, to apologize, to insult her some more. But Lottie just watched her go.

Franny had a clear path to the door, but now she was itching for a fight. Andy told a punchline, and as the room laughed and settled into her Showstopper, Franny marched right up onstage.

Andy blinked at her but then recovered. "Ladies and degenerates, give another round of applause for Peggy Blake." The room clapped tentatively. They didn't want her back. No one did.

"Why did you do it?" Franny said.

Andy pasted on an awkward smile and looked from the room to Franny and back again. "Excuse us while we pause for station identification." The room laughed. Andy pulled her offstage into the shadowed corner next to the bathroom.

"What do you think you're doing?" she said.

"You were so worried I'd blow it for you that you blew it for me, is that it? You just couldn't stand that I was getting better." Yeah, that was the ticket. "Maybe even better than *you*."

"Fat chance of that."

"You told Lottie I stole your jokes."

"I'm in the *middle* of my *set*. If you honestly think—I don't have time for this." Andy turned away, but Franny wasn't done yet.

"I guess now you get to be top dog forever," Franny said. "Big Andy, small pond."

Andy squinted at Franny. "Some of us worked hard to get where we are. Some of us give a shit, Peggy Blake."

"My name," Franny said, "is Franny." She left Andy standing there and burst past the sleeping Barb then pushed open the door into the humid, wheezy air. Cars zipped by. The world was too big, too much; it whirled around and around as if she weren't even there, and it wouldn't ever stop. Franny closed herself inside the telephone booth on the corner and tried to exist.

Michael Berman was probably out on a thousand dates with

a thousand pretty, short, thin, unfunny BBGs, who couldn't eat another bite, who hung on his every word.

"Michael," Franny said, when he picked up. She hadn't planned past this moment, but here it was, and she wasn't going to blow it, not this time. "It's…you."

Oh, Franny.

"I've never had so many phone calls from a girl I'm not going with," Michael said. "Your mother is looking for you, Franny Steinberg."

Franny pressed her forehead to the filthy glass and squeezed her eyes shut. "What did you tell her?"

"Will you tell me what's going on? I can't play a game I don't know the rules to," Michael said. He paused. "I don't like being the butt of a joke I don't understand."

"I'm not joking, I swear." Franny never wanted to joke again as long as she lived. "Hey, let's go out again. Let's go out right now."

What was she *doing*?

"Are you asking me on a date?"

She was losing it, whatever "it" was, as if she'd ever had "it" in the first place. Oh god, just hang up Franny, before you hurt yourself.

"I don't know, forget it, sorry I called."

"Wait." Michael sighed softly. Franny poked her finger in the coin release, let the little door swing, poked again. "I like you, Franny. I shouldn't, but I do. Just don't tell my mother. She doesn't like aggressive girls."

Franny was so relieved, she actually giggled. "Don't tell *my* mother either, please. Oh my gosh, don't tell her anything ever."

Franny squinted at her stupid watch. "Maybe we can still catch *Bedtime for Bonzo*. Meet you at the theater?"

"You are a funny one," Michael said. "You get the movie, I'll buy the popcorn."

"Deal."

The receiver dinged satisfyingly as she dropped it into the hook. Franny put in another nickel and dialed Mama, prepared with an excuse, an apology, a fast-talking alibi.

"Franny, thanks god," Mama said. "You need to come home."

"I'd love to, but I'm out with Michael Berman, and *Bedtime for Bonzo* starts in an hour," Franny said automatically, not considering that Mama had already spoken with Michael Berman. But she didn't interrogate Franny; it was like she hadn't even heard.

"We're leaving for the hospital," Mama said. "So maybe you should go there. I don't know." She started to weep, and Franny pressed the phone hard against her skull as though she could magic her way into the kitchen with Mama.

"What happened," she said, "to Leon?"

"It's Papa," Mama said. "It's Papa's heart."

CHAPTER ELEVEN

PAPA'S FACE WAS PALE AND CLAMMY AS GEFILTE FISH, A CUFF on his arm, a tube in his nose, machines everywhere. It was all wrong. He was supposed to be cracking wise, watching television, fixing people's plumbing.

Leon paced the floor, back and forth, running his fingers through his hair until it was a black rain cloud. He didn't like hospitals, having, at the insistence of the head doctor at the VA Hospital, spent a single day and night in psychiatric care there in July of 1945. Papa had rescued him, carried his skin-and-bones body over the threshold of 504, and Franny's strongest memory of that day was Papa's silent, vibrating fury, which she had never seen before or since. No one in the family talked about it, not even once. It wasn't until Franny saw the raw fear in Leon's eyes that she remembered the episode at all.

Mama hugged her tight, and Franny cried about everything.

"We were eating dinner—just sitting there like any evening," Mama said, staring at the empty air as though it were their dining table. "Papa was sitting in his seat here, and I had just walked in with the half of a roast chicken I had made. Since it was just the two of us eating alone. Again."

Leon stopped pacing. "I told you, I was on my way—"

Mama shooed his excuse away. "You kids have busy lives, hiding in garbage cans, phony dates with Michael Berman. Anyway, your papa goes deathly pale, and I think, nu, he's choking on a chicken bone, so I go to the other side of the table, ready to slap it out of him—"

Modern medicine, what a marvel.

"You were going to *slap* it out of him?" Franny said instead.

"But your papa clutches his chest and topples backward out of the chair, and then he's just lying there on the floor like a corpse, and it all came back to me, my training at the Red Cross. I pinched your father's nose and opened his mouth and leaned in to breathe into his lungs, when his eyes popped open and he said, 'I always knew you would do me in, but I didn't know it would be like this.'" Tears were streaming down Mama's cheeks, and she blotted them with an already-soaked handkerchief. "I knew then that he'd be all right."

"He doesn't look all right," Leon said.

"The human body can handle a lot," Mama said. She jutted her chin proudly. "And your papa's can handle more than most."

Staring at Papa's sleeping body, Franny felt uneasy. She shouldn't be seeing him like this—his collarbone exposed in the hospital gown, the swell of his belly under the sheet, his fingernails stained with grease below the plastic hospital bracelet. Franny patted her own collarbone, tucked safely away beneath her Peter Pan collar.

Seeing Papa so fragile brought to mind an image of him as a

young boy, as a teenager with fuzz on his lip, a too-big military cap with the czar's emblem covering his eyes. No, that couldn't have been him. Was it his papa? Had she imagined the photo? The details were so vivid in her memory, but Franny couldn't remember ever actually seeing it. The harder she tried to remember, the more unreal the image seemed. Papa wouldn't leave a photograph like that lying around for Franny to find. It seemed even less likely that he would have a photograph like that in the first place. Papa tucked his past away; if it ever popped up, he would swiftly cover it with a joke.

Franny didn't even know if Papa had been born in New York or Chicago or Russia (Kiev? Odessa? Vilna?). If he died here, in this hospital, would she ever know where she came from? What had been sacrificed to get her here? The last time Papa told his vaudeville story—she had wanted to ask questions. Why hadn't she asked questions? When did he stop crying and start laughing about the boys who tormented him? What had his papa left behind? How fast had he run to stay alive?

How ashamed they would be to see the results of their sacrifice. Franny Steinberg—world-class liar, professional sneak. Nightclub comedian. Well, not anymore. Every time she acted selfish, someone got hurt. Franny felt like vomit on legs.

Papa moaned. "Franny," he croaked. "Is that you?"

"Papa," she said, clutching his hand. Just hearing his voice, weak and croaky, was a relief.

"I'm sorry to be so much trouble," he said.

"You're no trouble," Franny said. "I'll take care of you. I'll spend all my time taking care of you, and that's a promise."

Papa motioned weakly. She leaned in closer. "What about," Papa said, "Michael Berman?"

"Yes, Franny," Mama said. "What about Michael Berman?"

Michael Berman was currently standing outside the Chicago Theater, angrily checking his watch because his date had stood him up. Franny would have to call him tomorrow and explain everything, ask for one more second chance. Would he give her one more chance? Michael Berman, who might not have been able to impress the Chicagoland BBG chapters, but surely had girls waiting for him back East. Why would he put up with more trouble from Franny?

Was Franny truly prepared to hang her future on Michael Berman?

Franny was saved from answering as the shift doctor entered the room, a blond shegetz with a movie-star jaw, who flipped through Papa's chart. "Looks like you had quite an evening, Mr. Steinberg. How are we feeling?" he said, without looking at Papa.

"Call me Isaac," Papa said. "I feel fine. Never better."

"Liar!" Mama said. "He doesn't feel fine!"

Standing over Papa's bed as the doctor took his pulse, Franny realized Andy had done her a favor. It took a painful betrayal to show Franny what was truly important. Family. Nursing Papa back to health. And then—yes, all right—marrying Michael Berman.

Mrs. Franny Berman. No, Mrs. Michael Berman. Swallowed whole in holy matrimony. Scrubbing kitchen floors on her hands and knees until she keeled over on them. Or would they have servants? What would Mrs. Michael Berman do if she couldn't scrub floors?

Would he know she wasn't a virgin? How on earth could she be a wife?

And there it was, that unwanted companion, Franny's crusty old memory of her twenty-first birthday. But this time, no matter how hard Franny pushed, it would not be ignored. She broke out in a cold sweat. Her vision sparkled, her ears started to ring, and she had to steady herself against the cool walls of Papa's room to keep from passing out. She conjured the image of Peter Finnegan right there in the doorway. Franny blinked. Twice. Three times.

No, he *was* standing in the doorway. Clutching a straw fedora in his fingertips.

Peter put a hateful hand on her bare arm. "I came as soon as I heard," he said.

"Franny, are you hearing this? Dr. Shegetz wants to strap me to this bed until next week!" Papa said.

It took all of Franny's energy not to scream. She was downright exhausted from all the not-screaming. "No one is strapping you to anything, Papa," she said.

"Mr. Steinberg—" the doctor said.

"Isaac."

"—you've just had a serious coronary event. It is not reasonable to think you'll be out of this hospital before the middle of next week."

"You see my daughter's face? Look how distraught she is. You've made her distraught."

"I'm not distraught," Franny snapped. Maybe if she ignored Peter's existence, he would eventually disappear. She forced herself to breathe. "Don't upset yourself."

"Upset?" Papa cried. "Who's upset? Bring on the leather straps, give me a wooden spoon to bite down on!"

Leon's face drained of all its color, and Peter released Franny's arm to help lower his friend into an available chair.

"For crying out loud, Isaac," Mama said. "Don't say things like that."

The doctor's eyes pinballed from one face to another, trying to predict who would speak next and what horrors they might say. "Visiting hours are over, aren't they?" the doctor said finally. "Mr. Steinberg really needs his rest."

"Isaac," Papa said.

Peter shook his head. "Doctor's right. Stress is a killer, Isaac."

"Mr. Steinberg," Papa said.

Franny bleated some unholy hybrid of a laugh and a sob. Peter frowned at her.

"I've been learning about it in my psychology course," he said, crossing his ankle over his knee and relaxing into the chair for a good, long visit. "Too much work, too much worry, it puts a burden on the heart. It's like shaking up a bottle of Coke—there's too much pressure, and one way or another, it'll explode."

"What would you know about it?" Franny snapped. Her composure teetered; her insides bubbled. Everyone turned to look at her, even Dr. Shegetz. What if, what if—she exploded right here in this hospital room? Would anyone stick around to clean her up? Fat chance.

"The body can't take it," Peter continued. "Eventually the stress leads to all kinds of problems, including heart attacks. It's science. Indisputable."

"Dr. Shegetz and now Dr. Pisher over here," Papa said. "Nu, if stress is such a killer, how did the Jews ever make it past Abraham? God tells old Abe to kill his own son, turns out He was just kidding. The world's first joke at the Jews' expense, handed down through the generations. Who would we be without stress, right, Ruth?"

Mama squeezed Franny's hand. Franny released a breath and remained intact, for now.

"If stress were a killer," Mama said, pointing at everyone in turn, "this room would be empty! Except for Dr. Pisher and Dr. Shegetz."

"Dr. Robinson," the doctor said, pointing at his name tag. "Actually."

"Leon," Papa said. "Go get your papa a hamburger and a chocolate malted."

The doctor sighed. "As a coronary patient, I can't allow you to—"

"It's my dying wish," Papa said.

"You're not dying," Franny said. "He's not dying, is he?"

"Of course not," Dr. Robinson said. "He just needs to—"

"Someday I *will* be dying," Papa said. "And on that day, you will all wish you had heeded my words. You're upsetting a man who will someday be dying."

The doctor left, muttering WASPishly, and Franny didn't need any other excuse to get out of that room. "Let's get Papa his hamburger," she said to Leon.

Leon looked up at her with a sadder, stubblier, handsomer version of her own face. He ran his fingers through his hair, and it stood straight up.

"I'm moving out," he said.

"Of what?" Franny said.

"Of the house," Leon said. He looked at Peter, who nodded encouragingly.

"Of *our* house?" Franny said dumbly. Franny never really believed one of them would actually *leave* 504, not for good. Leon was like Papa's TV—too loud, inconvenient, sometimes annoying—but just because she didn't *like* him all the time didn't mean he didn't belong there. "Where will you live?"

"With your father in his condition?" Mama said.

"You've been trying to push me out of the house for years," Leon said.

"To get *married*," Mama said. "Not just to leave, and with your poor papa so close to death."

"I feel fine," Papa said.

"Leon," Mama gasped and covered her mouth. "Are you getting married?"

Finally, the marriage guilt was heaped on someone else for a change, but Franny could hardly bring herself to enjoy it.

She had lived at 504 without Leon—during the war and for those six terrible, sickening months when they thought he was dead... But no, this would be different. He was just getting an apartment, not going missing. Franny tried to relax.

"I'm not getting married," Leon said. "The G.I. Bill will pay for me to go to college."

"That's how I'm learning about stress," Peter said, as if everyone were dying to know. "At Loyola."

Franny let out a mean little laugh at the idea of Peter Finnegan in college and caught a warning glare from Mama. "I'm sorry," she said. But then she thought of Leon collapsing at O'Hara's Grocery and laughed harder. It bubbled up from inside her like Peter's stupid Coke bottle, like Boopsie's beer. She was so tired. Peter continued to be realer than Franny could ever hope to be. Leon was helpless. Gal lived on a dirty mattress with cockroaches. Where did she hang her fancy outfits?

"And where is this lucky college, Leon?" Franny asked. "Loyola, I assume?"

"University of Miami," Leon said.

Florida? Franny stopped laughing. "That's not in Chicago."

Leon gave her a look.

"You're leaving?" Papa said.

"Why doesn't anyone listen to me?" Leon said.

He couldn't be serious. Could he? "But you hate the heat," Franny said.

"Don't worry," Mama said, patting Papa's hand. "It's summer. We have a year to get used to the idea. And just think, Isaac—Florida vacations!"

Leon shook his head. "I'm leaving in two weeks."

Tears gummed up Franny's sinuses, but she wouldn't let them out. Was he leaving because they fought so much? Was it because of—

"I tried to convince him to stay," Peter said. "I told him all about my psychology program, but he's not interested."

Oh good, just what she needed—Peter Finnegan's "help."

"Did you try reverse psychology?" Franny asked.

Peter frowned. "Where's that program?"

"My chest hurts," Papa said. "Where's Dr. Shegetz?"

"The whole neighborhood is at risk of heart attacks. Look at you, Leon. You look terrible. Everyone looks terrible," Peter said, apropos of exactly nothing. "Everything was fine until the Negroes moved in. That's when all the stress started. I'm going to do my thesis project on the psychological effects of racial integration. It isn't right that we should have to suffer because they think they can buy their way into our neighborhood. There are plenty of good neighborhoods where they can live."

Could Peter make threatening phone calls? Would he mean them?

"Knock it off, will you?" Leon said.

"I'm just saying what we're all thinking," Peter said.

"This is a hospital. We're all thinking about Papa."

And there you had it—practically a confession. Franny looked for more clues in Peter's handsome, pleasant, freckled face, perversely glad to have something to think about other than Leon leaving and Papa's health. But what exactly was she going to do about it, Franny of the grass-stained challah?

Mama quickly changed the subject, but no one else seemed to put all the pieces together. And why should they? No one else in the world, other than Franny, knew what Peter was capable of.

And there it was again—the hated memory. It bobbed about merrily, and Franny was too tired to push it away. Air would go out of her lungs but not back in. Franny couldn't move, her feet burdened by gravity. She was a sucker, a rube, for putting herself at Peter's mercy in the first place. She should have never gone out with him that night. She should have stopped him, kicked him, or, or—

They should award a Purple Head…to us girls. Franny snorted a laugh and tried to hold it in, but another snort escaped. Her shoulders shook from the effort of keeping the laughter in. It was about a thousand times better than crying, so she let it out.

Everyone stared.

"What's so funny?" Peter said. "Hello? Earth to Franny, come in, Franny." He waved his hand with the missing pinky finger in front of her face, which just made her laugh harder.

❧

"Is that car following us?" Leon asked, squinting over his shoulder.

"Watch the road," Mama said, clutching the door and the dashboard, as though worries could steer a car.

"It just seems that way," Franny said, "because you're driving like a grandmother. Why do you let him drive and not me?"

"Driving relaxes me," Leon said. "And I have a license."

"I have a license," Franny said.

"Expired doesn't count," Leon said. "It's against the law for you to drive."

"It's against the law to drive slower than a human being can walk," Franny said.

"Franny, luzzem," Mama said.

"At this rate we'll be home just in time for breakfast," Franny said.

"Ignore her," Leon said. "If you stay very still, sometimes she'll stop talking."

"Leon, be nice to your sister," Franny said. She certainly wasn't going to miss *this*. She breathed fog on the window and drew a squiggly line. "Boy," she said, "Peter really has it out for the Averys, huh?"

"Don't talk about things you don't understand," Leon said.

"I don't know," she said. "He seemed pretty angry. Like— threatening-phone-call angry."

The car swerved again as Leon whipped around to stare at Franny.

Mama lunged for the steering wheel.

"Peter just likes to talk; he doesn't mean anything by it. You're paranoid," Leon said. "Paranoia is poison."

A lot of people seemed to be doing a lot of things without meaning them. Franny wasn't sure what to make of it. Leon turned onto Euclid Avenue, and the car behind them sped past. "Speaking of paranoia," Franny said. "Looks like they just wanted to go the speed limit."

Leon parked and helped Mama out of the car. Mama stared at 504, gloomy with all the lights off, and sighed. "The house just doesn't feel the same without Papa," Mama said. "The only time we've been apart was when I was in the hospital when you kids were born. And even then, he slept on the floor next to me."

Franny and Leon bickered like children while Mama worried and Papa lay alone in a hospital bed. Franny was not cut out for taking care of people.

Leon enveloped Mama in a hug. "He'll be home soon," he said. "And then this will all be in the past."

As they hugged, Franny saw the outline of a familiar car silhou-etted across the street. The engine and headlights were off, but a shadow moved inside. It was Lottie, who else?

Franny followed Leon and Mama inside, feeling watched, wishing there were more locks to lock behind her, even as her heart pumped in anticipation.

                                         ❧

Franny was trying to read her dog-eared copy of *Robinson Crusoe* to calm herself when something clinked against her bedroom window. Then another clink and another and then they came fast and sharp—*rat-tat-tat* like a tommy gun. Franny laid her book on the bed and opened the window. A pebble caught her on the forehead.

Lottie wore a dark trench coat with the collar pulled up and a black fedora. She motioned for Franny to come downstairs.

"No," Franny whispered. "Go away."

Lottie shrugged, moved over to the adjacent window—Leon's—and picked up a handful of pebbles. She poised her arm as if to throw them, and Franny could imagine Lottie's delicate eyebrows raised in challenge. She would do it. The thought of unrolling the long tongue of lies to explain Lottie's existence was more than Franny could bear. For the sake of family, she would have to face Lottie.

She yanked on a robe over her pajamas and crept down the stairs, avoiding the squeaky spots. Her heart *whoosh*ed in her ears as she opened the front door.

"Nice robe, Granny," Lottie said.

"What do you want?"

"Aren't you going to invite me in?"

Franny turned to leave, and Lottie caught her arm. "Okay, okay, I'm sorry. I overreacted. But can you blame me?"

"You came here to ask if I blame you? Because I have a lot to say about—"

"No," Lottie said. She squared her shoulders. "I'm willing to let you make it up to me."

Franny went to close the door. "Good night, Lottie."

Lottie stuck out her foot. "Despite all evidence to the contrary, I still think you might have something special. I'm here to give you another chance."

"It's too late," Franny said. "I'm done with all that."

Lottie grabbed her and pressed soft lips to Franny's, the slick of her lipstick rubbing off. Franny's heart zinged through her whole body. A grin slid up Lottie's face. "You don't seem done."

"Are you crazy?" Franny wiped her mouth and left a red streak. She leaned out the doorway and looked up at Leon's window. Had the curtains moved? "This is my house. My family lives here. What if somebody sees?"

"I came all the way out here to grovel, and you won't even hear me out?"

Tears glistened on Lottie's cheeks. Franny had never seen her cry. Or grovel. Was she faking it? Franny tucked her robe tightly around her. "Thirty seconds. Then I slam the door in your face."

"Thank you. Believe it or not, I just want what's best for you girls," Lottie said, wiping her cheeks. "I really thought television comedy was a fad. Girls want to get out of their homes, not be stuck in them. Why squint at a tiny man slipping on a banana peel when you can experience real-life Boopsie Baxter? The boob tube is winning, and Showstoppers are losing. But I'm not ready to give up. We can't give up. Peggy, sometimes I lose my temper, but tomorrow is an important show. Maybe the most important in Blue Moon history." Lottie shook her head. "Look, I didn't want to tell you, but—"

"I know. Ed's coming," Franny said. "And you need me to go up, or he'll shut you down."

Franny didn't know what response she expected. Shock? Horror? Words like sharpened daggers? Instead, Lottie laughed. "Why, that lousy eavesdropping deviant. Fine, smart guy. Yes. I need you there because Ed is coming and he's expecting my new prodigy, Peggy Blake, whom I molded like Eve from my own funny bone."

Had that victory come a little *too* easy? Lottie could still be toying with her. Franny glanced up at Leon's window again. It was open; that's why the curtains were moving. Maybe she really was paranoid. Leon slept like the dead, unless he was having an episode, in which case he would be shouting so loudly, he wouldn't hear them anyway.

Franny could hold her own with Lottie. And anyway, what was thirty more seconds? She held a finger to her lips then moved them off the porch to the edge of the vacant lot so they wouldn't be overheard, just to be safe. The dead elm creaked in the light breeze.

"Even if I agreed, your plan's kaput before it's even started," Franny said. "No Showstopper, remember?"

"That's the beauty of it," Lottie said. "Ed's a man. Ain't a man in the whole world who can feel a Showstopper. Remember?"

Franny rolled her eyes. "Yes, obviously I remember, but—"

Lottie waved away her *but*. "He just has to believe that everyone else can feel it. I'll tell the book clubs your Showstopper feels like eating the Palmer House brownie…all the pleasure, none of the calories. They'll practically drool over the phone."

"That's all it takes?"

Lottie shrugged modestly. "The book clubs will gab about it—everyone's dying to know what you can do—and bam, you've got yourself a Showstopper. The brain is a powerful organ, very suggestible."

If a fake Showstopper could feel just like a real one, then what was the difference? Where was the magic?

"Faking a Showstopper to prove comedy has value. No irony there."

"Girls have to fake a lot of things to prove their worth. But if you come to the Blue Moon tomorrow—" Lottie let the promise dangle like a forkful of fettucine. Franny didn't bite. "Or it could end right here," she said, "both of us sore losers for no reason."

Was that a bottle of glycerin tucked up Lottie's sleeve? Franny never had to wonder if Mama and Papa or even Leon's tears were real. If Papa had faked a heart attack or Leon lied about an episode.

"Pass," Franny said.

Lottie looked genuinely surprised. "It's a teensy little white lie, a shuffle, ball, change around the truth. You've told worse in the past week."

"Good night, Lottie." Franny turned away, but Lottie was quicker, suddenly blocking her path.

"Okay, you got me," Lottie said. She took a deep breath. "I'm scared. The Blue Moon is my only escape; it's my whole world. Ed gets so angry… Without the club, I'm stuck with him." Lottie lowered herself onto her knees, right there on the grass Franny needed to mow, her hands clasped in prayer. "Not everyone gets to see Lottie Marcone grovel, you lucky duck. Please, come back." Tears streamed down her cheeks, and this time they looked alarmingly real.

The bruises, the split lip, the bravado…

I felt sorry for you. So timid for such a big girl.

"Sorry, Lottie," Franny said, pulling her up. "You're on your own."

❦

"Wow," Franny said, embracing Mary Kate, who wore a pretty, new flowered sundress from Hawaii. "You're so tan!"

"*Freckled* is more like it," Mary Kate said, patting her cheeks. "All the powder in the world can't cover this up. You would not believe the beaches in Hawaii. You really must go there sometime. Do you want a tour?"

Mary Kate and Walter had moved into a new housing development on the other side of town—street after street of gleaming white houses, all with new aluminum siding, no old-fashioned brick or wood in sight. It was within walking distance of her childhood home, but somehow it felt like a different world. Franny tried to feel like part of this world, tried to imagine herself in Mary Kate's place.

Mary Kate flitted like a dolphin, while Franny followed dumpily in her wake. She caressed their brand-new refrigerator, opened and closed the oven door like a magic cabinet she was about to disappear into.

"It only has three bedrooms," she said apologetically, "which isn't enough for a big family like Walter wants, but it's only a starter home. That's what I keep telling myself."

"Wow," Franny said for the thousandth time. She felt like a child next to Mary Kate's womanliness. Like she might never catch up.

"Now tell me all the gossip I missed. I heard you're going with Michael Berman?" Mary Kate asked, sitting on the front porch swing and arranging her dress prettily around her. She had placed a sweaty pitcher of lemonade on the table next to them before Franny had even arrived. She patted the swing, and Franny sat, grimacing as it squeaked under her weight.

"Oh, I don't know," Franny said. "We'll see."

"You're blushing!" Mary Kate said, poking her cheek. "If you marry Michael Berman, you could move out here, and we could be neighbors again. Our children could play together. Wouldn't that be wonderful?"

Franny thought seriously about leaping off the porch and running away at top speed. "That does sound wonderful," she said.

Would it be so bad? A nice new house, a wealthy husband, friends and children and neighbors? That was what people wanted. What else was there?

"I'm pregnant," Mary Kate said.

Franny turned to Mary Kate's profile. She stared out onto her impeccably manicured, bright green lawn. She had no particular expression on her face. "Mazel tov?" Franny tried.

Mary Kate burst into tears. There was nobody to hear her except Franny. Walter was at work. Most of the homes were so new that no one lived in them yet. All this tidiness and open space and shiny modernity suddenly felt hollow as a grave. Mary Kate had just returned from a monthlong honeymoon and was expected to dive headfirst into this new life. But maybe, her eyes revealed, just maybe, it was all a mistake. Her days stretched out endlessly, desolately. She had too much and too little at the same time. Franny rubbed Mary Kate's bare shoulders to keep her hands from shaking.

"Oh, Mary Kate, it's all right, it's going to be all right." Was it? "I don't live far away, and your family doesn't live far either. We can still—"

"Of course, it's going to be all right, silly," Mary Kate said brightly, dabbing her eyes. "It's better than all right. It's what I've always wanted."

Mr. Finnegan's car pulled up in the black driveway.

"And there's Daddy!" Mary Kate waved at the car so hard, her whole body shook.

"Hey, pumpkin," he said. "Or should I say *aloha* and… How do you say *pumpkin* in Hawaii?"

Mary Kate laughed loud and long, even though it wasn't funny. Franny attempted a moral-support chuckle.

Mr. Finnegan surveyed the neighborhood from the driveway and let out a contented sigh. "So quiet. So *peaceful* here. Maybe Mommy and I should move in next door, huh?" He smiled, lumbering toward them like Frankenstein's monster with his arms out for a hug.

"Oh shoot, I have to go," Franny said, evading him. "I just realized I'm late."

CHAPTER TWELVE

LOTTIE SAT AT THE U-SHAPED BOOTH—HER U-BOAT, ANDY called it, not that Franny cared what Andy called anything anymore—arms folded tight around herself, a barnacle attached to the man-size battleship to her left. A human interpretation of a stack of alphabet blocks. Ed "Fingers" Marcone.

Lottie's whole posture changed when she saw Franny. She brightened and sat up straight, and Franny felt a little stab of guilt to see relief wash over Lottie's face. She started to stand but stopped under the weight of Ed's hand.

Instead, Ed peeled himself out of the booth and limped over to Franny, who stood stiffly by the door. He grabbed her hand and shook it vigorously. He had at least twenty years on Lottie and was missing a thumb, which was ironic and also begged questions Franny didn't want answers to. The nub wiggled suggestively across the top of her hand like a tadpole.

"The mysterious Peggy Blake. Pleased to meet you," he said in a profound Southside accent. He grinned around a cigarillo. She hadn't expected Ed "Fingers" Marcone to be quite so affable.

"Likewise," she said, despite everything.

"You're tall," he said. "You funny?"

"I hope so," Franny said.

"Gotta do better than that," Ed said. He let go of her hand, and she tried not to rub the part where his thumb nub had been. "Lottie here tells me you've got a hell of a, what's it called, Showstopper. What was it? All the pleasure, none of the calories. Can't feel 'em myself, sounds like a lot of hocus-pocus to me, but if it puts butts in seats, you could be a devil worshipper for all I care. Have a drink. Enid!" he shouted, pointing at Franny. "Whiskey sour for the Heeb."

Ed steered her, a hand on her back, limping them back to Lottie. Lottie had that sun-behind-a-cloud look to her, trying and failing to look dim.

"You know my wife," Ed said. "Biblically, I assume." His grip tightened on Franny's sweaty lower back.

"Leave her alone, Ed."

"Hey, easy there. I'm just getting to know the girl," Ed said. He surveyed the room like he owned it, which he did. "Would you look at that. Didn't know comedy could still rake in the dough."

Clearly no one had told him about the book clubs' hired laughter. Lottie winked at Franny. Was she enjoying this?

"Nobody's got business sense like my Loretta. Even when she's milking me dry with this dump. I knew it when she was shaking her titties all over Times Square."

"Turn down the charm, Casanova," Lottie said.

Ed leaned across the table and patted her cheek, hard. "See,

Lottie and me, we've got a modern marriage. She gives me freedom, and I pretend I don't know she's a raging bull dyke."

Franny didn't know where to look; the ceiling seemed as good a place as any. There was that awful word again. If that's what Lottie was, what did it make Franny?

Gal was waving frantically at her from the periphery. Andy sat across from her, her back to Franny. No Hal anywhere. Surely not the bourbonic plague again? Was it Franny's fault? She ached to think of Hal, drunk and giggling, after Franny failed to conjure her Showstopper, right after Andy betrayed her to Lottie. Hal had always been supportive, in her way. Terrifying but supportive.

Franny pretended not to see Gal, which was ridiculous, given her exaggerated arm waving and the fact that she was shouting, "Hey, Peggy, over here!"

"That's funny, Ed." Lottie's voice snapped Franny like a rubber band. "Considering you don't know the first thing about what I like in bed."

Even facing Benedict Andy might be preferable to standing here, in the cross fire of the world's most dangerous lover's quarrel. A pistol bulged at the ankle of Ed's limping leg, matching the dainty der-ringer at Lottie's. So many guns on so many ankles; it didn't even surprise Franny anymore, which was the most surprising thing.

"Whiskey sour?" Enid said tentatively.

Ed squinted at her like he'd never seen her before in his life then pulled a dinner roll–sized lump of dollar bills from his pocket and flipped a few at her. "First round's on me, sheeny," Ed said. "Don't screw up."

"Thanks," Franny said, taking the drink.

"Screw up? Fat chance. Peggy's got a great new joke you're going to flip over," Lottie said. She pointed at Franny. "Start with that one."

Franny tried to subtly shake her head. Was Lottie losing her nerve already? It was too late to rearrange her whole set, especially on such an important night.

"That's my closer," Franny said.

"Well, make it your opener," Lottie said.

What could she do? At least this way she'd get the Peter joke out of the way first. Franny stood dumbly, clutching her drink. Even when she thought she was calling the shots, there was Lottie, changing the rules.

"Usually, when a man buys you a drink, you talk to him for a couple two-tree minutes," Ed said. "Have a seat."

Franny lowered herself into the booth, and Ed did not move over to accommodate, so she squeezed right up next to him as he examined her like a surgeon.

"So," Ed said. "What's your real name, Peggy Blake?"

"No prying," Lottie said.

"Who's prying? I just want to know who works for me, like everyone else."

"She doesn't work for you; she works for me."

"Oh, so you're the one who forks over the cash to keep this dump open?"

"Is one of your legs longer than the other?" Franny asked, instead of keeping her damn mouth shut. "I had an uncle with two different-sized legs, and he had to wear one shoe with a three-inch sole just to walk normal."

"Peggy is the master of the nervous joke," Lottie said.

"Didn't sound like a joke to me," Ed said.

"The limp," Franny said, as though the lack of that information was the problem. "I was just wondering."

Ed squinted piggily at her then broke into another disarming grin. "Beretta," he said, slapping his behind. "Took a nine-millimeter right in the ass."

"You're kidding," Franny said.

"That I am not. Spent a month in a field hospital outside Rome. They picked around inside me, told me they couldn't get it out without severing the whatsit, femoral artery, then they shipped me right back out to the front, to fight my mother's people." He picked up his whiskey shot, downed it, motioned to Enid for another.

"I'm sorry," Franny said.

"Don't be sorry," Ed said. "Be funny."

∽◌∾

"And now, please welcome the greenhorn of the Blue Moon... Peggy Blake!"

The room whistled and clapped, whipping up a whirlwind of perfume and smoke and whiskey that Franny would forever associate with the Blue Moon. There was no reason to be nervous; Lottie had fixed the show like a boxing match. So what if she didn't have a real Showstopper? She could knock them out even if she made up a bunch of rotten punch lines right there on the spot, even if she stood up there and read the back of a cereal box. She should feel relieved. There was no way to fail.

Except, Ed seemed like the sort of guy who could smell a scheme, the sort of guy who sniffed out schemes for a living. Sweat pricked Franny's temples. She ran over her rearranged set in her head one more time.

Gal clapped into the microphone and tried to shake Franny's hand, mouthed something that Franny didn't catch and didn't want to. Franny swerved around Gal to yank the microphone out of its stand, and feedback yowled. Hands were clapped over ears instead of together, and just like that, the room was against her.

Before Franny could try to turn things around, before she could utter even a single word, Lottie's angry voice boomed through the club.

"Bring that tramp one step closer, and I'll call the cops on you myself."

Lottie's palms pressed to the table, her small body bent forward at a dangerous angle, while Ed stood in front of her U-boat, arm wrapped around a willowy bottle blond in a low-cut dress. The barometer of her cleavage showed her to be several years older than Lottie. Didn't men usually pick younger women? The blond clomped like a nervous horse, but Ed and Lottie argued like they were the only people in the room.

"The only one making a scene is you," Ed said. "This is my club, and Varla can sit in this booth if I say so."

Franny whispered, "That's Varla?" forgetting she had a microphone pressed to her lips.

Ed pointed up at her. "Does she tell jokes or just eavesdrop?"

"Maybe if you'd shut your yap for once," Lottie said, "you might find out."

Ed slapped Lottie, knocking her backward, sending her sliding down the seat under the table. He rolled up his shirtsleeves and was about to yank Lottie off the floor to do it again. Varla clutched his bicep, tried to drag him away. He pushed her, hard, and she tottered backward on her high heels, toppling over and ripping her dress. The room was a breathless mausoleum. Fear seeped into every crevice, girls froze like deer who had faced this hunter before, in another forest, in another life. This was not what the Blue Moon was about. Franny despaired, her mouth glued together.

Ed grabbed the collar of Lottie's dress and yanked her out of the booth.

"You're embarrassing me," he said, quietly menacing. He was going to hit her again. Lottie cringed. In that moment, Franny knew she had really seen Lottie, maybe for the first time. It made her sick, and it made her mad. Lottie had asked for her help, and help was what Franny would give.

Franny had the microphone; she had the authority. If tonight was the last time a comedian would ever be allowed onstage at the Blue Moon, then that comedian was going to be Peggy Blake. And she would conjure a Showstopper, a real one.

"Being a kid is a cakewalk compared to becoming a woman, isn't it?" Franny said, voice wavering in the microphone. She planted her feet firmly and tried not to fall over. Faces turned to her. Franny was the last glass of water in a thirsty world. "The criteria for womanhood are a little different than we've been led to believe. It's not boobs, or marriage, or the first time a man steals your jokes—"

The room found its voice, tried laughing.

"—it's when a man thinks he can take whatever he wants from you."

Fear swallowed the laughter. *Stay with me*, Franny thought. *No way out but through.*

"My twenty-first birthday, a family 'friend' decided to make a woman out of me. He had his finger blown off in the war—but by the end of the night, I wished he had lost a different appendage. Sadly, they don't call him *Peter* for nothing."

Even Ed's pause was violent—his fist crumpling Lottie's collar, his face letting Franny know she was next. But inside Franny, the match had already been scraped, a tender yellow light wavered.

"Forget the Purple Heart," Franny said. "An injury like that, we should award a Purple Head. To us girls."

Laughter poured like gasoline, and the flame inside Franny roiled through her guts, up her gullet, burst out of her mouth, and disappeared into the darkness.

The joke was an incantation to the universe, a prayer for mercy. The first ancient fire that made human life possible. It burned away something Franny didn't need, and she felt light as meringue. She let go the microphone stand. So what if she floated away? *Float away, Franny, float away.*

Throughout the club, girls closed their eyes and licked their lips, raised imaginary spoons to their mouths, enjoying—the famous Palmer House brownie, guilt-free.

So that was that. Franny wasn't a comedian. She was a phony.

She waited for the violence that Ed's fist promised. He vibrated like the world's angriest statue—his face red then purple. He was going to pummel Lottie and then march up onstage and pummel her, and Mama would have to go to the hospital twice in two days.

A shrill hyena cackle filled the bar, and it took Franny a moment to realize it was coming out of Ed. Ed "Fingers" Marcone was laughing. He dropped Lottie, clutched his gut with his fist, stumbled around, and nearly toppled Varla again in her sky-high heels.

"Purple Head," he said. "Because it's his johnson!" He slapped Varla's arm and leaned on the bar to support himself. His laughter triggered another round of laughter, this time the manic whoops of relief. Franny imagined a faint yellow aura around Ed, like soft candlelight. She blinked, and it was gone.

His laughter died down, and he wiped tears from his eyes, picked Lottie off the floor, motioned for Enid the bartender.

"Ice!" Ed cried. "Or a slab of meat if you don't got ice. Lottie, honey, are you all right? I am so sorry, baby. I had no right to raise my fist in anger to you. Sometimes, I just feel threatened by your strength of character…so really, I should be punching myself! Ha! Please, sit, doll. Put some ice on that kisser. Enid! Refill her martini."

Lottie eyed him curiously, working her jaw to make sure it wasn't broken. "Are you feeling all right, Ed?"

Ed laughed and did a little hopping dance, the dance of a man who did not have a nine-millimeter shell in his tuchus, which should have surprised Franny but didn't. "I feel terrific," he said. "Top of the world."

Not a pair of eyes was looking at Franny. Ed sucked the air out of the room and inflated himself, stole her authority, marooned her onstage like Robinson Crusoe. How was it possible to feel abandoned and on display at the same time?

"You're dancing," Varla said. "With both legs."

"I feel like a million bucks. Two million bucks! Make that three martinis, Enid, sweetheart. Do you mind, Lottie, if Varla sits with us? Varla, why are you crying?"

"You scared me," Varla said.

"Then I owe you an apology as well. You are a sweet girl who couldn't hurt a fly. I, meanwhile, am a cad and a monster."

"You *could* make it up to me," Lottie said. "With the Blue Moon."

"Say no more," Ed said, tapping her nose affectionately. "I'm going to get the deed to the Blue Moon right now, and we're going to transfer it to you."

"Ed, honey." Varla petted his sleeve. "What's happening? What gives?"

"Drinks on me," Ed said. "We'll toast! Long live Lottie, queen of the Blue Moon!"

The room erupted into cheers, which devolved into loud gossiping. Ed King-Konged Varla out the door as she hollered for him to put her down. And then they were gone.

Meanwhile, Franny had only told one measly joke. The one joke, in fact, that Lottie had *specifically* asked her to tell.

And, speaking of Lottie, she wasn't shushing anyone or threatening to toss them to the curb. No, she was draped over the bar, giggling with Enid.

A piece clicked, a gear turned, thickheaded Franny finally got it. She watched herself walk offstage, where Gal intercepted her.

"Can you believe it? We did it! We saved the Blue Moon! Golly, I wish Hal were here to celebrate. Do you know where she is? Peggy?" But Franny brushed past her, leaned on the bar next to Lottie.

"Oh, are you done already?" Lottie said, looking at Enid's watch.

"People are talking over me."

"Don't sweat it," Lottie said. "You did great, kid, here, have a drink."

Franny cocked her head. "Very unlike you, not to care if people are talking during a show."

"Can't you just be happy for me—for us?" Lottie's eyes glittered, but not with tears this time.

"I see," Franny said. She did see, saw through Lottie like an X-ray. "Well, you got what you wanted. You don't need me anymore."

Lottie was the first to look away. She pretended it was to light a cigarette.

"You can't quit," Lottie said, blowing smoke. "What are you going to do, marry Michael Boreman?"

"I'm not quitting," Franny said. "I'm just quitting you." She walked out of the Blue Moon, feeling Lottie's eyes burn a hole in her back. Lottie would never grovel twice, and why should she? She won. Franny hadn't even realized they were playing a game. A snaky feeling constricted her gut. No one to turn to now; no one left to confide in. She was on her own.

Franny had conjured a Showstopper all right. Problem was, it only worked on men.

CHAPTER THIRTEEN

THE SEEDY SECTION OF RUSH STREET WAS CRAMMED WITH dingy burlesque theaters, rat-infested diners, and nightclubs owned by gangsters who made Ed Marcone look like Winston Churchill. Franny shook off a sheet of newspaper that had plastered itself to her shin and lowered the wool cap over eyes, tucking her hair up inside it. She had managed to sneak out of the house with a pair of Papa's work pants and a ratty old shirt she'd found in the laundry hamper. They had smudges of grease on the knees and elbows, were frayed at the collar and cuffs, and were tight at the hips and huge at the shoulders. But it was hard to look dapper in a hurry, and really, all Franny had to do to get onstage was look convincingly manly inside a hazy, dark nightclub. She was not convinced she had achieved even that. Franny squinted up at the glowing marquees—the Downtown Lounge, the Velvet Swing, the Happy Camper.

Who knew the Blue Moon had become so rare? Franny almost felt sorry for Lottie then got over it.

She had called every number in the Yellow Pages—every single comedy club listing was out of date. Closed, condemned, turned into a restaurant, coffeehouse, cocktail lounge. Was the Blue Moon really the last? Franny had been worried about sweet-talking the clubs into a special men's-only night, but there was no one to sweet-talk. Only place left do live comedy was Rush Street. Not exactly ideal. Franny had heard of these places, Lottie loved to tell the amateurs who bombed that they'd end up at one of these clubs as "spicy entertainment"—the girls usually ran out in tears.

The Rush Street clubs were run by men, populated by men, and advertised a hybrid smorgasbord of barely disguised gambling, burlesque dancers, lewd parody songs, and chintzy slapstick. All washed-up male comedians from before the war who couldn't get it into their thick skulls that stand-up moved on without them. *Very* occasionally, mostly during the war, you'd find one of them in a duo with a comedian trying to get her big break, but no one ever got her big break at clubs like these.

Franny consoled herself that she wasn't looking for a big break, not really. She was so tired of squeezing herself into things that didn't fit, just to make everyone else feel okay. *We were only trying to help*, she could hear Gal say.

"Mayday, mayday, Gal, stop helping," Franny murmured, mulling over which neon sign looked the most promising.

Okay, twist her arm, she'd love a second chance for a first day at the Blue Moon, to laugh with the girls and Hal, make jokes and eat Francheezies. Back when things were uncomplicated and anything could happen. She missed them, even Andy. A *little*. But were things ever uncomplicated? Didn't matter. The only person who could help

Franny was Franny. She tried to stop slouching, a bad habit. Time to focus on Franny for once.

What was her Showstopper exactly? That's what she was here to find out. Infamous gangster and amputator Ed "Fingers" Marcone could suddenly dance, his niceness like a pleasant truth serum, all because of a joke Franny told. What did it mean?

Franny fidgeted with her cap and decided on the Velvet Swing, tried not to consider why the door handle was sticky.

Inside, a burlesque show was in full swing onstage—as in, three girls in spangled panties were swinging their breasts in unison. Men stretched across tables, tossing change on the stage, shouting and hooting around their cigars. There was otherwise not a single girl in the room. A blue fog hung low, and the place stank of chewed cigars and sweat and male bodies. Franny's throat locked up, and she was about to turn around and walk back out the door, when a cocktail waitress in a getup not much demurer than the burlesque dancers' sidled up to her, looked her up and down.

"We got room for a girl in the five-o'clock show if you don't mind waiting," she said. "One of the dancers is puking her guts out in the alley. Pays two bucks, plus tips—not a bad gig. You in?"

"I, um," Franny said, trying to deepen her voice. She fixated on one burlesque dancer who was now shimmying center stage and leaning over, pressing her tasseled breasts into the face of a man whose tie was flung over his shoulder. "I think you're mistaken. I'm a man?"

The waitress giggle snorted. "Oh sure," she said. "And I'm Doris Day. Ain't nothing to be ashamed of. Girl's gotta eat." She looked Franny up and down, narrowed her eyes. "You ain't in here looking for your husband, are you? That is the one thing Sy don't tolerate. This is a private club." She stuck out her chin, and Franny suddenly saw a resemblance between her and Mary Kate and how in a slightly different life they might all be cocktail waitresses in a burlesque bar.

"I'm a comedian," Franny said. "I was hoping I might be able to do a set this afternoon?"

The girl's eyes widened. "Why didn't you say so? Come on in. We don't get a lot of solo lady comedians in here," she said.

"Between you and me, I'm a man comedian," Franny said, "remember?"

"Oh *right*." The waitress winked hugely and pushed through a knot of men leaning against the bar, and as she passed through, they stroked and patted and grabbed at her. Franny was horrified, but the waitress didn't even seem to notice. Then they turned their attention to Franny, who froze.

"What do we have here?" one of the men said. "Maybe we oughta unwrap the present to see what's inside."

The cocktail waitress whipped around. "If you touch her," she said, "I will punch your pecker inside out."

They all laughed mockingly, but not one of them took the chance. Franny was impressed.

"She ain't got nothing worth grabbing anyway," one muttered into his beer.

Franny walked through the scrum of men unmolested. "Who knew I was so ladylike?" she said, smoothing Papa's shirt. "It worked for Katharine Hepburn in *Sylvia Scarlett*."

"Movies ain't real life," the cocktail waitress said solemnly. Franny was about to retort with something smart, when the waitress laid a hand on her arm. "Your outside don't match your inside," she said. "Anybody can see that, even these jokers. Being a man ain't about playing dress-up. Or being a girl, for that matter." She nodded at her own getup and shrugged. "But sometimes a girl gotta dress up like a girl just to get paid, know what I mean?"

"Don't have to dress like a girl to get grabbed, apparently," Franny said, adjusting her shirtsleeves.

"No, they'll do that for free."

Franny tried to feel excited about the Velvet Swing, even a tiny crumb of the thrill she felt at the Empire Room or the Blue Moon. She had to make the best of it. She had to come up with just one thing that was good about the place.

The cocktail waitress seemed nice.

A man walked by, vomited into his own hand, shook it out onto the floor, wiped his pants, and took a swig of whiskey, all while walking toward the bathroom. It took all of Franny's energy not to run away screaming. Okay, so she would just scrub her skin with lye every time she left the joint. There were worse things, right?

Yes, there were worse things. The Velvet Swing may have been filthy on the outside, but the Blue Moon was rotten to the core. At least here she could spot the horrors across the room, instead of them sneaking up on her, dressed like friends.

"Is this what men are like on their day off?" Franny asked.

"This is what men are like, period," the waitress said. "Ain't you never met one before?" She looked at Franny with such curiosity, like maybe Franny really had never met a man before, that Franny started laughing. It felt good. All this comedy, but when was the last time she really laughed?

They stood in front of a tiny round table at the back corner of the club, occupied by a man like a square peg, a chewed-up cigar plugged into his face.

"Hey, Sy," the waitress said. "I got a girl comedian here who wants to do a set today."

"Just *comedian* is fine, actually," Franny said.

"Why's she dressed like that?" Sy said. "Where's her partner?"

"She ain't got one," the waitress said. "Or at least, I don't think so. You got a partner?"

"Just me," Franny said.

"She play the piano? Take off her clothes?" He looked Franny up and down quizzically. Was he talking to the waitress or to Franny?

"I tell jokes."

"Jokes, huh?"

"Yes, a regular comedian, telling jokes."

"Regular girl comedians got acts," Sy said. "They sing songs, they take off their clothes. This ain't the university glee club."

He looked like he should have a hand full of rings, but he did not. Franny caught a glimpse of a gold Star of David peeking out of a gnarl of chest hair.

"Bist a yid?" she asked.

He raised his eyebrows. "I've clobbered guys for less than that."

"I'm not a guy," she said.

"Coulda fooled me."

Well, which was it? "I'm a comedian. And I'll make your room laugh."

"You won't even take your top off?"

Franny sighed. Why was she wasting her time here? There were a hundred clubs all up and down Rush…but the thought of going through this again and again, perhaps without a protective waitress, exhausted her.

"A girl comedian," Sy mused. "All right. You got three minutes, between, uh, the magician and the headliner we got tonight. What's his name—Henry the Great Ape."

"Darwin fan?" Franny asked.

"*Henry*. You deaf?"

"No, his—"

"I can't pay you. But like I said, take your top off, and you might get—"

"Not happening."

"Suit yourself. Name?"

Franny almost used her stage name but stopped herself. Peggy Blake was Lottie's creation.

"Franny Steinberg."

"Kid, you need a manager. That is a rotten name."

"It's the one I came with."

Sy shrugged. "Okay—Franny Steinberg," he said in an exaggerated Yiddish accent. Why did everyone feel the need to do that? "You're on at four thirty-five. Don't be late, or we'll whack your kneecaps." He erupted into laughter at this, shaking his head. "Just kidding, what do you think I am, one of them greasy-haired Wops? I got a family. I'm a religious man." He winked, waggled his eyebrows like Ed Marcone.

"Okay, then," Franny said. "Point me to the ladies' room."

"Come with me," the waitress said. "There's no ladies' room, but the girls all get ready back here."

Back here was a curtained-off area next to the garbage chute, about the size of a fingernail, with a clothes rack on wheels, a hand mirror dangling from the ceiling, and a toilet sitting in the middle of the floor. "I'll keep watch," she said in a whisper. "We all watch for each other when we're getting ready, otherwise Sy or some drunk bastard will come back and try to get a glimpse of us in a state of dishabille."

Franny cocked her head at this odd use of French.

"I'm Margie, by the way." The waitress stuck out her hand. "Can't wait to see your set. I bet you have a Showstopper. What is it? No, don't tell me. I want it to be a surprise." She grinned so big and so hopefully that Franny wished, again, that she had a regular Showstopper Margie might enjoy. "We're not supposed to talk about 'em here," Margie whispered. "Just the word *Showstopper* makes Sy furious, but I've always wanted to feel one."

"Thanks for your help," Franny said, guts twisting at this bit of news. She ignored the pain.

Margie tugged on the curtain so it slid across the rope hanging from the ceiling. "Girls gotta take care of each other, don't we?" she said. "Won't nobody else do it."

"You should go to the Blue Moon," Franny said. "All the comedians have Showstoppers there. You won't believe some of the things they make you feel."

Margie's eyes got wide as saucers. "Oh, I couldn't," she said. "A classy place like that?"

⚬～⚬

The men at the Velvet Swing hooted and stomped their feet, beer sloshing over tables and stage and floor. The girl onstage gave one last grinning twirl then stooped to pick up her clothes and peel coins off the sticky, beery stage. Someone hurled another quarter and yelled, "Bull's-eye!" when it struck her in the rear.

You didn't have to be Einstein to see why Lottie refused to have men at the Blue Moon. Would girls have continued to try out their vulnerable new material on that stage? Would housewives let loose if the Blue Moon let in men, even one man?

Would Franny ever have ended up there in her terrible bridesmaid dress, seeking refuge?

But if Franny's Showstopper could fill the room with happy, pleasant dancing men—showering each other with drinks and compliments—that couldn't be so bad. Even Sy might be impressed.

"And now," Sy said, same chewed-up cigar between his fingers as he read his notes. "Please welcome girl comedian Franny Steinberg."

A couple drunken hoots and claps as Franny climbed up onstage. One *hubba-hubba* and one hopeful *take your top off* from an elderly man waving a one-dollar bill. Then the idea caught on. More men started chanting, "Take your top off," louder and louder. Franny took a deep breath. All she had to do was get them laughing. Just one laugh.

But they wouldn't stop shouting long enough for her to squeeze a single word in. Franny's authority slipped through her fingers. Her three minutes ticked down to two.

Franny yanked the microphone out of its stand, and the feedback shut the men up for a blessed second. She blurted the first thing she could think of, just to catch their attention. "If someone asked you to draw your own johnson...blindfolded... could you do it?" She walked to the edge of the stage, hoping they couldn't see her legs shaking, pointed to a man in the front row. "Could you?"

He shrugged. "Sure. Why, you wanna see it?"

The crowd guffawed.

"Nah," Franny said, "I didn't bring my magnifying glass."

Silence. The grandpa with the dollar bill waved the dollar bill around.

"Take your top off!" he said.

"Yeah! Take your top off!"

"You guys want me to take my top off?" she said.

Hoots, hollers, tumblers slammed on tables. Things were getting out of hand, or maybe this was just a normal Sunday afternoon. It wasn't the authority she was accustomed to, more like driving a car without brakes. But Franny wasn't about to let them get the last laugh. She clung to the steering wheel and hit the gas.

"You really want me to take my top off?" She moved her fingers to her top button and heard them all lean forward.

"Then you take your pants off," she said. "If every man in this bar takes his pants off, I'll take my top off."

Like snuffing a candle, the men fell silent. And, in the tension of that moment, Franny felt like a million bucks. Boy, had she got the hecklers good. And she still had a minute and a half to launch into her set and make them laugh. Now or never. If she could win over this room, she could do anything.

Then her blouse was wet. Something splashed her cheek. The men were throwing their drinks at her. She ducked to avoid getting a rocks glass to the head. She was dripping with whiskey. They chanted, "Take your top off," at her as whiskey slipped down her blouse and soaked through her undergarments, and then Sy hopped up onstage quicker than one might think for someone whose lungs were mostly cigar smoke, and he took the mic from her.

"Thank you very much, uh, Franny," he said, motioning with his head to get her offstage. "That was Franny Steinberg, everybody, and now let's get ready for a little spicy entertainment, my treat. A little palate cleanser, if you know what I mean."

The men cheered and hooted. Someone set up a record player to play some brassy burlesque tracks. Franny grabbed a dish towel Margie handed her and began blotting her hair. Now what—another club on the block, another hostile room?

"Well, I thought you were terrific," Margie said. "I would have listened to more."

"Great," Franny scoffed. "They didn't let me get through a single punch line."

"Oh, that's all right. They never listen to anyone, not even Henry the Great Ape."

Franny wrinkled her nose. And Sy thought her name was bad.

"But he's the one with the microphone, so he just keeps on

going, like they ain't even there. I think," Margie said, "I think you should keep going."

Franny stared at her open, hopeful face.

If this Henry the Great Ape could make it through a set, then so could Franny Steinberg. She handed the towel back to Margie like a boxing coach and hopped onstage, grabbed the microphone from Sy.

"No, kid, you're done here," he said.

"You said I have three minutes. I got one left."

The crowd booed, but Sy motioned for the music to cut out. "Your funeral."

Franny stood wide-legged onstage, her clothes clammy in the close heat of the dingy bar. She was humiliated, she was angry, she was sticky and wearing a middle-aged plumber's greasy getup. Might as well throw it all out there. There was one joke from her set that she would never dare tell at the Blue Moon. That she had never dared say out loud, ever. She had to muster every last bit of anger to get her mouth to move.

"War is a rotten thing," she said. She flipped the microphone cord over her foot and walked to the front of the stage. "They say war puts hair on your chest, makes you a man. But my brother…well, he did it backward. He went to war a man and came back a boy. The other day, Mama catches him playing with toy soldiers and wearing a diaper, if you can believe that. 'What do you think you're doing?' she says. 'Playing war,' he says. Next thing you know, he squats over the soldiers in his diaper and says, 'Bombs away!'"

Silence. No heckling, no airborne booze. Was it too late to take her top off? The light flickered inside Franny, heat gathering momentum, crawling up her belly. The silence pulled tight as a rubber band; the flames stuck in her throat like a swallowed cigarette. She had offended them—this audience of men who vomited into their own hands.

She shouldn't have told the joke. She shouldn't have *written* the joke. But it was done; it was out in the world, and she couldn't take it back. The only consolation was that Leon hadn't been here to see it.

Sweat trickled down her neck. The light inside her wasn't real—it was a metaphor—she wasn't actually on fire from the inside out, that was impossible, and yet. Her breath crackled in her chest. The heat scalded her throat worse than the flu. The lines on her palms glowed reddish gold, but that had to be the stage lights. What happened if the room was too angry to laugh, or too afraid, where did the Showstopper go? What happened to the comedian? Would Sy have to take a broom and sweep away her charred remains? She wished these men would throw their drinks again; a splash of cool whiskey on her face sounded pretty good.

Then: More of a rumble than a sound, felt rather than heard. Bubbling up from deep inside a body, somewhere between lungs and guts, a pocket of self even doctors didn't know how to probe. It reached the ears, low, gruff, a forest full of bears having a grand old time. The room rocked and trembled beneath Franny's feet. The light exploded from her mouth; she was Pompeii, Krakatoa, Pearl Harbor. The road flare that blew off Peter Finnegan's pinky. It lit up the whole city and was gone in an instant. But the laughter, it went on and on and on.

Franny was one with her audience—these men as they stomped

horsily to better squeeze out the laughs. She was herself—Franny Steinberg, grinning like a goon and crying at the same time, hollow-boned and heroic in Papa's damp clothes. She could have floated away on a cloud, but the show must go on. Franny searched for her tender voice as the laughter finally ebbed, a new joke rushing up the back of her throat. They liked that last one, huh? Wait till they got a load of this.

But before she could speak, two men burst out of the smoky dark, hooting like a monkey house, sweaty and toothy. They hurled themselves onstage, grabbed the curtains on either side of Franny and clawed their way up toward the stage lights. A ripping sound brought the heavier man down with a *thump*, knocking his hat from his head. He hopped to his feet, grinning at Franny. He kicked his hat out of the way and humped toward her, forelock in his eye. She backed away, but the other man blocked the stage exit.

"Sy," she rasped. What happened to polite honesty and buying each other drinks? What had she done?

Sy had his own problems. One man was doing a wobbly soft-shoe dance on a tabletop. Two men were doing the jitterbug with each other, cheek to cheek, swaying lustily. The rest, every other man in the room, had gathered around the door and were jostling to leave. Sy blocked the exit with his body. One by one the men embraced him, settled hats on their heads, said a polite *ope!* and squeezed around him out the door.

Meanwhile, Franny was tackled on both sides by the curtain climbers. She couldn't breathe. She was in Peter's car again; she was going to hyperventilate or pass out or dissolve into sweat droplets that would be wiped away and forgotten.

"Ma'am," one man murmured in her ear. "I am so very sorry to hear about your brother. I was also in the war, and it is not an experience I would care to repeat."

"I did terrible things in Europe," the other man cried. "I got no one to talk to. My wife would leave me if she knew."

They rocked her like a baby between them. Franny started to shake. "Please," she managed to whisper. "Let me go."

"Shh, shh," said the first man, stroking her hair now. "There, there."

Franny wanted to scream. She couldn't scream. She wrenched her body free, and the two men followed her as she stumbled, colt-legged, from the stage.

The jitterbugs stopped jitterbugging and came for her with out-stretched arms. She jerked away just as their fingertips brushed her sleeve, eyeing the exit like a parched woman would a desert oasis.

Men streamed past Sy like he wasn't even there. He was an old shipwreck; they were a school of fish with other priorities. Sy—the only one who hadn't gone bananas over her Showstopper. Because he was the only man who hadn't laughed. Sy had probably never laughed a day in his life! Franny had never been happier about a lousy sense of humor.

"Sy," she cried. "A little help?"

But Sy didn't help. Sy glared.

The soft-shoe man hopped off his table and blocked her path. She tried to swerve around him, but he swerved with her, doing a little spin and stumble, but he turned the stumble into a time step before finishing it off with a flourish of his hands. He looked like he expected applause, but Franny burst into tears instead. He embraced her, and the four other men who had been in pursuit piled on to the hug. She would be squeezed into oblivion. Franny felt absolutely nothing.

"I wanted to be Fred Astaire, and they laughed at me," the soft-shoer said, hot and breathy. He pointed to legs that bowed in different directions. "But I don't have to be perfect. I can still dance. No one told me I could still dance." He kissed Franny's hand and Charlestoned out the door. The other men tossed her aside like a deflated balloon.

One turned back. "If it feels this good, it can't be bad," he said. "Isn't that right?"

I did terrible things in Europe. I got no one to talk to. Laughing at her punch lines gave them relief from their pain. Relief manifested differently—some got giddy, some danced, some became more honest and self-aware, others emotional and clingy. Too honest, too handsy, too *much*. Was there a way to turn down the volume on their relief?

This was the Showstopper Franny intended to unleash on Chicago, on the world? Was this the kind of monstrousness Leon had locked up inside him? She fumbled for change. Forget finishing the set, she had to go *home*. Maybe hide in bed forever?

Franny was, frankly, jealous. When was the last time she had ever felt relief like that?

Sy clapped a hand on her shoulder, loomed over her like Mount Rushmorestein. "I'll need a good explanation for what just happened," he said. "Unless you think you got too many teeth."

Franny stared at the abandoned tables and chairs, overturned beer glasses, dripping onto the floor. Her whole body vibrated, slick with the sweat of strangers.

Franny looked at Margie, who had gone pale. "Sometimes the cure is worse than the disease?"

"A mol iz di refue erger far der make," Sy said. "And you, are you the cure or the disease?"

Sy rolled up his sleeves before grabbing Franny by her collar until it garroted her throat. Franny couldn't breathe. Or speak. Blood got trapped in her head and thumped like a downbeat.

"Sy!" Margie said. "Let's just laugh and forget about it, huh?"

"I only laugh when things are funny," Sy said. "Losing business is not funny, duping my customers is not funny."

"She didn't mean nothing by it." Margie slapped uselessly at his forearm. "They'll be back tomorrow, maybe even tonight. Show— it's not permanent, right, Franny? It wears off real fast."

Sy squinted at her, but something occurred to Franny, something even worse than being choked by the world's biggest Jew. She was so stupid. Showstoppers wear off. Every girl knew that, but you know who didn't?

What would Ed do to Lottie when it wore off?

"Well?" Sy shook her like a piggy bank. "Will they be back?" Sy asked.

Spit was dribbling out the side of Franny's mouth. Her face felt like it might pop right off her head. "Yes," she croaked.

Sy let go, and Franny dropped to the floor, rubbing her neck.

"Let me get you a glass of water," Margie said.

But Franny was already scrambling out the door, dread in her guts, fearing the worst had already happened.

CHAPTER FOURTEEN

THE SIGHT OF LOTTIE SILHOUETTED AGAINST THE BAR AT
the Blue Moon, all limbs intact, was such a relief that Franny's knees
buckled. She let Barb's empty stool catch her weight, freed the breath
she'd locked up in her chest.

But something was off. A sour note, a twang her heart vibrated to
before it even reached her ears. Why was Barb's stool still warm? Why
was Barb not sitting on it? No one was onstage, no one in the audience, no Enid behind the bar. Lottie was all alone, sitting in the dark.

"Why are you dressed like a drunk plumber?" Lottie asked.
"Never mind, I don't want to know."

That's when Franny saw the blood.

Lottie's face was puffy, a bloody goatee trailing past her chin,
down her neck, soaking the front of her blouse. She tried to laugh
and then winced, clutching her ribs.

"You should see the other guy," she said. "Make me a martini,
will you?"

Franny paced in front of Lottie, trying to find a way in, something she could do. She had raced all the way here, Franny who got

woozy at the sight of blood. If she had stuck with Mama and the Gray Ladies, she might have had some, any, a single useful skill. If Lottie had been a man, she might have hopped onstage and told a joke, relieved her of a little pain.

Which, of course, was why they were in this quagmire in the first place. Did anyone ever escape a quagmire? That was the point of quagmires, wasn't it? How inescapable they were?

"Lottie, you need a hospital," she said softly.

Lottie waved the notion away like an odor. "What do you care? You quit me."

She looked so lonely, so dejected, so broken that tears welled up in Franny's eyes. If Lottie didn't almost certainly have broken ribs, Franny would have given her a hug. "Showstoppers wear off," Franny said. "I worried Ed might not take that so well."

"Yeah, well," Lottie said. "I'm serious about that martini. Gin, if you would be so kind."

Franny had never made a martini in her life, but she went behind the bar and followed Lottie's instructions. Lottie sipped it and nodded.

"Enid couldn't get out the door fast enough," Lottie said bitterly. "Maybe you can be my new bartender."

Franny wrapped some ice in a dish towel like she did for Leon that time he twisted his ankle playing shortstop and handed it to Lottie. She pressed it to her eye. Her other hand slid across the bar, and Franny squeezed it.

"I'm glad you're here," Lottie said. "Don't tell anyone about this."

Franny bit her lip. Seeing her like this—it obviously wasn't the first time, why did she stay? "Lottie—"

"Why won't I divorce him."

Franny blinked. "You're a mind reader now?"

"You think you invented pity? Seen it a thousand times." Lottie sighed. "There's not a lawyer in this city that will take on Fingers Marcone. Even if there were, can you see Ed standing up in family court? And, okay, let's say hell does freeze over, no way would he sign a divorce decree." Lottie adjusted the ice on her face. "His mother would be devastated."

Franny laughed then smacked a hand over her mouth. "I'm sorry," she said through her fingers. "It's not funny."

"Only something that stupid could be so funny." Lottie smiled then winced. "I'm stuck with Ed. And I've lost the Blue Moon. That's the long and the short of it."

"You're giving up?"

Lottie's eyes flashed. "He was going to kill me." She left the words suspended between them, where they expanded, sucking all the oxygen out of the room. Finally, she looked away. "He thought I drugged him."

"But you didn't," Franny said.

"Your appetite for the obvious is truly astonishing. No, I *didn't*, but telling him he was the unwitting victim of an unprecedented Showstopper was not going to stop him from kicking me." Hearing Lottie call her Showstopper *unprecedented* made Franny's head swell, to her horror. "If that Showstopper had only lasted one more hour, if only he had signed that deed. If only, if only. Ed never makes mistakes, get it? Once that signature was inked, he would say it was all his idea. It would have been perfect." Lottie poked holes in her olives with the spear of her swizzle stick.

"What did olives ever do to you?" Franny said gently. Some jokes made people laugh, others helped them be kinder to themselves. They didn't all have to jab.

Lottie rested her head in her hands. "I said I was looking out for all of us, but I was just looking out for me. I'm sorry, Franny."

Lottie's use of her real name startled her. Franny's sticky clothes had dried stiff, the stink of the men who'd clung to her still assaulted her nose, the press of their bodies imprinted on her skin. But she was here. She'd survived. Her muscles still tensed with the desire to run away and hide forever, but Franny stayed. What's more, Franny wanted to stay.

"I begged to do a farewell show tomorrow night, no funny business. I promised him Boopsie." Lottie grimaced. "He may not believe in Showstoppers or the female orgasm, but if it puts Varla in the mood for *him*, he'll suspend disbelief. If Boopsie agrees—and that's a big *if*—she finishes her set tomorrow, I turn out the lights, hand Varla the keys, and it's goodbye Blue Moon."

The Blue Moon wasn't just a nightclub. It was a home, a family—dirty laundry, cobwebby corners, creepy basements, and all. It was also the last of its kind. That was worth something. That was worth a lot.

"Smell my shirt," Franny said.

Lottie wrinkled her nose. "Pass."

"I just went up at the Velvet Swing."

"Sy's joint?" Lottie snorted. "Fat chance."

"I'd say you should ask him yourself, but he wasn't a fan." She pulled down her collar. Lottie hesitated then gingerly touched her bruised neck. "You don't know what I can do. You don't know the half of it," Franny said. Hope was infinitely more intoxicating than vodka. "Lottie, what if we tried again?"

It would be weirdly easy. She'd go up first, do her whole set, make him laugh. Lottie would produce the deed, and he'd sign on the spot. Andy would apologize for betraying her; Franny would graciously accept. No more violence, no more pain, and all that pesky fear would melt away forever.

Was she talking about the Blue Moon or herself?

"No offense, but you're not exactly famous for courage under fire," Lottie said. "You'll freeze."

"I *won't*," Franny said. "I'll do it for Gal, for Hal and Andy. They need this place. Plus, it's like you said—if Ed thinks this is his idea, you can get him to do anything."

Lottie stared curiously at Franny. "That's true."

Franny was pacing back and forth, bursting with ideas, but Lottie was practically draped over the bar. She had almost forgotten how much pain Lottie must be in, how exhausted she must be. And here Franny was, yammering about plans to put her right back in the thick of it.

Lottie handed Franny the melted ice pack. "Under the bar, there's a pill bottle. And a glass of water, please." Franny handed them over. Lottie shook out two pills and downed them. "Now help me downstairs, will you?"

Franny lifted the trapdoor and gingerly held Lottie's arm while she hobbled down the ladder.

It was clammy and dark, and there was definitely a

scuttle-scratching sound echoing farther down the tunnel. It was all so sad, and Franny was reminded of Gal alone in her hotel. A lump swelled in her scratchy throat.

"Back off, Florence Nightingale, it's not *that* bad," Lottie said, reading her face again. She motioned to a folded cot tucked away in a corner. Franny unfolded the cot and spread a blanket over it. She tucked Lottie in and even kissed her on the forehead.

"You're a good girl. Lousy lay, but a good girl. Stay with me?" Lottie said. Boy, the way she could build up, knock down, and build up again in a single sentence. "I shouldn't have lost my temper when Hal confessed. If I had just stopped to think, could've spared myself a trip to the happy Steinblatt home in the suburbs." She shuddered at the word *suburbs*, or maybe *happy*.

"Steinberg," Franny said. "What are we talking about?"

"The night you told your Purple Head joke. Hal was acting very out of character. Yadda yadda, 'Peggy is so talented, it doesn't matter that she's not telling her own jokes.'"

Franny felt dumb and slow as she scrambled to catch up. That was the night Hal had called her *pretty*. Because Hal was drunk.

But...what if Hal wasn't?

Lottie sighed. "Honey, I know a Showstopper when I see one. I practically invented them. I know better than you what you're capable of." She paused for dramatic effect, or maybe she fell asleep. "And you owe Andy an apology."

Lottie could play her like a fiddle, but unfortunately, Franny liked this particular song. She had never felt so relieved to be betrayed. Andy hadn't told Lottie she was stealing jokes, Hal had.

Under the influence of Franny's own Showstopper. It was too perfect to be upsetting.

"Fine, twist my arm," Franny said. "I need this place too."

"Atta girl. We'll win the Blue Moon back," Lottie murmured. "With your great ideas, how could we fail?"

She giggled at this. Franny had never once heard Lottie giggle, so that had to be the pills kicking in. She turned to leave.

"Stay until I fall asleep," Lottie called out. "Please?"

Franny sighed. There was an old, uncomfortable-looking wooden chair in the corner, and she dragged it over. "Fall asleep fast," she said, stifling a yawn. Oh, to be crawling into her own bed!

Lottie snatched her hand like a mousetrap and wouldn't let go. The very *instant* her grip loosened, Franny would leave.

If only there were a magazine down here to read. Each time Franny blinked, her eyelids got heavier and heavier...

Then she was plunging through darkness, face-first.

Franny jerked her head up. She had just nodded off for a second. She wiped a bit of drool from her lip and realized Lottie wasn't holding her hand anymore. Her arm dangled limp over the side of the cot.

Franny squinted at her watch. Now that couldn't be right. She peered up at the clock on the wall.

Impossible.

She tapped her watch face like she might jostle time itself. She just couldn't have been asleep *that* long.

But there was no mistake. It was after midnight. And she had missed the last streetcar.

"Lottie, wake up. Please." Franny shook her shoulder. Lottie didn't budge. Franny shook harder, but Lottie's limbs were limp as a puppet's, her face more relaxed than Franny had ever seen it. She was out cold.

Franny had nowhere near enough money for a taxi home. She couldn't call Leon for reasons so obvious, they hurt to even imagine. Gal had never given her a phone number; she had no idea how to find Andy or Hal and couldn't even call the operator because she didn't know their real names—how was that possible?

And that was that. Franny was stuck in the city until dawn.

But wait, Mary Kate wasn't living at the Finnegans' anymore. She had her own home! Franny grabbed the phone behind the bar and dialed Mary Kate's new number. It rang and rang, and Franny strangled the headset to make it talk, just like Sy had done to her earlier—was that really today? *Oh, pick up, Mary Kate, pick up—*

"Hello?" Mary Kate's voice, slurred with sleep.

"Mary Kate, your voice is manna from heaven," Franny said.

"Franny?" Mary Kate's voice cleared. "What time is it?"

Walter's sleepy baritone in the background asked who it was.

"Nobody, Walter, go back to bed."

"I missed the last streetcar," Franny said. "Can you pick me up?"

"Are you in trouble? I'll get Walter."

"No," Franny said. Yelled, really. "I'm just—at the Blue Moon."

"Like…the *nightclub*?"

"No, like the song." Franny bonked herself with the phone for being mean. "I'm sorry, it's been a long day. Please? I wouldn't ask if I weren't desperate."

Mary Kate sighed. The wall clock taunted Franny with the passage of time. "Okay, I'll figure something out."

⚬ঔৎ⚬

Franny calculated that if Mary Kate threw on a housecoat and a pair of shoes and went straight to the car, it would take about forty minutes for her to arrive at the curb of the Blue Moon. Franny thought about making a stiff drink to calm her nerves. There were drops of blood on the bar. It was too eerie, the blue neon seeping through the front window, Lottie passed out in the tunnels. She shivered. At this hour, she might be mugged outside, but it was better than sitting in here. Franny peeked out the door, saw no muggers. She plopped down on the curb, straining for a glimpse of a car.

A pair of headlights blinked into view. Franny glanced at her watch. Couldn't be Mary Kate—that was much too fast. But the car slowed then slid up to the curb. Franny stood. Her heart was melted ice cream in her chest. It wasn't Mary Kate's car. It was Peter's.

He leaned across the seat and opened the door. "Déjà vu, huh?"

Franny's mouth shriveled in her face. Her feet cracked the sidewalk with their new roots. Not this déjà vu. Any car but this car. Any driver but this driver.

"Because I've picked you up here before? You can smile, Franny, it's a joke," Peter chuckled. Franny still couldn't move. "Or get in the back if you want to; I'll play chauffeur. Just—get in? Please? This neighborhood gives me the creeps."

What other option did she have? Franny got in the back. That leather smell, the brush of it on her skin… Franny gripped her knees and tried not to breathe. In forty short minutes, she'd be in her own bed, and all this would be over.

"You really gave Mary Kate a scare," he said. "She wouldn't even let me get decent." He motioned to his wine-red monogrammed robe, his striped pajamas, his strawberry-blond hair sticking up in the back. He grinned.

Franny couldn't remember where she'd last left her voice. It had to be somewhere. She managed to nod curtly.

Peter's grin melted, and he cleared his throat. "Okay, then," he said. "You're welcome."

He pulled away from the curb, but instead of turning around and going west, he continued east. To Lake Shore Drive. Fear exploded in Franny's chest, hot embers singed all the way down into her fingers and toes.

"Where are you taking me?" she said, trying for gravity but ending up with helium.

He frowned in the rearview mirror. "My apartment."

Franny gripped her own knees. "You have to take me home," she said.

Peter laughed. "At this hour? Are you kidding?"

Franny thought about opening the door and rolling out onto Lake Shore Drive, running into the lake and drowning. Anything but this. But she was trapped, frozen, hating herself for not thawing. She had felt so good, so hopeful. And now this.

From the car, Lake Michigan in the dark looked like a big black hole, the back of a giant throat, a sloppy interpretation of outer space.

✐

"Welcome to my humble abode." Peter opened the door to his apartment and gestured inside, smirking at her getup. "What the hell happened to you, anyway?"

"Costume party," she muttered.

He chuckled. "Shower's over there. Towels in the hall closet."

"I'm not taking my clothes off," Franny blurted. Her chest got hot and prickly. She nearly apologized, of all things, but forced herself to keep her mouth shut.

Peter frowned, concern in his blue eyes. The spacious sitting room felt suddenly cramped. A single row of narrow windows on the far side showed the lake from above, slightly darker than the sky and its city lights. A twinkling crystal chandelier dangled from the ceiling over a modern dining table. All the furniture was modern and sleek, including a sofa built on slick wooden legs that looked deeply uncomfortable.

"There's a pool with showers," Peter said. "But I think it's closed now." He cleared his throat. "You okay with the sofa? I'm sorry, I don't generally have houseguests."

"What about your fiancée?" What was her name again?

"Oh, that's over," Peter said. "Didn't Mary Kate tell you?"

The sofa was a prickly orange, and the floor a shiny pale wood, and Franny's whole body itched. "I should go," she said.

"Franny," Peter said, touching her arm. "Where are you going to go?"

"Don't touch me."

Peter pulled his hands away, palms forward in affable surrender. He squinted at her chest like he could see her heart pounding in it. "Is that *blood*?"

Franny looked down. A smear of Lottie's blood on the collar of Papa's shirt. The raw spot on her neck where Sy had grabbed her.

She would *not* cry. The chasm between the two Peters she had known was more maddening than the behavior of either one. "No," she said. "It's ketchup."

They sized each other up like cowboys. Finally, Peter relented, sighing. "If you leave now, your parents will tell my parents, and they'll never forgive me. Please, let me be a good host?"

A shower did sound divine, and Peter probably had that fluffy kind of towel, not the stiff, thin kind she had at home.

Franny locked the bathroom door behind her and undressed gingerly, stepping into the shower. She had never felt so scrubbed out and raw. So very *tired*. Water dripped from her hair to the tub. She touched her neck where Sy had grabbed her. Bruised and sore. It was starting to hurt to swallow, and she had no idea what to do about it. Any of it. She stood in the shower until her fingers pruned and the water turned cold.

The doorknob rattled. "Are you okay in there?"

Franny's breath came quick and shallow, and she pressed herself against the cold tile. She hugged her naked body, tried to get small.

The doorknob rattled harder. "Jesus, Franny. What are you doing? Please open the door." He knocked. Knocked harder. "You're not doing something stupid, are you?"

Stupid like what? Like staying out all night and sleeping over at the house of the man who...who... *Owl got your tongue?* She still couldn't even think it.

"You lock yourself in the bathroom for an hour with the water running—what am I supposed to think, Franny? You can't lock me out of my own home. This is my home!"

Franny's voice disappeared in a tiny peep into her throat. Her throat disappeared into her chest. Her mind floated out of her body, and the memory of her birthday bobbed up violently, repeating its horror in vivid Technicolor. She was floating away forever. She was shivering forever. Franny curled up in the bathtub and hyperventilated into her knees, watched her spirit leave her body.

A tiny wisp of a voice deep in her guts whispered, *They don't call him Peter for nothing.* The voice would not be deterred, not even now. It was there in Papa's hospital room. It told the joke about Leon at the Velvet Swing. It heckled a crowd of furious men. *I didn't bring my magnifying glass.* Franny opened her mouth, and the voice came out.

"Must be a peace-and-quiet shortage?" Franny said. "Next time I'll bring my ration stamps."

The rattling stopped.

She grabbed a fluffy white towel monogrammed with Peter's initials—was he worried he'd forget them?—and wrapped it tightly around herself before opening the door.

He turned away and handed her a robe. What a gentleman. The gesture filled Franny with rage.

"Why—" Franny's voice cracked. "Why did you do it, Peter?"

"Sue me for thinking the worst," Peter said. "You have to admit you haven't been yourself lately."

Her mouth puckered like there was a lemon in it. She was so tired. "I meant, on my *birthday*. I trusted you, and you...*hurt* me."

And just like that, it was spoken. She couldn't take it back. But Franny didn't feel any better, not a single iota of relief. She felt worse, actually. What was the point of telling the truth if it made you feel even more lousy?

Peter's eyes widened and a spot of red appeared on each cheek. "Franny!" he said. "You came on to me. I don't think of you that way. You're like my sister. I took you home."

The worst day of Franny's life was just another nice evening in Peter's. Franny felt the truth slipping like sand through her fingers. Like trying to pinch water. He was awfully confident about his lie. But it was a lie. Wasn't it? If believing lies was that easy, what if *she* was the one who had created the lie? How did this get so confusing?

"Just forget it," Franny muttered.

His eyes searched her face for something. "Franny, I took you home."

Franny didn't want to talk about it anymore, but this was just too much. "You want to lie to me, fine, I'm used to it," she said. "But you lied to Leon, and now he hates me."

"You're projecting," Peter said solemnly. "I learned all about this at Loyola."

Maybe it was a trick of the light, but suddenly Peter Finnegan looked like a paper doll cut out of the universe and stuck on the two-dimensional page of this apartment. His arms bent at a doll angle; his cheeks were smattered with drawn freckles. A handsome doll, a doll who could wear all kinds of different clothes. To puncture the lie was to puncture Peter. He wasn't powerful or solid; he was a flat piece of paper, drawn by someone else.

"I'm doing you a favor," he said. "Do you know what Leon would say if he knew where you were? That you spent the night here?"

What a twisted bit of logic. Twisted like Peter's mouth, tense as his shoulders, clenched as his jaw.

Just because he believed what he said didn't mean he was telling the truth.

Was what happened *really* her fault? Dependent on some minuscule different choice she might have made? One less giggle, a different dress, a gesture, a fidget, a word, a breath, a thought that would have sent the entire chain of events skittering in a different direction?

Why had it never occurred to her that Peter was the actor, the perpetrator, the one who made the choice? Not Franny. Franny had just been trying to celebrate her *fucking* birthday with a boy she'd thought was cute.

Franny's breath returned, slow and cool like Lake Michigan lapping at her toes.

"I'll need a blanket and a pillow," Franny said. "And if your fiancée left any pajamas, I'd like those as well, please."

Peter looked relieved. "Of course," he said. "Definitely."

Franny slept like a baby on that itchy orange couch.

⌐⊚⌐

Several hours later, Peter's telephone rang and rang and woke Franny. She pressed the pillow to her ears until it stopped. The sun shot beams through the narrow windows, the night's coolness gave way to humid air, and Franny glared at herself in the bathroom mirror. Her deep-set eyes underlined by the Steinberg smudge, the slept-on hair, the hated nose that looked so much better on Leon. But there was a glimmer of something different, something she had envied in the faces of the men at the Velvet Swing. Relief. So faint that when she looked directly at it, it disappeared. But it was there.

Peter's bedroom door was closed, and she was about to tiptoe out but changed her mind. She banged on his door with the full might of her fist. He flung open the door and looked around wild-eyed before his gaze landed on Franny. He tightened his robe around him as she smiled.

"Did I wake you?" Franny said, wide-eyed and innocent. "Just wanted to make sure you weren't doing something stupid in there."

She may have been wearing Papa's bloody, whiskey-drenched clothes, she may have appalled the noses of neighbors stuck in the elevator with her, but Franny had never felt more majestic.

CHAPTER FIFTEEN

THE NEIGHBORHOOD STANK OF STICKY-SWEET WET RUBBER
and hay, a strange and uneasy mix that took the strut right out of
Franny's walk. She hustled down North Euclid Avenue, breaking
into a run as the Averys' house came into view.

A crowd of neighbors huddled on the sidewalk across from the
Averys' home, though no one was talking to the Averys themselves. They
stood together in the shade of a tall oak. Mrs. Avery was bouncing and
comforting their little girl, Connie, who sobbed into her shoulder. Their
older daughter, Hannah, sat on the ground ripping up blades of grass.
Their stucco house had a blackened stripe up the front, and the bay
windows were shattered. Smoke curled upward from a circle of crackling grass. Up close, it smelled stomach-turningly like a carnival on fire,
burning cotton candy and powdered sugar. Dr. Avery was pointing at
Undercover Rod.

"And how exactly will you make sure this never happens again?"
Dr. Avery said evenly.

"No need to raise your voice. I'm doing everything I can."
Undercover Rod nodded at Connie. "And no one got hurt. That's
what matters most."

"No one got—" Dr. Avery paced back and forth. "Someone threw *dynamite* through my little girl's *window*."

"William," Mrs. Avery said.

He looked over at her, took a deep breath. "We need police protection, someone to watch the house."

Rod shook his head. "Which is it? Find the guy who did this or sit outside your house twiddling our thumbs?" he said. "We're not babysitters, Dr. Avery."

"No, you're public servants. But only for some of the public, isn't that right?"

"I don't like what you're implying," Rod said. "And I don't like your tone."

Undercover Rod had said not to worry. He had said the phone calls were from bored kids. Franny felt ill. That poor little girl—the Averys must feel terrified, suspicious of everyone and everything. Even Rod seemed a little too relaxed about the whole thing, and he was one of the good guys.

Why hadn't she brushed off the challah, brushed herself off, and given it to them? Why didn't she go over to them now instead of eavesdropping?

Guilt curdled in Franny's belly. But talking to them wouldn't erase what happened. And what was she supposed to say, anyway—*I'm sorry your house keeps getting bombed*? Franny watched the absurd conversation unfold in her head. What would they say, *Thank you*? And then what? Franny would squint up at the sky and say, *Sure is a hot one today*?

What a coward.

Franny remembered when the Averys moved in. She had peeked through the curtains to watch—just like everyone else on North Euclid Avenue. Franny had thought she was being sly, but they must have known they were being watched. They must know they were always being watched. How did Dr. Avery manage to stay so calm? Franny was sure she would have lost her marbles by now, would have actually raised her voice at Officer Rod. Or worse.

Like when Leon pushed him—and only got a "talking-to."

Another police officer walked out of 504, slamming the door behind him, and soggy fingers of dread slid up Franny's scalp. He passed her, crossing the street in long strides to join Rod. Franny hurried home, trying to look calm, heart pounding in her throat. *Please, Leon, please don't be skulking around neighborhood garbage cans late at night, looking for me.*

The blast had been powerful enough to send a window at 504 crashing down, cracking the glass in its frame. Leon was standing at the dining table, staring down at the eggs Mama had made him. He didn't look up when Franny came in. Mama wiped her hands on a dish towel, ran toward her with open arms.

"Nu, you smell terrible," Mama said, holding back at the last moment and hugging her tentatively. "Where have you been? What a morning we've had. If your father hadn't had a heart attack already, he would have had one this morning. The noise, Franny! It shook the house. The poor Averys. And this, in America! A shande." Mama clucked her tongue. "We were worried about you, where were you? We didn't know what to tell the police."

Franny's throat, full of lumps. "What did you tell them?"

"That you had stayed at the hospital all night with Papa," Leon said. "Like a dutiful daughter."

Poor Papa, lying alone in his hospital bed, while Franny nursed Lottie Marcone. So much for taking care of him. So much for turning over new leaves. Franny held on to the old ones until they browned and died, and she had to rake them into monstrous piles. "I'll visit today, I promise," she said. "Maybe tonight too." Already covering her own behind, so selfish. What a mess.

"You smell like whiskey and cigars," Mama said, sniffing. "I don't want to know. Where were you?"

"Are there any more eggs?" Franny asked. If she wanted to get Mama on to other topics, food was her best bet.

Mama shuffled away into the kitchen, muttering, "They live under my roof and come home at all hours, and I don't get to know where they've been? After all I've been through?"

Leon gazed at his glistening eggs like they were a crystal ball. "They think Peter did it," he said. "They think he bombed the Averys."

"Peter Finnegan?" Franny asked.

Leon looked up. "No, Peter Rabbit."

Franny opened and closed her mouth but couldn't figure out what words to put in it. "How do they know? Did he blow off another finger?" she asked.

"Do you always have to make jokes?" Leon asked.

Peter *would* do it—he had the motive, he had the experience with explosives, he had the disposition. The only problem was that he hadn't done it. No one should be punished for a crime they didn't commit, except…what if said person had committed another different heinous crime that had gone unpunished? In that case, wouldn't it be another form of justice?

"They telephoned him this morning, no answer. If he doesn't have an alibi," Leon said, "they're going to take him in."

Franny kept her face as still as a frozen lake. If she hadn't stayed with Peter last night, she would feel relief right now. She could still be this hypothetical, relieved Franny. Bring a criminal to justice, bring comfort to a neighbor. By saying one word, Franny could be the one to *help* the Averys. Be a hero.

"What makes them think it was Peter anyway?" she asked tentatively.

"Peter said some…things to me," Leon said. "About the Averys. Undercover Rod said he wouldn't do it. Peter volunteers at the Boys Club. He helps people. But I couldn't lie about some of the stuff he said."

"*You* told the police that Peter bombed the Averys?"

"I didn't say that. Did I say that?" He looked green. He slumped in the chair.

Franny sat next to him, tentatively touched his knee. When he didn't flinch, she patted it softly. This conversation was on thin ice, and she needed it to end as soon as possible. "I'm sure Peter didn't do it," she said. "They'll find the right guy."

"But what if he did?" Leon said. "Peter wants to please Mr. Finnegan so badly…what if he did it?" Leon pressed his face into his hands. Everyone in the house was so attuned to his moods, even Mama stopped puttering in the kitchen for a moment to see if things would escalate.

It hadn't occurred to Franny that Peter might have people in his life who were disappointed in him, people he might be trying to please. It hadn't occurred to her that Leon might be upset by it. This was all wrong. Franny did not want to be having this conversation, but she couldn't figure out how to get out of it. How did they end up worried about Peter anyway? Wasn't this about the Averys?

As good as it would feel to be a hero, as good as it would feel to see Peter finally punished, lying wasn't going to protect anyone except Franny.

"Peter didn't do it," she said miserably.

"I appreciate that you're trying to make me feel better," Leon said. "But this is bigger than your little crush."

Franny heated up like a nuclear reactor. "Nothing bad will ever happen to Peter Finnegan because Peter Finnegan gets away with everything."

Leon turned his dark, haunted eyes to her. "Well, Franny, which is it?" Leon said. "Did he do it, or didn't he?"

He did it, Leon, he did it. He just didn't do this.

"You're going to think the worst no matter what I say."

"I'm already thinking the worst. At least Peter is honest with me."

Franny would take ten Velvet Swings over the knife Leon just jammed in her heart.

If she didn't tell Leon the truth, he would think she couldn't be trusted. If she did, he would never trust her again. But Franny had endured worse. She had endured worse in the past twelve hours, for crying out loud.

Would she really stick her bruised neck out to save Peter Finnegan?

She tried to summon the warmth of her Showstopper—a bonfire on a cold night, the candles on Shabbat. She could remember the feeling, but she couldn't *feel* it. Lottie's voice scoffed in her head, her throat ached, her eyes burned, dread stagnated under everything like eggy well water. Didn't matter. The truth was what mattered.

She took a deep breath. No way out but through. "I slept at Peter's last night."

Leon was a statue, frozen in an expression halfway between agony and tears.

"I just needed a place to stay," Franny said.

"I bet that's not all you needed."

"You don't have the first measly clue what I need." Franny lifted her hand. She was going to slap him. She would do it. It would fix his brain, and he would finally see how very wrong he was about her.

He didn't flinch. He looked like he expected her to slap him, like that was exactly what his version of Franny *would* do.

There was no way to win.

"I'm more honest with you than Peter Finnegan will ever be," she muttered, lowering her hand.

"Then you had better go tell Undercover Rod," Leon said in a tight, low voice. "And you had better tell him fast."

Franny hadn't thought that far. Her stomach flipped. This was the problem with telling the truth. Undercover Rod would tell Mama, who would tell Papa. Two nights spent with two different boys? It was unthinkable.

He dug into his eggs, shoveling them into his mouth without tasting or chewing, like a person who had lost all his taste buds. Or one who was trying to choke himself to death with breakfast. Franny stared at the crown of his head, with its whirlpool cowlick.

"Franny, do you want jam with your toast?" Mama called from the kitchen, clattering plates. This house was so suffocating, everyone asking questions, everyone watching.

"Did I ask for toast?" Franny snapped.

Mama appeared in the kitchen doorway, clutching a spatula like a teddy bear. "I thought you liked toast."

"Don't talk to Mama that way," Leon said.

"Is okay," Mama said, "she always gets a little farbisn when she's hungry."

"I'm right here," Franny said. "Don't talk about me like I'm not." Mama retreated to the kitchen, and Franny snatched the plate of eggs from Leon.

"Hey," he said. "I was in the middle of not enjoying those."

"Don't you dare tell anyone," Franny said.

"Tell them what?" Leon said. "That you spent the night with Peter? That you have a hickey? That you spent another night with Michael Berman? Or that you kissed a strange man in a fedora on our porch after visiting Papa in the hospital? I can't keep up, Franny."

Franny's breath was knocked out of her body like the other team's home run.

"Trying to keep you from ruining your life is ruining mine. I can't do it anymore," Leon said. "When I get to Miami, do me a favor. Don't write."

Mama burst from the kitchen with a smile on her face and a plate of eggs and toast in her hand. She looked from Leon to

Franny, smile wilting. "Franny, those are Leon's eggs. Leon, eat your eggs."

"I'm not a child." Leon stood up fast, wiped his face on a napkin, and tossed it onto the plate. Without a word, he climbed up the stairs and slammed his bedroom door. Mama watched him go, longingly, like a tropical island she might never visit.

Franny felt sick. Somehow this was more final than the day he shipped off to Belgium, the day the hateful telegram arrived, and the day he returned as a skeleton in uniform combined.

Franny blinked away tears so Mama wouldn't see them, but Mama tugged gently on her collar.

"Oy gevalt," Mama said. "What happened to your neck?"

Franny lied. It was easy.

⌇⌇⌇

Mary Kate rang the doorbell later that afternoon, hands pressed over her flat belly as though she could squash whatever was growing inside.

"Thank you," she gushed, when Franny opened the door. She hugged Franny hard. "That was brave, what you did."

"I just want them to find the guy who actually did it." *Believe me*, Franny thought. *No one is more disappointed in Peter's innocence than me.*

"Of course," Mary Kate said, shaking her auburn curls. "But to sacrifice your own reputation to save my brother's life—it's not nothing."

"Oh, Mary Kate," Franny said. "If you think I still have a good reputation around here, you haven't been paying attention."

This made Mary Kate blush, and she looked down at her shoes. "I can't help but feel a teensy bit responsible," she said.

"Will you come in?" Franny said quickly. "Have some lemonade?"

"Remember when we tried to teach your mother to make lemonade, when we were kids?" Mary Kate said. "She thought we were crazy—vy vould you dringk leymon?"

Not a bad Mama voice. For a shiksa.

"And then she gave it to us, but she didn't put any sugar in it?"

"I remember."

Mary Kate nodded. "I should go. I'm meeting Mommy for lunch."

Franny smiled awkwardly. Mary Kate was squeezing her hands and wouldn't let go. "Don't tell, but your phone call got me thinking—were you really at the Blue Moon last night?" Franny glanced over her shoulder to see if anyone was listening, but Mary Kate didn't wait for her to respond. "I want to go too. I want to go with you," she said breathlessly. "Walter's out with his army buddies every night this week, and I just can't be cooped up in that house alone again. I can't, Franny. Say you'll come with me. Promise me."

Franny was pretty sure she was having a heart attack, right there in the doorway. Did they run in families? She forced herself to wrinkle up her face. "That old place?" she croaked unconvincingly. "Wouldn't you rather go somewhere else?"

*Any*where else?

"I'm going crazy out there alone," Mary Kate said.

"Mary Kate, you have a car."

"It's Walter's car."

"Still, you can drive over here any time," Franny said. Mary Kate's eyes shone like mirrors, and Franny did not like her reflection.

"I need to tell you something, but you have to promise not to blab," Mary Kate said. She lowered her voice to an excited whisper. "I joined a book club, except it's not a real book club. It's a bunch of girls who tell their *husbands* it's a book club and then go have a little fun, and tonight they're going to the Blue Moon. Boopsie Baxter's going to be there, Franny—"

Pinch me, Franny thought. *This is just a bad dream.*

"And some new girl that everyone's raving about—what's her name, you must know it—"

"Let's go next week," Franny said. "Next year?" How about never.

"—Peggy Blake, that's her name," Mary Kate said. "'All the pleasure, none of the calories.' Say you'll go with me. I won't take no for an answer. Come on, after what you did for Peter, you need to have a little fun. Show's at seven; pick you up at five?"

In the words of Lottie Marcone: *Christ on a toothpick.*

"What can I say?" Franny said. It was an honest question. What could she possibly say? *Can't, Mary Kate, I'll be too busy telling a dirty joke about your brother to trick a gangster with comedy magic?*

"Say yes!" Mary Kate smiled a Mrs. Finnegan smile. "It's my treat. Or, well. Walter's treat, anyway."

❧

It was Papa's last day in the hospital, so naturally, Franny snuck in a BBQ beef sandwich from Russell's and managed not to get a single spot of grease on her blouse.

"My daughter the mensch," Papa cried, unwrapping the sandwich carefully, so as not to alert any attendants to the crinkling paper. His eyes rolled back in his head as he chewed the first bite. "You wouldn't believe what they make me eat here, Franny. It's torture."

"Don't tell me. They make you eat real vegetables."

Papa set the sandwich on his stomach, squinting at Franny like she was a leaky faucet. "Okay, spill your beans," he said. "What's the matter?"

Franny laughed. "You're asking *me*?"

"No, I'm asking the sandwich," Papa said.

She tried to rearrange her face. "I'm not the one who has to eat mushy peas," she said.

"Don't change the subject," he cried. "I know that look. Your mama has that look."

"What look?"

"The look of a secret that wants out."

Tears pricked Franny's eyeballs. Why did he have to say that? Just moments ago, she had been feeling fine, great, peachy, not worried one bit about the many disasters on the horizon.

"Leon hates me," she said. She hadn't known this was what she was thinking until she said it. Then the waterworks flooded, and she wiped her snotty nose on her sleeve. "I can't do anything right."

"They have tissues for that, you know," Papa said, handing her one. "And he doesn't hate you."

Franny Steinberg: the only daughter in history to visit her papa in the hospital so he could console *her*.

"You're only saying that because you don't know what I did," Franny said.

"Bubbeleh, I know everything you do," Papa said. "I'm like Santy Claus that way."

Franny flinched. Just a coincidence. It had to be. But why would Papa invoke Christmas? Unless—he somehow *knew* what happened that Christmas Eve so many years ago? Impossible. Anyway, that was ancient history; she hardly thought about it anymore. And yet, it wasn't finished with her. The story crawled up her sore throat, demanding to be heard.

"Funny you should mention," she said. And now there was no way to turn back. "That Christmas Eve when we got the telegram—"

Papa stiffened, and please, oh, please, don't let her be responsible for another heart attack. "I sneaked away from Peter and Mary Kate and went to a nightclub all by myself. To see a famous comedian." She didn't dare look at Papa's face. "Leon was freezing on a Belgian battlefield, and all I could think was that I needed a break... I just wanted everything to stop, just for a few measly minutes so I could breathe. So I did." Franny knuckled away tears and more replaced them. "When I got home—when I saw you staring at the telegram—"

"Franny—"

"If I hadn't been so selfish, maybe Leon wouldn't have been captured, and everything would be terrific now. I'm always screwing everything up," Franny blurted. She hadn't known she really, truly believed this until she said it. Papa reached up to wipe her tears away, but she turned her head. "See what I mean? You need to get better, and here I am yammering at you like a priest at confession."

"You're going to confession now?" Papa asked.

"Figure of speech, Papa."

"Thanks god," Papa said, polishing off the sandwich and licking his fingers. "Sit down. Since we're telling secret stories, I've got one for you."

Franny crumpled the ball of greasy wax paper as tight as it could go and tossed it in the garbage. She pulled up a chair next to his bed.

Papa took a deep breath. "My papa was conscripted into the czar's army when I was in my mama's belly. When I was born, in Vilna, he was living in an army tent thousands of miles away, outside a city called Baku. The army didn't want to spend money on a Jew, so his uniform was old, it had holes in it, one boot was too tight, one was too loose. Every day they gave Papa a rifle with one single round and sent him into the woods to shoot his dinner." Papa chuckled. Franny had never heard any of this. She was afraid to move, to breathe, in case Papa might change his mind, worried the story would slip away and sink back into the deep, dark sea of his mind. But he continued. She exhaled.

"Somehow he survived. He never told me how. But as soon as I was born, Papa was determined to escape that army camp in Baku. He had a cousin in New York who would take us in. Mama prepared suitcases for us and placed them next to the front door, where they sat for months, gathering dust. I didn't meet my papa until I was two years old, but the first memory I have of him is hearing the stories he told about New York. We would eat ice cream for every meal. He would be a famous actor; we would have a big, gleaming white house with pillars. He saw a photograph of the White House once and wanted a house just like it. Our first night in New York City, my papa spent too much of his money buying ice cream for supper. Years later, he said it was one of the best suppers of his life.

"When he died, he made me promise to bring over his brothers and their families, to take them in like his cousin had taken us in. He clutched my hands, from a bed just like this one, nu, his grip was so strong. He cried, told me he never knew what had happened to his own mama and papa, if they had escaped Vilna or perished like so many others. Family, he said, is what connects you to history. It doesn't matter who your family is—if you like them, don't like them, respect them, or wish you could throw them in a lake in a potato sack. If you lose your family, you lose your place in the world.

"You don't remember my papa, maybe. He died in 1934, when you were only six. Nine years later, the rest of the family—" Papa stopped, cleared his throat. "I couldn't find them. It was all so confusing. Like a nightmare. I wrote letters, spent too much money on telephone calls overseas, and—as soon as I would find them, they slipped away, were moved somewhere else."

Franny had a fuzzy recollection of waking up before dawn to the sound of Papa yelling into the telephone in strange languages.

"I lost them. Every single one of them. I tried to keep it to myself, I didn't want to scare you or your brother or Mama. It all felt too real—the worst the world had to offer, right on our doorstep. Everything he escaped, it found us again. I was ashamed. I had failed at the one thing my own papa had asked me to do. But one night, your mama forced me to confess my shame. My mind refused, but my heart—I couldn't keep it locked up inside anymore. I cried on the sofa in her arms, I told her everything. My entire family, my link to history, to the past, to God Himself—destroyed.

"What I did not know is that Leon stood on the staircase that night like a ghost, listening to me wail. I had your mama to comfort me, but he endured my horrors alone. If I had known, if I had for one moment looked up from your mama's shoulder, I would have seen—I would have been able to comfort him. But I didn't. He was just a child, nu, but adult enough for the army to take him. And the next day, Leon enlisted. Maybe the day after that, who can remember." Papa wiped his tears away, blew out air. "Maybe they would have taken him anyway. But he chose to go, and it's my fault."

Franny remembered the day Leon enlisted. He came home in uniform. Framed in the doorway, Papa slapped him across the face. He had never laid a hand on either of them, ever. Leon's face crumpled. He had probably been expecting tears of gratitude. Franny had cried—out of fear for Leon, anger at Papa, confusion.

"You see? If it's my fault, it can't be your fault," Papa said.

"Papa."

Papa swatted her protest away. "But the biggest mistake I made? The most unforgivable? I didn't laugh about it. There was nothing funny, not a funny time in the least, but nu, it's easy to laugh when life is easy. It's when life hurts the most that you need to laugh."

Papa struggled to sit up, and Franny tried to help, but he made noises that meant he wanted to do it alone. "I need you to listen very closely. Your papa is old and wise and has been spending the week eating green Jell-O, so his constitution is weak."

Franny leaned in. "I'm listening."

"That Peter Finnegan is a real pisher, but he said something smart, I could hardly believe my ears. Stress and fear"—Papa poked his chest tenderly—"it breaks your heart. The heart needs to laugh. My papa knew this—freezing all alone in his old coat, trying to shoot rabbits. You knew this, Franny, that night with the telegram— the night you lied to us—don't do it again, by the way. You knew what your heart needed, and you were right. Leon hasn't figured it out yet. But—"

A nurse knocked and wheeled in a cart of food platters, plopping one on Papa's tray. Papa groaned.

"Mr. Steinberg, it's lunchtime," the nurse said. "You need to get your strength back."

"But what, Papa?" Franny asked.

"Let me guess," Papa said. "Green Jell-O?"

"You get to go home tonight," the nurse said. "So you've graduated to peas and carrots."

"Can't I skip a grade?" Papa groaned again.

"It's good for you," the nurse said. "Sometimes what your body needs the most is the thing you want the least."

The nurse threw open the curtains and the glow of sunlight on her blond hair was positively divine. Her name tag read NURSE MAGDALENE.

"A mol iz di refue erger far der make," Papa said, poking his peas. *Sometimes the cure is worse than the disease.*

"What did you call me?" asked Nurse Magdalene.

A baptism by boozy man sweat, an unwanted messenger. *I did terrible things in Europe. I got no one to talk to.*

Franny could fix Leon. She might be the only person in the whole world who could.

If Leon could feel her Showstopper, if that anvil of pain lifted off his chest, even for a few minutes, he would remember what it felt like to go out in public without needing to hide in the garbage, without screaming or freezing or hyperventilating, without Peter shoveling barbiturates at him. He would remember that he trusted her.

Leon would remember what he *used* to be like. He would be willing to find his way back to that person, and Franny would help him get there.

Tonight, on the stage of the Blue Moon, she'd unleash the full force of her Showstopper. She could save the Blue Moon *and* Leon in one fell swoop, why not? All she needed to do was get him there. All he needed to do was laugh.

Was it reckless? Yes. Dangerous? No question. But would it *work*? Probably not.

And yet.

"Enjoy your lunch," Franny said, leaping off the seat.

"Wait, won't you stay?" he asked. "At least until I finish my Gulag meal?"

"Mr. Steinberg, honestly," the nurse said.

"Wish I could," Franny said. "Busy, busy."

"Remember what I said," Papa said. "Hm?"

Franny pecked him on the cheek. "Thanks, Papa."

The nurse removed the silver dome off Papa's lunch with a flourish, and while Papa poked at his vegetables and the nurse chided him, Franny removed a five-dollar bill from his wallet. What did he need it for? Anyway, she was just borrowing it. Just for a little while. To save Leon! If Papa knew, he would demand she take it.

☙

Franny pressed her forehead to Leon's locked bedroom door and tried not to sound annoyed. "Please, open up," she said. "It's important."

No sound, no movement. A lesser Steinberg would think he was gone. Or dead. But Franny just had to figure out the right words, like a code breaker.

"Mary Kate needs you," she said.

Five, four, three, two—

The door opened a crack, revealing half of Leon's tired face. "What's the matter?"

Now was the delicate moment, keeping that door open. "She's all alone, cooped up in that house. Won't you take her out tonight?"

Leon opened the door wide enough to frame his broad shoulders. "Why doesn't Walter take her?"

"He's out with his army buddies," Franny said. "You got a problem with that, take it up with Peter."

"Don't start."

Franny wanted to start. She wanted to start and finish with him. But she couldn't lose track of the goal—get Leon to the Blue Moon, period. Nothing else mattered.

"Mary Kate has always been sweet on you, you know," Franny said. "Wouldn't hurt you to be nice to her."

"I know that," Leon said. A flush creeped up his neck. "She's married."

It had never occurred to Franny that Leon had been sweet on Mary Kate too. What had her wedding been like for *him*?

He folded his arms across his thin chest, and they stared each other down. "What does she have in mind?"

Franny grinned to cover up the ache in her chest. Used to be, it was Franny who could say *jump* and Leon would oblige. "She said she'd call you," Franny said.

"I'll call her." Leon started to squeeze past Franny.

"No, don't!" Franny stepped in front of him.

"Why not?"

"She…" She what? Doesn't know about this cockamamie plan? "She wanted to surprise you."

"So much for that plan," Leon said.

Franny took a deep breath. "Okay, you got me. Mary Kate wants to take you to a…special show for GIs," she said. "At the Blue Moon."

"The *Blue Moon*? Mary Kate's too classy for that dump." Leon narrowed his eyes. "A show for GIs? What are you up to?"

"Nice girl like me?"

Leon tried to shut the door on her, but Franny wedged her foot in. "Just act surprised when she calls? That's all I ask."

"You ask an awful lot these days."

"Hey," Franny said. "Don't shoot the messenger."

"Messengers are the ones who get shot," Leon said. "That's why they're messengers."

"That's the spirit," Franny said.

He snorted the faintest laugh, which surprised both of them. Leon nodded tersely and shut the door, softly, with a *click* instead of a slam.

Franny exhaled a lungful then bounded downstairs to the telephone. She dialed Mary Kate and pulled the cord as far as it would stretch, to the worn spot of carpet in Papa's TV room. She was more nervous about this phone call than going onstage tonight.

"Mary Kate," Franny said. "I need your help."

"What's the matter this time? Oh no." Mary Kate gasped. "It's the police, isn't it? They're after Peter—"

"No," Franny said. There would be no Peter talk on her dime. "I can't go with you to the Blue Moon tonight."

"Oh, Franny, you promised!"

Franny had definitely not promised, but she wasn't here to split hairs. She had to trust Mary Kate, and she had to get Mary Kate to trust her. She prepared her voice to sound like it just stumbled across a peachy keen idea. "Say, this is a crazy thought," Franny said. "But I saw in the paper that they're letting GIs in tonight. You should take Leon!"

Silence. Had Mary Kate hung up on her? Franny pressed her ear to the receiver then flinched as Mary Kate burst out laughing.

"You got a screw loose, Franny," she said. "*What* paper?"

Think fast, Franny. "The Jewish paper."

"Which Jewish paper."

"All of them."

"That's one heck of a scoop, Franny Steinberg. Well, I'm sorry, but you're not getting off the hook that easy. I'm going to make you have fun, and you can't stop me. Pick you up at five."

She was going to hang up. Franny racked her brain for another lie—but her mind was blank of anything but the truth.

"I'm Peggy Blake," Franny blurted.

Mary Kate laughed. "Boy, when you don't want to do something, you really pull out all the stops."

"I'm serious. I'm Peggy Blake, and I really do need you to sneak Leon into the club with you."

"Leon? At the Blue Moon?" Mary Kate could barely speak through hysterical laughter. "You should be a comedian because *that* is the funniest thing I've ever heard." Franny clutched the phone hard. If Mary Kate didn't believe the truth, what else could she possibly say?

Well. There *was* one more thing she could say.

"It's a little hard to explain—a lot hard to explain, actually—but." Franny took a deep breath. "Mary Kate, I can fix Leon. I can heal him with my Showstopper. We can get him back, the old Leon, the real Leon."

The laughing stopped.

Franny relaxed. Finally, she had gotten through that thick curly-haired skull. "But I can't do it without your help," she said. "I just need you to get him through the door. I'll take care of the rest."

Silence. For a beat too long. Many beats too long.

"You absolute hypocrite," Mary Kate cried. "How dare you? How could you do this to me?"

Franny switched the receiver to her other ear like maybe the first one was misbehaving.

"You said miracles were for babies and Catholics. You called me stupid. You said Daddy wished you had—" Mary Kate huffed through tears and didn't finish her sentence. "I invited you to my wedding, and you ruined that too. I don't ever want to speak to you again!"

There was the *click*. The judgmental drone of the dial tone. The pieces snapped into place, and Franny remembered.

❧

Right after the war, after a Leon-shaped stranger had returned, Mary Kate bounded over to 504 with a newspaper fluttering behind her like a kite. It was a Catholic newspaper, and a short article mentioned something called the French National Pilgrimage.

"To Lourdes," Mary Kate said breathlessly. "The whole country is taking a pilgrimage to Lourdes."

"What's that?" Franny asked. Mary Kate gaped.

"Only the biggest proof of miracles in the whole world," she said. "People go there and bathe in the holy water and are cured of all their ailments. It happens all the time."

Franny had had it up to here with Mary Kate's conversion efforts. "And I should care because?"

"Because now the French are going there," Mary Kate said gently, "and Leon should go too."

Franny ripped the newspaper out of Mary Kate's hands and tore it in half, in half again, and kept tearing until it would only bend, her palms smeared with sweaty newsprint. She threw the pieces at Mary Kate. "For the last time, we're not Catholic," she said.

"But it can heal him," Mary Kate said, tears in her eyes. "I just know it. Don't you want to heal your brother?"

"I don't believe in magic, Leon doesn't believe in magic, and there's no way in your Catholic hell that Leon's going back to Europe."

"You don't have to be so mean about it." Mary Kate sniffled.

"Your family doesn't respect us," Franny said. A terrible thought presented itself. "Your father wishes we died in a concentration camp."

Mary Kate's eyes widened. "Franny," she whispered. "You don't really believe that?"

Franny did not believe it, but the possibility of it made her so righteously angry, she slammed the door on Mary Kate's face.

They didn't speak after that. Mary Kate went to college. Franny didn't. They exchanged pleasantries in passing when Mary Kate was home for vacation, but they might as well have been strangers.

That is, until Mary Kate announced her betrothal at the end of her final year at Saint Mary's, extending the bridesmaid olive branch, and Franny decided to forget about it. She had apparently done a very good job of forgetting.

❧

Franny dialed Mary Kate again, but the phone rang and rang.

CHAPTER SIXTEEN

IN GRAMMAR SCHOOL, FRANNY WAS CAST AS MARY IN THE Nativity. It was a dream come true—a lead role! Well, the understudy anyway. And the director, her fourth-grade teacher, said it was important she rehearse with the rest of the cast every day so she could learn the story of Christmas. And have a costume fitted, which was the best part.

Mama cried and cried about it and pointed fingers at Papa. *You dragged us into this goyische wasteland, and now look what happened.*

Franny couldn't understand what she had done wrong. Who wouldn't love Mary? Calm, beautiful, hardly any lines to memorize. Franny practiced her angelic, closed-mouth smiles in the mirror in secret, draped bedsheets over her head to simulate the gauzy folds of her robe.

"What ever happened to separation of church and state?" Papa said at the parent-teacher meeting Mama had insisted upon.

"Mary was a Jew," the teacher said. "I don't understand the problem."

When Mary Number One came down with the flu, Mama and

Papa boycotted the play and demanded Franny stay home, but they didn't understand. She had to play Mary. The wise men and the donkeys and Joseph and the angels and everyone were counting on her. There was no understudy for the understudy. What's more, she *wanted* to do it.

On opening night, she scanned the gymnasium's folding chairs in the dark—someone waved at her from the front row—it was Leon. Leon! He had sneaked out of the house, against Mama and Papa's wishes. She felt rays of sparkly, magical starlight shooting out of her head, just like the pictures her fourth-grade teacher had shown her. "Mary is the mother of God," the teacher had said. "Do you believe? Do you believe yet?"

"You were even better than Jesus," Leon said after.

"Leon," Franny said, rolling her eyes, "Jesus was a rubber baby doll."

"Exactly," he said. "You were much more lifelike."

⌒☉⌒

Franny clutched the borrowed five-dollar bill like she could magic it into a diamond. She had called Mary Kate three more times—still no answer. She even considered borrowing Papa's car, going to Mary Kate's house, and begging her in person, but that was cutting it way too close.

Anyway, Mary Kate just needed to cool off. No way she'd choose hurt feelings over the chance to help Leon. No way Franny's plans would fall apart because of ancient history. She had to hope for the best.

Phase Two, then, was sneaking Leon through the door, and Barb was the troll under that particular bridge. All trolls had their weaknesses, and Barb would sing "Frère Jacques" in a tutu if you bribed her enough.

"What are you looking at?" Barb asked, baring her teeth. "I got something in my teeth?"

"I—"

"It's spinach, isn't it?" She picked at her incisors. "I never met the spanakopita that didn't leave something in my teeth."

"Your teeth are fine," Franny said. There was definitely a gob of spinach wedged in there. "I actually wanted to introduce you to my friend."

"I don't see no friend."

"How rude of me," Franny said. She opened her hand to reveal the crumpled bill. "Abe, meet Barb. Barb—Abe." She closed her fist as Barb leaned forward to examine it.

"Whatever it is, I ain't innerested." Barb turned away. "I got priors. And a husband in the clink."

Barb had a *husband*?

"When the book clubs get here," Franny said in a low voice, "they're going to have a man with them—tall fellow, dark hair. All I need you to do is let him in, keep him out of Lottie's sight."

Barb laughed, an unpleasant honk that certainly didn't sound like a yes. She pointed. "They're already here," she said. "If one of them's a man, he sure fooled me."

Sure enough, crammed into one of the booths on the shadowy side of the stage were the book club girls. No Leon. And no Mary Kate either.

Now that was startling. Mary Kate couldn't be so cross that she'd miss her chance to finally see Boopsie. Could she?

"I need to make a phone call," Franny said. "Got a nickel?"

Barb plucked the five from Franny's fist. "Sorry, kid," she said. "I'm flat broke." She commenced picking her teeth with the bill, daring Franny to ask for it back.

Lottie wasn't in her U-boat yet. If Franny was quick about it, she could duck behind the bar and use the phone there.

Barb grabbed her arm. "Wouldn't do that if I were you. Ain't so friendly downstairs at the moment."

Franny's intestines did a loop-the-loop. "Not Ed already."

"Boopsie."

Boopsie? Unfriendly? Franny squinted like that would help her hear better but couldn't hear anything over a rush of giggles from the book club girls. "You sure?"

Barb pulled out the gob of spinach and glared accusingly at Franny.

"I didn't see it," Franny said. "I swear."

From the girls' booth, Gal waved both arms like she was trying to find Franny at a war bond rally instead of a nearly empty nightclub. Still no Hal anywhere.

"Peggy!" Gal cried. "Over here."

The book clubs perked up at the sound of Gal hollering her name. They turned to ogle Franny, whispering and elbowing each other. What were they saying? What if they wanted to talk to her? Franny hustled to the girls' booth, red as a baboon's behind. Gal scooched over and patted the seat, but Franny sat next to Andy, who did not scooch over.

"You are not going to believe what just happened," Gal said.

Franny had a whole apology she had practiced in front of her mirror, and her reflection had been very forgiving. Andy, on the other hand, looked like she could hold a grudge to her grave. Now, Franny had one cheek hanging off the seat, everyone was staring, she had lost the five dollars she *stole* from her own father's hospital room, and it was already after five o'clock. She had less than two hours to figure out how to get Leon in the door. If Mary Kate was truly out of the picture, Franny's whole plan had already gone bust. What was she supposed to do now?

The last thing Franny needed right at this moment was another failure.

"Where's Hal?" she said instead.

"This is my side of the table," Andy said. "That's your side."

"So we get here, ready for a blessedly normal night of Amateur Hour, when Boopsie Baxter herself storms in and *slaps* Lottie," Gal said. "Across the face! *Then* she calls her a…the b-word. And they've been screaming in the tunnels ever since."

"I'm sorry," Franny blurted.

"*You* didn't use the b-word," Gal said.

"*I'm* about to use it, though," Andy said. "Scram."

How had this gotten so confusing? Franny took a breath and didn't have the chance to exhale it.

"Hal sold you out, you dolt," Andy blurted. "Says she didn't know what came over her. Says that suddenly, in the middle of the damn show, she was overcome by pure joy, which for some reason meant she *had* to blab to Lottie. I said, 'I know what came over you, it's brown and comes in a bottle.' She denied it, but I said I never wanted to see her lousy rat face here again." Andy played with the split ends of her ponytail. "Look, I may have been a little jealous of the attention you were getting. But I'm not a snitch."

"You told Lottie I couldn't dig deep enough."

"I tell you that to your face," Andy said. "Not the same thing."

Franny fingered the hem of her skirt. "I know," she said.

"We don't *do* that to each other," Andy said. "Or hadn't you noticed?"

She was going to have to crack open her chest and show Andy her heart. But what if Andy took a scalpel to it? Then she would have a mangled heart, a real purple one, not even a medal to brag about.

"I'm so sorry," Franny said. "For everything."

Andy flipped her ponytail over one shoulder and glared. "That's a long list."

"Please don't fight," Gal said nervously. "Remember? Boopsie? Slap? B-word?"

"I'm sorry I blamed you for ratting me out," Franny said, "and I'm sorry I interrupted your set."

"Twice."

"I'm sorry I interrupted your set *twice*," Franny said. She shook her head. "I have been a truly rotten friend."

Andy was silent.

There was no lousier friend than the one who couldn't trust anybody. Franny'd been so worried about herself, she hadn't even realized she *had* friends. Had she ever asked Andy a single question? Where she came from, what her dreams were? Was it too late to start?

"I'd love to hear your new material sometime," Franny said quietly.

Andy scratched at an old stain on the table. "It's just going to make you feel guilty."

"I'm a Jew," Franny said. "I always feel guilty."

Andy rolled her eyes, but her mouth twitched into a smile. Franny made her scooch over.

"I feel guilty too, you know," Andy said, looking at her hands. "I left. My family, my home. This country's trying to get rid of us, and I helped."

Franny snatched a skewer of olives from Gal's martini before Gal could protest and handed one to each of them.

"We have this saying—Gal, back me up here—that the theme of every Jewish holiday is *they tried to kill us, they failed, let's eat*." She held her olive aloft and raised her eyebrows at Andy.

Andy tried to make a serious face but pushed out a snort instead. "You goof."

"They failed," Franny said. "Come on, say it with me."

Andy groaned but toasted Franny's olive anyway. "They failed," she said. "Happy now?"

Franny popped the olive in her mouth and laid a fat smooch on Andy's cheek.

"Ick," Andy said. "I know where that mouth has been." But she smiled as she scrubbed her face with a cocktail napkin.

Gal held her head in her hands and sighed. "Making up almost makes fighting worth it." She looked pointedly at Andy. "I miss Hal."

"Yeah, well," Andy said. "She screwed up."

Franny had been so relieved to fix this one thing, she'd nearly forgotten how screwy everything else was. Was she really about to entangle them in her reckless plans? A Showstopper that healed men? She could hear them laughing—*Great punch line, Peggy, what's the joke?*

Of all the Showstoppers ever conjured since the dawn of Boopsie Baxter, from the dramatic to the mundane, never had there been one that worked on men. It was banana trees in Chicago, like Leon in Miami, a Jewish girl playing the Virgin Mary. Unnatural and a little gruesome.

But then again. What was that about trust? Franny was fresh out of plans and sick of secrets.

"What if she didn't screw up, though?" Franny tried. "What if…"

They stared expectantly. Last chance to back out. Toot, toot, *all aboard the coward train.* Franny let it chug on by.

"What if that was my Showstopper talking?"

"Showstoppers don't work on Hal," Andy said. "And you don't have one." Gal kicked her under the table. Andy winced. "You don't have one *yet*."

The irony of healing men's pain in order to save the only night-club left for girls was not lost on Franny. But what if Showstoppers could be for everyone without ruining it for anyone? Was that even possible?

"I do have one," Franny said quietly. "But it doesn't work on girls. It, ah, relieves pain. In men." Franny couldn't look them in the eye. "And Hal wasn't drunk that night."

The silence told Franny everything she needed to know. She was about to tell them to forget it, she was just trying out some new material—

"You're sure?" Gal said.

Franny swallowed. Her throat was still a little scratchy. "Unfortunately, yes."

"It does kind of add up," Andy said. "Hal is not a blabber. And, well, she isn't really a she, is she? Not, you know, on the inside? Or the outside, actually."

Gal nodded thoughtfully. "A Showstopper that heals men," she said. "Nurse Peggy, no—*Doctor*. 'Let Doctor Peggy Blake fix your trouser snake!'"

Andy fake vomited into Gal's drink. "There's my honest review."

"It's called workshopping, *Andy*."

Now that was a new sensation. Being believed.

"Bet you wouldn't guess," Franny said, "but conjuring a Showstopper for men is a bit...complicated."

She told them about the madness of the Velvet Swing, showed them the raw spot on her neck, and Andy couldn't stop laughing.

"You thought you were better off with *Sy*?" she cried. "He's a legendary prick. Ten times worse than Ed."

"He's my cousin," Gal said. Franny and Andy gawped. "Estranged, obviously."

"Well, I got to see what Ed's revenge looks like too. When my Showstopper wore off, he—" Franny couldn't say it through a haze of guilt. "He thought Lottie drugged him."

Andy grabbed her hand. "It's not your fault," she said. "You know that, right?"

"Doesn't matter. I can't let that happen to Lottie again," Franny said. "She needs this place. We all need it, and I'm the one who can fix it." Franny hesitated. "And there's something else—" Could she get any more selfish? Asking them to help with her piddly little family problems when something as big as the Blue Moon was on the line?

"Holy crow, *Leon*," Gal gasped. "Peggy, he's got to come tonight, he's just *got* to. How can we help?"

Gal Gardenia, who made her promise never to tell her family. Franny was amazed.

Gal snapped her fingers. "The Heeb grapevine," she said. "It's so obvious! Half the BBGs are sweet on him anyway. We'll get him here lickety-split." She popped out of the booth.

"Gal, wait," Franny said. "I don't think that's such a swell idea—" She tried to picture a gaggle of BBGs showing up at 504 and dragging Leon out of the house. It was not a pretty picture. But then again.

If Mary Kate really was *that* sore, if Gal could summon the *right* BBGs at the right time, if Mama added a pinch of guilt to get Leon out the door...it might work. In any case, this was no time to be choosy about secret plans.

"And I'll call Hal," Andy blurted awkwardly. "She'll do anything for the Blue Moon." She flushed a rainbow of reds. "Since we're going around apologizing."

The trapdoor to the tunnels flung open with a shotgun bang, giving Franny her third almost-heart attack of the week. Boopsie Baxter popped out of the floor, hair set in Dorothy Dandridge waves, looking cool and Grecian in a flowing white dress and heels, if a little shaken-not-stirred.

"Seven years bad luck," Lottie called up, voice echoing like a pissed-off choir. "That mirror wasn't cheap!"

"You want to talk cheap?" Boopsie said. "Ain't nothing cheaper than selling out a friend."

"Keep your voice down."

"Do you know how much she made, selling my jokes to that man?" Boopsie pointed at Andy, who froze with the phone stuck to her face.

"I don't, and I would never—" Andy stuttered.

"Bastard even showed me the contract, can you believe it? Thought he could squeeze more jokes out of the deal."

Lottie swore from the bowels of the Blue Moon.

Gal tapped Franny's hand. "See?" she whispered. "Didn't I tell you?"

"I have working ears, don't I?" Franny said.

Lottie clomped up the stairs and froze when she saw the book clubs staring at her. She mustered a haughty nod and then leaned in close to Boopsie. "Look," she said, "I didn't know he was going to do them on television. I swear."

"You swore you had no idea about *any* of it. You swore on your mother's grave."

"Christ on a toothpick. I did it to save the Blue Moon," Lottie said. "You only want to save Boopsie."

"Oh, the patron saint of stand-up comedy," Boopsie said. "The martyr of the Blue Moon. Spare me. Do you know how much a last-minute plane ticket costs? Of course you don't! You've never visited me, not even once."

"Why would I visit a dying nightclub in a shit neighborhood? I hear you can't even make rent."

Boopsie pulled herself up and glared at Lottie. "Good luck without me tonight." She spun around, breezed past Barb, and disappeared out the door.

The book clubs gasped.

Lottie composed her face. "All part of the show, girls," she said. "She'll be back with time to spare." She feigned calm, posed like a statue on a barstool. Enid tried to beg forgiveness with a five-olive martini, but Lottie wouldn't touch it.

Was she really going to let Boopsie leave? Had she lost her mind?

"Peggy," Lottie hollered. "Go fetch Boopsie, will you?"

All eyes glued to Franny. She slunk up to the bar. "Me?"

Lottie lit a cigarette. "Tell her about your Showstopper."

"You're joking."

"She thinks I'm a selfish shrew." Lottie tilted her head to blow out smoke, and Franny could see the bruises she had barely concealed with makeup. "But what she really wants is a reason to stay."

Franny burst out the door, scanning up and down Lawrence in a panic. There—right across the street at Peter Pan's—there she was, sitting at the window booth Franny and the girls always picked, stuffing her face with a Francheezie.

"Well, if it isn't Fran-cheesy," Boopsie said, dabbing her lips with a napkin.

Boopsie Baxter remembered her *name*?

"Peggy. Peggy Blake?" Franny thrust her hand out to shake. It arrived somewhere between Boopsie's neck and outer space. "We met earlier this summer?"

"Tell Lottie to blow her smoke up someone else's ass. I'm through being used," Boopsie said, delicately maneuvering away from Franny's hand. She leaned back and looked up at Franny through her thick eyelashes. "And you got some nerve. Just who do you think you are?"

"Me? I'm nobody!"

"Nobodies don't dictate the lineup."

"I don't dictate. I take dictation!" Franny plopped down in the booth like some big dumb animal next to Boopsie's goddess-starlet. "I'm just the opener; you're the main event." Boopsie looked surprised then scooched over to accommodate.

"I am the alpha *and* the omega, baby," Boopsie said. "I don't share the stage. Especially with an amateur. Lottie knows that. Everyone knows that."

"Tonight is different," Franny said. "We can save the Blue Moon."

Boopsie groaned. "Not this again."

Franny glanced out the window. The blue neon lights spelling out "Blue Moon Cocktail Lounge" flickered, a lighthouse for the lost.

"You're not going to believe what I'm about to tell you."

"Try me," Boopsie said. "Or don't. I don't care." She folded her arms, and Franny tried her.

Throughout Franny's story, Boopsie's expression didn't change, but Franny sensed a shift in energy. Boopsie was curious. About *her*.

"Oh, fabulous, so I'm the show's bed warmer?" Boopsie laughed, shook her head. "This is the state of my career."

"No, you're my *hero*. You changed my whole life." Franny stared at the table, its faded design. "If I hadn't seen you that Christmas Eve, I don't know where I'd be right now. I don't *want* to know."

And just like that, the last puzzle piece clicked. It was no longer a puzzle; it was a whole picture.

"Say it, don't spray it, kid." Boopsie blotted her arm with a napkin, but it was all show, and they both knew it. She shook her head. "Showstoppers that work on men, this I have to see. You can't fix anyone that doesn't want to fix himself, you know. Not even a Showstopper can do that."

"I know," Franny lied.

"Lottie's always got a plan five moves deep," Boopsie said. "Don't forget it for a second."

"So," Franny said quietly. "You'll do it?"

Boopsie looked at her long and hard, and Franny did not look away. "You better warm that room up good."

CHAPTER SEVENTEEN

THE BLUE MOON WAS STANDING-ROOM ONLY, PACKED TIT to tit. Every time the door opened, Franny's heart stopped. But it was never the BBGs, or Mary Kate, or Leon. And time was running out.

Varla's violin voice pierced through the clamor, like she was the solo act and everyone else was her orchestra.

"First, I'm putting in brand-new fluorescent lights to brighten up the joint," Varla said, waving a decorated arm around. "What's the point of looking this good if you can't be seen?"

"I couldn't agree more," Ed said, kissing her neck. Varla squealed.

"Ed, you're undermining my authority!"

"A regular Lottie Marcone over here," Ed said, patting Varla's cheek a little harder than necessary. "One's more than enough, doll."

Boopsie flipped open a silver cigarette case and offered it to Franny; cigarettes lined up neat as corpses. "Customary pre-gallows cigarette?"

"Thanks, but I'll stick with air," Franny said. "While I still can." Boopsie chuckled and lit her own cigarette. And then Lottie was standing there next to them, a vise grip on Franny's upper arm.

"Showtime, let's go."

Franny's throat clenched. "Show's not until seven," she said.

"Lottie, relax," Boopsie said. "No one's paying any attention yet. She'll have a hell of a time up there." Boopsie smiled sweetly around a mouthful of smoke.

"Whose side are you on?" Lottie said.

"Mine."

"The show starts when I say it starts," Lottie said, tugging on Franny. "And I say it starts now."

Franny looked wildly at Andy, who looked at Gal. What were they going to do?

Gal nodded, chugged her manhattan, and coughed.

"L'chaim!" she croaked.

"What is this, mutiny?" Lottie said.

"No." Gal stood, smacked her hands on the table, and made everyone flinch. "It's *Hebrew.*"

She slipped past Lottie, who was confused into speechlessness. And before anyone could stop her, Gal hopped onstage to wild applause, swinging the microphone cord around her like a lion tamer.

"Hello, all you lovely ladies!" Glorious, wonderful, stalling-for-time Gal. Franny shrugged like *what can you do?* Lottie let go of her arm, leaving tiny red smiles where her nails had been.

Maybe Gal's set was just the ticket. The tension was taut as panty hose in here; even the book club girls fidgeted in their seats. With Gal onstage, you just knew, no matter how desperately everything else was falling apart, she had one small corner of the world under control.

How else could she look so well-groomed while living in a rat hotel?

Franny was such a dolt. All this time they teased Gal about her snooze fest of a Showstopper, but they missed the whole point. Gal's Showstopper *was* her deepest yearning: to sit in the eye of the storm, the order at the heart of chaos, the joke at the core of a tragedy. Now was her time to shine.

But Gal had been silent for a few moments too long. She was just sort of smiling at the microphone, long after the room stopped clapping and cheering.

Finally, she perked up. "Boy," she said, waggling her eyebrows. "Have. We. Got." She smiled, paused. "The. Show. Of. A. Lifetime."

She drew out each word like it was the *Mona Lisa*. Taffeta rustled. Girls started murmuring and laughing, but not in a good way. Gal's set was only five minutes, but it felt like at least a week.

"I. Have. To. Say—"

The murmuring and rustling was a symphony of annoyance.

Andy leaned in. "She thinks she's helping. If you can believe that."

She was stalling for time all right. Franny could just scream. She wasn't helping; she was *bombing*. Even if Gal could stall until the BBGs brought Leon, Franny wouldn't be able to reach him. Even Boopsie Baxter would have a hard time wrestling authority back after this, and she was headlining.

"What is this crap?" Ed cried. "Where's Boopsie?"

The room murmured in agreement. Girls even started to chant, softly at first, then more boldly. Tapping their toes, slapping the tabletops. *Boop-sie. Boop-sie. Boop-sie.*

Gal blithely continued. "Isn't. Dating. Terr. I. Ble?" She winked at Franny like *hey, this is going great, huh?*

Lottie banged her glass on the table, and the stem broke, gin waterfalling to the floor.

"Gee, Lottie, I can't quite hear what name they're chanting," Boopsie said. "Can you?"

Gal gripped the microphone, pressed it right up to her mouth. "Ladies and degenerates," she said, "who here needs a free drink?"

The chattering stopped on a dime, on a penny, even. The room cheered. Lottie swore, motioning to Enid to get ready for a deluge of Mai Tais. Gal continued winking at Franny, now also nodding like a drinky bird toy. Franny nodded back, mouthed, *Thank you,* but Gal shook her head vigorously, then nodded again, then rolled her eyes.

"Look!" Gal cried, pointing at the door.

Everyone looked. In the doorway, a silhouette in uniform. Franny blinked to make sure she wasn't hallucinating.

It was Leon.

Finally, he had stumbled into the right place at the right time. She wasn't about to ask why or how. In that moment, he was better than one of Gal's buses.

"Hey, Peggy," Barb shouted. "Your boyfriend's here."

Franny stood shakily, trapped between the magnetic poles of stage and Leon.

"Grab those drinks lickety-split, ladies, because mark my words," Gal said, "our first comedian is going to be big, very big, and you'll be able to say you 'knew her when'—"

"Franny?" Leon's voice broke, and Franny wasn't sure she could mend it.

"Please welcome—Peggy Blake!"

Lottie snatched Franny's wrists and squeezed. "I will not let you choose *him*."

Barb hopped up and wrenched Leon's arms behind him. Franny and Leon faced off like prizefighters before a match. *Lemme at him,* Franny thought. *I can win this one.*

"Peggy Blake, ladies and degenerates!" Gal cried.

Not a single girl was watching Gal. She started an amateur soft-shoe routine, trying to grab their attention.

"Either he stays," Franny said to Lottie, "or I don't go up."

"Franny," Leon said. "We're leaving. Now."

"Peggy stays," Lottie said. "You go." She squeezed Franny's arm hard, but Franny refused to flinch.

"Who's Peggy?" Leon asked.

"No Leon," Franny said, "no jokes."

"Who's Leon?" Lottie asked.

"I am," Leon said.

"Nice try, Michael Boreman," Lottie said.

"Who?"

"Michael Berman," Franny said.

"That's what I said," Lottie said.

"This is Leon," Franny said.

"I don't care if he's a monkey's uncle," Lottie cried. "If he's not out of here in ten seconds, he'll be a monkey's *aunt*."

"Peggy Blake, ladies and degenerates!" Gal called helplessly.

They stared at each other in silence. The room had hushed, watching them like a movie. Ed struggled his way out of the booth, purple as a murderous eggplant. Lottie saw him and loosened her grip. She nodded at Barb, who released Leon.

"Make it quick," Lottie hissed.

Franny rushed over to Leon. He flinched, and it wedged in her heart like a splinter. "Leon. Give me five measly minutes. And then I'll leave with you, I'll explain everything, I promise."

Leon gazed at her with those haunted eyes and said nothing. She would have to take it as a yes.

The stage was Everest, and Franny climbed it alone. All attention was on her, every eye, every ear. A heavy weapon Franny hoped she could wield. She wouldn't get a second chance to save Leon.

Gal handed her the mic like Mama's wedding ring, the one Papa's papa smuggled across the sea. She took a deep breath then turned to face the room.

The room gazed up at Franny, mesmerized. They were on her side. Lord knew they were ready to laugh. And wouldn't that be something for Leon to see. Her authority over this room. A whole room of girls who believed Franny. She could make them laugh at anything. She could make them laugh at him, hurt him the way he hurt her by always taking Peter's side. *They say war puts hair on your chest, makes you a man. But my brother went to war and came back a boy.*

No, that wasn't right. She wanted to heal him, not hurt him. Didn't she?

She blinked out over the room of pretty, smiling faces. They didn't see her at all. They saw Peggy Blake. They didn't want her real Showstopper; they came for a fake one. And one thing was for sure: if she didn't deliver, their expectant smiles would slip like banana peels.

Franny was nobody, just like she told Boopsie.

But Boopsie was smiling at her too. Gal and Andy nodded encouragement. When was a nobody not a nobody? When they had friends.

Franny squared her shoulders and lifted her chin. "My twenty-first—"

The door banged open and in tumbled Hal. Her shorn hair combed neatly, wearing a stylish man's suit with a tie and cuff links and everything. There was a bulge inside the jacket that didn't seem to correspond to a body part.

Franny was treated to the back of everyone's heads. Hal always managed to command authority in a room. It just belonged to her, like another arm or a hat that fit exactly right.

"You want the Blue Moon to have a future?" Hal said. She opened her arms wide. "Well, you're looking at it."

Lottie raised her eyebrows. "And what *exactly* am I looking at?"

"I've been playing your game by your rules. But the only person who can win Lottie's game is Lottie. Took me too long to figure that out," Hal said. She reached into the inner, bulging pocket of her jacket. "So here's the only logic you will listen to."

For a moment, the entire club was suspended in disbelief, little orange bits floating in gelatin. Franny covered her heart like she could protect it.

Lottie scoffed. "You don't have anything in there but a banana," she said. "Matches the one in your pants—neither of them real."

Hal looked startled, but then a margarine smile spread across her face. "Always thinking the worst of me. Would you bet your life on it? How about Peggy's? Boopsie's?"

Andy stood shakily. "Hal, don't do this."

Hal looked at her. "Andy's?"

"What am I, chopped liver?" Gal muttered. Andy shushed her.

Enough was enough. Franny was going to speak if it killed her, even then.

"My twenty-first birthday," Franny said too loudly, making everyone jump, "a family friend decided to make a woman out of me. He had his finger blown off in the war—and by the end of the night, I wished he had lost a different appendage. They don't call him *Peter* for nothing."

Leon stiffened. A few girls in the book club chuckled, and the laugh caught on like measles, infecting the room.

Hal, her authority wobbling, turned to watch Franny. And in that second, Lottie reached for her ankle derringer.

A *pop* jangled Franny's rib cage. She had never heard a gunshot before, but now that she had, it was unmistakable. The body knows the sound of death on its way. She clutched her heart, expecting blood.

Leon crumpled to the floor.

"Man down!" Ed cried. "Friendly fire!"

Everyone screamed, hopping out of their chairs and plowing one another over to get the hell out of there. Barb and Enid were the first out the door. Hal rubbed the back of her neck, pacing in front of Leon while the crowd swarmed around them.

"Who are you? This wasn't supposed to happen." Hal pulled out the lump from her coat. It was an envelope, not a gun. And it was full of cash. "I got a job. I did everything legal." She looked like she wanted Leon to agree, but Leon just writhed on the floor, clutching his right leg. So much blood seeped through his pants. There was an important vein in the thigh, wasn't there? Mama would know.

"You shot my brother," Franny cried.

"If only," Lottie said, "there were someone here who could heal him."

That dastardly b-word. Franny started to run offstage to help Leon, but Lottie intercepted her.

"Not down here," she said. She waved her derringer at the stage. "Up there."

Lottie didn't need a weapon because she was one. But unfortunately, she also had a gun. And a paper and pen. Not just any paper—the deed to the Blue Moon. Franny's heart pounded.

Gal, Andy, and Boopsie huddled together in the booth. They didn't abandon ship. They didn't abandon Franny.

"You always need a push," Lottie said. "So this is what I do for you. I push."

Varla started shrieking. "I don't want this life. I was happy as a cigarette girl. Sure, I got some ass pinches, but nobody shot nobody. Nobody tried to turn me into Lottie Marcone."

"*You* hate this life? You don't know the half of it," Lottie said. She turned to Franny. "Time to make them laugh."

Ed helped Leon off the floor and plopped him in a chair. Leon stared up at him, pale and saucer-eyed.

"Looks like you got quite a scratch there, Private," Ed said. He loosened his tie, and Leon flinched. "Wrap this around your thigh."

Leon grabbed the tie. "Thanks, um," he said, "Fingers?"

Ed cackled. "Between you and me—the finger thing is a gimmick! You know how hard it is to get in the papers without a gimmick? Call me Sergeant Marcone."

Leon chuckled along nervously then seemed to realize Ed was serious. "Oh," he said, struggling to stand and salute, maybe the strangest salute in all of history.

"At ease, at ease," Ed said. He turned to Lottie. "You shot him. A man in uniform."

Lottie's face was a diamond, always out of reach. She glittered at Franny, holding the deed to the Blue Moon aloft.

"Tell the punch line, and you fix everything," Lottie said. "I see you, Peggy. I see you better than anyone. Most girls are trapped, but not us. Not today. Today you're Houdini, and you can magic us out of this mess."

Leon was getting paler by the second, his face slick with sweat. How powerful was Franny, exactly? What if she could save his life? Wouldn't now be the time to find out?

"By the end of the night, I wished he had lost a different appendage. They don't call him *Peter* for nothing." Franny spoke quiet as a prayer, hardly sounded like herself at all.

"Louder," Lottie said.

"Franny, get down from there before you say something you regret," Leon said. "You do not belong up on that stage."

"The hell she doesn't!" Andy said. "Peggy Blake is a star, and don't you forget it."

Damn right.

"Forget the Purple Heart," Franny said. She blinked back tears. "Leon, forget the goddamn Purple Heart already."

Leon's jaw worked like a piston.

"Have a little respect, this man is a war hero," Ed said, slapping Leon's battle ribbons and making him flinch. "He can take what he wants. He's earned it, isn't that right, Private?"

Leon's face changed. "Hold on now, I'm not the one—"

"And that's men for you," Lottie said. "They always protect their own. Why can't we do the same? Make them laugh at themselves for once?"

This was the moment Franny wanted, the moment she had lied and stole and manipulated for. She had made Leon laugh a million times, a million years ago. If she could just do it one more time, this *one* time when it really mattered, when that laugh had never felt so out of reach. Leon stood slowly, limped his way toward the stage, staring up at Franny with his haunted Steinberg eyes. They were just eyes. Franny had them too. So why were tears tickling her cheeks?

"God, you're pathetic," Lottie spat. "An innocent baby bunny, hunted by big bad Lottie the wolf? Oh, boo-hoo to you, I call bullshit. You know what animal skitters around in the dark, maneuvering, sneaking, stealing, covering their ass? A rat! You honestly think you're better than me." Lottie smiled up at her, serene as Mary. "Joke's on you, Franny Steinberg, you're just like me."

An egg sizzled in the pan of Franny's guts. Was it true?

"Hal has cash!" Andy cried, waving a stack of bills in front of Lottie's face. "Gotta be at least enough for a down payment!"

Franny watched the scene roiling at her feet—Leon, bleeding. Fingers Marcone, nursing. Lottie, vibrating with fury, the scales of justice balanced between a derringer and the crumpled deed, Gal and Andy and Hal and Boopsie, witnessing. An *aha* washed over Franny, and she knew exactly what to do.

Lottie always has a plan five moves deep.

Franny watched herself in slow motion as she snatched the papers out of Lottie's hand and held them up for everyone to see.

It wasn't the deed to the Blue Moon. It was divorce papers.

Lottie turned her derringer on Franny and cocked the hammer. "Fuck the Blue Moon."

A pause, a question mark, the top of the teeter-totter—who was heavier? Which way would it fall?

Leon tackled Franny, wrapping his arms around her legs and yanking her offstage. The divorce papers fluttered to the floor as he heaved her over his shoulder in a fireman's hold, limping and stumbling toward the side door then through it, into the shiny, oblivious bustle of Lawrence Avenue.

CHAPTER EIGHTEEN

LEON LIMPED INTO THE ALLEY BEHIND THE BUILDING AND heaved Franny into the dumpster, followed by himself. He fumbled with the bags of garbage, burrowing into them and covering Franny with squishy, slimy who-knew-what.

"I'm not your duffel bag," Franny cried. "You can't just throw me around." She struggled to get out, but Leon pulled her close and clamped a hand over her mouth.

"We're safe here," he said.

His hand smelled like iron filings and smeared her cheek wetly. Blood. Franny gagged, and he shushed her. Hiding only made everything worse; how had he not figured that out? He was in way over his head, and not just with garbage.

Footsteps approached the alley. The clacking metronome of high heels. "Peggy?" Lottie called. "I'm not going to hurt you." Franny clawed at Leon's hand, but he clamped down tighter. Just because he was bigger didn't mean his decisions were better. Franny tried to communicate this to Leon with her elbows, but her Morse code was a little rusty.

Lottie's footsteps approached the dumpster, paused for a long, filthy, stinking minute, and then finally retreated.

⤸❦⤷

Franny had nearly decomposed with the rest of the trash by the time Leon peeled his hand from her mouth. He peeked out of the dumpster then, satisfied, picked his way out. The humid August air felt cool and refreshing by comparison. Franny brushed what she hoped was just an ancient banana from the front of her dress. She was so mad, she was going to burst like a frozen pipe, Papa's winter nightmare.

"Now what, genius?" she said. "Or is hiding in dumpsters your new life plan?"

Leon slid down the brick wall and plopped on the filthy concrete. He gestured at the grimy alley, the dumpster, his bleeding leg, the smear of hopefully banana on Franny's dress.

"See? Safe. You're welcome."

He grimaced, wrapping Ed's tie tighter around his thigh. Blood squished through the fabric.

Franny crossed her arms to hold herself together. "You bled through your uniform," she snapped. "We need to go to the hospital."

"I'm fine," Leon snapped back. "At least it's finally doing its job."

"I thought you hated that uniform."

"*Someone* told me there was a GI night at the Blue Moon. *Someone* told me Mary Kate would be there," Leon said. "No one told me I was the punch line."

"You don't know anything about my punch lines."

"Okay, *Peggy Blake*. Bring on the laughs."

She could do it—she could conjure authority out here in the alley and *make* him laugh at her joke. She would watch him crumble under the power of her Showstopper. And then she would make him apologize.

"You have something to say? Say it to my face." Leon struggled to stand. Franny let him struggle.

"I've got a lot to say, but you'll just dive back into that dumpster to hide from it."

"Why, you want to poke fun of my service to this country? Or Peter's—I can't even say it, Franny!"

"You don't know the worst of it."

Leon punched the dumpster. "Then tell me," he said, "the fucking joke."

"Fine!" Franny leaned in close. She had never heard Leon swear in her whole life. "They say war puts hair on your chest, makes you a man. But my brother...well, he did it backward. He went to war a man and came back a boy."

Leon blinked in rapid Morse code. Franny did not retreat.

"The other day, Mama catches him playing with toy soldiers and wearing a diaper, if you can believe that. 'What do you think you're doing?' she says. 'Playing war,' he says. Next thing you know, he squats over the soldiers in his diaper and cries, 'Bombs away!'"

She tried to hold Leon's gaze, but he looked away first, the rattle of a gasp in his throat. She felt suddenly ashamed.

"It's a joke, not a court document," she muttered. "So sue me."

She had made herself believe that if the joke was funny, its ugliness didn't count. That if Leon didn't laugh, well, that was his fault. But Franny was just a lousy quack, using a scalpel to carve her initials in Leon's heart. Now that the joke was out there, dangling in the dank alley, Franny knew she didn't mean for Leon to laugh at it at all. She had wanted to hurt him with it, the way he could so casually hurt her.

"Peter was right," Leon said. "You don't think about anyone but yourself."

But this was too much.

"Oh, like when I saved him from going to prison?"

"You mocked him. Onstage. In front of people who might *know* him. You know what that could do to his reputation?"

Franny wanted to tear her rib cage open and throw her own scarred heart in his face.

Instead, she plunged into the deep, dark sea of her mind and found the memory—slimy, rank, and wriggling. She took a good hard look at it, the lousy fish, its greasy scales, the stench, the heft in her hands. She brought it to the surface and gutted it.

"I was always your kid sister, Mary Kate's little friend. I couldn't believe it when he asked me on a date. A real date, to see *Treasure of the Sierra Madre* at the Starlite Drive-In, just him and me on my birthday. Every girl in the neighborhood had a crush on Peter, but he was going to spend his Friday night with me. I wheedled Mama into buying me that dumb blue dress with the puffy sleeves. I borrowed her pearl earrings. I had my hair set and lacquered and stayed indoors so the breeze wouldn't mess it up. I was perfectly ridiculous. But I was determined. We'd be going steady by the time he dropped me off at 504.

"It all started off like a dream. He opened every door for me. He bought me popcorn with butter and didn't laugh when I dropped a handful on my skirt and got it all greasy. He talked about going to Loyola to get a good job so he could support a family, and he wrapped his arm around me as he said it."

Franny took a breath; Leon didn't.

"Next thing I knew, he was on top of me. I couldn't breathe. I couldn't move. I watched Bogart as he stole all that gold and wished I was there too."

"But Bogart doesn't make it," Leon said softly. "They kill him."

"Good old Peter," Franny said. "Boys Club, phony-shark-attack, funny, handsome, helpful, perfect-except-for-the-Catholic-part Peter. Wiggling his hand up my skirt while I kicked his shins. You think I didn't blame myself? Who would believe me over Peter? Who'd believe Peter's a monster?"

"Peter's not a monster."

"Gosh," Franny said. "And, to think, just yesterday you told the police he bombed a house."

Leon smacked the brick wall, which didn't even flinch. He threw his garrison cap at the ground. He limped around, trying to light a cigarette, but his hands shook, and he couldn't get the match to light, so he threw those on the ground too.

Franny picked up the matchbook and lit one. He leaned in close, the tips of his long eyelashes glowing.

"If Peter Finnegan is a monster," he said, "then so am I. You have no idea. What I had to do. What I have to remember." Leon pressed his face to the wall like there was a priest on the other side. "You make jokes, but Peter asks. Peter listens. Peter took my gun away when I wanted to use it."

Oh.

Oh.

Leon was afraid that if he told his secrets, he'd fall apart, go *kablooey*, disappear. Well, that sort of thing was awfully familiar to Franny.

Franny motioned for his cigarette case, took one for herself, and lit it.

"Some days I think Peter's the only thing keeping me from drowning," he said.

"Well, he *is* kind of a dinghy," Franny said then grimaced. "There I go again. With the jokes."

Leon stared at his cigarette like he'd never seen one before.

"You smoke it," Franny said, demonstrating. "Like this."

"I'm sorry, Franny."

Franny coughed so hard, he started smacking her on the back. "Stop it," she croaked, dodging his swats. "Why do people do that? It doesn't help."

"Sorry."

"You said that already."

"That's because I am," Leon said.

"For whacking my lungs out of my chest?"

Leon turned to look at her. "About Peter."

Franny had never believed those actresses who fainted from emotion, but she wished there were a fainting couch to catch her right about now. Instead, she sat on the concrete. Leon sat next to her, shoulder to shoulder, knee to knee.

"If I didn't find a way to laugh at this stuff, to laugh at you, I was going to lose my marbles. And then I thought," she said, "if I could make *you* laugh, we could pretend the war never happened, go back to the way things used to be, remind you who you really are."

"This is who I really am."

Franny thought about arguing, decided to believe him instead. "I know."

Leon held his cigarette loosely in his long fingers. "One hell of a speech, Hamlet."

Franny laughed. "I wouldn't guess you'd ever heard of Shakespeare."

"Oh sure, I played Romeo *and* Juliet in the POW theater troupe. Brought the house down."

The moment was a butterfly that alighted on Franny, thinking she was a flower.

"Wish we were still inside. I could use a bourbon," Leon said. "Look, Franny, I always wanted what everyone wanted. Family, house, steady paycheck. Then the war came, and it was just what we were supposed to do—fight the bad guys, come home a hero. Family, house, paycheck. Peter wouldn't shut up about how great the army was. Piña coladas, bathing beauties, the ocean. He said he could get me stationed in Hawaii, but he was out before I finished boot camp."

"Papa thinks you enlisted because you saw him crying," Franny said, "about his family."

"Only thing I've ever seen Papa cry over is key lime pie," Leon said. "I enlisted because Peter enlisted. Because everyone enlisted, or if they didn't, they were drafted. What was I supposed to do? Wait for the envelope to show up, while my friends were picked off one by one? Was I supposed to be the only man left standing, raking oak leaves at 504?"

"I'm the one who rakes the leaves."

"Is that what you call it?" Leon took a drag of the cigarette, exhaled like an old train. "We were just supposed to be cleanup crew, sweeping up after the war. The Panzer Army surprised us, marched us across frozen battlefields, fed us almost nothing. We had fleas and scurvy and dysentery. The only reason I survived—in the cot next to me—" Leon scrubbed his face with his hands.

"For a month, I was too weak to pick up a pen. But even if I could, I wouldn't have written. I survived the bombing of Dresden when braver men didn't. You thought your brother was a hero, meanwhile I was shitting gruel in an underground bunker, stealing stale bread, begging the enemy to keep me alive."

His cigarette was little more than a butt; he burnt his fingers and dropped it, smoldering, on the ground. "One day, they told the Jews to line up in the prison yard. They were going to shoot us. I was—I was..." Leon exhaled slowly. "*Grateful.* But my captain, he—he told our entire company to stand together, Jew and non-Jew. Not a single man objected. A German guard screamed in his face, shoved a Luger in his belly. But he wouldn't budge. He said, 'Today, we are all Jews.'" Leon's voice got so quiet, Franny had to strain to hear. "I stole a sick man's bread until he starved to death, and this stranger saved my life."

He flicked his eyes over to see her reaction. Franny didn't know how to react.

"The captain was just this Alabama farmer, never met a Jew

until he joined the army. But it was like he was enchanted. I can't explain it, but the prison guard just stormed off, and the Germans abandoned us there. No food or water and nothing to do but waste away and die. But then—we were saved by the British. And suddenly the war was over." Leon sighed. "It'll never be over."

Franny sniffled, and Leon started at the noise, like he had forgotten she existed. "Anyway," he said. "I was shipped off to France to go through a bunch of red tape before I could go home. And then to Leavenworth for more red tape. I don't know what's worse about war—the battles or the bureaucracy."

Franny hesitated then embraced Leon, leaning awkwardly over him. His body stiffened, but she refused to let go. She squeezed harder.

"Hug me, dammit," she said.

Leon wrapped his arms around her, just for a moment, but he did it.

"I didn't peg you as the type to be ashamed of your heritage," he said, pulling away.

"Excuse me?"

"Franny Steinberg isn't good enough for the stage?"

"If I had a nickel for every time you played hooky from Hebrew school—"

"You'd have about fifty cents. Hebrew school was boring. And happened during baseball practice."

"Look at you—Jake, the Yiddisher ball player—who thinks his heritage is boring."

"I fought real Nazis to defend my heritage," Leon said.

Franny rolled her eyes. "Sounds like you mostly ran from them."

Leon stiffened. Stupid big fat mouth. He had *just* opened up to her and what did she do?

But then he snorted. And something resembling a honk escaped his mouth. "Was that a laugh?" Franny said. "I'm serious, I'm not actually sure."

"You just reminded me of something," he said. "When our company was ambushed, me and my buddy Kurt, we were first in line. The Germans advanced, rifles drawn, and my whole body was shaking so hard, I could barely raise my arms in surrender. All I could think about was you, and Mama and Papa, and how scared and sad you were about to be. But nothing had happened *yet*. We were between moments when terrible things happened. And I thought—maybe I can stop this. Maybe I can fix everything. I figured my Yiddish was good enough to get them to understand me, but speaking Yiddish to a Nazi would be...not ideal."

"Understatement of the century."

"I had picked up a few German words and thought if I could say *don't shoot*, maybe they would take pity. At that time, I thought being a prisoner was better than being shot on a frozen Belgian battlefield. So I shouted, 'Nein scheissen! Nein scheissen!'"

Leon looked at her sheepishly, mouth caught in a half smirk. "And the Germans started laughing. They laughed so hard, they had to lower their rifles."

Franny wasn't familiar with the word. "What did you say?"

Leon grinned. "Don't shit! Don't shit!"

"Leon," Franny said. "That is the funniest thing that has ever come out of your mouth, and you wasted it on the Nazis."

Franny had forgotten how much Leon sounded like a donkey when he laughed. They laughed and laughed, and couldn't stop, and lowered their rifles.

⁓◈⁓

The windshield of Papa's Cadillac-sedan was smashed to smithereens. The roof was concave, V-shaped almost. And there was Lottie herself, leaning against the passenger-side door, turning her derringer over in her hand, a crowbar at her feet.

"What can I say?" Lottie said. "Nothing like a double dose of betrayal to make you want to let off a little steam."

Leon reached an arm out, slowly, trying to hide Franny behind him without attracting attention. Lottie smirked. "What a gentleman," she said. "Does he know what you are? She could fix you right now, brother, fix you right up, better than a doctor, even. Better than Freud himself."

The necktie wrapped around Leon's thigh was soaked in blood, though mercifully it had stopped dripping and was now crusting over. His face was slick and pale in the yellow sodium streetlights.

"That's not her job," Leon said. "It's mine."

"Sure it is, cowboy," Lottie said. She wasn't pointing the gun, just looking at it. "I don't know how you managed to unravel my entire life in a single summer. Truly impressive." The lights from the Blue Moon marquee reflected ghoulishly on her face.

Franny's heart clenched. "Ed tore up the divorce papers," she said, "didn't he?"

Lottie barked a laugh. "No, Peggy, he signed them."

Franny tried to laugh too, but something in Lottie's face stopped her. "You're serious."

Lottie raised her eyebrows in affirmation. "Ed and Hal, what a team. They negotiated me right out of my own club. 'The Blue Moon should be run by a comedian,' Hal says, 'Lottie's unhinged. Lottie's washed up.'" Lottie mimicked Hal in a shrill, girly voice. "Guffawed and shook hands like a couple of suits, and *I'm* the one squeezed out. Not queen of the Blue Moon. Not Mrs. Fingers Marcone. I'm nobody."

For a moment, Franny could see in Lottie's eyes that her feelings matched her words. No hidden agendas, no secret schemes. Just the gruesome truth of getting what you think you want, the way plans can slip out of your control like *that*, the long icy skid of real life. The thing about ice was that you had to go where it wanted to take you. It was only when you tried to take charge that you really hurt yourself. Franny knew that much from driver's education. And everything else.

"Why don't you take it out on someone else's car?" Leon said.

Lottie's eyes went shrewd again, and she stroked the derringer, nodded at Leon's thigh. "Don't think I won't aim higher this time, big boy."

Leon tensed, but Franny grabbed his arm. "We just want to go home, Lottie. No more trouble."

Lottie laughed. "No more trouble! Oh good. I think I've had about all the trouble I can stand."

She aimed the derringer at her own chest. "My corpse in front of the Blue Moon, can you imagine? That'll show them."

Time plunked down into space, dissolving like Papa's Alka-Seltzer. The fizz of space-time collapsed until there was nothing but the tether that bound Franny to Lottie.

Franny didn't want to be tethered anymore. She could not, she would not be part of Lottie's world for another minute, but the world still needed Lottie Marcone in it.

What the heck do you think you're you doing, Franny? Franny's mind screamed as her body leaped on Lottie and wrenched the gun away. The surprise of it made Lottie pull the trigger. They landed hard on the sidewalk, and the bullet pierced the passenger window of Papa's Cadillac, shattering it. The derringer skittered away, dropped through the slats of the gutter, and plunked into the sewer below. Lottie smacked her head on the sidewalk with a sickening *thump*.

Lottie groaned, blinking up at the streetlights. "I wasn't actually going to *do* it, you oaf." She touched the back of her head, looked at her fingertips as though she expected to see blood. "Nice to know you'd do something so stupid for me, though."

"Insulting me to the bitter end," Franny said. "You'll be all right."

She helped Lottie up from the sidewalk, and as she did, Lottie grabbed the back of her neck and kissed her on the mouth. Right there in front of Leon. Franny couldn't imagine what his face looked like right now, and she didn't intend to find out.

The kiss lasted for about a year, give or take, and then Lottie pulled a business card out of her cleavage and handed it over.

"Ever heard of a purse?" Franny muttered, wiping her lips.

"Boopsie wanted to give you this." It was soft with sweat and smelled like Lottie.

Franny took it.

Boopsie Baxter's Showstopper Club

In stunning Miami, Florida!

She flipped it over.

Stand-up comedy every night/Ladies, try your luck at Amateur Hour/All welcome/White men pay $5 cover.

"She needs comics," Lottie said. "Ever since the, ah, incident with the fella on TV, business hasn't been so hot."

"And whose fault would that be, I wonder?" Franny said.

Lottie rolled her eyes. "Now she's letting men in, and she thinks you and your Showstopper have a real bright future making money for Boopsie. I said to her, 'I thought she could save me too. And look what happened.' But that's Boopsie. Won't listen to no one but Boopsie."

"Showstopper?" Leon said. "Come on, lady, we weren't born yesterday."

That hurt more than Franny expected, and Lottie saw it.

"See? You can't save him. Can't save any of them." Lottie shrugged. "Should've stuck with me, kid."

"I'll keep that in mind," Franny said. She shoved the business card in her pocket. One final Boopsie Baxter clipping to cling to. *Once upon a time, Boopsie Baxter called me a waste of time, and then she gave me her card.* A fitting happily ever after.

"If you don't want it," Lottie said, reading her face again, "there's a trash can right there. Throw it away."

Franny put her hand on her pocket and thought about doing it. Really, she did.

A massive, squawking group of BBG girls tumbled around the corner—led by Nora Pushkin and Sarah something. Captains of the Heeb grapevine.

"Better never than late," Franny said.

"Franny!" Nora squealed, hugging her. "When Galit told Sarah you were here, I couldn't believe it, but here you are! And Leon, we looked everywhere for you!" She leaned in close to Franny but didn't lower her voice one decibel. "I always had a crush on him, Franny, did you know that? It was his hair, wasn't it, Sarah? Those wild curls just made me swoon. And it's not fair for a boy to have such long eyelashes, is it? Sometimes I thought I was more envious of him than attracted, but who knows! He hasn't been to shul in forever, has he? But then, war will do that to you. Nasty business. I was glad my brother had flat feet. The army wouldn't have him!"

"I'm right here," Leon said.

The BBG gaggle waved shyly.

"Gal keeps trying to get us to come to the Blue Moon, and we keep saying no, but here we are!" Nora said.

Silence. The girls took in a disheveled Lottie Marcone, the crowbar, the smashed car, Leon's bloody leg.

Leon yanked and yanked at the passenger door, until eventually it screeched open, sending a spray of glass tinkling everywhere. "At least let us give you a ride," he said to Lottie.

Lottie snorted. The snort became a chuckle, which became hysterical laughter.

"I thought you said he wasn't funny," Lottie said. "That was the funniest thing I've heard all night."

"So," Nora said, reaching for her purse. "Is there a cover or what?"

⁓❀⁓

Leon's injury being what it was, he agreed to let Franny drive. It was her very first time behind the wheel of Papa's Cadillac sedan, and she would have preferred if it weren't utterly destroyed, but somehow it still drove, and Franny would take what she could get. She managed to shoo away the BBGs, who stood around bickering about which of them would take Leon home. They didn't ask if Franny wanted a ride.

Franny brushed the shattered glass off the front seats, while Lottie watched grimly.

"I didn't touch the engine, I'll have you know," Lottie said. "I'm not a monster."

Franny adjusted the driver's seat and ran her hands along the steering wheel, feeling suddenly magnanimous. "Come on, Lottie," she said. "Let me take you somewhere. The Palmer House? The airport? You name it."

Lottie helped Leon into the passenger seat, and he draped an arm around her without even flinching. As though he let strangers touch him all the time, no big deal.

"Thanks, but no thanks," Lottie said. "I'm a big girl."

"It's late, you're alone—it's not safe."

"Here's looking at you," Lottie said in a Bogart-y voice as she stepped away from the car. "Here's hoping I don't have to do it again."

Franny put the car into gear. "Speaking from experience," she said, "everybody should be nobody sometimes."

"Goodbye, Peggy Blake," Lottie said. "Don't patronize me." She tapped the crumpled roof to send them on their way.

Lottie got smaller and smaller in the rearview, then they turned the corner, and she was gone. Just like that.

"Can I ask you," Leon said, "about what happened back there? Outside the club?"

Franny gripped the steering wheel and hunched into the wind. Her whole body ached, toenails to scalp. "Which part?" she said. "The shooting, the kiss, or the Showstopper?"

"Now you sound like Bogart."

"Can it wait?"

Leon *hmph*ed, flicked a shard of glass from his sleeve, but he didn't push it.

Franny exhaled a breath she had been holding for seconds, years.

Finally, they turned onto North Euclid Avenue, dreading the approach of 504. She pulled the car into park, and the lights inside the house immediately flashed on. They were in for it now.

"You ready?" she asked.

"I've never been less ready," he said. "And that's saying something."

CHAPTER NINETEEN

PAPA BURST OUT OF 504 WITH MAMA TRAILING BEHIND HIM. He clutched his chest over his brown robe.

"I can't look," Leon said. "Is he having another heart attack?"

Franny got out of the car. "Before you say anything, Papa," she said, "let's go inside and sit down and have a nice chat."

"Nice? Nice!" Papa said. "Look at this fakakta car! What did you kids do?"

Dogs started barking, and lights in the Averys' house flipped on. Franny wondered if they ever slept, if Dr. Avery sat up all night, spring-loaded and weary.

"Papa," Franny said, "you're scaring the neighbors."

"My car looks like a hot dog bun. I won't be able to drive to work, and if I can't drive to work, they'll fire me, and if they fire me—"

Leon limped out of the car, and Papa froze. "Blood! That is blood on my only son's leg! Why are you in uniform? Where's the war now?"

"Don't excite yourself, Isaac, think of your heart," Mama said.

"Aha!" Papa said, pointing. "And whose necktie is that?"

"Don't be such a nudnik. Get inside. Leon, let me take care of that."

"You're awfully calm," Leon said to Mama, hobbling inside. He let her undo the knot on Ed Marcone's necktie.

"I was a Gray Lady," Mama said proudly. "I can handle a little blood. Now sit." Leon sat obediently at the dining table while Mama went into the kitchen for a cloth, a bowl of water, rubbing alcohol, and a needle and thread, just in case.

"I'll pay for the car," Franny said. "It's my fault."

"It's the principle of the thing," Papa said. "You take the car, you bring it back in one piece."

"Technically, it is in one piece," Leon said.

"And we have insurance," Mama said, hugging Franny.

"What am I, chopped liver?" Papa said. "It's my car. And my five dollars, Franny."

Had that been *today*? Afternoon Franny had been so much more naive than middle-of-the-night Franny. "I'm sorry, Papa, I'll pay you back."

Satisfied, Papa flopped onto the sofa, and Mama propped him up with some pillows. "Now," he said. "What's this business about a nightclub?"

Leon and Franny looked at each other.

"Oh! Surprised your old papa knows some things, are you? Well, I have ways—"

"Is everything okay?" Halfway up the staircase, rubbing her eyes and wearing one of Franny's old nightgowns, was Mary Kate. "I heard yelling."

"I never reveal my sources," Papa said, folding his arms. "But sometimes they reveal themselves."

Franny felt ill. Mary Kate was not known for her secret-keeping capabilities.

"I couldn't go home to an empty house," Mary Kate said, toying with the shiny banister.

"Your parents live across the street," Franny said.

"I didn't want to wake them," Mary Kate said.

"Nu, she shows up on our doorstep like an urchin, throws her arms around me, and starts sobbing," Papa said.

"I just had the sniffles," Mary Kate said, blushing. "That's all."

"Like I said, sobbing." Papa crossed an ankle over his knee. "Now you, *Peggy Blake*. Out with it."

Franny lowered herself slowly onto the other end of the sofa, and exhaustion hit her like a tree. She sat flattened against the pillows. "Couldn't we talk about this tomorrow?" Or never.

Mama cut Leon's bloody pant leg and wrung out a cloth before dabbing his wound with it.

"She means *never*," Leon said, the traitor.

"I know what she means," Papa said. "I invented the brush-off!"

"No, you didn't, Isaac," Mama said.

"I'm sure Mary Kate's version was just terrific." Franny said through gritted teeth. Mary Kate didn't flinch. "You don't need to hear it from me."

"You think this is for *us*?" Papa said. "I have a heart condition. I should be asleep right now." A smile tickled the corner of Papa's face. He tapped his chest.

Pressure expanded. You couldn't be mad about it; that's just what pressure did. It could lead to the hospital or the morgue. *Or. You could let it out your big, fat mouth.*

"Stop me if you've heard this one," Franny said. "A fairy-tale wedding, ruined by a selfish bridesmaid, who—"

"Stop!" Mary Kate cried. "*Everyone's* heard this one."

"—who ran away to a nightclub and became a stand-up comedian."

Thunder cracked like a bone.

"Don't get on God's bad side," Leon said, pointing up. "He's like the Fingers Marcone of the sky."

"This schlemiel tells jokes now?" Papa said. "Franny, what have you done to your brother?"

∽◆∾

Time was marked by snacks in the Steinberg house, and by the time Franny finished her story, it was bread-crumbs-and-half-eaten-coffee-cake o'clock. Rain did a soft-shoe dance on the roof. Mama nibbled on a dry bialy, and Mary Kate stirred her tea idly, stifling a yawn.

"So," Mama said. "No Michael Berman, then?"

That was the moral of Franny's story for Mama. You had to admire her single-mindedness.

"Sorry, Mama."

Mama sighed. "So. When can we see your set?"

Mama knew what a set was, and Franny hadn't?

"Ruth!" Papa said. "She's not doing that anymore."

"Why not?" Mama said. "I always wanted to go to one of those clubs. Especially to see that Boopsie Baxter." She elbowed Franny and waggled her eyebrows.

"Mama!" Franny cried.

"Who, now? Do we know her?" Papa said.

"I heard about her from Mrs. Epstein, who heard it from Mrs. Goldman, who talked to someone after services on—"

"Never mind, Papa," Franny said, face hot.

"Nu, your papa gets to laugh at his boring TV shows, I can't have a good time too?"

"You can laugh at my shows," Papa said. "It's a free country."

Mama rolled her eyes. "They're not funny. A man *can't* be funny. Someone else washes his socks. What's he got to joke about?"

Mama and Lottie had the same opinion about something?

Papa flew into hysterics at the sight of blood, and Mama fixed up Leon? Papa was squeamish about night club comedy, and Mama wanted to see *Boopsie Baxter*? Papa started the lesson, and Mama finished it? It really was time to go to bed. Franny flung her arm around Mama and rested her head on her shoulder. Mama stroked her hair.

"There are other nightclubs, bubbeleh. Chicago is a big city."

Franny thought of the Velvet Swing, a part of the story she had studiously omitted. "Not as many as you might think. Not anymore."

"Franny wants to do this stand-up comedy," Papa said, "she can do it here, with her family, where no one gets shot and everyone keeps their fingers. We invite Finnegans over. I think the words you're looking for are *that's a great idea, Papa*."

"Her Showstopper won't work here; not enough...*authority*,"

Mama said, looking to Franny for confirmation. Franny nodded, pleased. "Haven't you been listening, Isaac?"

"Bah." Papa flicked his hand. "Not that nonsense again. Suddenly it's not enough to tell a funny joke and get a laugh? Suddenly family isn't as good as strangers? This Showstopper is phony baloney. Your family—*that's* real."

Mama and Papa started to bicker in earnest. Their voices filled the room like extra furniture, and suddenly the house was too cramped, the bialy too chewy, Mary Kate too silent, Leon too... Leon. Franny had finally told the truth, and now the truth was telling her something: she didn't fit here anymore. What did that mean? Where else would she possibly belong?

Franny felt the edges of Boopsie's card in her pocket. Why couldn't Boopsie have a club in Chicago? "I'll think about it, Papa," she said, just to get them to stop bickering.

"Don't forget the Averys," Leon said.

Everyone turned to look at him.

"They're our neighbors too, aren't they? You should invite them over," Leon said. "Whoever did that to their house—they'll see the Averys have friends on the block, and maybe they'll hesitate before trying it again."

"Seems like they prefer to keep to themselves," Mary Kate said. "And I don't care if they're purple, that's just not neighborly."

A fresh coat of shame painted Franny. She did not like hearing her own thoughts coming out of Mary Kate's mouth.

"The peanut gallery speaks," Papa said.

It occurred to Franny that shame *felt* useful, like it was making her a better person, but what if it was just a distraction? Like a sleight of hand or smoke and mirrors that actually *kept* her from seeing the truth? Could the truth be as obvious as knocking on the Averys' door?

"I'm worried someone will come for Daddy's house next," Mary Kate said.

"Don't be ridiculous, Mary Kate," Franny snapped. Mary Kate looked defiant, so she softened her tone. "Anyway, worrying is a waste of time. God takes it as a challenge: You call that worry? I'll show you worry."

"God doesn't have a Yiddish accent," Mary Kate said, wrinkling her nose.

"God doesn't exist," Leon said. "It's just us, making the best of it on this rock."

The thunder retorted in a language no one understood.

"See?" Mary Kate and Franny and Leon said.

❧

Franny felt oddly shy in her bedroom with Mary Kate and undressed demurely—pulling the nightgown over her dress and then sliding the dress off after she was fully covered. She couldn't quite explain why, something to do with the baby growing inside Mary Kate. They weren't kids anymore, whispering and giggling until the sun came up.

"I'll sleep on the floor," Franny said, even though they had had sleepovers in her double bed a million times. "I don't mind."

Mary Kate sat on the bed and smirked at the nightgown acrobatics. "I'm not a blimp yet," she said. "We can both fit."

Franny switched off the lights and crawled into bed. Mary Kate stared up at the ceiling, tears sliding into her ears. Franny propped herself on an elbow and wiped one away.

"Can you keep a secret?" Mary Kate said.

"Obviously."

Mary Kate sighed. "It all happened so fast. I mean, I know how these things work, I'm not a child. What's done is done. But I—" She pressed her hands to her face. A hiccuping sob escaped. "Franny, I don't want this baby."

Franny rubbed Mary Kate's shoulder. "It's okay to be scared."

She shook her head. "I feel so alone. Isn't that funny? Factually, I'm less alone than I ever have been."

The streetlights diffused through Franny's curtains. Mary Kate's eyelashes glistened like icicles. Franny pulled her close. Mary Kate nestled in her armpit and flung an arm across her chest, sighing contentedly. They lay in bed like that for a while, Mary Kate's sniffles punctuating the soft rain outside.

"I'm sorry I hurt you," Franny said finally. "I'm going to do better."

Mary Kate didn't respond. A light snore escaped her throat. And something about the shadows playing on her face brought out a resemblance to Peter not visible in daylight. Her face so close, her little arm oddly heavy on Franny's chest...Franny's throat started to clench.

She braced herself for the violent fish of memory to heave itself to the surface. It did, like it always would. But she picked it up by the tail, watched it wriggle in her fingertips, and then tossed it back in.

The truth was, fish belonged in the sea—all different kinds of fish. It didn't mean the ocean was broken.

～⌐∞⌐～

Franny slept like the dead; she slept a month's worth of sleeping. A loud noise finally startled her awake—a truck rattling over a curb. Or the dream echo of a derringer. She sat up in bed, heart pounding, searching her chest for holes. But she was fine. The house was intact. Everyone was alive. The bed was empty, the nightgown Mary Kate had been wearing shed on the carpet like snakeskin.

Downstairs, no one was awake yet, but there was a pot of filmed-over milk on the stove and a glass with white streaks down the side. Milk gave the Steinbergs the runs; it was the curse of the Jews, so it must have been Mary Kate's. Franny wished she had said goodbye, made sure Mary Kate was okay. She washed the glass, put on coffee, whisked up some eggs, and shoved toast in the toaster.

Out the front window, the big rotten elm in the adjacent vacant lot, the one Mama was always complaining to the village about, had toppled over, landing squarely on Papa's Cadillac. Franny stared, not quite believing her eyes. That was the noise she had heard, not a truck or a gunshot but the sound of a giant tree rending and smashing an already-smashed car.

She ran up the stairs, about to call for Papa, but paused at her open bedroom door. She grabbed a piece of paper and a pen and figured she would just jot down a few notes. Just to remember everything that had happened. But a joke bubbled up in her mind, and then another, and she was thinking so fast, her hand couldn't keep up. She wrote in a frenzy. She could barely read her own hand-writing. It wasn't funny, not yet. There was no premise yet, just the story. But it was in there. She just knew it.

"My car!" Papa cried, snapping Franny out of it. She ran down the stairs to see Papa standing in the open doorway, rain dripping on his bare head.

"I kept telling the village to take that tree down, didn't I?" Mama said, tightening her robe. "And now they're going to have to buy us a new car."

"The car was already smashed," Papa said.

"Who cares how it was smashed, the fact is that it was smashed," Mama cried. "Last night, you could drive it."

"She's right," Franny said. "I did drive it last night."

Their patter, so natural, almost a comedy routine in itself. Which came from living with the same people for twenty-plus years. But there wasn't anything new to unearth here. There was no hiding from the fact this was no longer her home. She had to leave, but she had no idea how to do it.

Mr. Finnegan opened his door and padded out to the sidewalk, staring. "Act of Yahweh, eh, Steinberg?" He chuckled. "Rough bit of luck."

"You should see the other guy," Papa said.

Neighbors ogled the car like it was this year's new model. People who only made an appearance at neighborhood catastrophes were now shaking their heads and murmuring nonsense at Papa:

Tough break.

Too bad, Steinberg. Too bad.

Hope you got insurance.

What are the odds?

Musta been that storm. Heckuva storm.

And the more they mulled over the impossibly bad luck of the situation, the more excited they got about its possibilities.

If you had just parked three feet farther up or on the other side of the street...

Coulda been my car; I parked in this very spot just two days ago.

What if someone had been in it, god forbid!

Undercover Rod pulled up behind a public works truck, shook hands all around, and then clapped Papa on the back. "We'll get you back on the road in no time. Man's gotta work, lovely wife has to do her shopping... Here's what I can do," He scribbled on his notepad and ripped off the sheet. "My brother-in-law owns a Cadillac dealership in Melrose Park, tell him I sent you, he'll give you a loaner for free and a great deal on a new model."

Papa looked at the paper like he had forgotten how to read. "I liked my old car," he said.

"Unless you want to move the family to the scrap heap," Rod smirked, "you'll need a new one."

Mama snatched the paper and gave Papa a look. "Thank you," Mama said. Papa muttered his forlorn thanks.

"Anything for the neighborhood," Rod said. "Want you to think of me as a friend, not just a policeman." He winked chummily at Franny.

This Rod bent over backward, went out of his way to help Papa but couldn't get away from the Averys fast enough. The sleight of hand revealed: tucked into the sleeve, pulled out at the right time. Is this your card?

We're not babysitters, was what he had said to Dr. Avery after his house was bombed. *I don't like your tone.*

Franny gathered her courage and stalked across the street. A dozen pairs of eyes burned a hole in her back. She walked right up to the Averys' front door and knocked without a moment of hesitation.

Dr. Avery opened the door wearing slacks and a short-sleeved collared shirt, pale green, a newspaper tucked under his arm.

"Yes?" he said.

Franny took a deep breath and smiled. "Dr. Avery, my name is Franny, I live across the street, and I am so sorry for everything you've been through. We're having coffee and pastries this morning, and I would like to invite your family over to join us."

Laughter burst out from inside the house, behind Dr. Avery. Franny flushed; her smile wilted. Was someone laughing at her?

But no—in the front room, his two daughters lay sprawled on the floor, comic books spread around them, giggling at something they had just read. They didn't even notice her.

Down the hallway, Franny caught a glimpse of Mrs. Avery in a sundress, smoking a cigarette and chatting on the phone. Franny didn't know what she was expecting—the family to be huddled together under a miserable blanket? Tearfully grateful that someone finally knocked on their door and offered Danishes?

"We're very busy today, Franny," Dr. Avery said. "But thank you for the offer." He started to close the door.

"Another time?" she called into the vanishing doorway.

The door closed and locked. Franny blinked. The neighbors stared and whispered as she walked stiffly back to 504. Didn't they have a tree-smashed car to ogle?

Mr. Finnegan met her halfway across the street, clapping a hand on her shoulder. "Why, *I'd* love to come inside for a cup. Thank you, Franny," he said loudly, winking as though they were conspirators. He held the door open to her own house. "*Now* do you see?" he whispered.

"Yeah," Franny said. She picked his hand off her shoulder. "Trust has to be earned."

❧

Inside, Papa looked up from a lapful of auto insurance paperwork. Mama was just cleaning the coffeepot.

"Mary Kate's expecting, you know," Mr. Finnegan said, plopping into the middle of the sofa and resting both arms along the back. Leon scooted away. "Cream, no sugar, please, Ruth."

Mama sighed, started up a new pot of coffee.

"Mazel tov," Papa said.

"Their new place has all the high-end electronics. Frigidaire, automatic washing machine, automatic dishwasher." Mr. Finnegan shook his head. "What's she going to do all day?"

Papa glared at the plate of carrots Mama fixed for him, looked wistfully at the gooey Danish she handed Mr. Finnegan.

"My boy is going to be a college graduate," Mama said, a real contender in the offspring-bragging arena. She beamed at Leon. "First in the family."

"Ma," Leon said, "I haven't even matriculated yet. It'll be years before I graduate."

"So I'm just *Ma* now? Now I'm a cow?" Mama said.

"My papa would be so proud," Papa said, wielding a carrot stick. "He came here with nothing. Nothing! Just him, Mama, me, a couple kopeks. Now look at us. We're like the Roosevelts."

Mr. Finnegan laughed so hard that coffee cake crumbs spewed everywhere. "That'll be the day, Steinberg." Mama handed him his coffee, but he waved her off. "Oh, I couldn't, I'd be buzzing like a streetlamp." He polished off the Danish and wiped his hands on the sofa. "I'd *love* to fritter the day away," he said, "But, you know. Idle hands—"

"Don't use napkins?" Franny said sweetly.

Mama gave her a sharp look but couldn't hide the twitch of a smile.

"So I've been thinking," Leon said.

"Don't hurt yourself, son," Mr. Finnegan said. No one laughed.

"Franny should come with me," Leon said. "To Miami."

A new star exploded in the cosmos of Franny's chest. She didn't dare speak, slowly setting her untouched Danish on the table.

"That nightclub is there," he said. "And anyway, the weather's better."

"Nightclub?" Mr. Finnegan frowned. "That's no place to find a husband."

Franny flicked the edges of Boopsie Baxter's card, which she had transferred to a new pocket this morning. It was just a keepsake, not a map.

Who would rake the leaves at 504? Would they pile up, year after year, a mountain of leaves Papa would climb every day, huffing and puffing and clutching his heart, desperate to reach his smashed Cadillac, while Mama wept over a brisket no one would eat: *If only Franny had stayed!*

She looked at Leon. Something was strange about his face.

"Leon," Mama said. "You're smiling."

"So," Leon said. "What do you say?"

"Nein scheissen," Franny said.

Leon laughed, the donkey. Franny loved that goofy sound.

Impatient with anything he didn't immediately understand, Mr. Finnegan opened his mouth to complain.

Papa winked at him. "Try some prunes, Franny," he said. "That always clears me right up."

⁓⦵⁓

After Leon left 504, the house took on a new personality. Mama and Papa seemed twenty years younger, giggling at each other like newlyweds, sleeping embarrassingly late. The day before Franny left for Miami, Mama wept into her Shabbos chicken, just like Franny had worried she might. But all it took was a reminder that they could visit the Miami horse races, and Mama's tears mysteriously dried up.

"It's not that we won't miss you," Mama said, dabbing those crocodile tears with her apron.

"It's just that we're so glad you're finally leaving," Papa finished. Mama giggled and Papa patted her on the tuchus.

"I think my chicken is coming back up," Franny said, covering her mouth.

"Such a burden to have parents like Mama and me," Papa said, pointing a fork at her. "You're lucky to have us."

"I'm lucky to have any appetite left," Franny said.

A letter had come, addressed to Miss Peggy Blake c/o Miss Franny Steinberg, with a return address in Chicago. It was from Gal, in the sort of neat, looping handwriting one might expect from her, and Franny tore it open and reread it until she had it memorized like a new set.

Gal had moved out of her sleezy hotel and found an apartment *in a lovely elevator building in Lincoln Park with an actual doorman, if you can believe that.* Andy Grand Canyon moved in with her, and Hal was trying to talk them into letting her move in too. *But I put my foot down. An unmarried couple, living together in my apartment? Of course, every time I say the word "married," Andy and Hal blush red as beets.* Still, Hal sprawled out on their sofa most nights and kept a toothbrush in the bathroom.

Not only was Hal running the Blue Moon, but she was also Andy's agent. *They're even flying out to Los Angeles, California, together! Turns out Lottie had some TV contacts squirreled away for an emergency. That's right—Lottie Marcone is "being helpful." When it suits her, anyway.* Meanwhile, Gal was doing stand-up at the new coffeehouses around town. *I haven't conjured a Showstopper, not even once. And some kid in a turtleneck called me a square, just for drinking a manhattan! But I don't mind. It's all so bohemian and moody! Luckily, I look good in black.*

Franny couldn't help thinking of Lottie's sad refrain: *The boob tube is winning, and Showstoppers are losing.*

But the last paragraph was the best part: If Franny wasn't done with stand-up for good, which Gal would *understand*, but she certainly *hoped* wasn't the case, the apartment had a squeaky Murphy bed with Franny's name on it. As long as they had the apartment, Franny had a home there too.

Franny tucked the letter into her pocket, next to Boopsie's business card.

✧

After years of avoiding Shabbat services on account of Leon, Mama and Papa had started going every Friday, staying late and gossiping with old friends at the Oneg. Franny got her cheeks pinched raw every time, so to save her skin, the night before she was to leave for Miami, she paid a visit to Mary Kate. The street was lined with gangly new trees.

"They're called green ash," Mary Kate said. "Apparently they're hardy and immune to Dutch elm disease. Sorry about the car by the way. Daddy told me."

"Papa's got a new one; he's already forgotten about the old." The new Cadillac, bought without Undercover Rod's "great deal," was nearly identical, slightly newer and shinier, and he spent his Saturdays waxing and buffing it. He wouldn't let Franny touch it. They started arriving at services fashionably late, just to draw attention to the new car.

"Do you like my flowers?" Mary Kate asked shyly. "I planted those myself."

"They're beautiful. I had no idea you were so horticultural." Franny sipped on a lemonade that was mostly lemon water, just like Mama's.

"Oh yes, I've joined the Ladies' Gardening Club and learned so many fascinating new things. Like did you know that without bees, we would have no fruits or vegetables?"

"I did not know that."

Mary Kate rested a hand on her belly, which was still no bigger than it had been at her wedding, but she rubbed it like a genie's lamp, like the baby might pop out and make all her wishes come true.

"I want you to know," Franny said, "that you're *not* alone. If you need me, I'm just an extremely expensive long-distance phone call away."

Mary Kate laughed and shook her auburn curls. "I'm sure I don't know what you mean, Franny, but that's very sweet all the same."

Franny searched her face for recognition, but her eyes were shining and vacant. Had she just pushed it down, locked it away? Franny wanted to warn her about that—about what it could do to a person.

"Are you still scared?" Franny asked instead.

"About what?"

"Being a mother," Franny said. "Getting older. All of it. I don't know."

"But it's perfectly natural," Mary Kate said, arranging her skirts. "In fact, there's no other option, is there?" For a split second, there was something on Mary Kate's face that was genuinely asking. *Is there another option?*

"Are *you* scared?" Mary Kate asked instead.

Franny laughed. "Terrified."

"Then why are you going?" Mary Kate cried. "Why would you want to leave everything you've ever known and everyone who's ever loved you?"

Franny couldn't answer because she didn't know. She just knew that not knowing felt right.

"I should go," Franny said, brushing cookie crumbs off her lap and standing. "I haven't even started packing."

"Wait," Mary Kate said. She hopped up and ran inside then ran back out with a tidily wrapped present, a flat box as big as a pancake. "For you."

"What is it?"

"Why do people always ask that? All you have to do is open it to find out."

Inside the box was a tam-o'-shanter with a massive red pom-pom, the plaid pattern so loud, it was almost screaming. Franny hadn't worn a hat like that since she was a little girl.

"Peter and I bought it for you that Christmas Eve. '44. But I can't remember why," Mary Kate said. "Didn't you have a hat? Anyway, I forgot all about it until I moved in with Walter, but it's just so cute, and I bet it looks terrific on you. A little something to remember me by."

A gift frozen in time, decades out of fashion, and completely oblivious to the fact that Franny was moving to a place with no winter.

Franny wrapped her arms around Mary Kate. "I love it," she said. Mary Kate beamed.

"Come visit me," Franny said. "Bring Walter, I don't care."

"All right," Mary Kate said. "Before the baby comes. Before I turn into a house."

"Yes! I want to see your big belly waddling around."

"Okay. I will."

They smiled at each other, both secretly happy because it would never happen. Franny stuck the tam on her head, knowing her hair would shoot out everywhere and make Mary Kate laugh.

CHAPTER TWENTY

FRANNY HAD BARELY DROPPED HER BAGS IN LEON'S DORMI-
tory before he was dragging her around like a new puppy, introduc-
ing her to every single solitary person he had met since arriving in
Miami. Meanwhile, she sweated more than seemed strictly reasonable. Chicago never fully emerged from the shroud of winter, even
on the hottest day, while Miami was where the whole concept of
Hades came from. Would she ever feel cool air on her skin again?
When was the next time she would see snow?

As if reading her mind, Leon had steered her past the latest Betty
or Liza and whispered, "How about we hit an air-conditioned hotel
for a drink?"

Leon hailed a taxi, and they drove down into Miami Beach, where
Franny could glimpse the ocean sparkling between the cranes and the
construction sites. She had never seen the ocean, and she knew it was supposed to be salty as a cracker. How was that possible? It looked refreshing.

"Not so different from the lake" She shrugged. "Big deal."

"Wait till there's a storm," Leon said. "Huge waves up to here.
Also smells a little better."

"I'm telling the lake you said that."

"How's Mama?" Leon asked.

"It's absolutely disgusting," Franny said, shuddering. "They're like teenagers. Groping each other, giggling. I couldn't leave fast enough. Of course, as I was walking out the door, Mama hugged me so tight, I couldn't breathe. 'Nu, call your poor mother sometime. Your brother—ach, he never calls, he never writes.'"

"I just called last week," Leon cried. "It's long-distance. She can't call me?"

"She doesn't want to bother you," Franny said. "She's just your mother." Franny's imitation of Mama made Leon snort.

"And who's going to rake the leaves, now that you're not there to complain about it?" Leon asked.

"Papa's got some scheme to hire Dr. Avery's daughter, Hannah."

"For money? Boy, we got scammed."

"And get this. Last week, the village chairman and a *priest* came by, asking Papa to be part of a group supporting the Averys and some new Negro families moving into the neighborhood."

"A priest! Asking the Steinbergs for help?" Leon grinned. "Boy, to have seen the look on Finnegan's face."

"They want to outlaw For Sale signs," Franny said. "Keep people from running away to restricted neighborhoods like Mary Kate did. Papa's job is to watch our street."

Franny made sure Papa took his new role seriously but also had to convince him that *constantly* scanning Euclid Avenue with his new binoculars was not exactly what the village had in mind.

"Look at this schlemiel," he had chuckled in response, pointing at a squirrel pushing a meatball down the street. "Squirrel Sisyphus beats Milton Berle any day!"

The cab pulled up to the Pink Lady Hotel, and Leon paid the driver. They walked in silence to the bar, where Leon ordered a round of Mai Tais.

"I've been meaning to ask you something," Leon said finally. "About the Blue Moon."

Franny's heart was instantaneously skewered and barbecued. After their dumpster heart-to-heart, Leon hadn't brought up his experience in the war again, or Peter, or *anything*. And in the chaos and excitement of the past couple months, Franny had managed to dodge the room-sized elephant of Lottie's kiss. It was as though they had left those parts of themselves at the Blue Moon. Which was a relief, frankly. Their relationship felt fragile and tender, and Franny didn't want to blow it by being too honest.

"What does your…Showstopper feel like?" Leon asked.

Franny laughed, exhaled, nearly collapsed into a pile of bones. "Is that all?" she said. "You don't believe in Showstoppers, remember?"

"I believe in my sister," he said.

Franny felt the shocked expression plastered on her face but couldn't seem to take it off. "You do?" She looked at her hands.

Leon cleared his throat. "Has anyone ever…panicked? Felt a Showstopper and, ah, run away screaming?"

"Yeah," she said. "Me."

Leon laughed. "No shit."

"Nein scheissen."

"So what happened?"

Was she really going to tell him? Now? What if the story destroyed what they had just started to rebuild? But then again, what if the story made the building *better*?

Or what if it was just a damn story, no more, no less?

"Well, in a nutshell." Franny took a deep breath and didn't want to give it back. "Boopsie Baxter's Showstopper gave me an orgasm that made me think I was responsible for your capture." She could *not* look him in the eye. "More or less."

Leon's Mai Tai went from mouth to lungs to nostrils to bar top in quick succession. "Less," he coughed. "Much less, please."

Franny's hands shook as she lifted her drink, which sloshed in its giant glass. She gulped down the slushy sweetness and instantly got a piercing headache.

"I'm sorry," Franny said. "By the way."

"I can't unhear what you just said. No point in apologizing." Leon shuddered.

Franny smacked his arm lightly. "No, dummy. For everything you went through," she said. "I didn't understand, and I made everything worse."

"Fair to say I made everything worse for you too." Leon sought out Franny's hand and squeezed. "You know, you probably don't remember this," he said. "But when you were really little, like six or seven, I took you to the movies, and one of the newsreels was about Hitler, right after his election. Papa had been talking about him for a while; he and Mama were worried and felt so helpless. It was the first time you or I had actually *seen* him—strutting around and yelling. You started to cry, and I had to take you home before the picture even started. But." Leon smiled and shook his head. "Soon as we got home, you bolted upstairs, slicked your hair back, and scribbled on a mustache and then stomped around the house screaming in what was actually pretty good gibberish German."

Franny covered her face. "I did that? Leon, that's *horrifying*."

Leon pulled her hands away. His eyes were soft and kind. "It was like an ice block melted in that house, Franny. You made us look at our fears and laugh at them."

Leon lifted his drink, carefully this time, and took a sip. "You know, this actually gives me an idea."

He grinned at Franny. She grinned back. It was nice to see his smile again.

"If you're thinking what I'm thinking," Franny said, "then technically, it was my idea."

"*Technically*," Leon said, "your idea was to lie to me. I'm just making it honest."

Franny *pshaw*ed. "Potato, potahto."

⁓꙳⁓

Boopsie's nightclub was not the swank affair on the beach that Franny had been expecting. It wasn't on Miami Beach at all but in Overtown, a Negro neighborhood. The name of the club—*Boopsie Baxter's Showstopper Club*—was lit up fetchingly in lights, similar to the Blue Moon, and the building was painted a fresh coral pink and bright white like practically every other building in Miami, but the street was narrow, there were no palm trees, and Franny felt, well, conspicuous. *Get over it, Franny*, she thought.

"Negroes can't live on Miami Beach," Leon said. He had taken to wearing short pants and a straw fedora and looked altogether too comfortable in both. When he picked her up at the airport, she had shaded her eyes from the sight of his legs and cried, "Put those away before you cause a shipwreck."

"But Boopsie always talked about working the clubs there."

"Oh, they can *work* there," Leon said. "But they have to be fingerprinted and carry ID. They're not even allowed on the beaches."

Franny thought back to Boopsie's stories about how much better Miami was than Chicago—how she never got stopped by the police. Boopsie had been trying to prove how well she was doing, when really, she was posturing as much as Lottie was. Miami seemed to have built two of everything just to keep whites and Negroes apart. The worst kind of Noah's ark.

Leon opened the door to Boopsie's club, but Franny hesitated.

"I don't know," she said. "Maybe this isn't such a good idea." What exactly was the point of trying to be funny in a world like this? What if it just made everything worse?

"I did not come all the way out here for you to back out at the last minute," Leon said. "No, ma'am. I will not let my great idea go to waste." He pulled the door open before Franny could argue again about whose idea it was.

Franny stepped into Boopsie's club and was stunned by the inside. Mirrored walls, shiny vinyl booths, clean floor without even a trace of stickiness. A cute girl bounced up to them and said the show didn't start for another three hours but could she show them to a booth? They specialized in vodka martinis, and did they want one to cool off with?

"Thanks," Franny said. "But I'm looking for Boopsie Baxter. She told me to look her up if I was ever in Miami."

The girl's eyes widened. "Miss Baxter is very busy," she said. "But I can, uh, I can tell her your name?"

"Oh," Franny said, and it came out as a relieved sigh. "I'll just come back another time."

Leon leaned over her shoulder. "Tell her Peggy Blake is here," he said. He fished in his pocket and handed over five dollars. "I hear there's a cover for white men."

The girl took the bill absently and walked to the back of the club, behind the stage, looking back at them curiously before disappearing.

A few seconds later, Boopsie burst out of the door in a loose-fitting man's button-down with the sleeves rolled up and short red shorts. She had red lipstick and red heels on, and she trotted over to Franny before scooping her up in a hug like they were best friends. She did smell terrific.

"Peggy Blake," she said in that smoky voice. "Never thought I'd actually see you again. And who is this handsome devil?" She extended one manicured hand, which Leon caught and smashed his lips on awkwardly, which made Franny snort.

"This is Leon, my brother."

"Pleased to meet you, Miss Boopsie, uh, Miss Baxter?" Leon was getting blotchy, no doubt thinking about the story Franny had just told him, which made Franny blush too.

"My goodness, the two of you look like you've been in the sun all

day. Have a seat, have a drink. Tell me when I can put you on the sched-
ule, Peggy." She grinned ear to ear and ushered them to a booth before
plopping down across from them and leaning over her folded hands.
"And tell me all the unfortunate gossip about Lottie, every gory detail."

"Actually," Franny said, ignoring the request, "we have a sort of
proposition for you."

Boopsie raised her delicate eyebrows. "A proposition, you say?"
She winked at Leon, who purpled.

"You never got to see my Showstopper," Franny said.

"The way you were babbling on, it must really be something.
Even Lottie wouldn't stop talking about you." Boopsie shook her
head. "Poor gal. Nostalgia is a hell of a drug, and she got hooked
hard. I should really call her."

Franny felt Leon's curious eyes on her, and she could not steer
the conversation away fast enough.

"I think we can help each other out," Franny said. "You need
butts in seats, and I need a room that won't try to kill me."

"I'm listening."

"My proposition is—*Leon's* proposition is," Franny said after he
elbowed her, "to do a special show for GIs. This Friday night."

Boopsie leaned back and regarded Franny through narrowed
eyes. "This Friday, huh?" she said. "You're assuming I don't have a
major headliner that night."

"Oh yeah?" Franny asked. "Who?"

"I've always got a backup plan," Boopsie said. "And a backup
plan to my backup plan." She pointed at Franny. "You're the one who
trucked her cookies all the way here. Sell me on *your* idea."

Franny looked at Leon, who motioned for her to proceed. "Leon's veterans' support group at the university," Franny said. "He can—"

"I can get thirty, maybe forty GIs in here for a show," Leon said. "Maybe more."

"You can get thirty white men in *here*?" Boopsie asked. "How are you going to do that?"

"Leave that to me," Leon said.

"This is a Negro club in a Negro neighborhood," Boopsie said. "White folks don't like it when they're not the center of the universe."

"They'll be here."

"And I *will* throw them out if they don't behave."

"Not if I throw them out first," Leon said. "They'll behave."

Franny looked from Boopsie to Leon and back again. This was happening. This was really going to happen.

"I can't guarantee payment if I don't know anyone will show," Boopsie said, crossing her arms. "But if you're right, we both stand to do pretty well. No nightclub I know of is doing anything like it." Boopsie stared at them for a moment then stuck her hand out. "Leon, Peggy. We have a deal."

"Franny," Franny said. "My name is Franny Steinberg, and that's my name onstage too."

"Franny Steinberg," Boopsie said. "Yeah, that looks good on you."

Franny grinned and shook her hand, then Leon did.

"No kisses this time, handsome?" Boopsie purred.

❧

White GIs whirled around the club like drunken dreidels, talking too loud, sloshing mugs of beer, downing them quicker than seemed physically possible. Dressed in full uniform, they periodically descended on the bar in tight battalions, demanding refills. The Negro patrons clustered at tables, clutching them like life rafts and trying to carry on civilized conversations.

"I swear, if even one of your buddies tells me to take my top off," Franny said.

"Believe me." Leon grimaced. "I'll be first in line to shut that down."

"Can you at least ask them to slow down on the booze?"

"Some of them, it's the only medicine they got," Leon said. "And all of them are nervous. But this is as bad as it gets. Probably." He tried to discreetly tug on the seat of his pants, and Franny snorted.

"Digging for gold?"

Leon had unearthed an extra pair of non-bloodied slacks, and now that he had finally filled out a little bit, his whole uniform was getting a little snug.

"What does this look like?" one Negro man called over the din. "*The Howdy Doody Show*?"

Franny laughed too loud and nodded vigorously in his direction. Not because she found it particularly funny, but if you come into someone else's house, you behave. What if Boopsie kicked them out?

"Maybe this was a bad idea," Franny said. "They're not ready. Maybe I should've started smaller, like my bathroom. By myself."

"You saying I had a bad idea?"

"*Again*, it was my—"

"Only person you have to worry about is me," Leon said. "Call me a baby again, and I'll get Lottie Marcone to come shoot you."

He grinned and Franny grinned back. She had written a whole new set, one that didn't rely on jokes at Leon's expense or even Peter's, and she'd mailed it back and forth with Gal and Andy and Hal, but she hadn't practiced it on a real human yet. Her own face in the mirror thought she was pretty funny, gave her a standing ovation, even. But would these GIs? Turns out, it was *much* harder to write jokes when you weren't angry.

On the other side of the club, a GI started mimicking the movements of a burlesque striptease while his buddies hooted and hollered. Emboldened, he climbed onto a shaky table to finish his show, causing quite a bit of irritated commotion.

"If you'll excuse me," Leon said, rushing over to pull him down. Leon gave them all a talking-to, and they nodded sheepishly.

Franny sweated ruthlessly in her short-sleeved blouse and skirt, a trickle of sweat dripping maddeningly down her new brassiere. She was about to run to the ladies' room to blot her entire body with a towel when Boopsie sidled up and nudged her. Somehow Boopsie always looked cool as Mary Kate's Frigidaire.

"You sure brought them in all right," Boopsie said. She nodded at Leon, who was now heaving the burlesque GI over his shoulder, to the delight of his buddies.

"I'm *so* sorry—"

Boopsie laughed. "Believe me, we've all seen worse. Make sure you bring your Showstopper, and all's forgiven."

"Losing faith in me already?"

Boopsie cocked her head. "Why, are you?"

Franny thought of the Velvet Swing and of her last time onstage at the Blue Moon. "Believe me," she said. "*I've* seen worse."

"That's the ticket, honeybuns." Boopsie nodded toward the barstools. "So don't get discouraged if Private Sourpuss over there doesn't crack a smile. Can't please everyone."

She nodded at a GI sitting alone at the bar. He was olive-skinned, short and lean and appealingly well-groomed, but he fidgeted constantly—now standing straight, hand on hip, now slouching, now leaning on the bar, like it was his first day in this body and he wasn't sure how it worked yet. Margie, the cocktail waitress from the Velvet Swing, popped into Franny's head like a clue without the mystery: *Your outside don't match your inside. Anybody can see that.*

An older Negro gentleman introduced himself to a knot of white soldiers standing by the door, announcing loudly that he had served in World War I as lieutenant of the 366th Infantry, and if they wanted to hear about a real war, then boy did he have a thing or two to tell them.

There was a tense pause, then one by one, the white GIs saluted the lieutenant, who regarded them through narrowed eyes before nodding tersely.

"At ease, soldiers," he said.

Then they all shook hands heartily, ushered the older man to the bar, and ordered him a beer. And slowly, like a ripple throughout the club, glasses were released from death grips. Smiles tentatively curled on lips. Shoulders untensed, just an inch. Another Negro man in uniform joined the circle.

"Cheers!" the group cried then launched into something vaguely musical called "Gorblimey," the lyrics of which made Franny blush to her ears.

Leon watched from a safe distance, mouthing the words but, thankfully, not actually singing. Franny stood next to him.

Sourpuss sat alone at the bar, his back to the carousing, sipping stiffly at a martini. "What's his story, anyway?" Franny asked.

"Oh, that's Richard," Leon said. "Whatever's going on with him started long before the war. It was like pulling teeth to get him here, but I figured he could use your…talents more than all the other guys put together."

"Even more than that striptease fella?"

When Leon wasn't looking, the GI had climbed back up on the table, now draping a napkin over his face and undulating in some jerky facsimile of a belly dance. Leon sighed and started to go over there, but Franny grabbed his arm.

"You're not the nanny."

"I promised I'd make them behave."

"Just give it a second," Franny said. Sure enough, the dancer's friends pulled him off the table, shaking their heads in dismay.

"You didn't come here for them. You came here for *those* guys," she said, pointing to the World War I vet and the GIs who had arms slung around each other, drenching each other's shoulders in spilled beer. They were singing "Boogie Woogie Bugle Boy" in surprisingly good harmony. "So go do it."

"Yeah, sure, it's time for my solo," Leon said.

"If you don't, I'll call you a baby *onstage* this time."

Leon mimed shooting Franny. She clutched her chest dramatically then pushed him toward the GIs. His voice rose atonally over the nice harmonies, but he was swept up into the group all the same.

Franny leaned on the bar in Richard's periphery. He swallowed the dregs of his martini.

"Why the long face, soldier?" Franny asked.

"None of your beeswax, magical sister."

She spotted a smear of red lipstick on his collar and grinned. "Wild night? You got a little lipstick on you."

Richard sat up, startled, and wiped his mouth. Franny saw, and Richard saw that Franny saw.

Franny also saw something in him that reminded her of Hal before she cut her hair and put on a suit: a longing to fly away.

"On your collar," she said softly.

"It's not what you think," the soldier said.

"I'm not thinking," Franny said. "I swear."

They watched each other for some indication of what should come next. Richard had neatly shaped eyebrows and clear green eyes, long-lashed and heart-stopping.

"I have to go," Richard said.

"Wait," Franny called, but he had already zipped out the door.

Then the room started clapping and cheering and whistling as Boopsie shimmied onstage in a winking blue sequined gown, without attendants, without a piano, without any distractions. Just Boopsie and the stage and a small spotlight.

"It has been a *very* long time since I've MC'd a comedy show," Boopsie said, "but this is a special occasion indeed. These young

white men, who so bravely served our country, have found the courage…to walk into a Negro neighborhood." The regulars laughed and
clapped, and a few stray feminine moans escaped.

Franny ran after Richard.

"Franny!" Leon cried as she zoomed past. "Where are you going?"

Franny held up a finger and hoped it was reassuring enough.
She pushed the door open and searched up and down the street. He
couldn't have just left, could he?

"He's gone, no use chasing him," Richard said with a smirk.
He was leaning against the coral exterior of the club, fiddling in his
breast pocket for cigarettes. Franny leaned against the wall next to
him.

"Spare a smoke?" she asked. He tapped one out, lit it on his, and
handed it to her.

"Shouldn't you be in there telling jokes?" he asked. "Why don't
you leave me alone?"

"You can't escape yourself, you know," Franny said. Her heart
pounded; what was she doing? "You're just wasting everyone's time."

Richard started coughing, mid-inhale, and ended up bent over
at the waist as she pounded him on the back.

"Stop," he croaked. "Why do people do that? It doesn't help."

Franny knew she liked this character.

"Don't go," Franny said. "Or I'll smack you on the back some
more."

Richard was silent for a moment. "You're taking this awfully
well."

"Can I be honest?" Franny asked.

"Why not."

"Red really isn't your color," she said.

Richard actually laughed. "Most girls run away screaming. Or call the police."

"No one has ever accused me of being most girls," Franny said.

His face lit up with a crooked grin, revealing bright little teeth. "They make 'em different in Chicago." He had a clipped East Coast accent—Boston, maybe.

"I'm not going back inside unless you do," she said.

He gazed at the door. "What I find funny and what they find funny are seldom the same."

"Then I'll make you a deal," Franny said. "If you laugh, I'll let you buy me a drink."

"A drink? I'll buy you a steak dinner if that Showstopper works on me."

Franny bristled. "Of course it'll—" Then she remembered Hal. Maybe the rules of her Showstopper were more flexible than they seemed. Maybe there was a lot she didn't understand yet. "—be a surprise for both of us."

"Your confidence is overwhelming."

"What, you don't like surprises?"

"Not usually." He looked directly at her with those eyes. She had to look away.

"But I get a date with a nice Jewish boy?" Franny said. "My parents will be thrilled."

He grimaced. "Don't call me that," he said.

"What, Jewish?"

He didn't laugh this time. Franny took a drag of her cigarette. A car sped past.

"What should I call you?" she asked.

He sighed. "I haven't decided."

It seemed the more things insisted on being only this or that, good or bad, girl or boy, the more they had an actual lot of space in the middle for not knowing. Like everybody, Franny was afraid of not knowing, but she was also getting pretty good at it.

"This is new territory for me," she said.

"New territory for me too." He hesitated then rested a hand lightly on her bare arm.

Her mouth dried up, and clearing her throat just made it worse. Tingles spread outward from his fingertips. It was overwhelming, the electricity in that small gesture.

There was a fleck of nail varnish on Richard's ring finger. Without thinking, she grabbed his hand, and a thrill zinged through her whole body. She opened the door with a flourish, and he smiled, then took a seat at the bar.

Leon was pacing in front of the door, and Franny nearly plowed right into him.

"Jesus, Franny," he hissed. "Don't do that to me."

"You didn't really think I'd run away?"

"Right, like you've never done *that* before," Leon said. But he wasn't mad, and he was sort of pretend worried, and Franny suddenly couldn't even remember the last time her stomach hurt.

"We're so glad you came out tonight," Boopsie said, pulling the microphone out of its stand. "Please relax and enjoy yourselves because we have a very special comedian here." She gazed over the room. "Me, of course." She paused for the laugh.

"But seriously," Boopsie said. "This comedian has made a Chicago mobster tap-dance, his heartless moll weep real tears. She's told jokes at gunpoint more times than *me*. I tell ya, this chick never gives up." Boopsie looked directly at Franny. "And goddamn if she makes me want to never give up too."

Franny inconveniently forgot how to breathe.

"Please give a warm Showstopper Club welcome to the future of stand-up comedy. All the way from Chicago, Illinois—Franny Steinberg!"

The room erupted in cheers and applause. Franny's feet were rooted to the floor. Boopsie Baxter called *her* the future of comedy. *The* Boopsie Baxter. The girls and Hal would never believe it. Heck, Franny Steinberg from Christmas Eve 1944 would never believe it.

Leon shoved her toward the stage. "That's my sister!" he shouted, as she took that long, solo walk.

Franny had to leave behind a whole life just to get *here*, where she had no idea what was coming next. Mary Kate wasn't wrong— she had willingly left behind nearly everyone who had ever loved her. But was she really leaving them behind? Change wasn't death; it was just the opposite. There had been so many endings, Franny had almost forgotten that new things were beginning too.

Boopsie enveloped her in a delicious-smelling hug—what *was* that, pancakes, lilacs?—left a lipstick stain on her cheek, and then thumbed it away.

She held the mic and looked out over the hazy, boozy, sweaty room. Its uneasy, anguished, hopeful crowd. They needed a laugh.

Franny took a deep breath and let 'em have it.

AUTHOR'S NOTE:

This book was inspired by real historical elements, which I've researched to the best of my ability. Any errors of portrayal or accuracy are mine and mine alone.

The Averys are inspired by Dr. Percy Lavon Julian and family, who lived in Oak Park and endured racism, threats, and two attacks on their home in 1950 and 1951. Eventually, Oak Park would devise many programs to support its Black residents: outlawing For Sale signs to prevent white flight, asking for support from sympathetic white residents, and training real estate agents to prevent racial steering and blockbusting. My dad lived across the street from the Julians in the 1950s, and so my anecdotal knowledge about the goings-on of that neighborhood came from the day Dad drove me around his old haunts and told me stories. The rest, of course, is made up.

Dr. Julian was a brilliant chemist whose body of work is so massive and wide-reaching, the mind boggles. He was granted more than 100 patents and authored more than 150 scientific articles, and if you like hormonal birth control or arthritis treatments, you essentially have Dr. Julian to thank. To learn more, you could do worse than the *NOVA* special on him. Or, frankly, the *Drunk History* episode featuring Jordan Peele.

Andy Grand Canyon's story of moving to Chicago is based on an era that began in the late '40s, after the Navajo (Diné) and Hopi peoples endured a blizzard that left many starving and destitute. Rather than invest in reservation infrastructure, Congress would eventually pass the atrocious Indian Relocation Act of 1956. The government, always eager to sabotage Native communities and get its hands on oil buried under the reservations, coerced Indigenous folks to leave home and move to cities, promising jobs, housing, and support that never materialized. So much more can be found in this great American Public Media story, including archival footage, much of it from Chicago: https://www.apmreports.org/episode/2019/11/01/uprooted-the-1950s-plan-to-erase-indian-country.

Confession: I rarely open anything from my family email chain since it's usually some variation of "Fw: Fw: Fw: A funny Passover joke." But one day, I randomly watched a video my aunt Myrna sent, which ended up being *nearly identical* to the scene I had *just* written about Leon's release from Nazi capture. I wrote my aunt, *I'm a little bit at a loss for words here. Not only because of the remarkable story, but also because I have been writing a fictionalized version of this story without realizing it was true.* Grab some tissues and watch: https://vimeo.com/198357872.

And finally, a shout-out to Kurt Vonnegut and his buddy Bernard V. O'Hare, who were captured at the Battle of the Bulge and shouted "Nein scheissen!" at the Nazis.

READING GROUP GUIDE

1. What are some of the different ways Franny Steinberg uses humor, and do they change over time? Do you think her humor helps her process her trauma or avoid dealing with it?

2. Did anything surprise you about the depiction of Judaism in the story? Is Judaism a religion, a culture, an ethnicity, or some combination thereof?

3. In our time, the language we use to talk about gender, race, sexuality, and more is in a state of refinement and flux. How does the story tackle such issues in a time where this refined language didn't exist? How do you think Hal would talk about themself if they lived in the twenty-first century?

4. When Hal finally explores their gender, they become more confident and comfortable in their skin. By contrast, Franny's exploration of her identities is more tentative and troubled. For many people, coming out is a process of fully

becoming themselves, but in what ways might exploring sexual and gender identity be uncomfortable and slippery? Does that discomfort make the identity less true?

5. Is there anything you believe can't be joked about? How does the idea of "punching up" apply in this context? Conversely, is humor possible without pain?

6. Boopsie Baxter conjured the world's first Showstopper by accident during World War II after learning about the death of her mother. Do you think Showstoppers were invented in that moment? Or could they always have existed unnoticed or undiscovered?

7. Franny was ambivalent about conjuring a Showstopper, and when she did manage to, it was unlike anything anyone had ever seen before. If you conjured your own Showstopper, what do you think it would be? How might it surprise you?

8. When it comes to the Averys, Franny and the rest of the Steinbergs take pains to distinguish their words and behavior from the overt racism of the Finnegans. In what ways can racism be subtle, even to the point people might not recognize it in themselves? If it cannot be recognized, how can it be changed?

9. What is the significance of Lottie Marcone's refrain of "men aren't funny," echoed by Mama at the end of the book? Have you ever heard someone say "women aren't funny"? What did you think when you heard that?

10. What is the role of magic in the story? What does a Showstopper make possible—for comedians and audiences—that would be impossible without its particular magic?

ACKNOWLEDGMENTS

Writing a novel requires the hearts and eyeballs of as many writers as will tolerate you, and I am embarrassed by my riches, which include Pamela Rentz, Tracy Harford-Porter, Kira Walsh, Shane Hoversten, Andrew Huff, Tom Underberg, Jessica Hilt, Jennifer Hsyu, Rory Kelly, Desirina Boskovich, Grá Linnaea, Rob Ziegler, Paolo Bacigalupi, Kelly Swails, Ysabeau Wilce, Les Howle, Neile Graham, Bill Shunn, the rest of Clarion West 2008 and Coastal Heaven 2018, and the whole Tuesday Funk community. Special thanks to Mary Winn Heider for the walks, advice, pep talks, and the occasional, necessary gift of alcohol.

If I got anything right about the highs and horrors of doing stand-up, it's because of the smart and hilarious comedian Alex Kumin, who endured many questions and taught my Fem Com workshop, the best stand-up class in Chicago. If I got anything right about the history, it's thanks to the excellent books *The Comedians: Drunks, Thieves, Scoundrels and the History of American Comedy* by Kliph Nesteroff and *We Killed: The Rise of Women in American Comedy* by Yael Kohen.

I also happen to have the world's greatest publishing team: my agent, Cameron McClure, who, lucky for me, never gives up; and my editor, Christa Désir, who is both a thoughtful editor and a tireless advocate. In fact, everyone who worked on this novel has been a dream: Jessica Thelander, Kelly Lawler, Rachel Gilmer, Findlay McCarthy, Brittany Vibbert, and Heather VenHuizen at Sourcebooks and the sensitivity readers at Tessera Editorial. I don't know how I got so lucky, but I'll take it.

I once heard an author say most of writing is emotional maintenance, and this is both exactly true and impossible to do alone. Thank you to every single relative and friend who supported me and listened over the years, and special thanks to Joshua Briggs, Matt Freeman, Jen Balkus, Sarah Rosenberg-Scott, Andrew Scott, Nick Mader, Michelle Rifken, Maria Argos, Sara Whitney, Rebecca Honig, and Bethany Caruso, my family from another mammary.

Hugs and endless thanks to my mom for always believing.

And to the women who came before—Mary Jane Mattingly, who deserved an audience for her poems; Ida Robins, who rocked leather pants well into her eighties; and Suzy Roberts, who used to clean her Navy barracks with maxi pads strapped to her feet, a detail I am devastated I couldn't find a way to use—their memories are a blessing.

Finally, without Kyle Thiessen's brains, heart, kindness, humor, and patience, this book (and I) would be lost.

ABOUT THE AUTHOR

Eden Robins loves writing novels, but they take forever so she also writes short stories and self-absorbed essays. She cohosts a science podcast called *No Such Thing as Boring* with an actual scientist and coproduces a monthly live lit show in Chicago called Tuesday Funk. Previously, she sold sex toys, wrote jokes for Big Pharma, and once did stand-up comedy for an audience who didn't boo. She lives in Chicago, has been to the bottom of the ocean, and will never go to space. This is her first novel.